IN THE CARE OF A MADMAN

The door opened, and the man came back with the lantern. He also carried a Pyrex mixing bowl with some kind of liquid sloshing around inside. Sis went immediately rigid with fear, but he ignored her. He went straight over to the man he had just killed and lifted a sponge from the bowl. He squeezed out the excess, set the bowl aside, and reached for the corpse's head. Now a new smell cut through the dead man's body odor and the stench of the lantern kerosene. It was a clean, fresh, soapy odor.

As it dawned on Sis what was happening, she actually laughed out loud. This had to be a nightmare. She pinched herself as hard as she could, but the dark apparition didn't go away. Then her senses snapped completely, and she giggled until her sides hurt, her insane laughter growing in volume as, just feet from where she lay chained, a lunatic sat naked on a bench and lovingly washed a dead man's hair.

VENOM

Jeffrey Ames

A SIGNET BOOK

SIGNET
Published by New American Library, a division of
Penguin Putnam Inc., 375 Hudson Street,
New York, New York 10014, U.S.A.
Penguin Books Ltd, 80 Strand,
London WC2R 0RL, England
Penguin Books Australia Ltd, Ringwood,
Victoria, Australia
Penguin Books Canada Ltd, 10 Alcorn Avenue,
Toronto, Ontario, Canada M4V 3B2
Penguin Books (N.Z.) Ltd, 182–190 Wairau Road,
Auckland 10, New Zealand

Penguin Books Ltd, Registered Offices:
Harmondsworth, Middlesex, England

First published by Signet, an imprint of New American Library,
a division of Penguin Putnam Inc.

First Printing, February 2002
10 9 8 7 6 5 4 3 2 1

PUBLISHER'S NOTE
This is a work of fiction. Names, characters, places, and incidents either
are the product of the author's imagination or are used fictitiously,
and any resemblance to actual persons, living or dead, business
establishments, events, or locales is entirely coincidental.

BOOKS ARE AVAILABLE AT QUANTITY DISCOUNTS WHEN USED TO PROMOTE
PRODUCTS OR SERVICES. FOR INFORMATION PLEASE WRITE TO PREMIUM
MARKETING DIVISION, PENGUIN PUTNAM INC., 375 HUDSON STREET, NEW
YORK, NEW YORK 10014.

Young fella come up, him name Jed, eighteen-year-old could pick 'im, oh, a hunnerd an' fitty pound in half a day, dat how strong he be. Bodacious-lookin' boy, had dem women comin' round. White women, too; Jed he had a lotta dem.

Marse Hatcher come home roun' middle o' th' day, catch him Jed up in de big house wid Miss Harriet, she Marse Hatcher's little girl. Marse an' fo', five white men whup Jed bloody, tie him up wid his head on de stump where ol' Fiddleback live. We never slep' none dat night, ol' Jed he be screamin' so, raisin' hell, an' next day Marse tell us, take Jed loose an' care fo' de boy. Seven, eight days, Jed got de fever like he gonna die. He don', but maybe he shoulda. Half de skin come off him face, he don' be pretty no mo'. Dem women don' come round rest o' his born days, time ol' Fiddleback through wid dat boy.

—excerpt from *Interviews with Slaves,*
by Thurman Wey, PhD

1

Sis Hargis thought that the farmer needed a reality check. Big-time. Old MacDonald here was living in a dream world. With a *quack-quack* here and a *fuck you* there. *Eee-iii, eee-iii, oh.*

Someone should have recited the facts of life to the guy: He couldn't afford the car, no way. Not with ten years' worth of drought-free corn crop, even if the stalks grew as high as an elephant's fuckin' eye. Not with a lifetime of milking cows. Nope, the farmer was strictly a used-pickup prospect, a lifelong loser whose kid raised cows or hogs in Future Farmers of America, saving up for tuition at Farmer Fuck U. Sis thought the kid would be better off selling tractors, long-haul trailers or something.

Nonetheless, Sis continued to smile down from the revolving stage at the Automobile Building, State Fair of Texas, opening day, with a snow-white Sebring convertible alongside her on the platform, showing gleaming magnesium wheels. All around her on the mammoth display floor were men, women, and kids in everything from shorts and halters to Jed Clampett overalls, all of them gaping at brand-new Fords, Chevys, Toyotas, scratching their heads while reading sticker prices. Here and there they sat behind steering wheels, honking horns or playing with gearshifts, all wondering what it would be like to tool around in an Eldorado or Beemer. As if ninety percent of the fair-goers could afford the fucking things.

Sis just couldn't take it, not for the fair's three-week duration. Not this year, not considering the other problems messing with her head. She didn't need the money, and she for damned sure didn't have to shake her ass around this platform to make a living.

Megan had called the work therapy. Keeping busy— just the thing Sis needed to chase her troubles away. *Okay, Megan,* Sis thought, *I've given it the old college try, and then some. Doesn't work. Fuck this. Who needs it?* Sis would tell Teresa at the agency this very afternoon.

The Sebring was the center of attention in the Chrysler display. Not to mention Sis herself as an at-traction, having not a half-bad set of wheels for a thirty-five-year-old. Terrific shape as well, in five-inch platforms and a shimmery silver minidress, dark skin contrasting with her sparkling white teeth, the laugh crinkles at the corners of her eyes working overtime, her outfit drawing every bit as much comment as the car. She knew she looked better than the majority of the car-show models, even the ones on whom she had ten or fifteen years, but she felt as if she'd traveled more bumpy roads than your average *fifty*-year-old.

According to Megan, Sis was merely stressed out. But *stressed out* didn't come close, not at the moment. Sis felt absolutely murderous, and the next person who crossed her . . .

The farmer reached up to tug at the hem of her dress, grinning as he asked her, "Mind if'n my boy tries that one on fer size?" while indicating the Sebring.

And Farmer Fuckface's son, a bohunk overweight youngster in an FFA jacket, tried to climb onstage beside her.

Sis at first maintained her cool, saying diplomatically, "This is a display platform, sir. Over there"—pointing over the farmer's head—"is one exactly like it except that it's green. Pale green leather upholstery, just gorgeous . . . Try that one, young man."

The teenager needed no further prompting, his fanny jiggling under gabardine as he trotted up to the green Sebring that sat alongside a yellow LeBaron, both cars at floor level and ripe for daydreaming, ready to have their gearshifts fondled like dildos. The boy dove in behind the wheel.

The father hung back, still looking up at Sis and now winking at her. "Well then," he drooled, "how 'bout if'n the boy's daddy tries *you* on fer size, darlin'?" He even hooked his thumbs through his suspenders and thrust his pelvis forward.

And that's what did it, the thumbs-through-the-suspenders routine, that and the dumb-looking, hick-farmer grin.

Sis sank down on her haunches like a stripper on the runway and looked the farmer in the eye. Using her best sugary Texas drawl she said, " 'Spect his mama wouldn't like that none, baby. Now fuck off, willya?" Then she rose and sashayed around the platform, smiling at the crowd. *Bumps and grinds ain't nothin' new to little Sis,* she thought. *You folks want some more?*

The farmer hesitated, dumbstruck, then took off in pursuit of his son.

As Sis handed out leaflets, Megan Harris approached, wearing a navy-blue courtroom suit and low heels, carrying her briefcase. She watched the Sebring rotate while Sis explained to a black man how the Jet Age–looking convertible's rear end functioned like a spoiler, cut down wind resistance, and improved gas mileage. As Sis turned away from the man, Megan caught her eye. Visible beyond the well-groomed attorney, a couple of five– or six-year-olds left greasy fingermarks on the SuperCab's windshield.

Sis paraded over to where Megan Harris waited, stopping on the way to hand out more leaflets. As she reached the edge of the platform she bent from the waist, maintaining her pleasant look as she whispered to Megan, "What'd the cocksucker have to say for himself?"

Megan had a plain round face, flabby hips and arms, and wore glasses with monster lenses. She had a reputation for going after soon-to-be ex-husbands like the Lord himself after the Temple's moneychangers. She patted her satchel. "We need to talk. Is there somewhere we can. . . ?" She peered around the building.

Sis checked her diamond-encrusted Piaget. "I'm off in fifteen. Meet me outside the east exit, the one where you can see Big Tex. There's a funnel-cake stand by the—"

"I know where it is." Megan lifted a foot and adjusted her shoe.

"Good. See you then." Before Sis resumed her strut, she bent over and said softly to Megan, "And if the bastard's not agreeable to every fucking thing, you can tell him he's wasting his time."

Sis paced back and forth in the late-September heat, smoking a Virginia Slim in rapid puffs. A hundred yards away a crowd surrounded Big Tex, necks craning upward as the three-story papier-mâché cowpoke boomed out, "Howdy" and "Welcome, pardner," its painted face grinning, its arms waving, its mechanical jaws opening and closing like a mammoth Charlie McCarthy. Sis scanned the rows of booths selling funnel cakes, snow cones and Fletcher's Corny Dogs. No Megan in sight. A man wearing a straw hat walked by leering, but Sis ignored him and put on sunglasses. She fished out her cell, called the valet service for her

car, paced, and smoked some more. What in hell had
happened to her lawyer?

Megan soon approached from behind and tapped
Sis on the shoulder. Sis jumped as if a cattle prod had
zapped her, dropped her cigarette, and ground the
butt into the asphalt with the toe of her shoe. "Jesus
Christ, Megan, where have you been?"

"Sorry." Megan balanced her satchel on her thigh
to open the snaps. "Had to call another client." She
produced a sheaf of papers. "Here's the proposed settlement," she said.

Sis draped her purse over her shoulder and began
to read. High above the midway a Ferris wheel spun
nearer by, and squeals came from the Bubble Bounce.
Sis arched an eyebrow as she flipped over a page. "I
want that little cunt out of my house, Megan."

The lawyer humbly shrugged. "The house was a gift
from Will Senior. It's Billy's as separate property. You
don't have a prenup, Sis, and—"

"I don't give a shit. I do not give one rat's ass about
all that legal crap. It's Billy craving the young pussy.
Let him pay for it. I get the house, or he and his whole
fucking family can start reading about themselves in
the *Dallas Morning News*. I'll walk right into the Com-
issioners' Court and wave their dirty underwear like
a flag if I have to."

"That's hardly a legal argument." Megan showed a
nasty grin, liking the idea, getting the picture.

"Fuck legal," Sis said. "Does he want to go his
merry way with the bitch blowing in his ear, or does
he want to spend the next millennium screwing around
down at the courthouse?"

A shiny black Mercedes four-door appeared half a
block away, poking along at five miles per, honking
for pedestrian fairgoers to get out of the way. Both
women watched the car approach.

Megan lowered her gaze to the pavement. "You're the client."

"Goddamn right I'm the client. My way or the highway." As the Mercedes pulled abreast and came to a stop, Sis reached for the passenger door handle.

Megan pointed at the settlement agreement. "There are other provisions in there you should—"

"Oh, I'll read it." Sis climbed in and slammed the door. She pressed a button and the window hummed down. "But no house, no deal."

"There are other attractive—"

"I'm getting the house, Megan. Period, the end. Otherwise Billy Hargis can have his balls in a vise 'till hell freezes over." The Mercedes began a slow U-turn to head for the fairground exit.

Megan shut her briefcase and emitted a long exasperated sigh.

"The house is mine," Sis yelled. "And lawyers are a helluva lot easier to get rid of than husbands. I wouldn't be forgetting that, if I were you."

By the time the driver had crept through the mob, skirted the Cotton Bowl, and neared the entrance to the valet lot, Sis wondered if steam was coming out her ears. What a bunch of horseshit! Five pages, four conditions, none of which she was giving into, no way. Billy wasn't going to have his young snatch and eat it, too, not while Sis was still breathing. She'd have the house, the CDs, the money-market accounts, every frigging nickel, and only then could Billy go his merry way with the teenybopper. Lose his head over some young stuff, would he? Well, Mr. Billy Hard-on Hargis was fixing to lose his ass as well.

Sis creased the papers in her lap and turned to the driver. "If it's okay I'll let you off here," she said, fishing a five-dollar bill out of her handbag. "Tip you extra for the walk you'll have to take, okay? I'm in a hurry. I've got, ha, ha, a husband to kill."

The driver kept both gloved hands on the wheel, the bill of his cap practically touching his nose. He eased the Mercedes past the valet entrance and, with the road ahead now clear of traffic, speeded up. The needle crept upward past ten, fifteen, twenty miles an hour.

Sis watched over her shoulder as the lot receded in the rear windshield. Her smile was hesitant. "Hey, excuse me. Didn't you miss your—?"

The driver floored the accelerator. The Mercedes leaped forward, signposts and railroad ties now zooming past in a blur.

Sis's throat constricted. She dropped the papers along with the five-dollar bill on the floorboard. "What in hell do you think you're doing? You want me to report this?"

They were doing sixty now, nearing the turnoff leading out of the fairgrounds onto Haskell Avenue. The driver jammed on the brakes and whipped the wheel to the right, tires squealing and burning rubber. Centrifugal force threw Sis across the seat against him. He shoved her away. The collision knocked the air from Sis's lungs; she fought to breathe as she gaped at him. The car hurtled toward the traffic light at Haskell.

Sis scrambled away from the lunatic and hugged the passenger door. "You let me out of this car, right now."

The driver pulled a pistol from his inside pocket and held the barrel inches from Sis's ear. He pulled back the hammer with a soft *click-click*.

She painfully choked out, "Jesus God."

He pistol-whipped her across the face. She fell back, her lip suddenly puffy, a trickle of blood running from her nose. There was a salty taste in her mouth. She

cringed against the door, tightly closing her eyes, praying silently as the Mercedes ran the light, missed a
pickup's fender by the width of an eyelash, and ca-
reened out onto Haskell Avenue.

By the time the driver brought the car to a
screeching standstill, he'd yanked off his cap. He had
sparse greasy hair combed over his bald spots, and a
broad sloping forehead. Sis was sprawled against the
passenger door, her head beneath the level of the
window.

He pointed the gun. "Get out." His voice was
hoarse, his tone as calm as windless air.

She moved in a daze. Get out? Of course she'd get
out. He could have the car, Christ, a piece of ass,
anything he wanted if he wouldn't hurt her. She held
up her purse. "Look, I don't have much money,
but—"

"Out." He prodded her with the barrel.

Slowly, carefully, her movements deliberate so as
not to set him off, her gaze locked on the pistol, Sis
eased the door open and stepped outside. The whirl-
wind journey hadn't taken over a minute or two; muf-
fled in the distance, Big Tex's mechanical voice boomed
out over the fairgrounds. They'd stopped just over the
tracks in a run-down neighborhood. On their left was a
tree-shaded vacant lot. On their right was a ramshackle
wooden house with worn-out tires and broken bottles
strewn across the yard. Sis was conscious of nearby freeway sounds of cars whispering past.

He slid across and came out after her. On the way
he thumbed a button and the trunk popped open.

Her head turned in reflex at the sound. Then he was
standing beside her. His breath stunk of garlic. He
shoved her toward the rear of the car.

She resisted. "No, please. I . . ."

He pushed harder. She stumbled and fell, ripping

her panty hose and skinning her knee. She winced at the sting as he grabbed her arm and yanked her to her feet, hauling her over to the open trunk.

Sis blinked in disbelief. There was already a woman in the trunk, with a blanket covering her body from the neck down. She was an olive-complected brunette with a stunning hairdo. Sis backed away.

Her captor slapped her, once, twice. "Get in," he ordered.

Sis moved woodenly, lifting her knee, setting her foot on the carpet inside the trunk. Her captor pushed from behind. She tumbled onto her side, her knees up in the fetal position. His eyes wild, the fearsome man brought the lid down until the trunk's electric motor kicked in, shutting out the light.

In the instant before blackness enveloped her, Sis had a single thought: the other woman must be dead as a stone. Otherwise, when the trunk had popped open, the woman would've run like hell.

2

DPD Patrolman Courtney Bedell spent the fair's opening day bored out of her mind, racking up overtime. She was tasked with crowd control, but mostly she stood by giving directions to people who thought just because someone wore a uniform they knew the way to anyfuckingplace. Which, around these parts at least, Courtney sort of did. While growing up in East Dallas she'd come to the fair every single year on free school-kid passes and had the major attractions memorized: the Automobile Building, the Electric Building, the Borden's Milk display, where Elsie the Cow was likely to pee on your shoe, the livestock exhibits, every ride worth riding on the midway. Also, mostly due to the approximately four thousand gallons of pop she'd consumed on these very same fairgrounds as a teenager, Courtney Bedell knew the location of every rest room on the premises. And that, she found, was her main contribution, pointing the way to the john.

For a while she stood around with two other cops, Rainey and Trevino, watching the crowd pass in front of the midway arcade while the two men argued about football. Or more to the point they argued about Michael Irvin, playmaker, pass receiver, drug convictee,

King of the Dallas Cowboys. Trevino thought that Irvin was right to retire when he did, earlier in the year. Rainey took the opposite view, opining that the playmaker could have made a difference, and that if he'd stayed another season the team would be worth more of a damn. Courtney thought that with the local school superintendent getting fired, thousands of homeless wandering the streets, and a drought that had strung out into seventy-four days in July, August, and September, Rainey and Trevino should have more on their minds than the Cowboys. But she didn't say so, not wanting to engage the guys in an argument. Dallas, Texas. My hometown, Courtney thought. Hotter'n hell, full of pickups and rednecks, totally bananas over its football team.

She stood with one hand resting on her holstered weapon, her elbow winged out behind her, as Rainey said to Trevino, "The thing is, Irvin could take the post route, open up the outside lanes for Rocket Ismail and the speed-burner guys. You need that: a big strong wideout with the hands down the middle, take away the double coverage at the corners."

Trevino pushed up his mirrored sunglasses, his biceps bulging from the hours spent at Gold's downtown. "So I'll give you that the guy had his day in the Super Bowls, back before Aikman got his bell rung so much he's hearing birds tweeting alla time. But the playmaker's what, thirty-four? Old for that league, the punishment. Plus the drugs and the strippers got to take their toll on a man. Days he's getting banged around by all those cornerbacks, nights they say he's taking on white girls two, three at a time. Guy's got to feel fifty by now." His Hispanic accent was faint but unmistakable.

Rainey was black, a head taller than Trevino, and with even bigger arms. He shifted a toothpick from one corner of his mouth to the other, corn-dog crumbs clinging to his mustache. "There you go with that racial shit again."

Trevino spread his hands, palms down. "Ain't nothing racial. It's the facts. They're dragging witnesses out of every titty bar in town. And him with a wife, those kids."

Rainey pointed a finger. "We are talking about the man's football ability."

"And I am talking about his *fucking* ability, which *affects* his football ability. When I was in the Gloves they used to tell me, 'No fooling around forty-eight hours before a bout.' Now here's this guy in a physical sport, doing coke and getting it on with women outside the locker room before the game. Thirty-four years old. He's going to break down. Hey, Courtney, you ever see a thirty-four-year-old guy that wouldn't break down doing all that?"

Idly watching the crowd, Courtney wasn't really listening. Over by the concessions were a bald man and gray-haired woman along with a child who was obviously the couple's granddaughter. As the woman bought the little girl a funnel cake the man looked in curiosity at the mismatched cops: the lithe young woman wearing an armored jacket alongside the black guy and the Hispanic guy, both men showing muscle-mag chests that looked as if bullets might bounce off of them. Courtney received funny glances often due to her size, her soft features, and her moist dark eyes, sidelong looks that said that people couldn't believe she was an officer even though she wore the same uniform as the guys.

Trevino poked Courtney on the arm. "You listening?"

Courtney tore her gaze away from the grandparents and the little girl.

"What's your take on it?" Trevino said.

Courtney dropped her hands to her sides. "Take on what?"

"Michael Irvin."

"The football player? I guess he's pretty good."

"*Was* pretty good. He's retired. So, Courtney, you going by Bethancourt's?"

Courtney decided she should get her head in the game. "What's Bethancourt's?"

"Jimmy Bethancourt. The guy at White Rock Precinct. You know him. He's partners with Belew."

"Oh, yeah, sure. Helped us run down the two assholes on 635 last month," Courtney said. "Brown hair, kind of tall?"

"Yeah, him," Trevino said. "Guy's giving a party, strictly for people on the job. You ain't heard?"

She shook her head. There was a booth nearby where people tossed rings over soft-drink bottles, trying to win a panda. As Courtney watched, a guy in a cowboy hat spun a ring through the air, missed, snapped his fingers in disgust, then dug more money out of his pocket.

Trevino's tone turned persuasive. "Bethancourt keeps asking about you since you met on that bust. He wants to get with you."

"Yeah? Sure, I remember Bethancourt. Pretty nice-looking, but he's going to have to wait. Tonight I have to get Jason."

"Aw. You could come by early," Rainey said. "I'll dance the Macarena. Could use more women to balance things."

"So could most cop parties. I'd like to, guys. But the shift ends at six and I promised the sitter I'd pick Jason up at eight o'clock. She's not going to be available many more times if I leave her hanging on what's supposed to be my day off. The overtime won't do me much good if I got no more child care." She lowered her head, but then raised her eyes and added, "Besides, I promised the little guy."

Rainey and Trevino exchanged a look. Rainey said, "So unpromise him. It's not like he's really your kid."

Anger surged through Courtney like a shockwave. "It *is* like he's my kid, Rainey. I'm all he's got, and you guys . . ." She chewed her lip. "The hell with it. I'm going to walk the park now. I'll keep radio contact. But for the rest of the shift I don't want another word about it. Just don't mess with me, okay?"

Courtney spent the rest of the shift patrolling, making occasional eye contact with Rainey or Trevino from across the midway, each time shaking her head to indicate, "Hey, us cops could've stayed at home." All in all the day went pretty well for her. She felt guilty about getting up in Rainey's face, but at the same time was certain that Rainey'd had it coming. As the afternoon wore on her anger softened, then left her completely. Rainey was all right, just another asshole with no responsibility.

In her mind Courtney went over the holes she could plug with her overtime check: the dress on layaway at Marshalls, a new outfit for Jason so he'd look nice at Sunday school, a couple of months' minimum on the credit cards, a Garth Brooks CD as a bonus. Her only problem right now was the heat. The armored vest was stifling. Rainey and Trevino could shun the vest if they wanted. Jesus, the guys were big enough that someone would think twice about taking that pair on, even with a gun. But Courtney felt she needed all the protection she could muster, so she went strictly by the book when working crowds. Even though the odds against a lunatic spraying bullets at the fair were a zillion to one, she kept the vest securely fastened and sweltered through the day.

Other than those two glitches her time on duty went
perfectly. Too perfectly. So, of course, something finally went very wrong.

Courtney's peaceful afternoon shift fell apart
around a quarter to six, as she walked the relatively
deserted area behind the Cotton Bowl. Later she
would wish she'd never noticed the long-haired guy in
ratty jeans and a Barenaked Ladies tee, that she'd
never caught movement in the corner of her eye as
the guy passed a Baggie to a couple of teenage girls
in exchange for some bills. She almost ignored the
transaction as it was. It was nearing the end of her
shift, and the penalty for possession wasn't much more
than for a parking ticket. Sale was a felony, of course,
but Courtney had been down that road; the girls
would swear that the dope was a gift and some ADA
would plead the dealer down to time served—couple
of days, max. The dealer himself might've been under-
age, a smooth-faced skinny kid with rings through his
nostrils and an addict's nervous twitch about him.
Courtney kept moving, her eyes averted, and did everything to avoid the bust short of sticking her hands
in her pockets and whistling a nervous tune.

But it was her rotten luck that the dealer noticed
her at the exact same instant when she noticed him.

He stared right at her just as he pocketed the
money, his eyes bugging out as he took in the uniform.
His mouth gaped open. And even as she thought,
Don't run, you dumb ass, he broke into a gallop. Curs-
ing under her breath, Courtney jogged into his path
and held up her hands, palms out.

The dealer lowered his shoulder like a running back,
slammed into her, and sent her tumbling across the
pavement. He sprinted off, never looking back. Courtney scraped her hip and skinned her thigh as she
rolled over. Then she was on her feet, thumbing the
button on her shortwave as the dealer's skinny butt

receded in the distance. As he disappeared around the west end of the Cotton Bowl and headed back toward the midway, she got Trevino on the horn and blurted out a description. Then she looked around for the girls.

They hadn't moved. Both were baby-fat pudgy, a redhead and a dishwater blonde whose hair hung to her waist. Fourteen, fifteen at the most. The blonde made a halfhearted motion as if to toss the baggie away.

Courtney went over fast. "Don't screw up like your buddy. You're juveniles. Won't spend a night in jail." Her forehead tightened. "For the record, what's your dealer's name?"

They gave it up, both kids sagging in defeat. The redhead sniffled, "Jeffrey."

"Hey, cute name." Courtney cuffed the girls together, left wrist to right, flagged down a passing park patrol cop and prepared to hand the teenagers over. Her radio crackled to life.

"Got him, Courtney. Coming your way." Trevino was out of breath, obviously yelling while at a dead run.

And damned if the dealer wasn't returning to the scene, the skinny Barenaked Ladies fan reappearing from the direction in which he'd fled, gasping, pipe-stem legs churning, his eyes wild, shooting glances over his shoulder like Ichabod Crane on the bridge with the horseman on his heels. In close pursuit came Rainey and Trevino galloping shoulder to shoulder, the burly cops with their neck muscles straining, their faces flushed from exertion.

Courtney stepped into the dealer's path with her weapon drawn, the Glock in her right hand with her left clamped around her wrist, in the classic shooter's pose. "You, Jeffrey. Don't be dumber than you already are. Put your hands behind your head and get down on your knees."

Jeffrey stopped in his tracks, arms flailing forward as he fought for balance, looking in fear behind him as the muscle brigade thundered up from the rear. He had had enough. He knelt with his fingers locked behind his neck, his expression as if he'd been here before and knew the drill. Courtney holstered the Glock and snapped the strap into place. Trevino stepped up and cuffed the suspect. He looked at Courtney. "You okay?" he said.

Courtney answered automatically. "Just bruised where he pushed me down." It was her collar, her decision what to do with the guy. In her mind she was already turning him over to the park patrol along with the girls, filing only a possession complaint, a misdemeanor, which would eliminate the paperwork required on a felony. Plus she'd be off duty in plenty of time to pick up Jason at the sitter's, take him to Chuck E. Cheese for pizza, let him crawl through the kiddie maze . . .

But then Rainey went off on the guy.

The black cop grabbed the dealer's hair, yanked him sideways, and sent him rolling. "You know what?" Rainey snarled. "You have assaulted a fucking officer, asshole, and you have got one pissed-off nigger on your ass. You know what that's going to get you?" He bunched the Barenaked Ladies tee in one hand and cocked his other fist.

Courtney made a lunge for Rainey's hand. She missed, and Rainey's punch landed square on Jeffrey's nose. The dealer's head snapped against the pavement and blood gushed from his nostrils.

Courtney shoved Rainey, hard. He staggered a step and righted himself. She stood her ground with hands on hips. "God*dammit,* Rainey. I already told you I promised Jason." She turned pleading eyes on Trevino. Trevino hesitated, looking from Courtney to Rainey to the dealer and then back again.

Jeffrey moaned. "You broke my jaw. You broke my fuckin' jaw." The area below his cheek was beginning to swell.

Trevino sadly shook his head. "Guy may be really hurt, Court. Too late to let it go. You know the rules. When the perp's fucked up there's no way around it. We got to call for backup now."

Patrolman Courtney Bedell had to fill out what seemed like ten thousand forms in order to satisfy the duty sergeant, charging the dealer with felony sale. She lied her fanny off to the on-the-spot IAD rep, backing up Rainey's story that it had looked as if the dealer was reaching for a weapon when the big black cop had decked the guy. As she left the IAD interview, Rainey squeezed her arm and said, "Thanks." She ignored him and stalked away.

She was more than an hour late leaving the fairgrounds, and hit the darkened gateside lot where she'd parked her Lumina at a dead run. It was already seven-thirty. She'd promised Jason's sitter she'd be there by eight o'clock, and the sitter's house was fifteen miles away. Piece of cake, Courtney thought, assuming she could rent a helicopter. Her boots made scraping noises on the gravel. Her armored vest flapped against her ribs. She reached her car and climbed inside, stowed her weapon in the glove compartment, fired up her engine, and left the parking lot in a cloud of dust. Working cops directed her to the exit, and she nodded to each in turn. She was glad she'd brought her own car and didn't have to waste more time turning a cruiser in at the motor pool. She drove out of the fairgrounds and headed for northbound Central Expressway.

She slammed on the brakes after traveling less than fifty feet. Westbound Martin Luther King Boulevard was stacked bumper-to-bumper from the fairground exit all the way to Central, as most of the fairgoers headed for home with the setting of the sun. The traffic barely crawled. Drivers honked horns, rolled down windows, and cursed the cars in front of them. One guy up ahead opened his door, stood out on the street, and shook his fist at the sky. Courtney gritted her teeth. At this rate she'd be lucky to reach the sitter's before the turn of the century. She punched the steering wheel in disgust, at the same time peering down a side street in search of an alternate route.

The side street led south, the opposite direction from home, but by traveling a mile or so Wrong Way Corrigan style she might find easier northbound freeway access, thus saving time in the long run. There was an opening in the eastbound traffic flow across the median.

Courtney floored the accelerator, cut across two lanes with her rear wheels burning rubber, and fishtailed away down a street on which she'd never been and whose name she didn't know. Central Expressway angled to the east as it ran south through the city, however, and with any luck at all she'd be in the northbound freeway lanes in no time, headed for home at a brisk seventy miles per. Who knew? She might even make it before her sitter turned Jason over to the welfare board.

Ten minutes later Courtney Bedell was hopelessly lost in her own hometown, and mad as hell to boot. She battled to control her temper. Central Expressway was in plain sight to the west, sodium lights burning brightly over the median, all lanes moving lickety-split in both directions, but try as she might she couldn't find an access. Every narrow westbound street led to

a dead end short of the freeway, so she'd have to
double back and go at it again. The fact that she
wasn't in the safest part of town didn't help; once
three Hispanic guys with bandanas around their heads
called her *puta*. Her response was to roll down her
window and exhibit the police shield stitched on her
sleeve, which caused the guys to snicker and call her
puta grande. She lost it then, and shot them the finger.

Grimly she continued on. She needed to make a
call to let the sitter know she was lost, but that she
was hauling ass and would get there as quickly as she
could. But unlike ninety percent of the in and with-it
population, Courtney didn't have a phone in her
pocket. She decided that by next month she'd have a
cell, even if she had to give up food in order to finance
the damned thing.

She pulled into the driveway fronting a closed 7-
Eleven. The lights were out, the gas pumps deep in
shadow, burglar bars raised over every window. On
the corner in front of the store was a glassed-in pay
phone. Courtney sat for a moment with her foot on
the brake. Ghetto residents had vandalized South Dallas pay stations to hell and gone so often that Southwestern Bell had given up sending repair crews on a
regular basis. More than likely the phone wouldn't
work. She looked up and down the street. The area
around the store seemed deserted. A half block down
on her right was a playground, complete with rusty
swings and jungle gyms, and alongside the playground
sat two vehicles. One was a black four-door Mercedes,
and the other was a two-tone pickup with a covered
bed. The pickup had a bumper sticker. Her cop's an-
tennae stood at alert; the expensive car was as out of
place in this neighborhood as a hooker in a monastery.
There was no sign of life in or near the park. She
killed her engine, took her keys and flashlight along

with her, hustled into the phone booth, and closed
the door.

She picked up, surprisingly heard a dial tone, and
spun a quarter into the slot. Warily scanning the area
for crazies lurking in the shadows, holding the receiver
between her cheek and shoulder and shining the
flashlight on the keypad, she punched in the sitter's
number. Mrs. Bailey answered on the second ring. Her
tone was anxious and angry.

Courtney said, "Hi, Mrs. Bailey. It's Courtney Bedell."

"We've discussed this before," Mrs. Bailey snapped.

"I swear to God, ma'am, it's unavoidable. Look, I'll
pay you extra for—"

"It ain't the money. My husband and me, we got
plans."

Courtney frowned. Visible through the glass, down by
the playground, a man had gotten out of the Mercedes.
He headed for the rear of the car, limping. He wore
dark clothing. Courtney said into the phone, "Twenty
minutes. Promise." And crossed her fingers as she did.

There were four beats of stony silence. "Not one
more minute than that," the sitter finally said.

"Hope to die, Mrs. Bailey. Hey, I don't know what
I'd do without . . ." The words stuck in Courtney's
throat. Down the way, the man had opened the trunk.
He reached inside and hauled a woman out by the
arm. The woman struggled, smoothing out her shimmery minidress.

Mrs. Bailey said, "I make allowances, sure, but this
is getting to be too much of a habit."

The man held the woman tightly around the waist
and steered her toward the pickup. He had something
pressed against the small of her back. As Courtney
watched, he opened the pickup's door and shoved the
woman inside. He climbed in after her.

Mrs. Bailey said, "Miss Bedell? You there?"

"Oh, Jesus God. I've got to go." Courtney hung up and doused her flashlight. She stepped quietly out of the booth. Warm night air blew on her cheek. The pickup and the sedan sat bumper to bumper in the moonlight, exactly as they had when she'd entered the booth.

A woman's panicked voice suddenly called out, "Someone help me, please!" The sound was faint, as if from far away.

Courtney sucked air. Terror gripped her. *You will not panic, Officer Dumbshitz,* she told herself. *Stay cool. Calm as ice. Procedure, procedure, procedure, straight from the old manualeroo.* She took a hesitant step, stumbled, and almost fell.

Get with it, Bedell. You're the cop. He's the fucking criminal.

Running in a crouch, her breath whistling between her teeth, her flashlight swinging beside her hip, Courtney moved down the block in a zigzag pattern, keeping the sedan between her and the pickup. The distance was no more than twenty yards, though it seemed like fifty miles. She knelt behind the bumper. The pickup was dead ahead, fifteen feet away.

The woman cried out once more for help.

Courtney crept alongside the Mercedes and peeked inside. There in the backseat, clearly visible in the moonlight, two bare feet were propped against the windowsill. Beyond the feet were olive-complected, splayed-out legs with flabby thighs. On both inner thighs were large craterlike sores, glistening with body fluids.

Courtney ducked down beside the car, gagged, and very nearly threw up on the pavement. *Oh fuck me,* she thought, *it's* him, *Jesus-H-Christ-in-a-candy-store, it has to be.*

Up ahead, the woman's screams increased in volume. Slowly, carefully, Courtney unsnapped her Sam

Browne holster and wrapped her fingers around . . .
around . . .

Thin air. She sagged against the fender. She'd left
her weapon in her car. The scene came back to her
in a flood; exhausted, her workday finally at an end,
she'd dropped the pistol into her glove compartment
as she'd left the fairgrounds. Patrolman Courtney Bedell, scatterbrain second to none, was wading into a
tense situation against a dangerous suspect, armed
with a fucking flashlight. She looked back toward her
car, thought about backtracking and getting her hands
on the Glock.

The pickup's starter chugged. The engine caught
and raced.

The woman inside the pickup yelled out, "Don't!
Please don't! Why are you *doing this*?"

There was no time. Any second now the pickup,
bad guy, woman and all, would be gone. Courtney
could stand here like a rock and let it happen . . .

Or she could fake it.

She inhaled through her nose, make up her mind in
a flash. Her fingers trembling, she thumbed the switch
and the flashlight came on. The beam illuminated her
feet and reflected from the Mercedes' bumper. She
stood and moved to her left, out in the open, and
trained the flash on the pickup's sideview mirror. A
man's startled face looked back at her. She took in
the craggy jaw, the ugly scar on the cheek, the eyes
wide in surprise.

Courtney yelled out, "Police. Step out and stand
away, and keep your hands where I can see them."
Her voice broke at the end.

The man didn't move. Just continued to watch in
the sideview, squinting against the flashlight's glare.

"Now," Courtney said forcefully.

The woman said tearfully, "Thank God. Thank God.
Thank God. Thank . . ."

A latch clicked. The pickup's door creaked slowly outward. Hands appeared with roughened skin. A foot wearing a jogging shoe pushed the door further open.

"Stand away from the truck, sir. Move." Courtney felt stronger. Maybe she wouldn't faint after all.

The woman continued to thank God, over and over.

The man slowly edged out on the curb. He had sparse thinning hair, combed over, and a broad sloping forehead. The glare from the flashlight painted a shadow outline of his nose on his cheek. He had thick muscular shoulders and stood with a slightly humped posture. He said in a high squeaky voice, "This isn't what you think." His eyes moved wildly from side to side in his head.

Courtney pointed at the ground. "Lie down flat on your face and put your hands behind you. Now."

The man wore a confused look. He opened his mouth.

Courtney wondered what could be so puzzling to the guy. Her right hand firmly gripped the flashlight. Her left index finger pointed at the pavement with authority . . .

She got it. Flashlight in her right hand. Left hand extending toward the ground. Two hands. No weapon in either.

She tried, more weakly now, "Lie down, sir."

The man turned to the pickup, reached inside on the seat, and produced a medium-bore revolver. The caliber didn't matter. From Courtney's vantage point, staring straight down the barrel, the gun might as well have been a fucking howitzer.

A loud boom sounded. Flame spurted in the darkness. Something slammed into the left side of Courtney's rib cage. She was suddenly airborne, her arms flailing for balance, then she was scooting over rough dirt on her butt as the flashlight clattered across the sidewalk. She sat there, stunned, as the man leaped back inside the pickup, slammed the door, gunned the engine. The pickup lurched away, picking up speed, careening around the corner and disappearing from view as Courtney watched helplessly, her life flashing before her eyes as if in a high-speed video.

The pickup was long gone before it dawned on Courtney that she wasn't going to die. She reached through the hole singed in her shirt, found the crater gouged into her armored vest, poked her finger into the hole and felt the soft metal slug. She lay down flat, closed her eyes and said a prayer. It was a full minute before she could breathe. Her backside was raw and her ribs hurt like the blazes. She struggled to her feet and started up the block toward her car, stumping along like Igor. She half stumbled to the phone booth, pushed open the folding glass door, leaned against the shelf, lifted the receiver, and punched in 911. The number rang a few times before the operator clicked in. "Nine-one-one. Your emergency?"

Courtney licked dry lips. "I'm a . . . police officer. Shot. I'm at . . ." She looked for a street sign. "Oh fuck, I don't even know where I am."

"I have your location, ma'am. It's on my screen."

"Send . . . there's a possible DOA. I'm . . . oh fuck, just get here, will you?" She slammed down the receiver, stumbled over to her Lumina, stretched out on the fender, and passed out cold.

3

Courtney Bedell couldn't remember ever feeling this kind of pain. Agony racked her body no matter in which direction she moved. Agony each time she breathed. Agony when she was sitting still.

She slumped in the back of the ambulance and held her shirttail bunched up around her bra as the Emergency Medical Unit guy finished wrapping her midsection. He checked the Ace bandage for tension, secured the clips, and at last seemed satisfied. He showed his satisfaction by giving her ribs a final pat. She closed her eyes to keep from screaming out loud.

From waist to sternum she was a mummy. She'd taken one look at the football-size, purple-and-yellowish bruise and had very nearly fainted again. According to the EMU tech, only X rays would tell for sure if anything was broken. Didn't really matter, though, he'd said, because a bruise in the rib area would hurt just as much as a fracture. *You bet your sweet ass,* Courtney thought.

The ambulance was backed to within yards of the Mercedes, which still was parked beside the playground. Visible through the open rear doors, techs from the Crime Scene Unit hunted, dusted, poked, probed, and shined flashlights here and there around the swings and jungle gyms. Three squad cars formed a semicircle around the Mercedes, with two more black-and-whites angled in across the street. Uniformed cops milled about, shooting the bull and scratching their behinds. Yellow tape hung at waist level, fore and aft, blocking traffic from both directions. One CSU rep, a hefty brunette, had already dug the bullet from Courtney's vest, looked her over thoughtfully, and then taken the vest and her uniform blouse as well. One of the techs had loaned her a tee shirt with DPD EMERGENCY MEDICAL UNIT stenciled across the front. Minutes ago, plainclothes detectives had arrived in an unmarked car.

The medical tech told her he was finished and handed her an X-ray authorization. She glanced at the slip of paper; she was to be at Parkland Hospital at nine in the morning. Courtney sagged in exhaustion.

The tech left the ambulance to join the group photographing the body, their cameras aimed into the backseat of the Mercedes, quick flashes of brilliance piercing the darkness, illuminating the corpse's splayed-out legs. Courtney stood and gingerly tested her ribs. She pictured the perp, his gun pointed at her midsection, his expression calm as flame spurted from the barrel. She felt once again the bullet's numbing impact, and was suddenly weak in the knees. She staggered slightly, and gripped the edge of a gurney for support.

She decided she'd better suck it up, put herself back together, and face the world. She inched into the corner to shield herself from prying eyes, dropped her uniform slacks to her knees, adjusted her panties so that they didn't feel put on sideways, and prepared to pull her shirt down around her hips.

A man stuck his head in. He was one of the suits, a rumpled-looking guy around forty with a thick neck, a wide face, and a nose that looked as if it had been broken several times.

Courtney, her trousers down to her knees as she daintily modeled black bikini panties, said angrily, "Ex*cuse* me?"

"Oops," the detective said, and darted back outside.

Courtney had had it. She pulled her shirt down, packed in the tail, buttoned her fly, then leaned outside and glared down at the intruder. "You ever hear of knocking?"

The detective took a step back, then folded his arms. "Yeah, I heard of it. You ever hear of not running around a crime scene in your underwear?"

"Yeah, I heard of . . . I wasn't running around a crime scene."

"Running around, walking around, standing around. You were in your underwear. If you're going to be parading in you skivvies somebody's going to look."

"I was in the privacy of—"

"You were in the privacy of a crime scene ambulance, on my crime scene. If you don't want to get embarrassed, keep your britches pulled up."

Both Courtney and the detective had been raising their voices, and the techs working near the Mercedes had stopped what they were doing to listen. A couple wore grins. One guy snickered out loud.

Courtney bent nearer to the detective and hissed under her breath, "Keep your voice down. Look, I was just getting dressed."

"And I was just trying to talk to you. The patrol sergeant said there was a witness, and that the witness was in the ambulance."

She felt a little silly. She tried a smile. "Look, can we start this conversation over? I'm Courtney Bedell."

"And I'm Lieutenant Jerry Gholer. And, no, I don't wanna start over with the underwear. I want to talk to you about what you saw tonight."

She blinked, recognition dawning. Gholer was the near-legend who ran Dallas' Crimes-Against-Persons Di-

vision, which in most major cities is known as Robbery/
Homicide. Whatever you called Gholer's unit, he was
the best-known murder cop in the state. Two years
ago he'd lectured her police academy class on crime
scene procedure, and during his talk he'd told them,
"Screw up most places on the job and the worst you
can expect is a bitch letter in your jacket. But you
fuck up one of my homicide scenes and I'll make sure,
personally, that you can kiss your ass good-bye."

Courtney decided that she'd walked the plank about
as far as she could go. "Look, Lieutenant, I'm sorry
I—"

"We've got no time for sorry, Bedell. We already
wasted enough time. Come on." He held up an arm
to help her down. She leaned on him as she stepped
down on the pavement. He was four or five inches
taller than her own five-five, and his off-the-rack suit
looked as if he might've slept in it. As if to prove the
point, he stifled a yawn.

Cops and techs returned to work, pretending not to
notice as Gholer escorted her to the unmarked detective car. Two more plainclothes, a man and a woman,
had a map spread out on the fender, marking an X at
the crime scene location.

Gholer interrupted the pair. "Guys, meet Officer
Courtney Bedell. She's the witness, and you'll be getting to know her. Miss Bedell, these two are Detectives Eddie Frizell and Jinx Madison. They ain't much,
but they're all we got."

Frizell was a medium-built man with a sharp nose
and pointed chin. One corner of his mouth turned up
in a half smirk. Madison was a tall black woman with
an athlete's body and frizzed-out hair. She winked at
Courtney and jerked her head in Gholer's direction.
"The loo don't bite," Madison said. "But he's not faking being an asshole." She grinned at Gholer, then
bent over the map once more.

"See, I get no respect." Gholer looked Courtney up and down. "Can you make it to there okay?" He pointed in the general direction of the Mercedes.

Courtney inhaled, holding her ribs. "Yes, sir. If I don't have to move too fast."

Gholer held up one finger in a teaching attitude. " 'Sir' don't get it. 'Jerry' gets it. 'Loo' gets it. 'Sir' is for the mayor and old farts drawin' pensions." He scratched his eyebrow. "You go by Courtney?"

She nodded. "Yes, sir."

He cocked his head.

She laughed nervously. "Okay, okay. Yeah, *Jerry*, then."

"That's better. You Courtney, me Jerry." He looked at his feet. "The patrol sergeant said you told him that you got a sitter?"

"Who's about to quit for me being late all the time," Courtney said.

"Well, listen, this may take a while. You want to call your husband to pick up your kid?"

"I've got no husband to call, Loo. And I already talked to the sitter. Twice. Once from the phone booth before all hell broke loose, telling her I was on the way. Another time from the ambulance cell over there, telling her I *wasn't* on the way. She doesn't like it, but . . . I've got a few minutes."

"You sure? While this stuff is fresh on your mind we need to do a few things. But I got kids myself."

"This isn't really my kid. It's the same as if he was, but really it's my nephew I'm raising."

Gholer took a step toward the Mercedes, then turned back. "I'll get you home soon as I can."

Courtney decided that this guy wasn't as tough as he was letting on. She firmed her mouth. "Loo?"

He looked at her. Visible beyond him, flashing rooflights illuminated the techs as they rolled a gurney alongside the Mercedes.

Courtney said, "It's the Fiddleback, isn't it? I saw those sores on that woman's legs."

Gholer remained deadpan. "What do you know about ol' Fiddleback?"

"Just what I've read. That he . . . supposedly he . . . tortures his victims with brown recluse spiders and then shoots them."

"Mmm-hmm. You told anybody else you think this might be him? Any of these cops around here?"

Courtney thought it over. "Now that you mention it, I don't remember anybody asking."

"Good. Keep it that way. You saw this guy up close?"

"Four or five feet. He was firing at me at the time, so I didn't walk off the distance."

Gholer gave a short dry chuckle. "Good you got a sense of humor. You're going to need it. Could you recognize the guy? Don't bullshit me now, Courtney. You know about eyewitness testimony good as I do."

Courtney did know. Eyewitnesses were great in court, with the DA's staff coaching them, but not much help in tracking a suspect. The truth was that eyewitnesses, especially the ones who'd glimpsed a suspect while the guy waved a gun in their faces, could seldom recall accurately the perp's hair color, build, even his race. There'd even been cases where the witness had gotten the perp's sex wrong. Courtney closed her eyes for a couple of seconds, picturing the crazy eyes, the scar, the thinning hair . . . She opened her eyes. "I can make him, Loo."

He clapped his hands. "Okay, tomorrow you'll look at photo spreads. Listen now. You know you've seen this guy. *I* know you've seen this guy. Detective Frizell and Detective Madison are gonna know. They're family. But don't tell anybody else. If the chief himself asks you, it was too dark for you to make a positive ID. Got it?"

Courtney blinked, confused. "I've got it. I don't know that I *get* it."

"For now let's just say that we don't want your name in the papers, and the best way to keep it out is for nobody to know we got a witness. That could change, depending on if I put my shorts on backwards tomorrow. You're injured. You're entitled to paid leave from the job till you heal. But while you're off duty we got rights to you as a witness, only that's not what we want to call you for public consumption. So I'm thinking, officially, you're temporarily assigned to my outfit for desk duty. That's done all the time with injured cops, and nobody'll even notice. In the morning I'll clear it with the Patrol Division. You good with that?" He watched her expectantly.

She felt a wave of resentment. It was clear that Gholer wasn't asking. "I suppose I'll have to be," she said, folding her arms.

He frowned. "Have to be what?"

"Good with it."

"Meaning you don't *want* to be?"

She didn't want to paint herself into a corner. But, no, Courtney Bedell hadn't gotten this far in the world by not speaking her mind. "Meaning," she said, "I'd rather be asked and not told. I'm pro-choice that way."

"You think I'm muscling you around."

She stood up straighter. "Yeah, Loo. After a fashion."

"Hmm," Gholer said softly, sizing her up. He turned toward the medics, who'd placed the corpse on a gurney, which they now rolled across the pavement. Gholer yelled, "You guys hold up a minute." The medics stopped short of the open ambulance doors. Gholer turned back to Courtney and crooked a finger. "C'mere," he said.

She followed him reluctantly over to the gurney.

Gholer nodded to one of the techs, then unzipped the body bag and spread back the flaps. The dead woman's eyes were in slits, her lips pulled back. Her hair was perfectly fixed and her teeth were sparkling white. There was a star-shaped wound in her chest, caused, Courtney knew, by a gun discharged with the barrel against the skin. Dark craterlike sores dotted the corpse's stomach, her inner thighs, one on each upper arm. A couple of the sores had swelled to the size of grapefruits. Courtney looked away.

"Right now," Gholer said, "I got eleven dead people to thank this same looney for. The lady that owns the Mercedes is missing, and I've already chalked her up as Number Twelve. Oh, we'll give the chief a lotta bullshit so he can tell the papers there's always hope, but anybody this guy gets his hands on, color 'em gone." He released his hold and nodded to the tech, who rezipped the bag and trundled on with his load. Gholer said, "Now that you've seen this guy, how you think he's going to react if he finds out he didn't kill you?"

Courtney lowered her gaze.

"Right," Gholer said. "He's going to think maybe you should be next. You're so important to this case you wouldn't believe it, and the best way to keep you in my sights is to keep you out of everybody else's, any way I can. So if you think I'm pushing you around, that's tough. So until we get this guy, you bet your ass you do what I tell you."

Courtney felt put in her place as she followed Gholer over to stand by the Mercedes. Inside she was seething, more at herself than anyone. Someday she'd take lessons in keeping her mouth shut. Gholer walked as if he was tired, shoulders slumping, palms to the rear. For Courtney it was also slow going. She stopped every five feet or so to gingerly touch her ribs.

Gholer backed away from the car, dusting his hands together, looking the Mercedes over from bumper to bumper. He said, "Where exactly was the pickup?"

Courtney kept her arms around her midsection and gestured with her head. "Right in front of the car. Tailgate was three or four feet away."

"Yeah, okay." Gholer dug a flashlight from his hip pocket. He thumbed the switch, then followed the beam along the ground to a point in front of the Mercedes. He stepped up on the curb and pointed down at the street. "About here?"

"Close enough," Courtney said.

Gholer bent from the waist, squinting. Then he stepped down from the curb, dragged his hand along the pavement, and examined his fingers. He murmured, "Yeah," then raised his voice. "Hey, Denny, got a minute?"

A CSU tech hustled up. Gholer leaned on the tech's shoulder and pointed down. "That brown powdery stuff," Gholer said. "Bag it, willya?"

The tech jogged away, then returned carrying a whisk broom and a Ziploc. He crouched and carefully brushed the pavement.

While the tech worked, Gholer came over to where Courtney stood. He massaged the back of his neck. "It's the same stuff we've found at other crime scenes attributed to this guy. Not all of his scenes, just four or five. Forensics will have to make it official, but I'll tell you off the record that it's resin. The same stuff pitchers used to keep in a bag beside the mound, to get a better grip on the ball. So maybe our guy's an old knuckleballer, but I'm not betting on it. The resin's the only consistent evidence we got. Evidence of what, though, don't ask me." He looked beyond Courtney and scowled. "Oh shit," Gholer said.

Courtney turned. A mobile news unit had pulled up beyond the yellow tape. Two cameramen and a chicly

coiffed female on-the-spot reporter stood near the
barrier, the guys hefting minicams while the lady
begged the cop on guard to let them through. The cop
stood firm with folded arms.

"'We got more leaks than a fifty-dollar rowboat,"
Gholer said. "I don't got to tell you, Courtney. Don't
talk to those people. *Especially* those people. I catch
whoever tipped them off . . ."

Courtney wondered if she'd ever figure out how to
take this guy. In the five minutes she'd known Gholer
he'd gone from combative to caring to going off on
her, and now he was back to surly. Her own fuse was
pretty short, but Gholer's was apparently burnt down
to the quick. She looked up the street, where her Lumina was still parked beside the phone booth. "Maybe
I should disappear," she said. "Go on home. Steer
clear of the press, plus my sitter . . ." She showed
Gholer a questioning look.

He firmly shook his head. "Nope. Can't turn you
loose just yet. I got one more thing for you." He stuck
his hands in his pockets. "The patrol sergeant told me
that you said you didn't have your weapon when this
guy shot you?"

"I forgot the damn gun in my car. Slapped leather
on an empty holster."

"And then you took the guy on anyway?"

"I didn't have a choice. It was either that or let him
go. The woman was screaming. I guess I wasn't thinking real clearly."

"I don't know whether to put you up for a comme-
dation or make you stand with your nose in the corner. Effective immediately, you don't go anywhere
without your weapon. If your lover objects 'cause you
got it in bed, tell him it's your turn-on. You're packing
heat at the grocery store, the shopping mall. What do
you carry?"

Courtney shrugged. "Glock."

"Good choice. Not much use unless you've got it with you." Gholer lifted his coat to show his nylon shoulder rig. "You got no better friend. What time you available in the morning?"

"I'm due at Parkland Hospital at nine for X rays."

"So, ten-thirty, eleven? You know where Irving Boulevard cuts through the Trinity industrial district?"

"Sure. A lot of warehouses, supply companies. I've driven through there lots of times."

"Good." Gholer pulled out a business card, scribbled an address and phone number, and handed the card over. "There is a task force there, working to get this guy, at least that's what it's supposed to be, which is a subject for debate. Officially it's us, the Texas Rangers, and the FBI. Jinx and Eddie are a hundred percent on this case. I'm ninety, which leaves ten percent of my time for the other three or four hundred open cases we got in Crimes-Against-Persons, for which we employ four detectives a shift. The Fiddleback's playing hell with our overall efficiency, you know? As for the FBI and Texas Rangers . . . well, if you've noticed there aren't any fibbies or Rangers around here doing any of this grunt work, then you got a leg up on getting the picture. Anytime there's a news conference you'll see people wearing Stetsons and guys in suits that cost more than fifty dollars, but unless we're on television you'll only see broke JC Penney customers like me. Listen, you got a partner you're going to leave hanging while you're on injury leave?"

Courtney coughed, nearly doubling over with the effort. "I'm riding relief this month. My regular partner got transferred."

"Good. You're not inconveniencing anybody." Gholer looked once more toward the yellow tape barricade. "Heads up. I think your first ID prospect just arrived."

A white Cadillac SUV had parked beside the news truck. Both of the SUV's front doors opened at once. The television crew geared up, the on-the-spot reporter hustling toward the Caddy with the minicam operators in hot pursuit.

Gholer lightly pounded his fist on the Mercedes' bumper. "Jesus Christ, we gotta figure out a way to keep Cokie Roberts Junior and her crew away from that guy." His expression grew intent. "Here's the deal, Courtney, so you'll know. Next few days you'll look at pictures till you may need glasses, and you're going to be seeing so many people from afar they'll be parading past in your sleep. Can't be helped. You're going to look at anybody where there's the remotest possibility. Some of the people I'll want you to eyeball, you're going to wonder if Gholer might need some funny-farm time to recuperate, but that's okay. Lots of folks have been thinking that way about me for years.

"So now we go on Wild-Goose Safari Number One. This Mercedes here belongs to a Mrs. William Hargis. She modeled at the state fair car show today, and we're pretty sure she's the woman you saw the guy dragging away. The corpse—well, we ain't sure who she is, but we're working on it. Point is, that's Mrs. William Hargis' husband who just drove up in the rich man's jungle buggy. I had Jinx call him, partly so he could confirm that the stiff we got here isn't his wife, but also 'cause I want you to look at this guy."

Gholer started to lead the way toward the barrier, motioning for Courtney to follow. "Odds are a million to one against," Gholer said, "but Mr. and Mrs. Hargis' divorce settlement was in the front seat of the Mercedes. You never know, right? Wouldn't be the first guy to off his old lady in the middle of a split. The bad news would be, if the husband's the guy you saw, then this would be a killing we couldn't hang on the Fiddleback. So put your game face on, Courtney. Your career as designated looker is about to begin."

Two men and a woman had arrived in the Cadillac, and at first Courtney couldn't figure out which of the guys she was supposed to zero in on. One man wore a dark suit and the other was decked out in Hilfiger slacks and an expensive Polo knit. The woman was early to mid-twenties, Barbie-doll cute with straight hair to her shoulders, dressed in designer jeans and five-inch, fuck-me platforms. She stayed close to the golf pro–looking guy.

At Gholer's insistence Courtney had positioned herself beside the cop who was guarding the barrier, looking the other way when the on-the-spot TV woman had thrown her a curious glance. As Courtney watched, Gholer approached the newcomers head-on. Detective Eddie Frizell and Detective Jinx Madison flanked Gholer. Frizell's half smirk reminded Courtney of a character in an old-time Western movie her dad used to watch over and over, the gunslinger hired by the rancher to scare the sheepherders away. Jack Palance had played the role, and Alan Ladd as Shane had gunned him down at the end. Jinx Madison walked catlike, erect, her shoulders back in a wary attitude.

Gholer had a driver's license photo, faxed over from the DMV to one of the radio cars. He compared the picture, first with the man in the suit and then with the guy in the Polo shirt. Polo-shirt was a match. Gholer extended his hand. "Lieutenant Jerry Gholer, Mr. Hargis, Crimes-Against-Persons. Thanks for coming down."

The Barbie doll clung to Hargis' arm. Courtney made Hargis to be early forties. He had striking good looks along with sun-bleached hair tousled just so; just the type to send tremors through the Barbie dolls of the world, Courtney thought, though a woman with substance would likely be put off by the guy. His tan was straight from the tennis court, his smooth-muscled body a result of personal-trainer workouts. Courtney pictured Hargis on a lounge by the pool, holding a double mirror under his chin for maximum sun exposure. Instinctively, her upper lip curled. Courtney's type or not, however, Mr. William Hargis no more resembled the crazy who'd shot her than Brad Pitt looked like the Hunchback of Notre Dame. The presence of the Barbie doll had a lot to say about his character; called to his wife's apparent abduction scene, Hargis had dragged his current sweetie along. Courtney hoped that in the divorce proceedings, Mr. William Hargis was getting screwed to the wall.

Hargis smiled blandly at Gholer while not saying anything, ignoring Gholer's extended hand.

The man in the suit stepped in between Hargis and Gholer, and produced a small printed card. "Larry Akin, Lieutenant. Akin and Gilchrist."

Oh, Courtney thought, his sweetie *and* his lawyer. Inside the lawyer's thousand-dollar suit were rounded shoulders and a slumped posture. Akin, in fact, looked more like the suspect than did William Hargis.

Gholer took the lawyer's card, which he stacked on top of Hargis' DMV photo. The lieutenant turned his head and appeared to be looking toward the murder car, but in the glare of the ambulance lights his nostrils were flared. *He's trying to get ahold of himself,* Courtney thought. Gholer took a deep breath, held it, then slowly emptied his lungs. He ignored the lawyer and said directly to Hargis, "Can you tell us if that's your car over there? Then, and this will be the hard part, we've got a body I'd like for you to—"

"It's my client's car," Akin cut in. "And I know Mrs. Hargis. I can identify the—"

"Mr. Hargis." Gholer stepped around the lawyer. "I guess I'm not understanding, Mr. Hargis. Are you being represented here?"

Hargis glanced down at the Barbie doll. She hugged his arm and snuggled up closer.

Akin kept the floor. "I've already told you, sir. I can provide whatever information you need. Billy, you and Heather get back in the car."

Hargis and Heather moved unhurriedly toward the Caddy.

Gholer blocked the couple's path. "Hold it a minute. I got to tell you, us calling a family member where we got a situation, a homicide, and then the family member bringing a lawyer along, that doesn't settle so good."

Jinx Madison walked over and leaned her rump on the SUV's fender, folding her arms. The tall black woman performed the move casually, expertly, her expression all business. She lifted her coat to rest a hand on her hip, revealing the handcuffs dangling from her belt.

Akin clung to his spokesman's role. "My presence here can set any way you want it to set, Lieutenant. I'm here as a friend."

"Friend?" Gholer said. "Well, I'll tell you, bud. The friendliest thing you can do is to tell Mr. Hargis to get his ass over there and have a look at that black car and tell us if it's his. Then the next-friendliest thing you can do is tell Mr. Hargis to get his ass over to that ambulance and tell us if the stiff in there is his wife. We don't want nobody collapsing with grief here, so maybe Mr. Hargis should take *her* along, to hold him up in case he faints." He pointed at Heather, who pooched her lips into a pout.

Hargis' smile faded. He took a step toward Gholer and opened his mouth as if to speak.

Akin charged in like a man on fire. "Keep quiet,

Billy. And, Lieutenant, I'm going to instruct you not to address my client again. Anything you have to say—"

"Client?" Gholer looked up at the sky as if searching for answers. "Not ten seconds ago you said you were a friend. Which one are you? You can't be a lawyer *and* a friend—that's not possible."

Akin spread his feet apart. "I can't believe we're having this discussion. Is Mr. Hargis a suspect here?"

"You're damn sure making him one with all this bullshit," Gholer said.

The lawyer's facial muscles tightened. "You asked for some Ids, car and corpse. We're prepared to give them. Otherwise we're finished here."

" 'We,' meaning you?" Gholer said.

"You're the one asking for help. Do you want me to view the body, or don't you?"

There were five seconds of silence, during which Courtney halfway expected Gholer to go into a fighter's crouch and put up his dukes. The lieutenant rubbed the back of his neck. Finally he said to Akin, "Yeah, okay. Go ahead. Detective Madison, escort Mr. Akin here over to the ambulance." Then as Jinx Madison fell in step alongside Akin, Gholer said, "I guess this investigation is going to be easier than most."

Akin halted. He seemed only mildly curious. "How so?"

"Well, in most cases," Gholer said, "the victim's family is a real pain in the ass. Usually we spend as much time keeping the loved ones up to snuff as we do chasing the perp. But in this instance here, I don't think the woman's husband gives much of a shit." He looked to Akin, then to Hargis, and back again. "That the situation?" Gholer said. "Or am I reading it wrong?"

*   *   *

Courtney hung out behind the barrier as Madison took the lawyer to the ambulance. Gholer came over to assume a hip-cocked stance a few feet from where Courtney stood. She raised up on tiptoes to peer over the lieutenant's shoulder. The mobile news crew followed Madison and Akin as far as they could, then adjusted their zoom lenses and continued to shoot the action from afar. Akin had to hustle in order to keep up with Jinx Madison's long flowing strides. As the pair approached the ambulance, the medics hovered over the gurney and unzipped the body bag. Madison stood aside while the lawyer bent for a look at the dead woman.

Gholer murmured to no one in particular, "Can you believe that fucking guy?" Then he called out, "Hey, Eddie. Over here." As Frizell jogged over, Gholer swiveled his head and shot Courtney an inquisitive look.

Courtney shook her head. "Not even close, Loo."

"Yeah, shit, I was afraid of that." Gholer rested a hand on Frizell's shoulder and pointed toward the SUV, where William Hargis held the door for his girlfriend. Gholer said, "Twenty-four/seven on that guy, Eddie. I want a report every time he takes a leak. The guy's dirty. We tell him his wife's missing, he shows up with Racehorse Haynes II running interference. I want to know why."

Frizell pulled on his earlobe. "What difference does it make why? Loo, your witness already told you this ain't the guy."

Gholer dejectedly lowered his chin. "He's jerking us around with that lawyer."

"Which is what he ought to do," Courtney said without thinking, then wished she could bite her tongue in two.

Both Gholer and Frizell stared at her. "So now

we're getting instructions from the witness box," Gholer said.

Courtney clasped her hands behind her back. "Don't mind me. Just thinking out loud."

Gholer made a beckoning gesture. "So think some more. You started, now you got to finish."

Courtney moved nearer the crime-scene tape. "I'm not the detective here."

"Yeah, you are," Gholer said. "I have just appointed you Detective for a Minute. Now talk."

Courtney expelled breath. "Okay, look. The guy was shacked up for the night when he gets this call from the police demanding that he hook 'em over to South Dallas where there's this murder scene. Something about his wife being missing, when he's currently in the midst of a messy divorce. Rich people like that, their lawyer's the first person they'd call in a situation. That's all I'm saying, loo. The lawyer being here, that's not a suspicious circumstance on its own."

Gholer studied the ground.

Frizell chipped in, "Lady's right, Jerry. In addition to which, we ain't exactly got a posse on call we can send around every time you happen to get a hard-on for a guy."

Gholer lifted his head. "How come everybody's got to have a better point than me? Hey, Courtney, didn't you say you got a baby-sitter to look after? Go on home and I'll see you in the morning. Jesus Christ, we got too many people cooking the soup around here."

4

Sis Hargis was burning hot, sweat glistening on her naked body, frightened to the point of madness. Chained to a bench inside a pitch-dark room.

Alone except for a sleeping man.

She'd realized that she had a fellow captive early on, almost the instant that Captain Asshole—she'd assigned the nickname to the phony valet parking attendant within minutes after he'd kidnapped her—had brought her here, stripped her, and shackled her wrist. She hadn't seen the moon or stars since he'd first stopped the pickup someplace in the middle of nowhere right after he'd shot the policewoman and had slipped the blindfold over her eyes. But the second that he'd pushed her, struggling and begging for mercy, into this prison of a room, she'd been aware of a presence nearby other than the creep himself. She'd smelled the faint body odor even before Captain Asshole had left, locking the door behind him. The other captive's loud breathing had at first frightened Sis, and then had settled into background noise. For what seemed like an eternity the other person stirred and mumbled incoherently. Sis tried whispering, speaking, even shouting, all to no avail; the sleep-breaths and gentle snores continued on and on. Once she stood up and struggled in the darkness toward the

seemingly sleeping person until her restraints held her
back, her outstretched fingers touching empty air.

In minutes—or could it be hours?—a rasping sound
grated her senses as Captain Asshole twisted the handle and pushed the door open. *If I'm going to die,* she
thought, *please let me do so without having to smell
his stinking breath again.* Into the room he shuffled.
Sis was going to be brave. No way would this bastard
make her crawl.

She managed to get mad. "You'll regret this, you
son of a bitch," she screamed.

The slice of dim lighting lasted only a heartbeat
before he shut the door. He stood over her, his rapid
panting interspersed with the sleeping captive's mea-
sured breathing. There was a metallic *clink,* a nauseat-
ing whiff of kerosene, the scratching of a match, and
finally a reddish glow as a lantern flickered and
glowed.

Her heartbeat quickened. Jesus, he was naked as a
jaybird. He'd slipped on a ski mask. In the flickering
dimness she made out a featureless head and three
pale slashes where his mouth and eyes showed
through. He carried a pistol, giving her the juiciest of
choices: Did she care to look at the ski mask, his flac-
cid dick swinging a foot or so in front of her face, or
stare down the barrel of the gun? *Your choice, Madam
Hargis.* She lowered her lashes and watched the floor.

He prodded her with the pistol. "Lie down flat," he
ordered, the first words he'd spoken to her since he'd
locked her in the trunk of her own car. He put a hand
on her shoulder and pushed her down.

The shackle and chain made rattling noises as Sis
stretched out on her back. So it had come to this.
She'd assumed that he'd eventually rape her ever since
he'd kidnapped her—had even strengthened her resolve to put up with it, not to resist—but as time had
passed her hopes had built. She'd hoped against hope

that her captor wouldn't be interested in sex, that he got his jollies by merely scaring the shit out of people, but now that fantasy fled out the window. This disgusting asshole was about to climb on top of her and force her legs apart.

"Anything, just . . . please don't hurt me." She no longer felt brave. She'd submit to anything just to get out alive. Her voice sounded whiny and far away.

He sat on the bench, one fuzzy buttock touching her hip. There was a huge tattoo between his shoulder blades. He reeked of cheap aftershave. Bile rose in her throat. "Be still," he said. "If you move I will shoot you."

Sis flexed her arms and legs and lay stiff as a stone. *You want to rape a statue?* In the light from the lantern, the ceiling rippled like choppy water.

For long seconds he sat motionless. Then he reached underneath the bench and removed a palm-sized plastic box along with a latex glove, which he pulled on and snapped up around his wrist. He opened the box and reached inside.

Lunge at the bastard, Sis thought. *A quick hard one to the nuts, claw his fucking eyes out.*

But she couldn't move. She couldn't . . . fucking . . . *move.*

He dropped something small from within the box onto her stomach, letting his hand fall back into his lap, and watched her.

An insect crawled on her skin.

Was she *imagining this*? Jesus, was it a cockroach? Tiny scrabbling legs paraded up her body and came to a standstill a couple of inches beneath her left breast. The bug sat motionless, as if waiting for orders.

Oh Jesus, Captain Asshole had an erection. His eyes widened behind the ski mask. He reached with the pistol and prodded her ribs where the insect had stopped. He pulled back, waited, and then poked at the bug a second time.

And then the fucking thing bit her.

As the insect sunk its probe into her flesh she bit her lips. Whatever it was it was no cockroach. *A scorpion,* she thought, *it's got to be.* This sadist bastard had put a scorpion on her, and now the fucking thing was stinging the shit out of her.

But aside from a tiny pinprick, she felt nothing. No sudden blast of pain, no agony spreading from the wound. A slight itching, nothing more. The bite of a butterfly.

Captain Asshole snatched the insect up and returned the crawly thing to its carrier. He held the lantern aloft and, as Sis held her breath, bent near and examined the insect bite. Apparently satisfied, he stood up and crossed the room to where the sleeping man lay.

The light from the lantern gave Sis her first look at her cellmate. He was a young guy with smooth features, an olive tint to his skin, and several days' growth of beard. His eyes were partway open.

Captain Asshole nudged the man with his foot. Then he extended the gun and fired.

The explosion in the tightly enclosed space was deafening. The stench of burned gunpowder filled the room. The young man's body jerked once. The labored breathing was at once interspersed with rattles from deep in the throat. Then came a long sigh as the last air escaped from the lungs. There was slight movement, a rustling of limbs as the body relaxed for the final time.

Sis yelled, jumped up from the bench, and struggled toward the door. The shackle dug into her wrist so hard that tears came up in her eyes. She sagged in defeat and collapsed, sobbing.

Her captor stood over her, holding the lantern aloft, and for a long instant Sis was certain he'd shoot her as well. But then he turned and left the room, slamming the door behind him. A deadbolt thunked into place. Bare feet thudded on wooden floors, receding into silence.

Sis stared helplessly at the ceiling in the darkness. One down, one to go, she thought with little emotion. *And as the one to go next I'm casting my vote for a final glimpse of daylight. Just one more look at the outside world before he kills me.*

She struggled to get a hold on herself. She would remain upbeat no matter what. Right down to her death rattle, she'd leave 'em laughing. Nothing matters but the show, kid.

She supposed that she should say a eulogy for the dead man. But, Christ, she didn't know his name, where he was from, what his favorite song might be, or any of the other shit that eulogists were supposed to have at their fingertips.

She lay in the darkness and dreamed up a history for the guy, and for no particular reason decided that he must be a hick from Oklahoma, Arkansas, or, worst of all, East Fucking Texas. Only bumpkins, she thought, and ditzos like yours truly, would fall for Captain Asshole's bullshit to begin with; anyone with half a brain would never have gotten in the car with the guy. *Besides,* she thought, *I'm the one putting on this funeral, so the stiff can be from wherever in hell I say.* She licked dry lips, whistled a few bars of "Okie from Muskogee," then giggled insanely before her laughter dissolved in chest-racking sobs.

Quit being a crybaby, she told herself. *Look on the bright side. At least there'll be no more divorce proceedings and no more lawyers to pay. When I'm gone,* Sis thought, *the women at the Park Cities Book and Luncheon Club will shed a tear, have a moment of*

silence, hoist a spot of tea. And my dear estranged hus-
band Billy, bless his heart, will be so grief-stricken that
he'll ejaculate all over my grave.

She lay as if paralyzed and waited for a delayed
reaction to the insect bite, but none came. Slowly, her
fear subsided into numb acceptance.

The door opened, and Captain Asshole came back
in with the lantern. He also carried a Pyrex mixing
bowl with liquid of some kind sloshing around inside.
Sis went immediately rigid with fear, but he ignored
her. He went straight over to the dead man and lifted
a sponge from the bowl. He squeezed out the excess,
set the bowl aside, and reached for the corpse's head.
Now a new smell cut through the dead man's body
odor and the stench of kerosene. It was a clean, fresh,
soapy odor.

As it dawned on Sis what was happening, she actually laughed out loud. This had to be a fucking dream.
She pinched herself as hard as she could, but the apparition didn't go away. Her senses then left her completely and she giggled until her sides hurt, her insane
laughter growing in volume as, just feet from where
she lay, a lunatic sat naked on a bench, and washed
a dead man's hair.

5

At six A.M. the bedside radio came on, blasting, "I Heard It Through the Grapevine," over Magic 102 Jammin' Oldies. Courtney Bedell's throat was dry and her ribs ached. She'd had five hours' sleep and a host of nightmares. The crazy who'd shot her was still out there, waiting.

Jason stirred and giggled, from somewhere off in the Land of Nod. He slept on his side on top of the covers, dressed in his Jockeys. His thumb was an inch from his lips. Courtney had read countless child-rearing books, most of which told her that Jason's thumb-sucking wasn't cause for alarm; by the age of five, the experts agreed, the child should grow out of the habit. But Christ, Courtney thought, this kid's already four and shows no sign of slowing down. She resisted the urge to yank Jason's hand away from his mouth. As quietly as she could, she pushed the blanket off of her and prepared to rise.

She scootched on her back to the edge of the king-size mattress and tried to get on her feet. The pain in her midsection flared up; she laid flat until she could breathe, rolled over, and came out of bed crab fashion with her rump in the air.

I owe you one, Fiddleback. Do I fucking ever.

She flicked on the bedside lamp, and stood looking

around in panties and T-shirt as Marvin Gaye finished his rocking number and the Beatles cut in with "I Wanna Hold Your Hand." Normally Courtney went through a sit-up and leg-lift routine in time with the music, but today she'd be lucky to make it into the bathroom. She staggered through the door, leaning on the jamb for support, stripped down her panties, and sat on the john.

When she was finished she cast her T-shirt into a hamper, carefully unwrapped the Ace bandage from around her midsection, pulled the curtain aside, and turned on the shower. As she waited for the water to heat up she stepped on the scale. One twenty-seven, five pounds over ideal, three pounds below the point where she felt like a tub. She looked in the mirror, at her raven short-cut hair, at her dark Italian eyes, her smooth Sicilian coppery skin immune to sunburn. She thought she looked beat to hell.

When the water was hot enough she stood under the spray and soaped down, letting the torrent pound her injured ribs as she winced in pain. She washed her hair, managed not to get shampoo in her eyes as she rinsed, turned off the shower, and stepped out on the mat, dripping. She felt half alive, which was more than she could have said for herself ten minutes ago. After she dried her body and her hair, she rewrapped her torso and returned to the bedroom.

She hauled out a clean uniform, looked it over, then stowed the navy-blue slacks and blouse, emblems and all, back inside the closet; she was on injured leave from the Patrol Division, and civvies would be her dress of the day. She dug in her drawer for Levi's and a loose cotton shortsleeve sweater with a collar, and reached under the bed for gray running shoes.

When she was dressed she pinched her chin in thought. The Glock gave her a problem. Gholer had told her to be armed at all times, but wearing the

holster over her jeans would have her looking like
Pistol-Packin' Annie. Finally she wrapped the thick
leather belt around the Glock, holster and all, and
shoved the whole mess into a shopping bag. She stood
over Jason, reached out to wake him, then stopped,
stood back, and spent a few seconds just watching the
little guy.

She adored him.

No way could she love Jason more if he'd been her
own child. He had dark Bedell skin and dark Bedell
eyes. As he grew older the baby fat in his cheeks
would recede to show sharp Bedell facial bones. He
couldn't look more like her if she'd carried him in
her womb.

The resemblance wasn't any mystery. Courtney's father's genes had been dominant in the family. All
through their growing-up years people had taken
Courtney and Jan for twins, even though Jan was in
fact two years older, and Jason was the spitting image
of his mother.

Jesus, Courtney thought. Jan.

She didn't like thinking about Jan, but daily contact
with Jason kept her older sister's image rooted firmly
in her mind. Courtney moved up nearer to the bed.

She squeezed Jason's arm. His thick dark lashes
fluttered, then lifted. Sleepy confusion crossed his features, followed by a grin of recognition. "Read to me,
Coatney?" he said.

"Pronounce your R's, Jason. *Court*ney. Say it
again."

He frowned in puzzlement. "Coatney?"

"Courtney, you little stinker. Court. Court. *Court*ney."

He giggled. "Will you read to me?"

Her insides melted. "Of course I will."

He held out his arms.

She gingerly touched her side. "Can't lift you, baby.
Courtney hurt herself."

He raised up and laid a pudgy hand against her ribs. "Coatney hurt?"

"You betchum, Little Beaver."

"Jason make it better."

She leaned over and planted a kiss on his forehead. "Know what, buddy? I'll just bet that you can."

Twenty minutes later Courtney had finished Jason's morning reading session, and decided that she'd picked the wrong before-breakfast literature. Sam I Am was an asshole. She wished that she could bust Dr. Seuss for contributing to the delinquency of a minor. She would have loved to get Seuss down to the station, grill him about his motives.

For the fourth or fifth time she maneuvered a plate over in front of Jason. The plate held two crisp bacon strips and one fluffily scrambled egg. A yellow egg, not a green egg. Bacon, not ham. "Please eat, baby," she said.

Jason shoved the plate away. A strip of bacon fell on the table. Jason grinned and tightly shut his eyes. "I do not like them, Sam I Am." He was being difficult as hell, and was just cute enough to get away with it.

Green Eggs and Ham lay open near Courtney's elbow. She thought that Sam I Am looked just like the Cat in the Hat, the star of Jason's second-favorite Dr. Seuss. Nothing original about old Seuss, the guy wrote the same book over and over.

I would not eat them with a fox, I would not eat them in a box.

How about if you were handcuffed, Seuss? Courtney thought. *In the backseat of a squad car, with me shoving them down your throat, would you eat the fuckers then?*

Time to employ the old psychology. Remain calm. Do not allow the child to know he's upsetting you. Be pleasant but firm.

"As soon as you eat your breakfast you may play in your room until it's time to go." Courtney got up, went to the sink and turned on the hot water. She plugged the drain, Dawn dish detergent held ready.

Her grandfather had bought the tiny East Dallas home long before automatic dishwashers had come into being. Her mom and dad, when they'd inherited the house, had wanted to redo the kitchen and add a dishwasher if Sears would extend them credit. Sears had approved, but her dad had backed out when his paycheck simply wouldn't stretch to meet the payments, and also continue to fund a lawyer for Jan.

Fucking Jan.

Following in her father's footsteps, Courtney had visited Sears two months ago, and they'd approved her credit as well. But her cop's salary wouldn't extend any farther than her father's bus driver's pay, not once you figured in Jan's *current* lawyer. Jesus Christ, Courtney couldn't remember when Jan hadn't needed a lawyer, or when someone in the family—her dad, her uncle, and now Courtney herself—wasn't paying her bills.

Until her ship came in Courtney would continue washing dishes by hand. Not to mention put up with plumbing that creaked and groaned as if every night was Halloween.

Jason kicked his feet. "I do not like them, Sam I Am." He was getting mad. What had begun as a game was progressing toward a tantrum. He made as if to throw a piece of bacon.

Courtney touched a glass figurine that had been her mother's—a woman wearing a bustle, riding a bike—and held her hand under the faucet until the water was hot enough. She squeezed a stream of soap to mix with the flow from the nozzle; in a minisecond, suds appeared. She said calmly to Jason, "When you're finished, you may play."

Jason tried a different ploy. "Does Coatney like green eggs and ham?"

"Mmm. Love 'em." As she washed her plate, silverware and coffee cup, her gaze drifted out the window. The back yard was tiny, with the same waist-high cyclone fence her grandfather had erected stretched across the back of the property. Metal cans stood beyond the fence on a wooden stand. The alley consisted of twin tire ruts on a bed of dirt; on days when it rained, the city collectors required that the trash be placed in front of the house. The home behind Courtney's was vacant. It would be no trick at all for an intruder to creep up the alley, vault over the fence . . .

"Does Mr. Trevino like green eggs and ham?" Jason interrupted her thoughts as he played with his spoon. His resolve was weakening since his antics weren't producing the desired reaction.

Bulletin: *Woman triumphs over difficult kid.*

Courtney grinned at Jason's question. A couple of weeks ago she'd partnered with Trevino on patrol, and had gotten a call from the sitter telling her that Jason was ill. They'd detoured by the sitter's in the squad car, and all the way home the muscular Hispanic cop had bounced Jason on his knee. "Officer Trevino *loooves* eggs," Courtney said. "Eat your breakfast now." Courtney's own mother had always given in, allowing her and Jan to pretty much do as they pleased. Courtney wondered if the lack of discipline had been the start of her sister's downfall. *That's it, Court,* the voice inside her said. *When you can't deal with the problem yourself, blame it on poor old departed Mom.*

Jason's look grew suddenly cunning. He paused for effect before asking, "Does *my mommy* like green eggs and ham?"

Courtney's grip on the plate tightened convulsively. Even at four, Jason knew which buttons to push.

Courtney blinked away a tear, at the same time struggling with the answer. At times she'd blown it over discussions pertaining to Jan. This morning she was going to be in control. *That's not really your insides coming apart, old girl,* she told herself. *It only feels as if they are.*

She finished washing the plate then placed it on the drainboard alongside her cup and spoon. "Just eat your breakfast, Jason," she calmly said.

At first Courtney was stunned speechless. She was unable to speak until she and Mrs. Bailey were out of Jason's earshot. As the older woman followed her onto the front porch, Courtney turned back and folded her arms. "Look, couldn't I have a week or two?"

Mrs. Bailey was in her mid-sixties with wispy gray hair. She wore a shapeless housedress with a flower-print design. "No, it's final," she said. Visible behind her, through the screen, Jason sat on the sofa watching *Sesame Street.* The little boy's legs were straight out in front of him, with his toes pointed at the ceiling. His pose was carefree and innocent. Unsuspecting.

Courtney began, "It's just . . ." Then she collected her thoughts and said, "I'm going to be on injury leave for a while. I can promise that I won't be late after this."

"You promised that before, Miss Bedell. I'm takin' no more promises."

"I know I've promised. But you also know that I'm a cop. Sometimes I can't just—"

"It ain't my decision. It's my husband's."

Courtney knew it was an out-and-out lie. Mrs. Bailey's husband was on railroad retirement and worked part-time at Wal-Mart, grinning at customers and handing out shopping carts. When he wasn't working, he was sleeping and couldn't have cared less about his wife's child-care duties. The truth was that Courtney being late so often cut into the older woman's *I Dream of Genie* reruns. Courtney bit her inner cheek. "You know I can't just produce someone else out of thin air, Mrs. Bailey. I have to interview people, make arrangements . . ."

"Afraid that's your problem," Mrs. Bailey's smile wasn't friendly. "Tonight will have to be it."

Courtney looked toward the street where her Lumina was parked, then down at her shoes, and finally back at Mrs. Bailey. "I'll bring you a check," Courtney said. "And believe me, I hope I can return the favor someday."

At least Courtney's rib wasn't broken entirely in two. The Parkland Hospital ER's resident-on-duty pointed to the hairline fracture on the X-ray as if exhibiting something wonderful. She showed gleaming straight teeth as if posing for a toothpaste ad. "You'll be a hundred percent in no time."

Courtney sat on a stainless steel examining table in a hunched-over posture. She inhaled and winced. "How long is no time, Doctor?"

The resident toyed with the stethoscope dangling between her breasts. Her pale green scrubs showed coffee stains and spatters of blood. Her smile dissolved into a look of uncertainty. "Twenty or thirty days."

"During which I can't do what?"

"Lift heavy objects. No, on second thought, change that to *most* objects. Things that didn't seem heavy before will now weigh a ton. Do you have someone who can help you around the house?"

Courtney stood, blinking with the effort. When the X-ray tech had told her to flatten her chest against the hard plastic screen while he took a series of pictures, she'd very nearly screamed. Between the Fiddleback shooting her, Mrs. Bailey's sudden announcement, and now the fractured rib news from this ER doctor, things weren't going really well. Courtney felt like collapsing in a heap and crying her eyes out. If it wouldn't have ruined her tough lady-cop image, she would have. She straightened the hem of her sweater around her hips, and started to walk away.

The doctor stepped after her. "Well, do you?"

Courtney reached for the shopping bag containing her weapon. "Do I what?"

"Have someone who can help you?"

Courtney tried to lift the Glock one-handed, found she couldn't, then grasped the bag's handles in both hands and let the weight of the gun hang between her thighs. "Not unless a genie appears," she finally said.

6

Courtney finally allowed the tears to flow as she drove
through the Trinity Industrial District on her way to
report to Gholer and his task force. Her blurred vision
distorted the images of box manufacturers, freight
haulers, and software companies that paraded past on
either side of the car. Damn the Fiddleback, damn
Mrs. Bailey and while she was at it, damn the ER
doctor as well.

The address that Gholer had given her was a con-
verted warehouse across the street from a rustic
wooden-front restaurant named Danny's Barbecue,
and was a story-and-a-half, brick-veneered building
with a flat roof. Across the front of the building were
glassed-in office suites. Courtney parked her Lumina,
wiped a final tear of frustration away, got out of the
car, and locked the doors.

She paused for a moment to clear her head.

Profession front and center, all else to the rear.
Deadpan cop expression in place, not a sign to let
anyone know there was a thing out of whack in her
life. Jan no longer existed. Mrs. Bailey was a figment
of her imagination.

She squared her shoulders, took a firm grip on her
pistol-laden shopping bag, and marched ahead.

Only one of the suites across the front of the building had a sign on the entry. The sign read, SPIDER.COM. Courtney thought wryly that the task force must employ a few comedians. She tested the door, found it open, and went inside.

There was a reception area with no receptionist, mundane prints of flowers and meadow scenes hung on the walls, and a clock that read a quarter past ten. She painfully shifted the bag to her good side—her right—passed the reception desk and entered a bull pen.

The work area was set up with four desks in the middle and cubicle offices around the perimeter. Papers were stacked on every desk alongside Gateway PCs. There was a coffee bar, a paper shredder, and a copying machine. There were nameplates on the doors of three offices across the back: Special Agent Miller in the center, Captain Trent on the left, Lieutenant Gholer on the right.

All that office equipment, not a worker in sight.

Courtney went to Gholer's cubicle. His light was off. She reached around the jamb and flipped on the switch.

A bulletin board hung on the wall behind a government-issue desk of gunmetal gray. Twelve grisly murders were outlined on the board, in newspaper clippings, crime scene photos and investigators' reports with portions highlighted in yellow. On a separate, smaller board was a map of North Texas. The map was dotted with colored and numbered stickpins. The numbers corresponded with those hung on the detail board, one for each crime. Courtney stepped around the lieutenant's desk for a closer look.

Victim Number One, Carla Ruth Rabinowitz, had been twenty-eight. The picture showed her limp nude body tied to a tree, her neck oddly bent, her head hanging to one side. Dark craterlike sores marred her arms, her stomach, and her breastbone. Courtney

looked at the map to pinpoint Crime Scene Number
One's location, in far southeast Dallas County near
the town of Wilmer. She went to the investigator's
report and began to read.

She jumped in shock as, behind her, Lieutenant
Jerry Gholer said, "Carla was the first one. We don't
have much on her. Or Vic Two, or Vic Three. They
all turned up in different local jurisdictions, with no
reason to tie 'em together. You'll find more detail on
the later vics, the ones after we knew we had a
pattern."

Courtney turned. Gholer was dressed in navy-blue
cotton pants and a white shortsleeve knit. His slacks
had lost their crease and his shirt hung limply around
his shoulders and arms. His eyes were bloodshot.
There was a scar near his left elbow, another below
his right ear.

Courtney came from behind the lieutenant's desk.
"Sorry to barge on in. There was nobody around, so
I came on in." She looked toward the reception area.

Gholer stumped around to sit in his wooden swivel
chair. "Yeah, we got Eddie and Jinx out at the fair
asking around, and as far as staff goes, they're it until
noon when I got an administrative person coming in
from downtown. There's some other people in the
back, on loan from the medical examiner, but they
stay outta sight. These guys"—he gestured toward the
two adjoining offices—"are usually invisible. Who's
purported to be in there are Texas Ranger Captain
Mason Trent and FBI Agent Donald Miller. But do
you see 'em? You won't, unless a news van drives up
outside. Then they'll suddenly materialize. And, hey,
I didn't intend to leave you hanging, but they brought
last night's victim in."

Courtney frowned in puzzlement.

He pointed to the rear of the office. "We've got
our own forensics people back there, doing our own

autopsies. They're cutting last night's vic open as we speak, and we'll have a full report this morning instead of a week from now. We're a miniature juggernaut, Courtney. But we just can't seem to catch the guy." He raised an eyebrow. "Coffee?"

"If you don't have anything stronger." Her gaze was riveted on the bulletin board. Jesus, all those bodies, hung by the hands, the feet, upside down and sideways.

He looked at the board as well. "Yeah, sometimes we all wish we could get roaring drunk." He got up, reached across and took her bag, and looked inside at her Glock. "You'll need something besides this Quick Draw McGraw holster to carry that in plainclothes."

"That's the only rig I own, Loo."

"No sweat. We'll dig something up. Follow me." He left the office and went through the bullpen with Courtney on his heels.

He led her to a storage room with built-in lockers. "Blunderbuss deposit," he said, grinning.

She stuffed her Sam Browne inside, locked the door and pocketed the key. When she turned back, Gholer was already at the coffee bar with one Styrofoam cup filled and another under the spout. "You doctor yours?"

She shook her head. He carried both steaming cups inside his office. She crossed the open area, went in, and sat across from him.

He indicated the bulletin board. "You need to memorize every detail you see up there. Jinx and Eddie will be in later with material to add, like the photos and reports on last night's vic."

He set her coffee on the front of his desk. She picked up the cup and sipped. The liquid tasted bitter, coffee mixed with chicory. She looked through the glass into the adjoining office. FBI Agent Miller's desk was bare, and there was nothing on the walls.

Gholer followed her gaze. "He thinks he's the chief," Gholer said, "and we're the Indians. As I told you, this is supposed to be a local project with the FBI and Rangers only in for consulting. In practice the feds try to take over everything they touch. There's friction. You'll feel it. But remember that you're my witness. Agent Miller will find out about you, sooner or later, and when he does he'll try to bypass me and question you on his own. When he does, tell him to buzz off. Don't let this guy scare you. He's got no authority to make you do a damned thing. There's nothing you can do about these feds, they're always around like roaches in the wall. We just do our best, okay? Our only purpose is to take out the Fiddleback. If we do that, who the hell cares who gets the credit? Agent Miller cares. We don't care."

Courtney wasn't sure how to react. She opted to say, "Gotcha, Loo."

"Now Texas Ranger Trent is a little different," Gholer said, "only because he's a step below the FBI on the food chain and knows it. If it was just us and the Rangers, Miller would be trying to take over like the Fibbies are, but with the FBI involved his main function is to make sure the Texas Rangers get named in the newspapers when they're describing the task force. Bottom line, Miller doesn't have a lot to do. But he'll make some noise. Just ignore him.

"One good thing," Gholer continued, "is that Miller and Trent spend most of their time at their agencies' offices and aren't around here very much. But when they're here they'll throw their weight around. Learn to live with it. I gotta see Miller and Trent once a day, like it or not, at main police headquarters when we play *Meet the Press*. Dealing with reporters at a separate location lets us keep the newsies away from here and out of our hair. It also allows us to spoon-feed whatever information we want public. Most of what you'll learn today has never been in the newspaper. Keep it that way."

Courtney set her cup aside. "Where's this going? Last I heard I'm only a witness. Are you saying I'm more?"

"Your record says you were military police." Gholer reached inside his desk and opened a folder. "Courtney Catherine Bedell," he read, then recited her social security number. "That you?" he said.

She was too surprised to do anything but nod. She'd expected him to order a report on her, but Jesus, the turnaround time had to be a record. Normally any request made in the city bureaucracy took weeks for a response.

He propped his shin against the edge of his desk and rested the open folder against his thigh. "Born and raised in Dallas, it says here. Both parents deceased." He frowned and scratched his forehead. "You're what, twenty-five?"

"Six," Courtney said. "A month ago."

"Yeah, right. Twenty-six. Your folks must have passed away young."

She vacantly studied the map on the wall. "Dad was forty-eight. Mom was forty-three."

"An accident?"

Courtney crossed her legs and brushed something off her jeans. She didn't say anything.

Gholer closed the file. "I gotta let you in on something. You're critical to me as a witness. You're not critical as a file clerk. I already got one of those. So I lied to Patrol when I had you transferred. How's your ribs?"

"They hurt like hell."

"They broken?"

"Just one cracked. Hairline."

"So you'll be getting around slow, which is better than not getting around at all. There's some errands that, frankly, we don't have time for, what with questioning people and chasing spiders and shit. I'm nosing around in your background because likely I'm gonna need you for those errands. I like the fact that you went up against this suspect unarmed. Not a lot of cops would've done that. From where I'm sitting, a warm injured body is better than no body at all." Gholer opened the file with a pop. "So your folks die in an accident?"

"No," Courtney said.

Gholer watched expectantly.

"I was eighteen. A senior. My dad took a second job at an Exxon station to try to help pay for my college. My mother went to pick him up one night around midnight. She got there early and went inside to wait for him. She drank a Coke. Two assholes came in and shot them both and took the money." Courtney looked down, then back up. "They found my dad behind the counter and my mother in the ladies' room. Means they had to march her back there . . ."

"Jesus. They get the guys?"

She focused on the front edge of Gholer's desk. "I don't know. If they did, no one told me."

He drummed his fingers. "Drive-in robberies are hard as hell to solve, but I'm not telling you anything you don't already know."

"That doesn't help my parents, does it?"

He pyramided his fingers under his chin. "Did you blame the department for not running them down?"

"I did. Not anymore. There's nobody *to* blame. I don't know if I even blame the perps that much, with what I know now. It's just the way things are. There are people who do bad things. Mom and Dad just happened to be unlucky. If it hadn't have been them that died that night, it would've been someone else."

"You don't strike me as a forgiver and forgetter," Gholer said.

"Oh, I'm not, Loo. If I ever busted those two and knew it was them, they'd never make it to jail. But I try not to go around wild-eyed all the time. I've met victims' family members since I've been on the job, people so obsessed that they can't get on with their lives. I'm trying to get on with mine. The guys are at the back of the file drawer, where I can bring them out if I get the chance."

Gholer inhaled, then let his breath out slowly. "You have to be that way, especially as a cop. I quit apologizing for the unsolved cases a long time ago, because I know it's a miracle that we close any of 'em. But I am sorry about your folks. I understand, being just a kid, how tough it must have been on you."

"Tough things happen to a lot of people." Courtney feared she might break down for the second time this morning, only this time in front of Gholer, God, everyone else. "Can we talk about something else?" she said.

Gholer studied her for a moment, then went back to the file. "You enlisted in the army right out of high school. Did what happened to your folks have anything to do with your career choice in the military police?"

"Some. My enlistment had everything to do with it. I wanted some time, you know? After basic training I put the MPs down, as my second choice actually, but there weren't any openings in missile training."

"Says here you prevented a rape in Germany while you were off duty, and held the perps for the Berlin police."

"I didn't have much choice. I just happened onto it."

"Happened onto it in the Tattered Angel? That's a place near where the Berlin Wall used to be, isn't it?"

She adjusted her position in the chair and looked Gholer a question.

"I did Berlin duty myself," Gholer said, "about twenty years before you passed through there. That's a shitty part of town. Jesus, the Tattered Angel was off limits even in my day."

Courtney's lashes went down. "It still is."

"Then what in hell were you doing there?"

"I had a girlfriend in the MPs who was sort of adventurous. Plus we were broke most of the time, and we could get German beer in the Tattered Angel cheaper even than in the enlisted personnel club on the base. Sixty U.S. cents a bottle, if you can believe."

"So you were risking getting your throat cut over cheap beer?"

"We weren't in that much danger—at least we didn't think so. The regulars all knew we were military cops. We were armed."

"How did the incident come down?"

Courtney did her best to sound matter-of-fact, but a pulse jumped in her neck. "Not much to tell. There'd been this woman in the bar getting pretty drunk, and as my friend and I were leaving three guys had dragged her into an alley. I didn't see how I could keep my nose out of it."

"Most American military personnel would have. You were off limits and could've gotten your ass in a sling for just being in the neighborhood."

"None of that occurred to me when I heard that woman screaming, Loo."

Gholer's look was respectful. "So where most women your age were going to rock concerts and hunting for husbands, you were up an alley in Berlin cleaning some bad guys' clocks in a section of Berlin where the baddest-assed soldiers in the army won't go. I call that pretty gutsy."

Courtney gave a wry smile. "Some would call it stupid."

"How did you feel while it was going on?"

"Terrified. I'd had quite a few beers, or I don't think I could have gotten up the nerve. The barrel of my weapon was wavering so much, if the guys hadn't given it up I might have shot myself."

"I don't think being drunk had anything to do with it," Gholer said. "I think nerve had everything to do with it. Were you drunk when you took out after Fiddleback last night?"

"I don't drink on the job. I don't drink much at all anymore. And I think I was even more scared last night than that time in Berlin."

"Which didn't stop you from doing what you had to." Gholer was once again absorbed in the file. He selected a piece of paper, which he held between a thumb and forefinger. "Says you've got some college credits."

"Eighteen," Courtney said. "Three semesters at Richland College, at night. At this rate I'll be graduating when I'm sixty."

"You considered taking the detective's exam?"

"I haven't had a lot of time to consider much of anything."

"Well you ought to think seriously," Gholer said. "Listen, don't think you'll spend all your time here giving details to sketch artists. There'll be a lot of that, but . . ."

All of this was coming straight from left field. Courtney said, "I'll try to point the guy out, Loo. Other than that, I don't think I'll be much help."

"Well, regarding your injury, we're not going to ask you to—"

"I don't expect you to put me in hand-to-hand combat," Courtney said. "But my child-care person quit me this morning. While I'm on injured leave I thought I'd look for someone else. Until I can make arrangements, don't depend on me for any eight-hour gigs."

"Hmm. This is your nephew you're raising?"

Courtney's gaze shifted to the file folder.

"That information isn't in here," Gholer said. "It's what you told me last night. I'm just wondering, in a pinch, if his mother or father could—"

"No. As for his father, I've never met him. And my sister's not available. Please don't ask why."

"You don't think it's any of the department's business?" Gholer looked peeved.

"Or anyone else's," Courtney said. "Just don't ask about it, okay?"

Gholer opened, then closed his mouth. Then he said, "Yeah, all right. Moving along. Once the autopsy's over things will get crazy around here. I'm gonna talk to you for a minute, in general, about the Fiddleback. I'm doing something here which I haven't done with many people. Because of the position you're in I'm going to get down and dirty with you about this guy. You need to understand what we're up against.

"What you're seeing here," Gholer went on, "is the damnedest psycho-serial case anyone around here has ever heard of. None of the profiles seem to fit this guy, and it's Fiddleback's deviation from the norm that makes catching him so goddamned difficult. He doesn't follow the patterns."

Courtney settled back in her chair, mesmerized.

"First," Gholer said, "I'll give you what's normal for the abnormal. Like every nutso, Fiddleback thinks no more of killing his victims than a scientist would fret over a laboratory rat. Just part of the ball game. We don't even think he sees what he's doing as murders. To him it's like throwing out the garbage after he's finished with his ritual. The spider bites, the single shot to the chest, the body makeovers. The hair, the nails, the pubic areas, all clean as a whistle. The guy takes as much time with the corpses as a mortician would take, except for going ahead with the embalming. Which plays hell with any trace evidence on the body, but I don't think Fiddleback's concerned with that. I think he's saying, 'Look, world, see how pretty they are.' "

Courtney finished off her coffee. She balanced the empty cup on her knee. "He's probably got a sexual motive."

Gholer fiddled with his ear. "Now you sound like those FBI profilers. Sex this and sex that. And maybe sex does figure into it. But if it does, I don't think Fiddleback's victims are what turns him on. I think he's got a stiff one for somebody else altogether."

Courtney set the cup on Gholer's desk and rested her chin on her clenched fist. "One of the courses I took at Richland College was in criminal justice, and we had a guest speaker with Violent Criminal Apprehension who happened to be in town from Quantico. He gave us what he called the FBI crash course in serial killing 101. According to the textbook—"

"I know just what you're about to say." Gholer held up his hand, palm out. "According to Professor Fibbie, all these fruitcakes have got sexual motives. Their mother or their father grabbed their dongs at some point, so their retaliation is to go around slaughtering people. The subject picks victims of all the same gender, and *which* gender depends on whether the guy's boat floats upstream or downstream, which in turn depends on which parent grabbed his dong. That's, basically, FBI profiling in a nutshell. Right or wrong?"

Courtney was feeling just a bit miffed. "I was just quoting the lecturer. The man was supposed to be an expert on the subject, Loo."

"Everybody in the FBI is supposed to be an expert, to hear my pal Agent Miller tell it. Only Fiddleback hasn't read their book. He's taken men *and* women, from three or four different racial groups. And he's not choosing these people at random. If we can figure

out what his victim criteria is, I think that's going a
long way toward catching the guy."

Gholer rose and paced back and forth, waving a
pointer. He placed the tip on the photo of Victim
Number Four, Matthew Rhepan, who'd been hung
head-down from the Cadiz Street Viaduct over the
Trinity River. "Mr. Rhepan here," Gholer said, "was
a gay rights advocate. He disappeared en route to an
activist's meeting in the Oak Lawn area, and we think
Fiddleback grabbed him as he got out of his car.
His . . . soul mate, or whatever you call it, a guy
named Thomas Heard, was found dead inside the car
in front of the meeting hall. Our guess is, Fiddleback
wanted Rhepan, and to get Rhepan he had to take
out the other guy. Heard's killing was pretty conven-
tional, a bullet to the head. A .45 instead of the .22
he uses in his ritual murders, which could be a match
to the slug they took out of your armored vest last
night and the casing they found on the playground.
I'll let you know. It's the only instance we know of
where he's offed somebody other than the target vic,
which demonstrates the ends Fiddleback will go to
when he picks out someone."

"I remember the Rhepan case," Courtney said. "It
was a while before his killing was connected to Fiddleback, wasn't it?"

Gholer pointed a finger. "Exactly my point. We
didn't attribute Rhepan to ol' Fiddleback at first because of the sexual angle. Or in his case, the *homo-
sexual* angle. Originally, thanks to FBI profiling, we
were questioning a bunch of poor innocent gay guys.
When Matthew Rhepan finally did turn up, four days
later, he had fourteen insect bites and his hair was
done in ringlets. The rope used to hang him from the
bridge matches ends with the rope used to tie Vic
Two, Sally Benedict, to a railroad trestle. The mere

fact that Rhepan was gay had us running around chasing our tails. No telling how many leads we might've missed."

"According to the lecture I heard," Courtney said, "your FBI people zero in on similarities."

"Yeah, they do. Not that that's a bad investigation procedure, but the problem is that it eliminates any study of *dis*similarities. I believe that what's different between two cases is just as important as what's the same about them. All of the weirdos that the FBI trainers have studied had a sexual motive, so they try to assign a sexual motive to this guy regardless of whether there is one or not.

"All I see here is opposites," Gholer said. "First of all, of Fiddleback's twelve vics, four are men. Gacy, Dahmer, every one of those guys, they lured their victims to a private place. Fiddleback thrives on taking his from crowded public areas. Look at the bulletin board. From Carla Rabinowitz' disappearance at the halftime of a Cowboy game a year ago, to yesterday's abduction at the state fair."

Courtney was beginning to feel as if she was getting it. "Your stereotypes," she said, "your Gacys and whatnot had all hidden their victims' corpses. Buried them, or in Dahmer's case eaten them and hidden the bones. Fiddleback dresses his leftovers up and puts them where you can't miss 'em."

"Now you're cookin', Courtney. So does Fiddleback have a sexual motive? Maybe, maybe not. Maybe he gets a hard-on every time one of his spiders bites somebody, but knowing that isn't helping us catch the guy. In this area the FBI is totally full of shit."

Courtney covered her mouth and forced a cough.

Gholer raved on. "So the FBI and me go to fist city a lot. They deal in theory, want to play getting inside the killer's head just like in the movies. Me, I'm just a gumshoe murder cop. I believe you catch murderers by going over evidence and wearing out your footsies. We got no Hannibal the Cannibal, no goof locked up who shoots us clues while he's dazzling us with mind games. There's just us on one side and Fiddleback on the other. And right now, our side's getting lonesome as hell."

Gholer seemed all at once very tired. Courtney wondered how much sleep he'd gotten. She had copped only five hours herself, and Gholer had still been at the crime scene when she'd headed for home.

Gholer showed her a questioning look. "You know anything about these spiders?"

Courtney put her elbows on her armrests. "Brown recluse? Only what I've read, which you could put in a thimble."

Gholer dug in his top drawer, then tossed a thick booklet over in front of her. Courtney examined the slick-covered paperback, a U.S. Department of Agriculture publication entitled, *Brown Recluse Spider* (Loxosceles reclusa *Gertsch & Malaik;* Loxoscleles rufescens *DuFour*). On the cover was a drawing of a benign-looking arachnid. She thumbed through the booklet, then dropped it into her lap. She turned her helpless gaze on Gholer.

"My sentiments exactly," Gholer said. "In about one minute's discussion I'm going to save you the three days the FBI made us spend with two USDA bug scientists, one of which wrote that fascinating thing you're holding there. Anybody that gets involved in this case I'm supposed to lock in a room with that booklet and not let 'em out until they can answer five hundred test questions. If anybody asks you, that's what I did. Okay?"

Courtney nodded appreciatively. She flipped the booklet onto Gholer's desk.

"Not that the spider isn't an important part to the puzzle," Gholer said, "because it is. But Jesus Christ, we spent a whole day learning that there are four poisonous arachnids in the U.S., getting details on the three that don't have anything to do with this case, and another day learning about the spider's body parts, the cephalathorax and all that crap. About the only thing worth telling is, the spider's got no ding-a-ling. Why's that important? Don't ask me, but it's about all I remember."

Courtney chuckled. A sharp twinge went through her ribs.

"You should study the picture on the cover of that booklet," Gholer said, "so you'll recognize a brown recluse if you see one. That part's easy. The recluse is light brown except for a dark violin-shaped marking on its back, with the bow pointed toward its butt. If you see a guy going around with one of these things riding on his shoulder, petting it, then that guy's automatically a suspect."

Courtney laughed even harder, and the constriction of her diaphragm hurt like the blazes. She winced and held her side.

Gholer turned serious. "Another thing you should remember about this bug is, if it bites you, you're probably going to need a skin graft. The nickname 'Fiddleback' comes from the violin marking. Go to east Texas, there are a lot of scary nursery rhymes with Ol' Fiddleback as the monster. Little piney woods kids learn to spot a brown recluse spider before they do a bullfrog, and their mothers warn them that if they see Ol' Fiddleback, they're to get the hell away. Twenty-four hours after the brown recluse bites you, you'll be running a high fever, and you'll probably lapse into a coma. About the second day, the skin around the bite will slough away and leave a wound like a crater, sometimes as big around as the span of your hand. The recluse venom affects some lighter-skinned people no more than a mosquito bite. I believe that the way our boy Fiddleback chooses his victims is by how juicy the wound is gonna turn out.

"Dark-complected people," Gholer said, "react more than people with fair skin. By the way, the FBI will tell you that there's no scientific evidence to support that theory, but you go ask the people in Longview, Nacogdoches, all over east Texas. Just because there's no scientific evidence doesn't mean something isn't true. Dark-skinned people have worse reactions, period. And Fiddleback knows it, too. He's dark-skinned himself. Bet on it.

"That's the one thing that every single victim so far has in common: dark skin. We've got blacks, Hispanics, three Jews, two Arabs. Not a single Nordic blond. Otherwise Fiddleback's selection seems at random. If he does anything else to single out his victim in advance, we got no evidence of it. We've broken our necks trying to find a connection between any of the victims, but so far we haven't scored shit. Best we can determine, none of these people ever saw each other before."

Courtney's stomach did flip-flops. "You said last night you didn't think he was torturing them. What makes you think not?"

Gholer closed, then opened his eyes. "You'd call it torture. So would I. But I'm not sure that *Fiddleback* would call it torture. 'Torture' means one thing to some folks, something else to others. Obviously these victims don't think it's very funny when these spiders start crawling on them. But there are no other signs of abuse—beatings, bruises, genital mutilations—none of the shit we associate with torturing a captive. It's almost like Fiddleback is watching the spiders, not the victims, to see what the insect is going to do. He doesn't seem to care one way or the other whether he's hurting the vic, and once he's finished with these people he kills them pretty painlessly. One gunshot to

the heart, right against the skin. Easiest way there is
to go, next to sleeping pills.

"These spiders themselves are passive," Gholer
said. "What can I say? It's how they got their name.
They're reclusive. They hunt at night, kill and eat
cockroaches, sometimes a mouse or two, but they bite
humans only through accidental contact. Maybe the
spider is hiding in a shoe the person puts on, and
injects its venom 'cause it's disturbed. You can set one
of these Fiddlebacks in the palm of your hand, and as
long as you don't fuck with him he'll sit there for
hours. Fiddleback has to put a brown recluse on the
vic and then stir it up somehow, poke at it, get it
to bite.

"And there's one other thing Fiddleback does that's
out of the norm for these weirdos," Gholer said. "Take
John Wayne Gacy or any of the FBI prototypes—they
get rid of the body like they're sort of apologizing. Bodies have been found with pillows under their heads,
that's not uncommon at all. The shrinks tell us it's a
showing of regret for what the killer's done. But not
only does Fiddleback not show any particular malice
for his vics, he doesn't show pity, either. He uses these
people, kills them, and then puts them on display after
cleaning them up. It's as if they don't mean shit to
him one way or the other. It's the showing off of the
bodies that turns the Fiddleback on."

"Maybe he's playing, like, a sick joke," Courtney
said.

"Taunting the cops? That's what the FBI thinks he's
doing. But your psychopaths who get their jollies from
publicity do more than just taunt. We haven't seen
any Son of Sam notes to journalists claiming somebody's dog made him do it. Ask me? I think Fiddleback puts these corpses on display for someone's
benefit other than ours or the public's. And I think

determining who he's putting on the show for, I think that's going to eventually identify the guy.

"Keep in mind that no matter where he's dumped the body, there's always rope involved, either in hanging up the corpse or tying it to something. Vic Eight, Sharon Ruiz, he left her in the median on Highway 114 with a rope dangling around her neck, with no marks to indicate he'd ever tightened the noose. He sure as hell didn't have to tie her up after she was already dead. I think the use of rope is significant. How, I got no idea."

Gholer paused as his phone buzzed. He looked irritated, and held up a finger in Courtney's direction as he picked up the receiver. "Gholer," he said, then looked more pleasant as he said, "Well, I'll be damned." He hung up. "Son of a bitch if they aren't already finished with the autopsy. Ranger Trent is already back there, and Agent Miller is gracing us with his presence." Gholer appeared thoughtful. He reached in his drawer and tossed a thick bound volume on his desk. "Bad-guy photo album, Courtney, courtesy of the FBI, something to keep you busy. I doubt if our guy's in there, but any port and all that crap. I'll get back to you. And if anybody asks, you're reading a magazine. I don't want anybody knowing what you're doing in here, okay?"

He walked around his desk and stopped in the doorway. "Oh, and don't worry. No spiders in here. I had the place fumigated." He took a step to leave, then cocked his head and showed a crooked grin. "What, you think I'm kidding?" Gholer said.

7

Gholer took his time leaving the main office, dawdling near the exit, going through a stack of mail that he'd already seen. He watched from the corner of his eye as, visible inside his own cubicle, Courtney Bedell reviewed the suspect photos. Her back was military-posture straight, her head inclined intently over the open volume, her dark short bangs falling loosely over her forehead. She was one good-looking woman, and carried herself more like one of the college-graduate, daiquiri-drinking types from over at the DA's office than a patrol cop who'd showed nerve in more than one intense situation. Gholer hadn't built a crackerjack Crimes-Against-Persons staff without stepping on a few departmental toes, stealing some of the best and brightest from other divisions, and he was getting ideas about Courtney Bedell. He dropped the mail and left the office.

He moved with confidence down a twisty corridor, his head turning watchfully from side to side. He skirted rolling gurneys and aluminum tables loaded down with scalpels and specimen bottles. White-coated techs roamed the hallway, Gholer nodding to each in turn as he passed them by. He came alongside a window that was set into the wall. Visible through the glass, a young Asian woman hand-vacuumed a piece of carpet. Gholer pointed at her; she grinned and nodded. Gholer came to a door marked HARRIS SANDS, AME, drew a shallow breath, and went on through.

Hail, hail, the gang was all there.

The crowded office held a desk and a conference table, and on the walls were multi-colored charts of the human arterial system, digestive tract, and skeletal structure. On one side of the table sat Texas Ranger Captain Mason Trent and FBI Agent Donald Miller. Trent, a tall, straight-off-the-cow-patty drink of water, was playing Ranger to the hilt, complete with cream-colored Stetson and gray hand-tooled boots. The toe of one of his boots was propped against the edge of the table and his arms hugged his knee. He made a pistol with his thumb and forefinger and shot Gholer with an imaginary bullet.

Agent Miller sat on Trent's right. Miller was second-in-command to the Special Agent-in-Charge of the Dallas FBI office, and was a native Minnesotan with the accent to prove it. He had big shoulders and skinny hips, along with brown hair thinning into a widow's peak. More than anyone Gholer had ever met, Miller loved to hear himself talk. He spent a lot of on-the-job down time bullshitting about a psycho nicknamed the Duluth Dangler, as in, "I remember one time when we were after the Dangler," this and that and so forth. Detectives Jinx Madison and Eddie Frizell called Miller Donald the Dangler. Gholer tried to discourage his cops from using the monicker when Miller was in earshot, but sometimes they slipped, the result being that Miller didn't get along with Gholer's detectives very well. Or Gholer himself, for that matter; Gholer couldn't stand the guy. He nodded curtly to Miller and sat down across the table.

Gholer now said a brief hello to Angela Mart, the FBI's straight-from-Quantico profiler whom Miller

brought to every meeting concerning the Fiddleback,
and who served as backup whenever Miller didn't
know where the fuck the conversation was going.
Which, in Gholer's estimation, was most of the time.
Angela Mart was a frail woman in her thirties who
could recite the particulars of every serial murder case
in U.S. history from memory. Every time he was in
the same room with her, Gholer felt as if she was
profiling him.

Strung out along the wall in the background were
Captain Helen Dilbergast, a deputy chief and the
highest-ranking woman in the DPD, and Arnold
Slanter from the city manager's office. Slanter's function in this meeting had to do with keeping the mayor
up to snuff on the Fiddleback. He wore his hair in a
buzz cut. Wire-framed I'm-smart glasses rode the
bridge of his nose. Captain Dilbergast, a severe gray-
haired woman, was a devoted muscular jogger with
gold stripes on her uniform shoulder boards. She was
here because the last Fiddleback conference had
ended in a near fistfight between Gholer, Miller, and
Texas Ranger Trent, so Dilbergast, at the chief's in-
struction, had come along to referee. Dilbergast's nod
to Gholer was part greeting, part warning. Gholer returned the nod, then folded his hands and waited to
hear what the medical examiner's people had to say.
The odor of formaldehyde drifted up his nose.

AME Harris Sands co-occupied the head of the
table along with his assistant, Carol Neely. Sands wore
glasses in dark plastic frames and had his white hair
combed back. He had a narrow face and sunken
cheeks. Carol Neely was strikingly pretty, though a bit
on the hefty side, with enormous breasts and wide
shoulders. Both AMEs nodded hello.

Gholer kept his mouth shut while FBI Agent Miller
nodded broadly at Sands. "Okay, Harris," Miller said,
"solve our case for us."

"Hah." Sands removed his glasses, showing red nosepiece marks. There were pinkish stains on his lab coat. "You want a step-by-step, or can I just xerox the other eleven autopsy reports?"

Miller folded his hands. "Same old, same old?"

"And more just like it to follow," Sands said. "The victim is a Hispanic female between thirty and forty years old, at this point unidentified though we've printed her and put out the feelers. First I'll go over what you already know. From experience. Cause of death in this instance, one .22 bullet to the heart from point-blank range. The slug was lodged behind the left shoulder blade. The lesions on the vic are loaded with enzymes and buthidae-class toxins. Spider venom. The body was groomed postmortem, hair washed and set, finger and toenails polished and lacquered. A comb-out of the head and pubic hair produces not a sign of trace." He pointed to a stack of folders at the opposite end of the table. "It's all in those files, copy for each of you folks, which you can gather on your way out. There's also a morgue photo of the vic in there."

Miller laid his palms on the table. "So what's new?"

Sands looked hopeful. "Surprisingly, quite a bit. Carol?" He pointed at his assistant.

Neely smiled like the class egghead ready to strut her stuff at the blackboard. There was an eager-beaver lilt to her voice. "This victim had some personal effects, Lieutenant Gholer, found on the floorboard of the car. We've already turned them over to the Rangers."

Ranger Trent exhibited a cheap cloth purse. "In here, Jerry. I got 'em." He tipped his Stetson.

"See you don't make a career out of keeping them," Gholer said. Captain Dilbergast shot him a warning glare. Gholer averted his gaze.

"Sure thing," Trent said. "As soon as we take a little thumbnail inventory."

Which would take a week or more, once the evidence left the Rangers' hands and then passed through the FBI's. Gholer extended an upturned palm across the table. "Rather than put you guys out, we'll do the inventory for you. Copy to you, copy to Agent Miller. Any problem with that?"

Trent hesitated. His grin was strained. He slid the victim's bagged purse across the table. "Sure thing, Jerry. 'Preciate the help."

"No sweat, Mason." Gholer hauled the purse over by the drawstring. "No ID, right?"

Neely looked apologetic. "Afraid not. She kept chewing gum and a couple of stale candy bars. That's it except for two pari-mutuel betting tickets from Lone Star Park, meaning that four days ago the victim was out in Grand Prairie playing the ponies. And her teeth were capped, recently."

"Which without ID to use in tracking dental records," Gholer said, "gives us zero."

"Well . . . not exactly." Neely exchanged a look with Harris Sands before saying, "The teeth were capped postmortem."

Gholer's mouth twisted in revulsion. The more he learned about the Fiddleback, the more he couldn't believe the guy.

Agent Miller said, "Come again?"

Neely seemed pleased with herself. "There's no residue on the caps, meaning she hadn't eaten since they were installed. The adhesive is brand-new, hadn't set completely, and we were able to remove some of the caps with finger pressure. There's no saliva on the caps, either, meaning that her glands weren't producing when whoever fixed the teeth went to work. Someone forced those caps onto her teeth after she was dead."

Miller rubbed his cheek. "Jesus Christ. What motive could there be for that?"

"Maybe he didn't like her smile," Gholer said. Captain Dilbergast stared daggers at him.

Harris Sands cut in, leaning forward. "It's the same motive this asshole has for everything. To make her presentable. The new porcelain was all in front. I'm no dentist, but I know rotten teeth when I see 'em. Under the caps the fronts have cavities you wouldn't believe. Two rear molars broken off at the gum line. I'd be surprised if this woman had ever been to a dentist in her life. The teeth aren't even filed down, which is part of the standard capping procedure. The porcelain caps are pushed on over the original teeth. Two of the fronts are broken, likely from the pressure of forcing the caps into place. The teeth are rotten to begin with, so it didn't take a very hard push to snap 'em right off."

"We're not looking for a dentist, then," Gholer said.

Neely tried to speak up, but Sands cut her off. "Not unless he was in one helluva hurry, and that's not the case with this guy. Our female techs couldn't believe the care it took to fix that hair. I think you're looking for someone with zero knowledge of technique, but access to dental supplies. I'd check crime reports for a burglary on a dentist's office. Also get a list of the employees of every dental supply house in the Dallas–Fort Worth area."

"What about the makeup? Another professional job?" Gholer said.

"And a damn sight more than just a facial makeover," Sands said. "There was a layer of flesh-tone powder all over the body. Hid the yellowish tint to the skin. Plenty of mascara to hide the fact that her eyes were sunk in her head. With the exception that he didn't go ahead and embalm her, this guy took as much care as a funeral home."

Now Angela Mart spoke up. "Yellowish, as in jaundice?" She folded her hands professionally. Agent

Miller threw her a curious look, as if she was talking over his head. Mart lowered her chin and doodled on a legal pad.

"Yeah, jaundice." Sands nodded and looked to Carol Neely for confirmation. Neely nodded as well, wrinkling her nose *I Dream of Genie*-fashion. Sands said, "All in all, the yellowing indicates liver dysfunction, which can be a hepatitis symptom, but not in this case. The jaundice combined with the bone deterioration and the sunken eyes, plus the incredible looseness of her skin and total lack of muscle tone, all that points to a severe vitamin deficiency. There was very little fecal material in her intestines, and the urine in her bladder was crystal clear."

Gholer looked at Miller, then at Trent, then concentrated once more on Sands. "Which tells us?" Gholer said.

"She had virtually zero body waste to eliminate. The urine was damn near pure water. No outgo of waste material means minimum food intake over an extended period." Sands spread his hands in a shrugging gesture. "She was starving. She's either a longtime street person or a recent transient from south of the border. She hasn't been eating right."

"But she had enough money to bet the horses?" Gholer said. "Doesn't equate."

"I don't know if I buy that, Jerry," Sands said. "A lot of gamblers don't eat so good." He picked up a pad and went over his notes. "That's it for the autopsy. Physical evidence, not much new."

Gholer hitched forward. "How 'bout the resin?"

"Oh, Jesus," Agent Miller groaned, looking up from whatever Angela Mart was pointing out on a graph. Miller pushed the graph away. "Here we go with the resin again."

Gholer ignored Miller and concentrated on Sands.

"Yeah, there was resin residue," Sands said. "For whatever it's worth."

Gholer pulled a palm-sized spiral notebook from his pocket, wrote down, "Thursday," and tucked it away. He rested his chin on his touched-together fingertips.

Miller couldn't stand the suspense. "You want to share with the class, Jerry?"

Gholer raised his eyebrows. "I thought you didn't want to hear about the resin."

Miller rested his ankle on his knee. "Well, let's pretend I do. Bore me."

Gholer was conscious of Captain Dilbergast sitting forward intensely, like a woman needing desperately to go to the bathroom. He wondered if she had a goon squad waiting outside, ready to haul him away if he got out of line. He smiled at Miller, though the effort hurt his jaws. "I think I got it figured out," Gholer said, "that Fiddleback uses resin on his job." And folded his arms.

"Oh come on," Miller said. "We've got this guy pretty well profiled. His movements throughout the area, the around-the-clock times of his abductions—"

"If I may." Angela Mart referred to her graph. "You're looking for a white male between twenty-five and forty with a flexible schedule. Likely has a strained relationship with his mother. The periods between incidents he's—"

"The pertinent phrase being," Miller interrupted, " 'flexible schedule.' This guy doesn't work. This guy hunts. These serial murderers are too obsessed to hold a steady job."

Gholer's ears were suddenly warm. "Well, maybe this particular serial murderer has to eat. Pay rent and shit. Every one of these fruitcakes doesn't have to have a trust fund. You want to know why I think he uses resin on his job, or you want to hear your head rattle?"

Miller's mouth turned down at the corners. Dilbergast stared wide-eyed. Gholer pictured the captain giving him the hook, his body jerking sideways as she yanked him away from the table. Slanter, the city manager's man, seemed ready to faint.

Miller spread his hands. "Okay, Mr. Gholer. Enlighten us."

"Be glad to. The way my notes read we've found resin at five crime scenes attributed to this guy. Every one of those abductions happened on a weekday evening between five and seven P.M. The rest of the kidnappings occurred on a Saturday or Sunday, and no resin was found at any of those locations. Five to seven on a weekday, the guy'd been to work and was on his way home." Gholer rested his cheek on his fist.

There were several seconds of silence, during which Miller and Mart frantically searched their charts. Sands murmured, "Makes sense." Even Trent nodded his head. Captain Dilbergast relaxed somewhat. Mart leaned over to Miller and, while pointing at her chart, whispered something.

Miller's head snapped up. "Could be he's got a hobby. Woodworking, maybe—"

"Oh bullshit." Gholer slapped the table. "This guy's hobby is killing people. He's got a job. We need to research every business that works with resin. *Powdered* resin, meaning we can eliminate most construction sites going in. Likely it's used for traction, to get a grip on something."

Miller and Mart had another confab. Miller said, "Yeah, okay. We'll kick it around."

"Kick it. . . ?" Gholer breathed in, then out. "Well, while you're kicking it around, I got work to do." He used his palms on the table to push himself into a standing position. "We through here?"

Both AMEs began putting their gear away. Captain Dilbergast stood hopefully and moved toward the exit, as did Arnold Slanter. Miller lifted a restraining hand. "Not quite yet. I still have a couple of questions."

Everyone sat. Gholer eye-measured the distance across the table, picturing himself grabbing Miller by the throat.

Mart pointed to something on the chart while Miller read over her shoulder. Then Miller said to Sands, "On this latest victim. Any sign she was molested?"

Gholer rolled his eyes.

Sands seemed resigned. He said merely, "None that we've found," and waited for Gholer to bail him out.

Gholer did his best. "Well, I guess that's that." He stood once more, this time dusting his palms together.

But Miller wasn't about to let it drop. "Doctor, when you say none that you've found, do you mean it's possible there was molestation and you just didn't see it?"

Gholer sat back and waited for the shoe to fall.

He didn't have long to wait. Sands opened and then closed his mouth. He thumbed his lapel. "Agent Miller, the answer is the same as the last eleven times you've asked the same question, in connection with every other victim we've looked at in this case. There was no penetration, rectal or vaginal. No semen in her mouth. Or her hair." He paused.

Easy now, Harris, Gholer thought.

Miller waited attentively. Mart had pen in hand and legal pad ready.

Sands licked his lips. "Or her ears. Or her goddamned nose. If he stood back and flogged his dong at her, he was far enough away that he didn't drop any load on her. Anything else?" He exchanged a glance with Gholer. Carol Neely looked horrified.

Miller said, "You sound resentful, Doctor."

Sands said, "You bet your ass I'm resentful. We keep telling you. You keep ignoring us. Fuck it."

Miller and the AME locked gazes.

Gholer clapped his hands. "Great. If we're all through here, I'll just—"

"Not so fast." Miller came to his feet. "I'm not through. Not just yet. I said *two* questions."

Gholer was conscious of the captain arching her eyebrow in the background. He looked at Miller as if he adored the guy. "Why, sure, Don. What's on your mind?"

"What's on my mind? Why, gee, Jerry, not a helluva lot. Just that the word's around that you're hiding a witness who can identify the Fiddleback. Anything to that?"

Gholer did his best to remain deadpan but wasn't sure if he was pulling it off. He searched his memory bank. Who was at last night's crime scene? Jesus, with all those cops and techs running around, the leak could be about anyplace. He said to Miller, "Uh, witness?"

"Yeah. A witness." Miller turned around and addressed the lady captain. "Mrs. Dilbergast, is this the kind of cooperation I can expect? If he has a witness, I'm entitled to access. Shabby treatment, you ask me."

Uh-oh, Gholer thought, *he's screwed up now, FBI or no.* Captain Helen Dilbergast was one female whose face you did not want to get up in.

Dilbergast's eyes narrowed, just enough for her rancid mood to show. She said, "What's shabby about it, Agent? Other than your accusation, I haven't heard anyone say that there *is* a witness."

She comes to referee, Gholer thought, *now she's in the middle of it, swinging for his balls. Love ya, Captain,* Gholer thought.

Miller alternated his gaze between Dilbergast and Gholer. "Yeah, but there is, Jerry. Isn't there?"

Gholer first checked out Dilbergast, whose expression now told him not to give the fed the time of day. Gholer grinned at Miller, and spread his hands in a show of innocence. "Gee, I don't know, Don. But if I run into one, I'll be sure and let you know."

8

Gholer reentered his office bullpen with the victim's purse bumping his hip and the AMEs' autopsy folder shoved under his arm. Things had picked up while he was gone. Topper Moore, the administrative assistant who was splitting time between downtown headquarters and the Fiddleback unit, was at a computer entering data from a file. Jinx Madison and Eddie Frizell had returned from the fairgrounds and were waiting outside Gholer's office, drinking coffee. Courtney Bedell was still bent over the FBI's suspect album, looking at pictures. Gholer thought that Courtney seemed glassy-eyed. He raised a just-a-minute finger to Madison and Frizell, then went over to the desk where Topper Moore worked the computer.

Moore was a trim forty-year-old with dyed red hair and an attitude. She wore loose-fitting tan slacks and brown loafers with squared toes. She looked exhausted. *Hell,* Gholer thought, *we're all exhausted.* As Gholer approached, Moore stopped typing and looked up.

"I need a favor," Gholer said.

Moore thumbed over her shoulder. "Wait in line."

"Well, let's say this favor take priority." Gholer sifted through the autopsy folder and brought out the victim's photo—dead eyes, lids at half-mast, the mouth

partway open to reveal dazzling white bicuspids alongside rotten front teeth. Gholer dropped the picture on
top of the computer monitor. "About fifteen copies,
Topper, huh? You know, show-around stuff to give
the units."

Moore picked up the picture and looked it over.
"Who's her dentist?" she said. "She must've only had
money for half a treatment."

Gholer ignored the question. He now had dug inside
the purse and held an evidence Ziploc between a
thumb and forefinger. Inside the bag were the vic's
two Lone Star Park pari-mutuel tickets. He said, "And
I need Monday's *Dallas Morning News*. That's . . ."
He checked the dates on the tickets. "September the
twenty-sixth, okay? Sports section."

"That's two favors. You asked for one." Moore continued to look at the picture.

"Well, let's say I'm ordering the two-for-one special.
September twenty-sixth sports section, Topper. I don't
have time to screw around. We got a woman out there
about to die."

She smiled sweetly. "You mean me?"

Gholer frowned at her. "Nine/twenty-six/two thousand. Get it."

Moore dropped the photo on the desk. "That's four
days ago. Do I look like the archives?"

"I can count days, Topper. Somebody around here's
got one. Check with the AMEs back there. If they
don't have it, walk across the street to the barbecue
joint. See Tommy the cook, he's never thrown away
a Monday sports page in his life, not during football
season. I need the racetrack results for Sunday, that's
the twenty-fifth."

Her chin tilted. "Racetrack results."

He nodded. "Time's a-wastin'. Go."

She didn't look pleased, but got it in gear. She wrote
down DMN—9/26 on a Post-it, took the note with her,

and disappeared through the back toward Harris Sands' office.

Gholer watched her go, then walked up to Frizell and Madison. Frizell watched Topper Moore leave the office. He said, "What's got her? Must be on the rag or something."

"Yeah, or something," Gholer said.

Jinx Madison had been reading an employee benefits pamphlet, which she now discarded. "You two male chauvinists are harassing me. Wait till I see my union rep."

"Wait till I see mine," Frizell said. "Tell 'im about you looking at my ass all the time."

"Yeah, I look. I'm wondering why you don't pull your britches up," Madison said. "Guy going around with his crack showing. It's sick."

Gholer didn't laugh. "Say, can we discuss business now?"

"Sure," Frizell said. "Jinx is just getting her thrills. In here?" He indicated Gholer's office, where Courtney Bedell was now perched on the edge of the lieutenant's desk with the photo album open on her thigh.

Gholer paused. "No," he said. "I don't want to disturb the witness. We can use Miller's place. After the meeting we just had, I doubt he'll be coming in." He went into the FBI agent's cubicle, flopped down behind the desk, and laid the purse and the autopsy folder out in front of him.

Madison came in with Frizell close behind. The detectives sat in visitors' chairs.

Madison scooted her fanny forward and crossed her legs.

Frizell showed a crooked grin and rested his ankle on his knee. "You met with Donald the Dangler?"

Gholer dug out his notepad and ballpoint. "He don't like us."

"Fuck 'im," Frizell said. "We don't like him, either."

"Someone's told him we got a witness." Gholer glanced through the glass at Courtney Bedell.

Frizell had droopy eyelids. "Son of a bitch. Who?"

"Likely we'll never know," Gholer said. "So, you've been out to the fairgrounds. You win a teddy bear, or what?"

The two looked at each other. Madison dropped her chin. "Our spider guy's got himself another victim."

"You mean one we don't know about?"

Madison nodded her head. "Not until today."

Gholer wrote, VIC 13, followed by a colon. "And we know this how?"

"The valet parking manager," Madison replied, "told us one of his regular drivers called in sick and sent a substitute. The substitute's the one who took Sis Hargis' car to pick her up. Last they ever saw of the guy."

"And we think that means the Fiddleback got the regular driver?" Gholer said.

Frizell bent forward and rested his forearms on his thighs. "David Og's the regular's name. O-G. He's worked the fair for four or five years. His fulltime gig is driving a limo. He's not answering his phone, so me and Jinx dropped by his apartment on the way back in from the fairgrounds. Got the apartment manager to admit us. No one home, but the guy's got a little dog. The dog had shit all over the place and had no food in his dish. A whole rackful of leashes just inside the front door, and nobody's walked the dog. Mr. Og hasn't been in in several days."

Gholer entered DAVID OG after the colon on his pad. "We know the name of the limo service he works for?"

"Yeah," Frizell said. "We got that information from the fairground valet parking manager. The limo service has been searching for Mr. Og, too, and have issued a stolen car complaint downtown regarding his limo. He's vanished, along with the limo he had checked out."

"Jesus." Gholer pressed hard on his ballpoint. "The bastard's escalating. We find out where Mr. Og was headed when last seen?"

Now Madison cut in. "Sure. We talked to his supervisor at the limo company. Last Sunday Og takes a party of out-of-towners to the racetrack, and he's supposed to wait out front for them. When the people finished playing the ponies, the limo was gone and so was Og. The Fiddleback must have picked him off as he sat outside the track."

Gholer's chin lifted. "Track? Lone Star Park?"

"Sure, Loo. What other track is there around here?" Madison said.

"We're starting to connect," Gholer said. "Last night's stiff had a couple of pari-mutuel tickets in her purse. From Sunday. Two plus two. Listen, did the valet lot manager say anything about recognizing the voice on the phone that told him Og was sending a substitute?"

Madison and Frizell exchanged a look. "We didn't ask," Frizell said.

"Well, ask," Gholer said. "I'd like to know if Fiddleback made the call himself, or if he had the other guy do it. Tells us whether the other guy, Og, was in shape to make the call, and also raises the possibility that Fiddleback's not in this alone. You make it down to the auto show?"

"That was our first stop," Frizell said. "That new Cougar's a ride, man."

Gholer blinked. "You're telling me, you went by the auto show and this is what you learned?"

"No way, Loo," Madison said. "We also learned that the new 'Vette is an even better ride. Plus, this Sis Hargis has got a history."

"Which is more important than which is the bossest ride," Gholer said.

"Depends on your perspective. A guy in a 'Vette has a better chance of spreading my legs than a guy in a Cougar. For Sis Hargis it apparently took a Beemer and upward."

Gholer slipped off his wedding ring, massaged his naked finger, then slipped the ring back on over his knuckle. "She was screwing around?"

"That we don't know," Madison said. "We get this from the guy that hires the models for the show. Sis Hargis, formerly Frazier, is a Highland Park lady who started out in *Low*land Park. Garland, Trailer-park Texas to be exact. She took up quote, modeling, un-quote when she was a teenager, worked style shows, skimpy underwear, bikinis, you name it, and has been doing the fair for about fifteen years. Mr. William Hargis picked her off a car show stage about ten years ago. She quit fulltime modeling then, but kept working the fair for something to do. Six months ago Hargis apparently decided to trade her in for a newer model."

"This is the asshole last night with the lawyer?" Gholer said.

Madison nodded. "Big money. Old-time money. Hargis Junior is apparently bent on spending every nickel on things Hargis Senior wouldn't approve of."

"Such as Sis what's-her-name," Frizell said.

"And the cutie pie last night," Madison said.

"Okay," Gholer said. "And in view of that, why is my idea to put twenty-four/seven on William Hargis full of shit?"

"Well, the guy's . . ." Frizell looked to Madison for help. "We are looking for a psycho here," Frizell finally said. "If it was just Hargis' wife missing, yeah. But Hargis is no fruitcake."

"And we know that how?" Gholer said.

"Because he . . ." Frizell trailed off, stumped.

Topper Moore stalked in from the bullpen and tossed a newspaper on the desk in front of Gholer along with some copies of the dead victim's morgue photos. She said, "The drops on the corner of the paper, that's barbecue sauce. The place across the street is filthy. Yuck." She turned around and left.

Gholer picked up the paper and looked at the date. "Just what I like. Service with a smile." He tossed the paper aside. "Aside from Sis Hargis' life history, you learn anything more recent? Such as, does anybody remember anything about yesterday?"

"Yeah," Madison said. "The security guard at the south entrance to the building. A woman visited Sis Hargis while she was on the platform, showcasing a Sebring. Which is a ride I might also spread 'em for. Not as wide as for a 'Vette, but, you know."

"How 'bout my five-year-old Buick Skylark?" Frizell said.

"Wouldn't get you a sniff," Madison said. "In your case it would take a Rolls."

"This woman," Gholer said. "You get any particulars?"

"Carrying a briefcase," Frizell said. "Dressed in a business suit. The guard said they talked, then the woman left. Later on he saw the same woman talking to Sis Hargis outside the building, after Sis had left for the day."

"This woman look like a lawyer?" Gholer asked.

Both detectives looked at him. Madison said, "Could be. Why?"

"Because Sis Hargis' divorce settlement was on the floorboard of her Mercedes." Gholer thumbed through the newspaper and plucked out the sports page. "Logic says the woman's her divorce lawyer and she was delivering the settlement papers. Look, just because the husband's not a fruitloop himself doesn't mean he don't *know* a fruitloop. We got, what, twelve abductions so far?" He made a come-hither gesture. "So what's different about this one?"

Madison and Frizell looked confused. Frizell said, "Doesn't seem any different to me."

Gholer said, "Wrong. It's quite a bit different. While we figure the Fiddleback has stalked all these people, he's grabbed the others when he had an open opportunity. They were walking somewhere or pulling up someplace in their car. Here, we got additional prior planning. We got the guy going to the trouble of posing as a valet parker, picking Sis Hargis' vehicle out of a parking lot full of cars, and personally going to pick her up when she called. He knew before he went to the fair exactly who he was going to snatch, what her car looked like. We got to assume that before he drove to the auto show to get her, he didn't know what she looked like unless someone told him. So how'd he pick her out of the crowd?" Gholer found the racing page in the sports section, folded back the paper and began to read.

"I get the feeling," Madison said, "that we're about to meet Sis Hargis' divorce attorney."

"Now for that," Gholer said, scanning the page, "you win the teddy bear. Make that your next stop. Since the Hargises have filed for divorce, county records will tell you the lawyer's name. Visit with her. Then go by and see William Hargis. I want heat on this guy."

Madison sat up straighter in her chair. "His lawyer told us to leave him alone, Loo."

"Fuck his lawyer," Gholer said. "We're not arresting the guy. We're only doing an investigation." He held the newspaper closer, rubbed his eyes, and said, "Jesus Christ."

"Your horse come in?" Frizell said.

"Somebody's damn sure did." Gholer laid the newspaper down. "I think you should be getting a move on."

"What's with the horse, Loo?" Madison said.

"You let me worry about the horse. Go worry about the lawyer first, then Hargis second. And next time I tell you I want twenty-four/seven on a guy, don't give me a lot of shit about it, okay?"

The pictures had long since begun to run together in Courtney's mind. One man's mustache became another's eyebrow, one man's nose the dimple in another's chin, the images overlapping like a series of double, triple, or in some cases quadruple exposures. And none of the FBI photos remotely resembled the man they were calling Fiddleback.

Oh, a few appeared crazy enough. There was one guy who even had an almost-matching scar, but that particular suspect was thin and sallow-faced. Courtney was worried that seeing thousands of pictures would flaw her memory.

She pretended not to notice when Gholer hauled Madison and Frizell into the FBI agent's office next door, then she spent the entire time while the trio met watching Jinx Madison out of the corner of her eye. Seen in the light of day, Madison's skin was lighter than Courtney remembered. The tall athletic detective walked gracefully and sat with confidence. Courtney wished that she had Madison's demeanor, that she herself looked more like a cop. She needed more time to run, maybe work out in the weight room.

By the clock on Gholer's desk the meeting lasted seven minutes, Courtney counting every second as she held the photo album in her lap. As Frizell and Madison exited the office side by side, Courtney considered approaching Gholer and screaming in his face, demanding that he let her sweep the floor, clean the toilets, anything but look at any more photos.

Gholer came out of Miller's office and walked into his own, carrying a cloth purse inside a Ziploc bag, a file jacket, and a folded-over newspaper. Courtney quickly vacated the corner of his desk and sat in a visitor's chair. Gholer thumped the file down, set the purse on top, snapped open the paper, and flopped down.

Gholer said, "You feeling any stronger?" He patted his own ribs.

"I feel like tearing this photo album in two," Courtney said.

"You won't find Fiddleback in there," Gholer said.

"Then why am I looking for him?"

"Agent Miller gave me that book. I think some of the guys in there are dead. A lot of 'em are bank robbers, swindlers on the run. It's the same suspect album they'd show to a robbery victim. Everybody on the wanted list is in there. But Fiddleback isn't wanted. If he was, we'd have him by now."

Courtney pinched the bridge of her nose. "Then why was I even bothering?"

"I didn't want you getting bored," Gholer said.

"Watching grass grow would be less boring than this."

"Then you'll enjoy the spice I'm about to put in your life. You like the races?"

"Horse races?"

Gholer nodded. "As in Lone Star Park. I want to send you there."

"To look at more photos?"

"To aid in our rapidly expanding investigation as it draws relentlessly to a close. I got Jinx and Eddie doing something else. I could get one of our detectives from downtown to do this in about a week, but I need it today. Won't require any, you know, heavy-duty physical stuff. Strictly questions and answers."

"What is it you want me to do?"

"First things first." Gholer reached inside his desk and produced a white nylon holster, which he dropped over in front of her. "It'll support the Glock and fit on your belt. You got a cell phone?"

Courtney made no move to touch the holster. "Odd you should ask. I was just thinking about getting a phone before I got shot last night."

Gholer now pulled out a Primestar with a flip-out mouthpiece. "It's in my name, so don't be calling Berlin, okay?"

Courtney took the phone and holster and held them in her lap.

Gholer waved a hand as if shooing flies. "This assignment's top priority, but it's pretty much a piece of cake." He extracted the betting tickets from the purse and tossed one of the morgue photos over to her. "Take this along to flash around in case someone can ID the victim."

Courtney was completely puzzled, and said so. Running around at Lone Star Park didn't sound like a piece of cake to her. She'd never felt so fucking inadequate. Twenty-four hours ago she was directing fairgoers to the bathroom, for God's sake.

"The pari-mutuel tickets belonged to the vic," Gholer said. "Or possibly the perp, though since they were in the victim's belongings we got to assume they're hers. You been to Lone Star Park before, or you need directions?"

"I went with a guy once. Horse races are almost as boring as looking at pictures, Loo."

"You're not going to watch the races, anyway. Start at track security. There'll be identifying numbers on those tickets telling which window sold 'em and what time. Then once you find the person that sold these, show the seller the picture. I don't see what's so hard."

"What's so hard is, I've never done anything like this. Besides, there are thousands of these tickets laying around out there. How can you expect anyone to remember who bought a couple nearly a week ago? You can pick hundreds off the floor."

"Not hundreds like these," Gholer said. He picked up the newspaper. "Sunday the twenty-fifth. Eighth race. Wonder Girl beat Misty's Dan by a length and a half, Two Pair by three lengths."

"I'm sure that's nice for Wonder Girl, but—"

"Which paid $60.40 for a show ticket on Two Pair, thirty bucks for a place ticket on Misty's Dan. And these babies"—he tapped the baggie holding the tickets—"are five-dollar trifecta bets. They're worth a shade over twenty-five hundred bucks apiece. You got any idea what that means?"

Courtney stared at the tickets. "It means I wish I'd bought them."

"Don't we all," Gholer said. "It also means that the winner would have cashed them in quicker than God can get a weather report. Unless something interfered. The Fiddleback had to've grabbed this woman in between the time she bought the tickets and the end of the race. On a payoff this size there won't be over a dozen winners, and I'm betting these are the only ones left uncashed. Also increases the odds of someone remembering selling the tickets.

"The racetrack beckons, Officer Bedell," Gholer said. "If I can be blunt, get your butt in gear." He thought for a moment, then grinned and spread his hands. "If you don't come back with the buyer's name," he said, "then your sentence will be a week looking at that photo album. We're desperate, Courtney, what can I say?" His smile faded fast, and his hands dropped listlessly into his lap. "I want these people to stop getting dead."

9

Madison and Frizell were driving a turd-brown, four-door Mercury Sable, the motor pool's idea of an inconspicuous detectives' car. After the two left Gholer, Jinx Madison sat behind the wheel in the parking lot while Eddie Frizell used the cell phone to check for the name of Sis Hargis' attorney. Madison watched bobtail trucks and forty-foot tractor-trailer rigs rumble back and forth on Irving Boulevard, drumming her fingers on the steering wheel. Frizell stood by the passenger door out in the open where there'd be less interference, and talked to the clerk at family court. He jotted information on a legal pad that he'd laid on the Sable's roof.

Frizell finished his conversation and stuck his head in. He popped the phone's antenna down with the heel of his hand and tossed the legal pad on the floorboard. "Attorney Megan Harris," he said. "Highland Park Shopping Village."

Madison turned the key in the ignition. The starter chugged and the engine caught and raced. "Ooo, uptown," she said. "Same address as your divorce attorney, right?"

"Shit, which one? My first was a retired lady in Mesquite. My second was somebody legal aid referred me to. I'm still paying the guy." Frizell climbed in and slammed the door. "I think the Loo's full of it. We should be hunting the nut, not chasing around after normal people."

Madison looked through the rear window and poked her tongue inside her cheek as she backed out of the parking lot. She didn't answer.

"Don't you think he's full of it?" Frizell said.

"The Loo?"

"Yeah."

Madison dropped the gearshift into drive. The car lurched forward. "Maybe so, maybe not."

"Hell. We've got a psycho here. The husband and the lawyer aren't going to know anything about any nutso."

"By a certain way of thinking," Madison said. "But by another, this case was front page headlines this morning. If this lawyer was with the missing woman yesterday, and was actually the last person to see the victim before she disappeared, then why has she not already contacted the police department?"

Frizell propped a knee against the dashboard. "Good point."

"Damn right, good point." Madison eased the Sable into the southbound traffic on Irving Boulevard. "Anybody thinking the Loo just climbed off a load of turnips is as full of it as you said you thought *he* is."

Frizell rolled down the window a couple of turns. "What's your take on the witness, Jinxie?"

"Patrolman Bedell? I never met her before last night, but she's ballsy, going up against that guy like she did. I think the Loo's got his eye on her."

Frizell snorted through his nose. "You kidding? The Loo don't screw around on his old lady."

"No, I mean for the unit. I was on patrol when he drafted me. Worked a crime scene with Gholer out in South Dallas, and I got to admit I was pretty much on my toes that night. The next day I come in for work, there's a transfer slip in my box. You watch what I'm telling you."

The blinker clicked monotonously as Madison steered into the left-turn lanes leading onto Inwood Road. Frizell said, "Be okay with me if he recruits her. Woman's got some body on her. Could stand some new talent."

"Come on, Eddie. You can't be messin' with no woman. Your palm would get jealous."

"Fuck you, Jinx."

"In your dreams." Madison took her foot off the brake, let the Sable roll up closer to the yellow DART bus idling in front of her, then applied the brakes once more. "Highland Park Shopping Village. I won't be seein' too many sisters out there."

"You can't stay the Fiddleback's not giving us a tour. First the state fair, now the rich man's neighborhood. We're seeing the sights."

"You can keep the sights," Madison said. "The farther I can stay from the fairgrounds, the better."

"What are you talking about? Us Dallas kids' pleasantest memories are at the Texas state fair."

"Pleasant memories for people from *your* neighborhood, maybe," Madison said. "I ever tell you my father worked at the fair?"

"Yeah? Concessions? Sideshow barker, what?"

"My old man *was* the sideshow." Madison's smile faded, a rare occasion for her. She looked down at her lap. "Up until the sixties and early seventies they had this midway attraction named the African Dip. That was the official name, but you honky kids called it the Nigger Dunk."

"Oh shit. I remember it. Jinx, you're not saying . . ."

"Yep. Bunch of black men sitting on a board inside a cage over a tank filled with nasty water. For a quarter you could throw three balls at a target. Hit the target, release the board, dunk the nigger in the tank.

I remember standing there holding my mama's hand while my daddy danced around on that board yelling, 'Up your ass, white boy, you can't throw baseballs for shit.' Eggin' 'em on. Real fun days." She shook her head. "Most embarrassed I've ever been. No little girl deserves to see her daddy carrying on like that." Up ahead, the light turned green. The bus rolled sluggishly ahead. Madison gave the Sable a little gas, stayed close behind the bus as she turned the wheel to the left. She wiped at her eye. "I hate that fuckin' fair."

Jinx Madison had called it correctly. There were no sisters in sight within the confines of Highland Park Shopping Village. No brothers, either. Nor were there any Asians, Hispanics, Native Americans, or Lebanese. Madison thought that this was the lily-whitest fucking place she'd ever seen. The Fiddleback would play hell trying to score around here.

The shopping village was built on a square just a few blocks from the Dallas Country Club, in a neighborhood of homes like English castles behind lawns the size of polo fields. Madison steered the Sable past Mercedeses, Porches, and Beemers, looking for a parking place. Women roamed the sidewalks in St. John knits worn over sunlamp tans. There were college-age girls wearing dressy black pants, boots, and sorority tees. There were boutiques whose display windows showed crystal goblets and pewter vases, Ralph Lauren, Harold's, Banana Republic. The buildings were Spanish architecture, with adobe walls and slanted, red-tiled roofs. As Madison parked in between a Porsche and a Bentley, Eddie Frizell murmured, "Holy shit." Madison thought about the movie *The Stepford Wives*.

The late-September sun burned down; the thermometer on the tower across the way showed ninety-two degrees. The detectives got out and locked up the Sable. Two women in tennis dresses crossed the street, headed for their cars, and sniffed down their noses at Madison as they passed her by. Jinx hitched up her tight-fitting pants and showed the ladies a couple of extra-saucy wiggles as she walked up under the awning.

The lawyer's office was one flight above street level, overlooking a restaurant with sidewalk seating and a sign reading CAFÉ DALLAS over the entry, and down the block from a four-screen theater. The detectives mounted the steps and hustled along the landing. There was an iron railing on their right and lattice-work arches overhead. As they pushed through a glass-paneled door into the lawyer's reception room, a cowbell jangled.

They stood on brown flatweave carpet with spongy padding underneath. Ahead on their left was a French provincial sofa with a rose-pattern design, uncomfortable-looking chairs to match, and a coffee table that was probably teakwood. Across the room from the seating area, a young man sat at a computer workstation. He had tousled brown hair and wore a white shirt, tie, vest, and light-colored slacks. His nameplate identified him as Wilson Wright, Paralegal. He looked up and said in a soft tenor voice, "Hi. May I help you?"

Frizell stepped forward. "Megan Harris, please."

The guy examined a calendar. "You have an appointment? Ms. Harris is just—"

Frizell had his wallet open, flashing his badge.

The paralegal stared uncertainly at the shield. "What does this concern?"

"Police business," Frizell said. "She in?"

The paralegal and the cops looked at each other. The paralegal reached for the phone.

A cultured female voice said from off in the corner, "I'll handle it, Wilson."

Madison looked toward the sound. A woman stood

in an inner doorway wearing a silk blouse, tan skirt, and medium-heeled square-toed shoes. She had a round face, a soft body, and wore glasses in monstrous frames. She offered Frizell her hand. "I'm Megan Harris. What can I do for you?"

Frizell shook the hand and introduced himself. "Detective Edward Frizell, ma'am. Investigating Mrs. William Hargis."

Megan Harris showed surprise. "Sis? You're investigating Sis?"

"Her disappearance, ma'am."

"Oh. It's horrible, isn't it?"

Madison stepped up and joined the group. "I'm Detective Jinx Madison, Ms. Harris. Can we talk someplace?"

Harris gave the black woman a fleeting glance, then addressed Frizell once more. "I don't know what I can—"

"Hey, begging your pardon," Madison said. "You didn't know Mrs. Hargis was missing?"

Harris' gaze flicked at Madison. The lawyer licked her lips before answering. "Yes, of course I . . ." She turned to the paralegal. "Hold my calls, Wilson," she said, then turned and led the way into the back office.

A minute later the detectives sat before Megan Harris' desk, with the lawyer in a high-backed leather swivel chair across from them. Framed needlepoints adorned the walls. There was a bookcase by the window displaying black-bound Vernon's *Annotated Civil Statutes of Texas,* red-bound U.S. legal code volumes, and tan-jacketed *Southwestern Reporters.* That day's *Dallas Morning News* lay on Harris' desk, the headline FIDDLEBACK CLAIMS TWELFTH VICTIM in plain view. There were no family pictures within the office. Madison eyed the lawyer's hands. She wasn't wearing a wedding ring. Madison didn't think that Megan Harris was a lesbian; she didn't have the look about her.

Here was a plain-looking woman, still single in her thirties, who substituted humping a law book for what was missing in her life. Megan Harris likely resented all men, and took her frustrations out on her clients' soon-to-be-exes with a passion.

Madison pointedly eyed the newspaper. "I see you've been reading up."

Harris reached for the paper, picked it up. "Oh yes, I . . ."

"So you already knew that Mrs. Hargis has disappeared," Frizell said.

"Yes, of course. After all, she's my client."

"I guess we misunderstood you," Madison said. "Out there a few minutes ago I got the impression that this was news to you."

"No, I . . ." Harris obviously fought for composure. Her expression firmed. "I was just surprised that the police would be calling on me."

"Why wouldn't we be calling on you? Our information is that you visited Mrs. Hargis while she was modeling at the car show yesterday." Madison sat at ease, watching the lawyer's reaction closely.

There was the barest flicker in Harris' gaze. "That's right." Then the mask was back in place, the lawyer once again in control.

Frizell slouched down in his chair, his ankle resting on his knee. "Mind if we ask why you met with Mrs. Hargis?"

"That would be confidential."

"Oh, we understand privilege," Frizell said. "But, I got to tell you, we found a copy of a divorce settlement in Mrs. Hargis' car. Along with a dead woman. Can we assume the settlement is something you put together?"

"Yes, you could assume that."

"Ms. Harris," Madison said, "let's approach this from a different angle. We honestly don't give a shit about the Hargises' divorce proceedings, other than as they pertain to the woman being kidnapped. But I'm sure you understand, we have a woman who's suddenly disappeared, and now a husband who could have . . . well, he and his wife aren't exactly doing it regularly, you know?"

Harris eyed Madison with distaste.

"I suppose I could be more delicate," Madison said. "But you get the idea."

"What am I missing, detectives?" Harris said. "I've just read in the newspaper that this lunatic has taken Sis. Surely you don't think Billy—"

"You mean, Mr. Hargis?" Frizell interrupted.

"Of course I mean Mr. Hargis. This case is unusual for me in that I knew both husband and wife before, on a first-name basis."

"Oh?" Frizell steadied a ballpoint. "From where?"

"The club. Various social functions. I'm sure you're aware, Park Cities is a small community."

"A whole lot smaller than mine," Madison said. "Knowing them both didn't give you a conflict?"

"Not per se. I'd never *represented* either of them before. Just knew them socially."

"Okay," Madison said. "Without you revealing any of the down-and-dirty about the divorce, suppose you just tell us about yesterday afternoon. You came into the Automobile Building while she was modeling?"

"Yes. I met with Mr. Hargis and his lawyer yesterday at noon. By the way, Mr. Hargis' lawyer is named—"

"Larry Akin," Madison said. "We had the pleasure last night at the crime scene."

"Larry came to the crime scene?" Harris' surprise looked genuine.

"Along with Mr. Hargis," Madison said. "I got to say, Ms. Harris, we're not surprised that Mr. Hargis' lawyer is less than thrilled to have us talk to his client.

But we'd expect *Mrs.* Hargis' attorney to show a little bit different attitude."

"I'm not being difficult," Harris said.

"You could have fooled me." Madison locked gazes with the lawyer.

Harris lowered her eyes. "Of course. I'm sorry I . . . What is it, exactly, that you want to . . . ?"

"Just an overall description of the events," Frizell said.

Harris drew breath, then slowly let the air out of her lungs. "Sure. After I met with Larry Akin and Billy—Mr. Hargis—I reduced my understanding of the settlement terms to writing. I went to the fair to deliver a copy. I spoke to Sis as she was working on the revolving stage. Then when her shift ended I walked outside with her, where she called for her car from the valet service while we finished our chat."

Madison's forehead tightened in surprise. "During the time you talked to her, did she say anything that might make you think she was in distress?"

"All people in the middle of a divorce are in distress, Detective. Sis was up in the air over the terms of the settlement. Of which I assume you still have a copy."

"Sure do," Madison said. "And anybody who'll give me what Mrs. Hargis was getting can divorce me any time."

Harris smiled condescendingly. "People in the Hargises' bracket look at things differently."

"Oh?" Madison said. "What bracket is that?"

"People used to having unlimited funds. In those cases money often takes a backseat to . . . call it one-upmanship. Certain things become a matter of pride."

"Yeah, we call 'em pissing contests," Madison said.

"That's a rather vulgar description," Harris said.

Madison leaned back and watched the lawyer. "So,

after you and Mrs. Hargis talked things over inside the auto show, you went outside to finish the conversation?"

"Yes. To clear up a few things."

Madison waved a hand, a signal for Frizell to pick up the ball and run with it.

Frizell came out of his trance. "You were with her when she phoned for her car?"

"Yes. And stayed with her until the driver arrived." Harris put her hand in front of her mouth. "My Lord. The driver."

"Did you get a look at him?" Frizell asked.

"He was . . ." Harris seemed deep in thought. "Not really a close look. He wore a chauffeur's cap. The bill pretty much obscured his face."

"And the whole time," Madison said, "you and Mrs. Hargis were discussing this divorce settlement?"

"That's the way I recall it," Harris said.

"Was the chauffeur's cap dark-colored?"

"It was . . . dark blue, I think."

"Blue," Madison said. "Not black?"

"I'm certain it was blue."

"Mmm-hmm," Madison said.

Frizell took a note, then looked up. "Do you remember if the guy was—"

"I think," Madison said, "we've got enough for now." She laid one of her business cards on Harris' desk. "If you think of anything else, Ms. Harris."

"Of course." Harris snatched up the card with a look of surprised relief. "And if you need me, I'm certainly available."

Madison crossed her legs and jiggled her foot up and down. "I wouldn't be surprised if we will be needing you," she said. "In fact, I'm close to a hundred percent sure that we will."

*   *   *

When the detectives had left the attorney and were seated in their car, Frizell said, "The fuck was all that?"

Madison paused with her thumb and forefinger on the ignition switch. "An interview with Sis Hargis' attorney. The fuck did it look like?"

"No, I mean, why are we leaving so quick? I had a bunch more questions to ask."

Madison watched two women come out of the Ralph Lauren shop. One was dressed in designer jeans, the other in blousy pleated pants. Madison said, "Waste of time asking her anything more. That chick was lying through her asshole."

"Sounded pretty straight to me," Frizell said.

"Get the wax out of your ears, Eddie. Jesus Christ, we're going to have to go to the fair again and talk to that security guard."

"Everything she said sounds reasonable. She met with the other lawyer in the divorce, went out to give the news to her client."

Madison started the car, raced the motor. "In case you don't remember, Doctor Watson," she said, "the security guard told us this morning that this lawyer came in to talk to Hargis, and then left. Later, he says, he saw the lawyer talking to Hargis outside the building. Megan Bullshit Harris just told us she stayed with Hargis till she got off, then walked outside with her."

"Shit. She could have just forgot."

"She might have forgotten one little aspect. But she also just told us she was talking to Hargis about the divorce and doesn't remember what the valet driver looked like. But think. She wasn't paying attention to the driver, yet she remembers exactly what color of hat he had on and how he was wearing it. You notice the two women that just left that Ralph Lauren shop over there?"

Frizell was studying his notes. "Yeah, sort of."

"You were just aware of them walking by. But you weren't really paying attention to them, right?"

Frizell rubbed his chin with the end of his ballpoint. "Yeah, I remember 'em. Two women shopping. So what?"

"Okay," Madison said. "What did the women have on?"

"The fuck could I know that?" Frizell said.

"Exactly. But that lawyer just told us she wasn't really paying any attention to the valet driver, but she described his hat to a *T*. Like maybe she knew in advance what he was going to be wearing. Like maybe she'd seen the guy before, but wanted us to think she couldn't describe him." Madison put the car in reverse. "Chick's lying, Eddie," Madison said. "Once we talk to some other people and get our shit more together, we'll take a shot at Ms. Megan Harris again. You're partnered with Sherlock, bud. This here sister knows what's happenin'."

10

Courtney Bedell left westbound Interstate 30 and headed south for Lone Star Park in bumper-to-bumper, stop-and-go traffic. Visible on both sides of the road were tall elms and sycamores, high weeds, and swampy riverbottom land. A quarter-mile in the distance was the marquee atop the Texas Sports Hall of Fame. A few miles beyond the Hall of Fame lay Six Flags Over Texas and Wet n' Wild. Behind her on the interstate cars and trucks whizzed past in both directions, headed west for Cowtown, east for Big D. The tractor-trailer in front of her came to a stop with a hiss of air brakes. Courtney stopped as well and impatiently patted the dashboard. Her Glock dug into the small of her back; she twisted around in order to get comfortable.

There was a sudden ringing near her hip. She jumped, dug for the Glock, and very nearly rear-ended the forty-footer in the process. She frantically looked around inside the car for the cell phone. She picked it up, flipped open the mouthpiece, jammed the receiver against her ear. "Uh, hello."

"Gholer here. It works, huh?"

"I'm talking on it, Loo."

"Listen, I'm giving you a heads up. I've called ahead of you out there."

The traffic ahead moved sluggishly on. Courtney gave her Lumina a little gas, following the tractor-trailer around the curve, headed north now toward the racetrack. "Called out where?" Courtney said.

"To track security. See a Captain Dennis Rush. He's expecting you. I faxed him a picture."

She looked in puzzlement at the portfolio she'd brought along. "I've got several copies of the vic's photo in the folder with the betting tickets."

"Different picture. A guy named David Og, a limo driver who vanished from the racetrack parking lot the same day as last night's vic. I've asked Rush to show Og's picture around out there. He won't be much help in doing that, but we got to try. Track security's not known for being a ball of fire. So you'll know the connection, the Fiddleback showed up at the fair as Og's replacement yesterday, as a valet parker. Which is how he got to be the driver on Mrs. Hargis' car. Now we're pretty sure Fiddleback picked Og off as he sat outside the track last Sunday, and we're dead certain that last night's vic was out there the same day. How he managed to take two victims at once, I got no idea. Courtney?"

Lone Star Park loomed on her right. There were two structures at the track, the towering grandstand and, closer to the street, the low-slung building where gamblers could bet on races year-round, via simulcast from Oak Lawn, Aqueduct, Saratoga, and other tracks around the country. Courtney said, "I'm here, Loo."

"Likely after last night I don't got to tell you this. But beginning a year ago the Fiddleback began to abduct people, maybe one a month at first. Now he's taken three people we know of in the past week, not to mention trying to kill you. As the shrinks would say, it means he's escalating. You keep your eyes and ears open, Courtney, and one hand on your weapon. If you ever come face to face with this guy a second time, and you're not ready, odds are we'll never be talking again."

She parked six rows out from the main track entrance, in between two SuperCab pickups. She then took inventory—thirteen rounds in the Glock's magazine, thirteen more in the spare clip, safety on—hefted the portfolio holding the morgue photos and pari-mutuel tickets, then got out and locked the car. She took a couple of steps in the direction of the grandstand, then stopped and leaned shakily on the Lumina's fender.

Thoughts assaulted her brain in waves: Jason, Mrs. Bailey, Jan, Gholer, all in a jumble and in no particular pattern. And over all these mental images towered the Fiddleback, the scar on his face pulsing red, the barrel of his pistol pointed at her midsection. And right there in late-September Texas heat, Courtney Bedell was suddenly cold.

She flashed her badge on her way in and learned from the ticket-taker that track security was on the second level. She mounted an escalator. Riding two steps above her was a man in overalls. As Courtney leaned on the moving handrail, the man tore a ticket into shreds. He dropped the pieces over the side, the bits of pasteboard swirling in the updraft like confetti. Near the top of the escalator was a television monitor showing live action from the track outside; visible on the screen, a jockey booted a winner home. The grandstand roar reached a fevered peak, the noise reverberating throughout the building and causing the escalator steps to vibrate. As she reached the top and stepped off, the jockey guided his mount into the winner's circle. She stepped past the monitor and walked through an open area containing more TV monitors along with a row of betting and payoff windows. Lines were already forming in front of the sellers in anticipation of the next race, while a few lucky winners waited for the payout workers to confirm the results and post the numbers. As Courtney passed the entry to the upstairs bar and grill, a man inside lifted his glass and offered her a toast. She permitted herself a responsive smile, then quickened her pace and hurried on.

Ten minutes later she sat off to one side of Captain Dennis Rush's desk in the track security office. Rush was about fifty, bald with a graying fringe and a big stomach. His uniform shirt was pale blue and his pants were too tight. As he'd ushered her in he'd checked out her ass. Each time he smiled at her, her skin crawled.

Rush was saying, "And guess who the perp turned out to be. The landlord, the guy who'd called us in to begin with. I says to myself, you miss one that obvious it's time to retire. Left the force in 'ninety-two, and been here ever since. A lot easier out here, not so much bullshit to put up with. You work with Gholer, huh?"

Courtney didn't want to go into detail with this guy. She said merely, "Yes, sir." She opened the folder and pulled out the copies of the betting tickets. "Listen, Captain, I've got some things here I wish you could—"

"Good man," Rush said. He surveyed her up and down, tits, waist, thighs, finally her face. "Me and Jerry used to do a few things together."

"These tickets," Courtney said. "I wonder if you could look them over and tell me—"

"Back then they didn't have any women in Crimes-Against-Persons. Must be something new, huh?" He ogled her again.

Courtney inwardly squirmed. "I wouldn't know about that. I've only got three years on the force. There have been female detectives ever since I went through the academy. Could you look these tickets over and tell me, possibly, what window sold them?"

His gaze continuing to roam, he tossed a copy of a picture over in front of her. "I'm supposed to give you this. Jerry Gholer faxed it out here. I got copies for our people, but I got to tell you, picking one face out of a crowd is pretty tough. Unless you happen to accidentally know the guy. Whatcha shooting?" He pointed at her holster.

"I prefer the Glock, sir." Courtney picked up the photocopy. It was a driver's license picture, a dark-complexioned man around thirty-five with thick black hair, a mustache, and beard. Looked Middle Eastern. She stowed the photo inside her folder. "I've got a picture for you to look over as well," she said. "As soon as we can identify the ticket seller that sold these trifectas, and possibly get the seller in here to have a look at the photo at the same time you do."

"The Glock's lighter and easy for a woman to handle," Rush said. "My day we all carried the .38 Special. But we were all men." His look grew cunning. "Say, is this about that stuff that's been in the papers?"

"What stuff is that, sir?" Courtney felt sudden agony in her ribs as she shifted in her chair. She gingerly touched her side.

"You know, the asshole with the spiders."

"I'm not at liberty, Captain. But I'll tell you it's front-burner stuff."

"Yeah, right." *Tits, waist, thighs.* Rush picked up the pari-mutuel copies and leaned back. "Thousands of these laying around on the floors out here. You know the odds of somebody remembering who they sold these to?"

"The odds are long. But those are winning tickets, sir, big winners. We thought that might narrow the percentages."

Rush squinted at the tickets. "Last Sunday? Let's see, window forty-three. That's on the general admin level downstairs. And on the twenty-fifth, that's . . ." He opened a log, ran his finger down the page. "Lester Fine sold them tickets. And you're in luck, he's working today. You want me to get ol' Lester in here?"

Courtney did her best to look grateful. "That would be great, Captain, if you could."

"Sure thing. When I tell him a pretty lady's waitin', ol' Lester will pick up his feet." He reached for his phone and grinned. "Tell me, pretty thing, you spoke for?"

Horny old goat, Courtney thought. She leaned in nearer the desk, and forced herself to smile. "Why, I don't know as I should answer that one, Captain. Handsome men can kind of put a girl in the middle, you know?"

Lester Fine acted like a man under surveillance, which Courtney supposed he often was, with hidden cameras trained on his betting window in case he stuck his fingers in the till. Fine was around forty, thin as a shadow, and wore a pencil mustache. His eyes moved constantly, as if he was searching for the nearest escape route. He was dressed in a short-sleeve white shirt and black slim tie. He sat on the corner of Captain Rush's desk and held the pari-mutuel tickets about three inches from his nose. Finally, he said, "Whatcha askin' for?"

Courtney dug out her wallet and flashed her shield. Lone Star Park was in the City of Grand Prairie, outside DPD jurisdiction, and if Fine felt like telling her to take a hike there wasn't a thing that Courtney Bedell could have done about it. She felt a wave of relief when Fine barely glanced at her badge, then nodded. "It's part of a homicide investigation," Courtney said.

Fine used the copies of the tickets to fan himself. "Just so happens, I'm holdin' copies o' these under my counter."

Captain Rush frowned at the ticket seller. "You mean, you know who they belong to?"

"Sure. Trash Rosita and the combine." Fine shrugged as if to say, Who else?

"Naw." Rush had a closer look at the morgue photo of the victim. "No way that's her."

Fine stroked his mustache. "I sold Rosita the tickets and she bummed our Xerox to make distribution to the others. Only six winning tickets purchased on that particular trifecta, and four of 'em cashed in within five minutes after the results posted. I been thinking it's odd I ain't seen Rosita, 'cause with a payoff that size you woulda thought she'd of knocked down the window to get her money. That's how come I'm holding the copies, in case the wrong party tries to cash 'em in."

Rush's interest picked up. "How much they worth?"

"Shade over five thousand."

"Jesus Christ. Trash Rosita finally picked one."

Courtney felt like a spectator at a tennis match. She butted in. "Excuse me? Trash Rosita and the combine sounds like a musical group."

The racetrack men looked at each other. Fine turned his face away. Rush leaned over his desk. "Trash Rosita's not exactly your standard horse player."

"Obviously," Courtney said. "Mind telling me what she is?"

Rush turned to Fine. "How long since you've seen her?" the captain asked.

Fine pulled out a knife and cleaned his nails. "Ain't laid eyes on her since she bought the tickets. Sunday."

Rush turned to Courtney and gestured in the general direction of the racetrack exit. "Across the road and a piece to the south, there's this colony. You'd call 'em street people. My old man woulda called 'em hoboes. Same difference. They live in crates, Dumpsters, overturned trash cans, anything to keep 'em out of the rain. Nights they build fires and cook wild rabbit, raccoon, hell, anything they can get their hands on. We let 'em in here after the track closes, and they can have whatever trash they can haul away. Get some pretty good aluminum cans, all kindsa junk, sell it for scrap metal. Trash Rosita's one of them.

" 'Bout once a week when the season's on," Rush said, "they pool whatever dollars they can scrape together and send Rosita over to place a bet. Them people figure, what the hell, if all they got's twenty bucks to their name, why not try and run it into something? We sorta look the other way while the people at the front gate let Rosita in without charging her admission. Jesus Christ, five thousand dollars. Rosita finally hits the jackpot, suddenly she ain't around no more."

Courtney felt a surge of pity. She pictured the wretch, the one good fortune of her life hidden in her purse as the creep had taken her to God-knew-where, for abuse, unspeakable torture, and finally to die. Courtney reached to Rush's desk for the morgue photo, which she handed over to Lester Fine. "Please look carefully, Mr. Fine," Courtney said. "Have you ever seen this woman before?"

Fine perched on the corner of the captain's desk and crossed his ankles. He held the picture at arm's length. "Might've. Ain't Trash Rosita, though."

"Look again, please. Are you sure?"

"Rosita's face is always sooty. Those nasty front teeth look like hers, but the pearly-white teeth, no way. And the hair? You kidding? Rosita ain't bathed in forever. You could plant corn under her fingernails. You can smell her comin'."

Courtney had a thought. "Look here, guys." She took the picture away from Fine and smoothed it flat. Then she pulled a sheet of notepaper from Rush's pad, and tore the paper into strips. She carefully arranged the strips over the photo, covering the hair on top and on both sides of the head. "Concentrate just on the face, okay?" Courtney said. "Any better?"

Fine hunkered over the picture, scratching his head. Rush stood and bent from the waist, peering at the morgue photo as well. The men looked at each other. Fine lifted the picture, shook off the strips of paper, and held the photo at arm's length. "Jesus Christ, it *is* Trash Rosita," Lester Fine said. "Somebody done transformed her into a beauty queen."

Courtney steered her Lumina over twin tire ruts leading from Loop 12 into marshy riverbottom land, and entered a forest of elms, sycamores, and tangled kudzu vines. Thus far Rush's directions had been right on target. The sawed-off stump that the racetrack cop had described loomed directly ahead over the Lumina's hood ornament. The clearing where the street people lived should lie just beyond the stump. Courtney stopped the car, took a deep breath, and looked fearfully all around. The last time she'd ventured into the toolies alone, the Fiddleback had tried to kill her. She pressed her back more firmly against the seat. The pressure of the Glock against her spine steadied her nerves. She gave the Lumina a little gas and continued on, lowering her window as the suspension bumped and rattled. Blue jays screeched and locusts whirred.

She passed the landmark stump and entered a clearing overgrown with ragweed, moss, and dandelions. The tire ruts ended where the clearing began, so she parked and cut her engine. About fifty yards in front of her was a ragged circle of homes for the homeless: packing crates, overturned Dumpsters, and plastic shipping boxes. Piles of charred wood lay here and there. A lone wisp of smoke rose from one of the piles, and near the dying fire were animal bones. They looked like rabbit remains, and Courtney thought that the rural homeless were luckier than those in the inner city; under the bridges on Cadiz Street and Zangs Boulevard, the wretches cooked rat and alligator gar.

She scanned the clearing. Johnson grass waved in the breeze, but otherwise nothing moved. She reached to the small of her back, touched the Glock, and eased the safety off. She clutched the portfolio to her chest. Slowly, carefully, looking warily in every direction, she slid out of the car and crossed the clearing. The wind was hot and humid. Ragweed clung to her pants legs. She sneezed.

She approached the makeshift village and peered inside an overturned Dumpster. There on the ground were a gunnysack stuffed with rags, a rusty folding chair, and a tattered paperback Jack'e Collins novel. The book gave her an idea. She'd r :treat to the car for a pad and pen, and leave a note giving the task force's phone number and hinting reward. She left the Dumpster and started back across the clearing.

A gruff male voice screamed in her ear, "Whatcha doin' fuckin' with my stuff, woman? Knock yer ass off."

Courtney jumped sideways, stumbled, and fell into a thicket of ragweed. Fear clogged her throat. Pain razored through her aching ribs. She put up her hands and shielded her face.

A lunatic towered over her, waving a tree limb. He was filthy, with an unkempt beard and red-rimmed eyes. He swayed on his feet, wearing an army jacket and jeans with holes in the knees. He raised the limb. "Answer me 'fore I bash yer fuckin' brains."

She scrabbled away from him. The Glock pressed hard against her backbone. "Sir, back off. I'm a police officer, and you could be in serious trouble." She reached for her pocket. "I'm going to show you my badge."

He continued to hold the branch aloft. "Be quick about it."

She opened up her wallet. "I'm not lying, sir."

He bent over and squinted at the badge, then lowered the tree limb. "It figgers you'd come now, after them people already died. You gonna arrest us?"

Courtney climbed wearily to her feet. Her hands trembled and her mouth was dry.

He yelled out, "She's a cop, y'all."

There was movement all around. First a woman stepped out from behind some kudzu vines, then a man. One at a time the others came from their hiding places, a dozen human wrecks, their faces covered in grime. The men's hair was as long as the women's. They shuffled hopelessly over and surrounded her where she stood.

She turned to the man holding the tree limb. "I showed you ID, sir. Mind giving me your name?"

He spoke in a monotone. "They call me Weasel. My real name don't matter, not anymore."

She tried staring him down. "It might matter to us."

His face was expressionless. "I don't give a shit, lady. You want to put me in jail? Hell jail's better'n this. My name's Weasel, and that's all yer gettin' from me."

Courtney watched the hopeless red-rimmed eyes. She picked up the folder and held out the morgue photo. "You know her?" Courtney asked.

A woman standing nearby came up to look over Weasel's shoulder. The woman said, "Oh, shit."

A second woman shuffled over, sniffled, and wiped her eyes. A bearded man had a look at the picture as well, then knelt in prayer.

Weasel looked resigned. "Yeah, we do. Rosita. Sumbitch killed 'er."

Courtney dropped the photo to her side. "You're not surprised she's dead?"

"Hell, lady, she was dead the minute that sumbitch hauled her away from here. She was breathin' air, but she was dead all right." Weasel's lip quivered. Tears ran down his face, streaking the grime.

Courtney gently touched Weasel's shoulder. "Tell me," she said.

All around her the homeless sank to their knees.

Weasel said, "You ain't gonna arrest us?"

"Did you kill her, sir?"

"Hell, no. I was affeared of gettin' killed my ownself."

"Then there's nothing to arrest you for." She stepped toward him. "Tell me what happened," she said.

He sorrowfully hung his head. "Last Sunday it was. Rosita and Bulldog an' Pretzelhead, they'd gone over to the track to make our bet. We watched 'em comin' back down that road yonder. Just 'fore they reached the woods this long black car drove up beside 'em, and one crazy-lookin' sumbitch got out wavin' a gun. Goddamn, lady, who'd want to rob Rosita and them?"

"The car," Courtney said. "Was it a limousine?"

Weasel used his sleeve to wipe his nose. "Yeah, though the likes of us ain't never rode in one. Couldn't hear whatall the guy was sayin' to Rosita and them, they was too far away. But Bulldog stepped up and said somethin' back, and then Pretzelhead said somethin', too. Bastard shot both of 'em where they stood, pushed Rosita inside the car, and hauled ass on outta here. Last time we seen Rosita. We kept hid and kept quiet. If we hadn'a, sumbitch woulda killed us surer'n hell."

"My God," Courtney said. "You didn't report this?"

"Report it to who? Police don't give a shit about us, lady, lessen we steal somethin'."

"What about the two wounded men?"

"They wasn't wounded. They was dead."

"And you didn't call for an ambulance?"

Weasel snorted through his nose. "For what? So the county could take 'em for cadavers? We take care of our own, lady. Give 'em a better funeral than they would have got otherwise. Said a right nice send-off speech, I did."

A filthy woman nodded in agreement. "Weasel, he said him a right *smart* send-off speech."

Courtney pictured them all, their heads bowed as Weasel said the eulogy under a canopy of trees. She was practically in awe. "And the bodies?"

"Buried 'em," Weasel said. "Right over there in them woods. Shit, Rosita *would* be the one carryin' our bettin' slips from the track. We never even knew which horses we was pullin' for to win. We always lose, lady. Every single time, but we keep hopin'. Bettin' them races once a week, that's the only fun we got left in the world."

11

Harold Bays hated for people to bug him while he was working. Or eating. Or sleeping. Harold Bays wanted everyone to leave him alone. Once the Change was over and done with, no one would fuck with Harold Bays ever again.

His current tormentor was Melvin Pure. Harold hated Melvin Pure even more than he hated most people. He would love to kill Melvin Pure right here, right now, but too many other humans were watching. Humans who would realize just how powerful Harold was becoming and interfere. Harold would bide his time. Once the Change was complete, Melvin Pure could be the first to die.

Pure stood at the edge of the loading dock, peering inside the forty-foot trailer where Harold hid in the shadows behind a stack of Tide liquid detergent cartons. Harold loved the musty smell inside the trailer, loved the darkness even more. Pure squinted, searching with his eyes. "Yo, Harold. You in there? Gotcher pay." He waved a window envelope with a computer-printer check inside.

Harold didn't move. There was a time in his life when he would have laid in wait and slit Pure's throat when the dock boss left work for home. But unless Melvin Pure got in the way of the Change he was safe for now. Pure was a redheaded, white-skinned human, and therefore not a proper instrument. The Change was all that mattered to Harold; all else was fuck-and-be-damned.

Pure stayed on the dock and flapped the envelope up and down. "Goddammit, Harold, I ain't got all day. You wantcher money, or don'tcha?"

Harold left the shadows and moved out in the open in a crablike shuffle. Melvin Pure recoiled in fear, then tried to laugh it off and act as if he'd only been startled. Harold knew better. Everyone on the dock thought that Harold was spooky. Even those who weren't afraid of him kept their distance.

Harold neared the edge of the dock. He removed his thick gloves and slapped them together. A cloud of powdered resin flew. Harold's two-piece worker's uniform was green, while Pure wore supervisor's white coveralls. Visible beyond the dock boss, the loading dock was twice the length and half again the breadth of a football field. There was a glass-enclosed office dead center in the floor. Here and there along the dock Hyster forklifts whined, inching forward, going in reverse, inserting their blades under wooden pallets, lifting heavy loads. Tacked on a corkboard was a notice of an extra deduction from this week's pay for union dues.

Across the floor from where Harold labored was the break-out line, where pickups and bobtails stood backed in to the dock. The smaller trucks had hauled in deliveries from customers' warehouses throughout North Texas. Break-out workers—sweaty men and even a few women, many with long hair tied back in ponytails, all with weightlifters' builds—loaded freight onto dollies, marked the cargo's destination on a chalkboard, and hooked the dollies onto a conveyor for transfer over to the stacking side of the dock. On

the stacking side, freightloaders took the carts from
the line and packed their contents onto eighteen-
wheelers bound for San Antonio, Chicago, Atlanta,
LA, points north, south, east, west, and in between.
TEXAS MOTOR FREIGHT was emblazoned on each of the
trailers in block letters over the company logo, TMF in
cursive script with lightning bolts above and below.

Harold Bays was the stacker in the forty-seven hole,
which meant that he loaded freight bound exclusively for
the Midland-Odessa area in far West Texas. Intrastate
shipping wasn't subject to border-station weight limits,
so it was nothing for TMP to load Midland-Odessa
trucks with seventy, eighty thousand pounds, sometimes
more. It was murderous work. Most freightloaders shied
away from the Midland-Odessa hole, preferring instead
to work the longer-haul trucks that carried fewer
pounds, but not Harold Bays. The more weight that
Harold could stuff into one trailer the better; bigger
loads meant longer hours to toil in solitude. No one
worked alongside Harold Bays, and no one wanted to.

Harold stumped into the light, a squatty man thirty
years old with Indian-dark skin, wearing a turtleneck
sweater under his shirt along with a Texas Rangers batting helmet pulled low over his eyes. Every other male
worker on the dock was stripped to the waist, the
women down to their tees; sweat poured from every
freightloader in sight, yet Harold was dry as a bone.
He had a crooked nose and a nasty scar on his cheek.
His shoulders were sloping and powerful.

Melvin Pure turned his clipboard around so that
Harold could sign for his pay. As Harold limped closer
and grabbed the pen, Pure removed the stump of a
cigar from between his teeth. "You know Art Moseley's old lady domino'd, don'tcha?" Pure said. "Had
'erself a girl." Art Moseley was the supervisor on the
break-out side.

Harold didn't answer. He scribbled his signature on the space beside his name, released the clipboard, and reached for his check.

"Anyhow," Pure went on, "we're takin' a collection. Only three dollars if you want to—"

"No." Harold spoke in a high squeaky voice. He folded the envelope in half and stuffed it into his breast pocket. Without another word he limped into the shadows inside the trailer and returned to work, dipping into the resin barrel as he passed.

Melvin Pure stood for a moment with his head cocked to one side, then poked his cigar back into his mouth and bit down hard. He shoved the clipboard under his arm and moved on toward the next trailer in line. "Crazy sonofabitch," he muttered, loud enough for Harold to hear.

There was a time when Harold Bays would have flown into a rage and attacked Melvin Pure on the spot for making such a remark, but that time had given way to the Change. Now, Harold hated in silence.

He'd been subject to uncontrollable fits since the day he was born. At the age of twelve he'd beaten a girl to death for giggling at the way he walked, and had lived in a reformatory until he'd reached eighteen. For ten years thereafter he'd been involved in brawl after brawl, once having beaten his Lithuanian wife until she'd gotten a restraining order. But today all that mattered to Harold was the Change. He was a tireless worker, strong as a bull, and if every other TMF employee thought he was a crazy sonofabitch, well, fuck them, once the Change was complete he'd kill them all.

He worked the Midland-Odessa hole until a siren blew at five P.M. The trailer was almost full and Harold could have finished the job in another five minutes, but today he had important business. He stripped off

his gloves at the siren's first beep, hung the gloves
over the resin barrel, and crossed the dock to wait in
line to punch his time card. All around him men told
smutty jokes, talked about stopping off for a few cool
ones, patted willing coworker women on the ass,
tapped cigarettes from crumpled packs and lit them
up. Harold kept his head down and minded his
business.

Once he'd punched out, he vaulted down from the
dock and crossed the parking lot to his pickup. His
left leg was four inches longer than his right, a birth
defect, which resulted in a step-and-drag gait. A few
years earlier a doctor had prescribed an orthopedic shoe,
which Harold had worn faithfully until the Change had
begun. Just recently he'd discarded the shoe; as the
Change took place, his shorter leg would grow.

His pickup was a ten-year-old GMC, maroon and
white with a covered bed. An Aggie Twelfth Man sticker
adorned the pickup's bumper. Harold had bought the
truck from a secondhand dealer, and knew from the
papers left in the glove compartment that the original
owner had graduated from Texas A&M. Occasionally
passing Aggies would flash Harold the gig-'em sign.
Until the Change had begun Harold would snarl and
shoot the signaling Aggies the finger, but now he ignored them all.

Harold climbed into the cab and slammed the door.
The sun was nearing the horizon and he adjusted the
visor to block the rays from his eyes. It was ninety
degrees outside, and stifling inside the truck, but Harold made no move to turn the AC on. He peered
through the rear cab window and through the opening
into the covered bed. The chains and shackles were
secured so they would not rattle, and the miniboulders
with which he'd weighed down the tarp-covered body
were safely in place. He started the engine and cruised
slowly onto Irving Boulevard.

He left the industrial district and went north on Stemmons Freeway in crawling rush-hour traffic. He was careful not to break any traffic laws; he'd never received a ticket since getting his license at eighteen, shortly after his release from the reformatory, and since that time he'd never spent a night in jail and had even carefully complied with his wife's civil restraining order. Since his juvenile record was expunged by law, his fingerprints weren't on record with any law-enforcement agency.

As he bounced along the expressway a sound emerged from his lips. It was an eerie noise, not quite a humming, a toneless monotone of Harold's own creation. The noise didn't seem human at all, in fact, and resembled nothing so much as an insect's angry buzz.

He left Stemmons Freeway at Grauwyler Road, a deserted two-lane blacktop that angled off toward the City of Irving a mile south of Texas Stadium. On both sides of the road were rows of stubby mesquite shrubs, head-high Johnson grass, and gravelly floodplain soil. Thousands of tire ruts wound among the trees, evidence of Sunday Cowboy fans who used Grauwyler Road as an unofficial parking lot. The sun had dipped beneath the horizon as purple dusk set in. Harold switched on his headlights, raising the visor to its normal position and squinting as he peered off among the trees.

A thousand yards west of the freeway Harold slowed, turned to the right, and bumped off into the scraggly forest. He stopped fifty yards from the blacktop, and left the engine running while he went back and opened the tailgate. He climbed up inside the covered bed and sat on the floor.

He groped around for a flashlight, found it, and clicked it on. The beam swept over the blue tarp that covered the body and came to rest on an accordion-

type carrying case. Harold dragged the case over between his legs and opened it up as he laid the flashlight aside. From within the case he took a sterile
cotton pad, a hypodermic syringe, and a bottle with a
rubber stopper. He shook the bottle and examined the
amber liquid with the aid of the flashlight. He didn't
like the color.

After carefully placing the syringe on the cotton
pad, Harold looked inside the case and found a surgeon's scalpel. Clutching the bottle and the scalpel, he
crawled over to the tarp-covered body. Straining with
the effort, he rolled away the miniboulders and cast
the tarpaulin aside. The nude body lay on its back,
the young man's mouth partway open, the beard thick
on both cheeks. Though the corpse's coal-black hair
was brushed and groomed as if by a stylist, there was
still a faint odor of decay.

Harold retrieved the flashlight once more, and
shined the beam along the length of the corpse. On
the body's dark skin were eight craterlike wounds, several the size of a half-dollar, others as big as Harold's
fist. He used the scalpel to test each sore for moisture;
most were dry, but he located a wound on the corpse's
buttock that glistened with fluid. Harold uncapped the
bottle, scraped mucous from the sore, deposited the
scrapings into the fluid, and wiped the scalpel across
the bottle's neck like a man removing peanut butter
from a bread knife. He shook the bottle and looked
at the liquid, which was a shade darker in color than
before. He replaced the stopper, scrambled across the
floor and picked up the syringe.

He injected the fluid into his arm, pushing hard on
the plunger to force the syrupy stuff into his body.
Then he lay back, feeling the strength flow into his
limbs. At the beginning of the Change the injections
had made Harold deathly sick, but now he'd developed immunity. Now the Change was nearing comple-

tion. He thought that the hair on his arms and legs was thicker than in the past, and a knot had developed below his ribcage. To Harold, the knot was evidence that one of his six additional legs was beginning to grow. He opened his mouth and made the hissing sound. The dead man watched through one half-open, unseeing eye.

Feeling strong, his pulse quickening with pleasure, Harold hung a hundred feet of coiled rope over his shoulder and climbed out on the ground. He limped back to Grauwyler Road and looked in both directions. No cars were coming and the only sounds were the wind stirring the trees and the faraway hoot of an owl. He crossed the blacktop, located a mesquite whose branches began at eye level, and tied the rope to one of the lower limbs.

Harold then uncoiled the rope and, being careful to avoid all snags, retraced his steps to the pickup. He dragged the corpse out and let the body tumble to the ground. The young man's body landed face-up, arms akimbo. Harold tied the rope around the corpse's ankle, then draped the line over a tree and brought up the slack until the rope was suspended three feet over Grauwyler Road. He tugged to be certain that the knots were secure.

Working quickly now, Harold vaulted once more up into the pickup's bed. He put the syringe, bottle, sterile pad, and scalpel back into the carrying case, folded the tarp, then hopped nimbly to the ground. He slammed the tailgate, returned to the cab, revved the engine and dropped the lever into gear. He alternated backing up and inching forward until the truck's nose was pointed toward the road, then bumped slowly away. His headlights illuminated a buzzard as it sat on a limb. Harold beeped twice on the horn, but the buzzard stood its ground.

The huge bird sat on its perch until Harold had

driven away. As soon as the pickup disappeared over
a crest in the road, the buzzard swooped. It landed
hard, sank its talons into the corpse's chest, and prepared to enjoy its evening meal.

Harold Bays rented a crash pad in Oak Cliff for
two-fifty a month, where he kept a few raggedy clothes
along with a foldout sleep sofa. He dropped by the
place a couple of times a week to empty the trash, set
out rat poison, and check his mail. But where he really
lived was on a rundown farm fifteen miles southeast
of the Dallas city limit, a stone's throw west of the
federal penitentiary at Seagoville. In the summer he
could sit on the porch and, using binoculars, watch the
inmates play softball beyond double fences topped
with razor wire.

Harold's secret place was impossible to find unless
you'd been there, a two-mile jaunt on blacktop road
from I-45, then a sharp left turn on a gravel road that
one had to slow down in order to see. He arrived an
hour after dark, left the pickup's engine running while
he opened the barbed-wire gate, then twisted his way
through a maze of tangled vines, mostly dead oak and
pecan trees, and washed-out fields that hadn't been
cultivated in years. Once he stopped when a skunk
wandered into his path and, silhouetted in his headlight beams, turned its back and raised its tail. Harold
waited patiently until ol' skunky lowered his tail and
ambled away. Once Harold would have run the crea-
ture down, but no longer. The current version of Harold Bays lived at peace with the animals of the world.

The property had been in Harold's family for gener-
ations, and his ancestors had grown cotton and wheat
here. The ancient barn still stood in the moonlight, a
hulk from the past, its roof sagging as if it might col-
lapse at any minute. Beside the barn sat a rusting
forties-vintage harvester with rotary blades.

The house was a hundred yards behind the barn, and was two stories high with flaking paint, rotten wood walls, and shutters that hung from single hinges. At the peak of the roof was a boarded-up window, and beyond the window was the room where Harold had remained locked up as a child. He steered carefully up the path and parked in a circular drive, which once had been gravel but now was mostly mud.

He got out of the pickup. On his left was the post where his mother once tied him for punishment. Harold curled his lip. He wished that his mother was still alive, just so that he could kill the old woman in tribute to the Change.

The inside of the house was dark. A single bulb glowed on the porch. Harold wiped his boots on a straw mat before stepping over the threshold. He didn't bother to turn on a light; he could find his way through the maze of corridors and rooms with his eyes closed.

He skirted the staircase banister and passed the sitting room where his mother used to sew. One day she'd gotten drunk, jabbed a needle through the fleshy part of her hand, ripped open a six-inch gash while extracting the needle, then had died in a head-on with a semi while trying to drive herself to the hospital. According to the police report she'd been doing ninety on the wrong side of the median. When the accident had happened, Harold was only ten.

Halfway down the hallway was the room that was his as a child. Harold's boots made squeaky step-and-drag noises as he passed the door. From inside the room a panicked female voice called out, "Help! Please help me. I . . ."

Harold ignored the cries and continued on. He stopped beside a hallway pantry, picked up a jar from a shelf, and twisted off the lid. Inside the jar two fat cockroaches wiggled and squirmed. He tossed the roaches into the cupboard and slammed the door. In seconds he listened to the scuttling of tiny hairy spider legs.

Once inside the master bedroom he switched on the lamp. Harold lived in a Spartan environment; the room contained an iron twin bed, a single dresser with a mirror, and one lone rocking chair. He pulled off his boots, stripped out of his dock uniform, socks and underwear, and tossed the clothing into the corner. His Rangers batting helmet was the last to go. Bareheaded, he carefully arranged his hair to cover his bald spots.

He examined his back in the mirror. While his shoulders and arms were strictly muscle magazine material, his spine was hideously curved. Disks and spinal bone stood out from ruddy skin. The upside-down violin tattooed between his shoulder blades was the painstaking work of a parlor artist in Deep Ellum. The artist's picture now hung on Lieutenant Jerry Gholer's wall and was identified as Victim Number Three.

Naked, Harold limped into the kitchen. He scratched his privates with one hand as he opened the fridge. Inside the fridge was a lump of moldy cheese, a six-pack of Pilsner beer, and a Pyrex mixing bowl. He reached inside the bowl and found a bone with strips of chicken hanging from it, which he hungrily gnawed as he exited the house through the back screen door. He stepped down into the yard.

He crossed the lawn at a rapid pace; despite the limp, Harold Bays could move very quickly when the occasion arose. Going naked did not bother him one iota; in fact he felt better without his clothes. He considered his love of nudity more evidence that the Change was progressing successfully.

He passed the neatly kept garden where he grew squash, zucchini, and watermelon in the summertime, and approached the sagging toolshed that stood at the rear of his yard. He skirted the shed and stood looking about as he finished his meal.

Here behind the shed, hidden from anyone standing inside the house, the earth was soft. Dallas County existed above a shelf of limestone which made digging impossible; through the years Harold had piled six feet of potting soil on top of the natural dirt and had installed drip irrigation lines to moisten the ground to a precise degree. The plot he'd prepared was a forty-foot square, and inside the square were numerous mounds.

As Harold ate, he counted the piles. There were fourteen graves in all, some fresh, others in various stages of erosion. Harold's brow knitted in puzzlement as he counted a second time. Could there be that many? He supposed there could; he might've lost count somewhere along the way. He needed to keep better track, though once the Change was complete the number would no longer matter. Stark naked, his spine curved into a parentheses, his tattoo dark against his skin, Harold Bays stood in the moonlight. He racked his brain, trying to remember who was buried where as he finished his supper and prayed for the Change.

Sis Hargis' cry for help had been pure reaction. She had heard someone—at this point anyone would do—outside in the hall and had begged for mercy in her sleep. She burned with fever and lingered between coma and delirium. No longer did she scream or make little jokes to keep her spirits up. In fact she made very little noise aside from her labored breathing. Though her wrist was still shackled to the metal cot, the restraint was no longer necessary to keep her in the room; she lacked the strength to get up even if she'd been free as a bird.

The spider bite below her breast had grown and

festered, and now formed a dark wet circle four inches
in circumference. That morning, before Harold had
left for work, he'd placed another spider on her, this
time on her thigh. The second wound had formed an
off-white blister. Within a day it would be larger than
the first sore. Sis's movements were now limited to an
occasional twitching of arms and legs. Her comatose
condition was actually a blessing of sorts, because as
long as she slept she could feel no pain.

Just after ten P.M. Brother Abner Benedict, driving
a three-year-old Pontiac Grand Marquis, left Stemmons Freeway at ninety miles an hour, ran the red
light at Grauwyler Road, made a left turn with two
wheels off the pavement, and barreled on through the
night. Hot on his tail were two DPD cruisers with
sirens blaring and rooflights flashing. Three miles up
ahead, the Irving Police, having received a radio alert
from DPD, stretched barriers across the Loop 12
intersection.

Brother Benedict, pastor of the Hager Road Church
of Christ in Grapevine, was up to his ass in alligators
due to a series of events that the Lord himself couldn't
have foreseen. On the seat beside him, blasted out of
her gourd, sat fifteen-year-old Rachel Gore. Rachel's
father was one of Brother Benedict's most fervent
faithful. Between the preacher's ankles was a half-
empty liter of Jack Daniel's Black Label whiskey; a
fourth of the liquor rested warm in Brother Benedict's
belly, an eighth was inside Rachel Gore, and another
eighth was on the floor along with Rachel's dinner.
The car's interior reeked of whiskey and vomit. To
make matters worse, Rachel's shorts and panties lay
tangled in the backseat and Brother Benedict's pants
were around his knees.

The evening hadn't started out as a disaster, not at
all. As late as eight P.M. Brother Benedict was leading

the evening young people's class in prayer, and after
the meeting he'd listened benevolently as Rachel—
who, in the preacher's favor, had been the one asking
for the private conference—confessed tearfully that
she'd slept with her soccer coach, at which point
Brother Benedict decided that Rachel was in need of
further counseling. And not ten minutes ago he was
driving lawfully north on Stemmons Freeway as Rachel gave him a hand job. Oh glorious night, the
preacher'd thought, and had lifted his voice to sing
hosannas.

A faulty taillight had done Brother Benedict in,
flickering at first, finally blinking out, thus drawing the
attention of a patrol car without a helluva lot to do.
The cops had given a peaceful blast on their siren and
a friendly flash from their rooflights. Their original
intention was merely to give the driver a warning. But
when Brother Benedict responded by pouring on the
coal, the chase was on for real.

And now, as Rachel gagged and threatened to lose
more of her cookies, Brother Benedict put the pedal
to the metal. Blacktop flashed underneath the Grand
Marquis and mesquite trees whipped past on both
sides of the road.

Lord Jehovah, the preacher thought. He didn't
know what to do, though he was certain he needed
guidance. He couldn't stop, that was out of the question. Between images of his wife beating him to death
with a curling iron, the elders at the church holding
his excommunication conference, and Rachel's father
blowing his head off with a .30-06, Brother Benedict
found ample inspiration to keep on truckin' down
the road.

A thousand yards west of the freeway something
loomed in his path, a rope strung across the road three
feet off the ground. The rope caught on the Grand
Marquis' grille, twisted, then hung on the bumper as

the car hurtled forward. Something with flapping arms
and legs bounced wildly out of the trees and slammed
the side of the car a foot from Brother Benedict.

The preacher threw on the brakes and the Grand
Marquis fishtailed. A man's nude body skidded across
the hood and banged hard into the windshield. The
glass cracked in a spiderweb pattern. Brother Benedict
covered his face and prayed to God Almighty. The
car spun round and round, slammed into a tree, recoiled, and bumped to a halt.

Brother Benedict opened his eyes. The Grand
Marquis' nose was now aimed back toward Stemmons
Freeway. A bloody corpse stared at him through the
broken windshield. Visible over the hood ornament,
uniformed cops piled out of the squad cars with pistols drawn.

Rachel Gore said drunkenly, "Wow." She then
retched and threw up.

Brother Benedict had had enough. His career in the
pulpit almost certainly at an end, he slowly opened
his door and stood. His arms in stick-'em-up position,
his pants around his knees impeding his progress, he
moved slowly to the middle of the road. Tears of
shame ran down his face. His dick hung limply for all
to see. His head humbly bowed, his hands held high
in supplication, Brother Abner Benedict thus surrend-
ered his ass to the cops, and his soul to the Lord
on high.

12

The detectives didn't have a lot to do while the Crime
Scene Unit unearthed the bodies near Lone Star Park,
so Lieutenant Gholer stood by and watched the process
with Courtney Bedell at his side. Meanwhile, Madison
and Frizell picked the homeless people's brains for
details of the shooting. The corpses were buried two
feet down. Two beefy CSU techs wearing coveralls
and rubber gloves did the digging. Earlier, Weasel had
led a group of techs over near the road leading from
the racetrack, and had pointed out the spot where the
crazy had done the killing. The techs had found a set
of tire tracks and now searched the area in a grid
pattern using flashlights. Occasionally one of the
white-coats would bend over and pick something up.
The bodies came out of the ground naked, with dirt-
filled mouths. Only after Gholer issued threats did the
homeless surrender the dead men's clothing.

It was after ten o'clock and a fall thunderstorm was
headed in. Far in the distance, thunder rolled and
lightning flashed. Gholer asked one of the diggers how
long before the deluge arrived.

The man had put his shovel down and now helped
his partner string yellow tape around the shallow open
graves. "Forecast says around midnight, Loo."

Gholer looked toward the road, where the techs

searched for evidence. "Those people need to get their asses in gear, then."

"They know about the storm," the digger said, wrapping a strip of tape around a tree trunk.

"Guess they do," Gholer said. He patted Courtney on the shoulder. "You look at every one of those people?" He pointed in the general direction of the racetrack.

Courtney had. Beyond the area where the techs searched, the flashing lights had attracted a crowd. Men and women stood watching, some with babies in their arms, emphasizing disaster's role as the ultimate attention-getter. *Watch closely, kids, and you might see a dead guy.* As a patrolman, Courtney had dealt with mobs around traffic accidents, and was finding that public curiosity seemed to double at murder scenes. At Gholer's direction Courtney had circulated among the onlookers. "Got up in every face," Courtney said. "He's not there, Loo."

"Didn't figure to be. Say, you hungry? They got doughnuts in the CSU truck. Chocolate sprinkles, some cinnamon sugar."

"I don't believe I could eat anything now."

"You don't know what's good, young lady." Gholer raised his voice in the direction of the van. "George. Hey, Georgie, bring me a couple of sprinkles, will you?" Then he turned toward the makeshift village, where Madison and Frizell interviewed the homeless beside the overturned Dumpster. "You guys learning anything?" Gholer yelled.

Jinx Madison was talking to a scruffy man with a kerchief over his head. She turned away from the witness. "Yeah. We're learning that you're a prick."

Gholer laughed. "But you already knew that, didn't you?"

A tech trotted over with two doughnuts wrapped in a napkin. Gholer took both, bit into one. "Man, we're brimming with information. We know our unidentified vic is named Trash Rosita and that these two dead guys are named Pretzelhead and Bulldog, or so they've been identified by a party named Weasel. Jesus Christ, if the Fiddleback's watching he's laughing his ass off about now."

The temperature had dipped rapidly as the front moved in. Courtney had found an old windbreaker in her trunk and slipped it on. She stood with her hands deep in her jacket pockets. Tomorrow was the first of October, and the rainstorm was bringing the first real hint of fall. "I can't stay any longer," she said. "My nephew."

"Yeah, right. We'll have a little confab with Jinx and Eddie and then you can—"

"I need to go now, Loo."

"Now's not possible." Gholer finished off one of the doughnuts and started on the other one. "Half hour, maybe."

"Jesus, it's the middle of the fucking night."

"Yeah, okay, I'll put an ad in the paper. 'Fiddleback: From now on all murders will be between the hours of eight and five, so Courtney Bedell can—' "

"Listen." Courtney's eyes flashed fire. "I happen to be on injured leave. You can save funny for one of your troops. I shouldn't be out here to begin with."

Gholer paused with a doughnut inches from his lips. He lowered his hand. "Shouldn't any of us be out here. Shouldn't any of these people be dead, but they are. So it's up to us to make the extra effort."

"I'm not part of 'us.' "

Gholer stuffed his mouth full and chewed. He swallowed. "Oh yeah, you are."

"Yeah, as temporary office help while I'm injured. You see me filing? Typing anything? Unless you've got some quick dictation to give, I'm going home."

"You're doing what you're supposed to do, help us supervise a crime scene."

"Have you been smoking something funny? That's a detective's job."

Gholer checked his watch. "As of, let's see, six hours ago, that's what you are."

"I haven't even taken the exam."

"Well, sometimes we cut a few corners. I've had you reassigned permanently."

"Oh?" Courtney felt the anger building from within. "Just like that, huh? I don't remember turning in any written request."

"This is a transfer under emergency circumstances."

Courtney turned her back and walked five paces in a huff, then retraced her steps. "Well, I just got *un*transferred. I can't do full-time shit here, Loo. I've lost my child-care. As of right now I'm about five hours late and hoping my sitter doesn't toss the kid out with the trash. As of tomorrow I'm staying at home until I can find somebody to stay with Jason."

Gholer held the doughnut between his thumb and middle finger and pointed with his index. "We'll hire you somebody. Department expense until the case winds up. How's that?"

"That's bullshit. I'm not turning the kid over to just anybody."

"You're getting upset," Gholer said.

"That's putting it mildly," Courtney said. "You can't just up and switch me to another unit. Tomorrow I'm putting in a call to my patrol supervisor."

"You don't have a patrol supervisor anymore. *I'm* your supervisor."

"Not if I don't want you to be."

"Look," Gholer said. "Your only choice is, you can resign from the force."

"Which I just might do."

"Which could cause me to hold you as a material witness. I got to have your input on this case."

"And a little kid needs my input as his guardian. That's no choice for me. Oh Jesus, we're wasting a lot of time. Good night, Loo." Courtney turned and started to stalk away.

Behind her, Gholer said, "Hold it there, *Detective* Bedell."

She walked back, quivering. "Up yours, *Lieutenant* Gholer."

The two stood nose to nose as EMU people rolled one of the bodies toward the ambulance.

"Okay, call me out of line." Gholer dropped his gaze and stood back. "But could you do me one favor?"

"I've already done you more than one," Courtney said.

"Give us ten minutes. Me and Jinx and Eddie. Just describe in detail what happened from the time you left for the racetrack. Then you can go. Tomorrow we can take your temperature, see how you feel when you wake up."

"Don't expect me to feel any different. Not tomorrow, not six months from now, unless my nephew's taken care of to my satisfaction. For all I know you'd hire some sex offender."

Gholer showed a slowly spreading grin. "I was thinking more in the line of a snitch that owes me a few favors."

"Jesus Christ, Loo . . ."

"Just kidding." Gholer raised a hand, palm out. "Just kidding, okay? Come on, Courtney, give me the ten minutes. Tomorrow is tomorrow, we can talk about it then."

Courtney looked down at her feet, then she checked her watch. "Time's running, Loo. The ten minutes started thirty seconds ago."

*　　　*　　　*

"So then this butler comes back and says"—Jinx Madison held her nose and talked in a falsetto—" 'Mr. Hargis is indisposed, madam. You should address your inquiries to this gentleman.' " She handed Gholer a business card.

Madison, Frizell, Gholer, and Courtney stood near the turd-brown detectivemobile. As they talked, the ambulance carrying the dead men bumped away over the open field toward Loop 12 and the interstate beyond. Courtney had already described her meeting with racetrack security and her encounter with the homeless people, giving ample detail while Madison and Frizell made a few notes. Courtney was beginning to fidget. Mrs. Bailey's final day with Jason would be one for the older woman to remember.

Gholer looked at the business card while Courtney read over his shoulder. The card belonged to Larry Akin, Attorney. Akin & Gilchrest. "Shit. I already seen this last night," Gholer said.

"Apparently that's all you're *going* to see," Madison said, resting a hip against the side of the car. "We've got the missing woman's lawyer lying to our faces and the missing woman's husband referring us to counsel. Sounds suspicious."

"They didn't even let you in the house?" Gholer was angry, his nostrils flared.

"Never got off the porch," Madison said, "and never got to talk to anyone other than the butler. The whole thing stinks to beat hell. Still, I've got to side with Eddie in that I don't see how any of these people connect to any fruitcake killer."

"They connect," Gholer said. "Somehow, they connect. Tomorrow you get back on this guy. See the lawyer, Akin, and ask him to arrange a meeting with his client. If he won't, then we'll see about probable cause for some kind of warrant."

Frizell folded his arms in disgust. "Loo, the guy lives

to fuck-and-gone in Preston Trails, and the lawyer's right down the road from there. In traffic it's a half-day's drive, to and from. We all get resentful of people stonewalling, but we should be sure we're not spinning our wheels. While me and Jinxie are running around after the husband, who's going to be tracking the Fiddle-back? If it turns out there's no connection, we're all going to look like assholes."

"*The rest of us* are going to look like assholes, Eddie," Madison said. "You already do."

"We've got additional assistance in the case." Gholer extended a hand in Courtney's direction. "Meet Detective Bedell, the newest member of the staff."

Courtney glared at Gholer.

Madison grinned at Frizell. "Told you so," Madison said.

Courtney scratched her jacket sleeve with a thumbnail. "There's nothing final about any transfer."

"That's what *I* thought, when the Loo moved me over from Patrol, without me knowing about it. That was four years ago," Madison said.

"For me it was four *minutes* ago," Courtney said. "And I don't think it's going to last."

"We can thrash it out later," Gholer said. "For now . . . Jinx, Eddie, first thing in the morning. You be at Hargis' lawyer's office when the doors open."

Madison stifled a yawn. "What's your definition of 'first thing'? We've been on duty for fifteen hours."

"Tell you what. Tomorrow you can have an extra fifteen-minute break. But be at the lawyer's at nine. Bedell and I will be holding down the fort. Remember, we've got a woman who's probably alive right now, but who's going to be dead in a few days if we don't get a move on."

Madison and Frizell watched the ground. Courtney

concentrated on the rapidly approaching thunderstorm.

"Everybody got the program?" Gholer said.

Madison and Frizell slowly nodded their heads.

Courtney's jaws clenched. "Sorry, but as far as I'm concerned I've fulfilled my duty. I've told everything I know, and then some." She checked her watch. "Ten minutes goes by in a hurry, Loo. And I wish you lots of luck in catching this guy."

13

Mrs. Bailey didn't launch into the tirade Courtney had expected. The older woman offered the silent treatment instead, which might have been tougher to take than an all-out assault. As Courtney walked over to the sofa and gently shook Jason out of his slumber, then scooped up the tote bag holding his extra clothing, Mrs. Bailey stood near the exit with her arms folded and a good-riddance smirk on her face. Courtney took Jason's hand and led him, barefoot and in his pajamas, past Mrs. Bailey onto the porch where she handed the woman a check. Mrs. Bailey closely examined the figures to be certain she was getting the full amount, then slammed the door in Courtney's face. Good-bye, nice knowing you, and go to hell.

Courtney led Jason across the yard toward her Lumina. The wind had picked up, rustling leaves and rattling branches. Lightning flashed and thunder rolled. She'd just deposited Jason on the passenger side and climbed in behind the wheel when the first drops of rain spattered the fenders. Jason murmured sleepily, stretched out across the seat and laid his head in her lap. Courtney softly rested her palm on the little boy's cheek and, steering and changing gears left-handed, headed for home with Jason snoring away.

She'd made it halfway to the house when the

shower became a downpour. Downpour hell, it was a freaking deluge—she could barely see beyond the hood. She turned on her high beams. The result was even worse; the reflection from the heavy rain was absolutely blinding. The wipers couldn't complete their arcs before the cascade jellied the windshield. The gutters on both sides of the street were rushing rapids, carrying branches and flotsam along to hang up in the sewer drains.

With Jason sound asleep, Courtney crept grimly on. Every intersection was an adventure; as she steered through the overflowing speed bumps, waves slammed the Lumina's underbody. Once the car planed sideways in the torrent, and Courtney held her breath until the tires settled onto the pavement.

When she finally lurched into her driveway the dashboard clock showed half past midnight. The driveway ran past the house to a free-standing garage backed up to the alley, but no way was Courtney going that far. Jesus, to make it from the garage to the house she'd need a rowboat. She pulled up even with the front porch, doused the lights, and killed the engine. And there she sat for a full five minutes while she decided what to do.

She hadn't brought any rain gear, of course; far be it from her to engage in any sort of emergency planning. She owned two umbrellas, both of which rested in a barrel she kept just inside the entry. Also folded inside the barrel were raincoats and galoshes. She considered snuggling up beside Jason and sleeping in the car.

She'd have to make two mad dashes in order to get Jason safely into the house. During the first dash she'd take the tote bag inside, and then she'd return with an umbrella along with the child's galoshes and raincoat. She eye-measured the distance to the porch through the curtain of rain. Drowning en route was a definite possibility. She reached across Jason and hefted the tote bag, gently removed Jason's head from her lap, clutched her keys firmly in her hand, shouldered the door open, and made a run for it.

She stumbled and almost fell on the way, but she made it onto the porch with water running into her eyes and her wet hair clinging to her ears. Her windbreaker was drenched and so was the tote bag. Her soaked Levi's felt as if they weighed a hundred pounds. She set the bag aside, located her house key, and reached for the door handle.

The front door was six inches ajar. As Courtney stood frozen with her hand touching the handle, a gust of wind slammed the door against the frame.

For a couple of seconds Courtney couldn't breathe. When she was able, she sucked air deep into her lungs. She pictured herself that morning, locking doors and checking windows as she'd left. As she'd exited the house with Jason in tow, she'd twisted the knob and given a final outward tug on the door. Dammit, the house had been secure and the deadbolt in place. She peered back through the rain at her car. Gholer's cell phone was in the glove compartment, and her first impulse was to retreat and call 911. Jesus, what if the Fiddleback was crouched in the entry hall waiting for her?

Her face muscles relaxed and her pulse slowed. If the man with the hideous scar on his face was actually inside her house, wasn't this the perfect opportunity to kill the bastard?

Wasn't it?

She slowly eased the Glock out and disengaged the safety. She flattened against the wall beside the door with her weapon aimed at the ceiling.

Cops're comin', Fiddleback. You scared?

You'd damned sure better be. This time I didn't forget my gun.

She eased the door all the way open and stuck her upper body around the jamb with the Glock held ready. There was no one in sight, so she stepped on into the entry hall. Water dripped from her jeans and formed damp circles on the rug. The old windup clock on the mantel in the living room ticked and tocked loudly in the dead quiet inside the house. Lifting first one foot and then the other, Courtney removed her shoes.

She held her weapon in both hands beside her ear as, sweeping her gaze watchfully in both directions and moving at a snail's pace, she traversed the entry hall and neared the kitchen. The swinging door leading into the breakfast nook was closed. Light streamed through the cracks, both underneath and on both sides.

Courtney lowered the Glock and peered through the door crack. Someone was sitting at the breakfast table. She made out the outline of shoulders and a head. She inhaled and raised her weapon into the ready position.

She pushed off her right instep and barged on through, leaping to her right as she cleared the doorframe, steadying her pistol at the intruder as the door swung closed. "Don't move a muscle, fucker," Courtney hissed.

At the table sat a young woman with eyes the same deep brown color as Courtney's. Olive-complexioned skin tightened as facial muscles flexed over prominent cheekbones. A mouth shaped identically to Jason's opened in surprise.

Courtney let the pistol hang beside her hip. She sagged back against the wall. "Oh Jesus," she breathed, hung her head, and then looked up in anger. "Jesus *Christ,* Jannie," Courtney said. "Why can't you just leave us alone?"

*   *   *

While Courtney loaded hers and Jason's wet clothes into the washer, Jan told her that she was turning her life around. As Courtney dumped in two capfuls of liquid Free, Jan said that she'd been clean for a couple of months and was looking for a job.

Courtney set the temperature selector on warm, cold rinse. "What kind of job?" She selected normal wash, pulled on the knob, and the washer began to fill.

"I can wait tables. I'm a good waitress, Courtney."

"You were once," Courtney agreed coldly. She sat down across the breakfast table from her sister. As Jan had waited in the kitchen she'd put Jason down for the night after stripping him out of wet pajamas. Then she'd slipped a man's dress shirt—a remnant of her last serious relationship two years ago—on over her panties and bra. "Correction. You were a good waitress several times," Courtney said. "Three restaurants in two months that I remember. All three jobs ended in drug busts, didn't they?"

"I was in the wrong crowd." Jan leaned on her elbows.

"Oh, hell, Jannie, you *are* the wrong crowd. Why don't you just tell me what it is this time? If I can scrape up the money I will, but I'll tell you in advance that I probably can't. I'm still paying that fucking lawyer from the last time."

Jan sniffled. "I don't know why you're being so mean to me."

Courtney herself wasn't sure why. No matter what Jan had done, she was after all the only member of Courtney's immediate family left alive. Even now, with an addict's frailty and the nervous twitches to go with it, Jan was breathtakingly beautiful. Just a handful of years ago Courtney had worshipped the ground her older sister walked on, and had adoringly forgiven Jan the two boyfriends she'd stolen while the girls had been in high school. Even in the harsh light inside the kitchen and minus her makeup, Jan looked soft and vulnerable. She'd removed the rings from her nose and ears for her visit, though the two holes in her left nostril and the four in her right lobe were clearly visible. She wore jeans, sandals, and an imitation leather vest over a denim shirt—all clean for a change.

Jan continued, "I am family. Mom always said—"

"—That family's the most important thing in the world. And she believed it. So did Dad. Over and over and over, and they both went to their graves thinking that the next time would be the charm. So what's this, Jan? The hundredth time? Oh Jesus, how much do you want?"

Jan showed a touch of petulance. "I see you're still into that tough-shit stuff."

"Tough *love*. And obviously I don't have what it takes for the program; otherwise I wouldn't be sitting here talking to you. What I should have done is put you out in the rain." Courtney looked instinctively at the ceiling in the far corner. As the drumbeat of rain on the roof continued, the water stain on the wallpaper continued to spread.

"I'm not here just for money, little sister. Why don't you believe me?"

"Emphasis on the word *just*. I can't imagine what else you'd want."

"To see you." Jan's gaze steadied. "And to see my little boy."

It was shocking that Jan would even ask about Jason. Fifteen minutes earlier Courtney had made Jan hide in the kitchen while she brought him in from the car, and Courtney had stayed in the bedroom until she was certain that the little boy was fast asleep. Only then had she returned to confront her sister. "Not on your life," Courtney said.

Jan broke down in tears. "He's my flesh and blood."

"And was born with your dope in his veins. You're not getting near him."

"I could take him if I wanted to. I'm still his mother, you're not."

"And I can visit with your parole officer. Don't think I won't, Jannie, if it comes to Jason's welfare. Goddamn you, you tried to *sell* him, and would have if Mom hadn't bailed you out."

"I'd . . . never! I'd never, Courtney, not my little boy."

"Who you've seen maybe four times since he was born. I want you out of here, Jan. Don't make me take you downtown."

"For doing what? Coming into my own home? Don't give me that big bad policewoman shit."

"You should get your brain unfried for long enough to read up on the law. You gave up your rights and got extra money from the estate for your half of this house. Which you spent in a month or so. You've got no rights here, Jannie, and don't think I won't arrest your ass before I'll let you spoil that child's life."

"You'd put your own sister in handcuffs?"

"And leg irons and a gag, if it would help. Jason is one subject where you don't want to fuck with me." Courtney was almost as angry with herself as she was upset over Jan's being here. The tough love people said never to lose your composure, and that every request for a handout should be met with a firm but friendly no, but Courtney had never been able to follow either principle when it came to her sister. Until addicts hit rock bottom and made up their minds to confront the problem, lecturing them was a waste of time. A police psychologist had described Courtney's confusion over her feelings in a single word: codependence. Until she could cast her own albatross aside, she'd never be able to shoulder the burden of Jan's. Courtney had a thought and went to the dining room window. The rain had slackened to the point that she could see both ends of the block. The only car in sight—other than her own in the drive and the neighbor's across the street—was parked three houses down with its lights off. She went back in and sat across from Jan. "How the hell did you get here, anyway?" Courtney said.

Jan's look became suddenly cunning. "How do you know I didn't walk?"

"Because I know you, and walking would take too much effort. In the rain? Bullshit, Jannie, how did you get here?"

Jan looked down at the table. "Got a ride."

"With that worthless fuck of a boyfriend?"

Jan hugged herself. Her fingers were beginning to tremble. "James is not worthless."

"Jesus Christ, you're not even supposed to have contact with that asshole. He was your codefendant. If your parole officer finds out . . ."

"They've got no right to keep us apart, Courtney."

"The law says they do. I can't keep playing, 'see no evil, hear no evil' with this crap. You're my sister. That cocksucker's not even related to me."

"Soon as me and James get jobs, we're getting married."

"Well, don't ask me to be your maid of honor. That's him parked down the block, isn't it?"

Jan bit her lower lip and didn't answer. She touched one of the piercings in her ear.

Courtney bent over the table and looked her sister in the eye. "How much, Jan? Tell me now, so I can get rid of you."

Jan worried with her ear and watched the far corner of the room. "Do you . . . ? Do you have to make me feel so ashamed?"

Courtney's gaze remained steady. "How much, Jan?"

Jan breathed out through her nose. "Can you spare a hundred?"

"Now that I can manage. I've got some money hidden in a jar." She held out a hand, palm up. "And I want your key to the house. Don't you dare ever come here again without calling first."

Jan reached quickly for her pocket. "It's my home, Courtney." She pulled out a single key on a chain.

"No it isn't. As long as you're on dope, I don't know where you live and don't want to know. Your key in exchange for a hundred dollars, Jan. That should be a no-brainer deal. Beats hooking, doesn't it? And believe me, that will be next if you don't figure a way to turn your life around."

Courtney folded the five twenties and slid them into her sister's hand as the two stood on the porch, looking out at the street. The rain had slowed to a drizzle and the lightning had moved off to the east. The temperature had plummeted into the fifties. Courtney shivered as she surveyed the block. The car with its lights off hadn't moved. "When's gonad-brains gonna pick you up?" Courtney said.

Jan thumbed through the money, counting. "His name is James."

"Okay," Courtney said. "What's the pickup signal?"

Jan stuffed the money in her pocket and didn't answer.

"I'll bet it's the same as you used when Mom and Dad were alive." Courtney reached inside and flicked the porch light on and off, then on and off again. "I'll also bet that the only reason you waited around until I got home was that you couldn't find any money by poking around on your own. You left my underwear drawer open. I've moved the emergency cash, Jan. If you look for it again you'll be wasting your time."

"I don't have a key any longer," said Jan. "I guess it's too much, asking my own sister to trust me."

"Goddamn right. And as soon as I can get someone to change the locks, those spare keys you've made won't do you any good, either. I don't want you coming around anymore. This well's run dry, Jan. Look for a different supply."

Half a block down the street, headlights came on. The car pulled away from the curb and cruised slowly toward the house.

"What a gutless fuck," Courtney said.

Jan glared at her.

"Even the creeps we handle on the job," Courtney said, "at least they go in and pull the burglary themselves, and leave the girlfriend out in the car."

"It isn't like that. You've got no right to talk about James."

"Oh yes, I do. I've earned the right." Courtney stepped back inside and prepared to shut the door. "Don't come here again," Courtney said. "I've paid for your lawyer for the very last time, so if you're busted again you're on your own. And if I catch you in my home uninvited, your ass is going straight to jail."

After she'd checked every door and window—and vowed to get an attack-trained Doberman or Rottweiler to leave in the house while she was gone—Courtney went to bed. She snuggled up behind Jason and pressed the sleeping little boy to her bosom. And as she lay there wide awake, she shed tears of sorrow for Jan.

Jesus, one-thirty in the morning, she was crying over a junkie burnout who'd just tried to rob her. Injury leave, hell. She should be on insanity leave. Courtney sobbed even harder, her tears wetting Jason's hair.

Codependent? You fuckin' betcha. Every time Jan

turned up in Courtney's life, cash and dignity drifted away.

And, *SHAZAM*, here she was again.

Courtney came out of her trance as a small pudgy hand touched her cheek. Jason had rolled over beneath her, and was wiping her tears away. "Coatney sad?" the little boy mumbled sleepily.

Courtney raised her head from a pillow soaked with her tears. She looked down at Jason and forced herself to smile. "Nah, Courtney isn't sad. Courtney's never sad. You go back to sleep now, buddy. Tomorrow's gonna be another happy day."

14

Thud-thud-thud. Dingdong, dingdong. Thud-thud-thud. Dingdong, dingdong.

The pounding at the front door alternated with the ringing of the chimes dragged Courtney slowly into wakefulness. She looked at the clock with her one open eye.

Seven-oh-five. Morning or evening? Oh Jesus, whoever it is should go the fuck away.

Thud-thud-thud. Dingdong, dingdong. Thud-thud-thud. Dingdong, dingdong.

She tried to remember where she'd stored her weapon, picturing herself sticking the Glock in some salesman's face, chasing him from the neighborhood.

She looked down at Jason, still snuggled into the crook of her arm. The little boy was fast asleep.

Thud-thud-thud. Dingdong, dingdong.

She threw off the covers and stumbled out of bed, crying out in pain and clutching at her side as she did. Someone was in for it. She dug in the closet for her bathrobe, and slipped the garment on as she stomped through the living room to the front of the house. She looked outside through the peephole.

Gholer.

She sagged in the entry hall. Jesus Christ, it couldn't be. She looked outside again.

Gholer in the flesh. Rumpled brown suit and all, his tie done in a terrible half-Windsor knot, his lips puckered as he whistled a silent tune. He reached out to ring the bell.

Courtney threw open the door. "If you wake up Jason I'm shooting you."

He froze with his arm extended. "That would be murder."

"Justified. You were attempting a break-in."

Gholer laughing agreeably. He grabbed the handle and tried to pull open the screen. The eyebolt held.

"It's locked, Loo," Courtney said.

"Yeah, well, lemme in. I gotta talk to you."

She watched him. "How'd you find me, anyway?"

"Helluva question to ask a detective. Your address is in your file. Us brilliant cops got Mapscos."

"Okay, a better question. How do I get you to lose me?"

"It's about the Fiddleback," Gholer said.

"The who?"

"Come on. We don't have much time."

"Oh, I've got time. Didn't I make myself clear last night?"

"Yeah, but now that you've thought it over . . ."

"I'm still not coming. I'm still without child-care. I'm still on injured leave."

"And we've got another stiff on our hands."

"*You've* got another stiff on your hands. I've got a little kid on mine."

"I've had some thoughts on that. Listen, I'm good at making noise. You don't want to piss off your neighbors this early."

Courtney undid the bolt, trudged over to the sofa, and flopped down with her arms folded.

Gholer came in behind her and sat in an easy chair. He crossed thick legs. "The chauffeur. Og."

"He's dead?"

"Found around midnight, south of Texas Stadium. Fiddleback's MO. The bites, the washed hair, all of it. The bastard tied a rope to his foot, strung the rope across the road. A pedophile preacher running from some squad cars dragged the corpse out in the open."

"How do you know the preacher was a pedophile?"

"He had one of his pedos along for the ride. But that asshole is somebody else's problem. The body was Og. We got a print match plus his photo."

Courtney drew up her legs and sat on her ankles. "Jesus. Listen, I'm sorry if I don't sound interested."

"Quit being sorry and start getting interested, then."

"What is it you want me to do?"

"Go with me, first to the office and then to the scene where they found Og. We'll have crews out there all day gathering evidence, which means there'll also be onlookers. I want you to take a look at anybody hanging around, just like last night by the racetrack."

"Why do I feel like this guy won't be there? That once he's finished with the vic, he could care less what happens to the body or how many cops invade the scene?"

"Because that's the way you should feel. Because it's the same way I feel. But even if it's a million-to-one shot we have to take it. You know I got Jinx and Eddie calling on Hargis' lawyer today. I got to have you."

Courtney gestured toward the bedroom. "Jason's asleep back there. I can't go off and leave him."

"I told you I had thoughts on that. For now, we're taking him to the office. What do you think about that?"

"I think you don't know what you're getting into, Loo. A child around the office? You've got to be kidding."

"Would I kid about a thing like that? Get dressed, Courtney, you and the boy both. You can drive while I sit in back with him. You might be surprised. I'm pretty good with little kids."

Gholer was better than pretty good. By the time Courtney had driven the motor-pool car to the industrial district, Jason was giggling so hard that she was afraid he might wet his pants. The child spent half his time on Gholer's knee, part of his time climbing all over the lieutenant's shoulders, and part of the time hiding his eyes while he and Gholer played some version of hide-and-seek. Courtney wondered what it was about so many men, that they could be such a buddy to someone else's children but still a hated tyrant toward their own. She hoped that Gholer wasn't that way.

As they drove into the lot Gholer said, "Stop right here."

Courtney applied the brakes and turned around in the seat. Gholer had Jason in a playful half nelson, but his gaze was outside the car. Courtney followed the lieutenant's look. He was watching the turd-brown detective's Sable, which was parked nose-on to the entry.

"That's Eddie and Jinx's," Gholer said. "Only they're not supposed to be here. They're supposed to be on Hargis' trail."

Courtney nodded. It was the car, all right, complete with the small dent beside the gas tank, which she'd noticed last night out by the track. "I got no idea, Loo," Courtney said.

"Here, buddy," Gholer said, lifting Jason bodily over the seat to deposit him in the shotgun position. Jason giggled and squirmed. Gholer's smile dissolved as he continued to look at the detectives' car. "They're not supposed to be here, Courtney," Gholer said.

"Something's stopped them from going. Jesus, what else could go wrong?"

What had gone wrong became apparent as Gholer, holding Jason's hand and with Courtney Bedell on his heels, walked into the bullpen. Topper Moore, the half-day admin from downtown, was rattling computer keys. She looked up as Gholer came in and shook her head. Madison and Frizell sat at two of the desks. Frizell's ankles were crossed and a baseball cap was pulled low over his eyes. Madison was reading a magazine. She noticed Gholer, made a face, thumbed toward the offices in back, and shrugged with her hands. Gholer followed her direction.

His own cubbyhole was deserted and the light was off, but a mob had gathered inside FBI Agent Donald Miller's office. Miller was in there, behind his desk, and Texas Ranger Mason Trent sat against the wall with his Stetson tilted back. Beside Trent was Captain Helen Dilbergast, wearing full-parade dress, and alongside Dilbergast was Arnold Slanter the city manager's stooge. The handsome bushy-haired guy seated next to Slanter was Clifford Nance, the chief of police. On the far end of the office was a guy who Gholer had seen just recently but at first couldn't place. The man had thinning hair and rounded shoulders, and wore a suit that had cost eight hundred minimum. As Gholer studied the stranger's profile the answer came to him. Larry Akin. Akin & Gilchrest. William Hargis' lawyer. *Jesus Christ,* Gholer thought, *there's no room in there for anyone else to sit.*

Gholer couldn't figure out what the fuck was going on. He walked up to Madison and Frizell and asked them, "Am I wrong that you guys are supposed to be traveling today?"

Frizell took his feet off the desk. "Shit, Loo, we're trying to travel. That captain stopped us."

Gholer shot a look to the back. "Dilbergast?"

"None other," Frizell said.

"You tell her you had orders from me?"

"Didn't have to tell her. First words out of her mouth was, all other instructions cancelled until further notice. I assume she knew who'd been giving those instructions."

Madison was making little goo-goo noises at Jason, who stood beside Courtney about twelve steps away. She said, lowering her voice, "You know you give the word, Loo, we're outta here. If I get fired I'll take a couple of weeks, I haven't had a good hump in a while."

Frizell brightened. "Yeah, me and Jinxie could stand the time."

"I said a *good* hump, Eddie," Madison said. "You tellum, we do 'em, Loo."

"I 'preciate it," Gholer said. "But you stay put. The way I see it, if anybody's about to get fired, it's gonna be me."

Gholer walked innocently toward the back, and stopped in feigned surprise when Miller pointed through the glass, first at Gholer, then at the only vacant seat left inside his jam-packed office. Gholer relaxed his mouth and laid a hand flat on his breastbone. Who, me? He stepped inside the FBI agent's door, looking around and said, "Hiya. How y'all doing?"

Miller once again jabbed a finger at the empty chair.

Gholer sat down, looking pleasantly curious. He nodded in turn, first at Captain Dilbergast and then at Chief Nance. Both high-ranking cops studied their laps.

Miller leaned forward. "We're not doing so well. None of us. Maybe you can explain that, Jerry."

Gholer grinned around. "I know, Fiddleback's whacked another one. That what this is about?"

Miller started to answer, but Nance stopped him. The chief said, "Only in a peripheral manner of speaking, Lieutenant. Part of this meeting has to do with the Fiddleback, but the main thrust is why we're apparently investigating people who can't possibly have anything to do with these crimes."

Gholer solemnly folded his hands. Nance's expression was dead serious. Under Dallas' city-council form of government, the chief of police was a political hire. Nance had come from Kansas City two years earlier, and up until ten seconds ago he and Gholer had been on a first-name basis. The fact that Nance had addressed Gholer as "Lieutenant" meant that the shit was very close to hitting the fan.

Miller took charge once more. "Mr. Akin tells us your people have been harassing his client Mr. Hargis. This man's wife is missing, Jerry. How come you're bugging him?"

"We're just covering all bases," Gholer tried. He glanced at Dilbergast, who didn't respond. In yesterday's meeting she'd sided with Gholer toward the end, but now her own boss was present. Nance was the Man here, and the captain would do nothing to pull Gholer's chestnuts out of the fire.

Nance said, "That's your answer?"

"It's standard," Gholer said. "A woman disappears. Her estranged husband is immediately suspect."

"Sure, unless you're looking for a psycho. Which in this case you are, so you don't start questioning sane people." Nance fiddled with his breast pocket. "I'd hoped for a more logical response, Lieutenant."

Lawyer Akin butted in. "How about this for more logical, Chief? Lieutenant Gholer is completely stumped, and wants to use my client merely to show he isn't sitting on his ass. Give the newspapers something more to write about."

Gholer's temper flared. "Now that's a lie. You see

me giving any interviews? That's somebody else's department. Chief, you know we're not just screwing around here. If we didn't have reason to think Mr. Hargis might know more than he's letting on, we wouldn't be trying to talk to the guy."

"Against his lawyer's permission," Akin said. He looked at Nance. "I instructed this man not to contact my client except through me, and he's ignored that. Yesterday afternoon two of his detectives were out pounding on my client's door."

"And that," Gholer said, "is one of the main reasons we're looking at Mr. Hargis. Nobody suspected him of anything until he shows up to make some IDs with his lawyer running interference. And until Hargis is officially the target of the investigation, we don't have to jump just because this attorney says so." He locked gazes with Akin. Akin looked to Chief Nance.

"So you're going to let Lieutenant *Gofer* here punish my client for exercising his right to counsel?" Akin dismissively waved a hand. "This isn't some rummy your department is tracking here, Chief. William Hargis Jr. and his father have been some of the mayor's strongest supporters. These family roots go back to the eighteen hundreds."

"And my great-great grandpappy fought in the Alamo," Gholer said. "That means I get to go around murdering people?"

Akin extended a palm-up hand in Gholer's direction while speaking to Nance. "See there?" Akin said, then leaned back and folded his arms.

"This conversation," Nance said, "is going nowhere. Mr. Akin, we're not going to tell our people to lay off merely because your client knows the mayor. By the same token, Lieutenant, we're not going to continue to investigate someone like Mr. Hargis without our ducks in a row." He exchanged a look with Agent

Miller. "What's this about a witness, Lieutenant Gholer?" Nance said.

"Who we get no access to," Miller said.

Gholer scooted his rump forward. He didn't say anything.

Nance took a legal pad from Captain Dilbergast, and read some of her notes. He laid the pad aside. "Okay, let's cut through the crap. Lieutenant Gholer, is there a witness, or isn't there?"

Gholer decided he'd better give it up. Part of it, anyway. "Yeah, there's a wit. Who I'm not willing to put in any danger by—"

"Now we're finally getting somewhere," Nance broke in. "Okay, I won't argue the pros and cons of revealing this witness's identity, all that goes without saying. But among ourselves?"

"Discussing it just among ourselves," Gholer said. "Meaning within the department? I got no problem with that. I'm just opposed to telling people who got no business knowing."

"Yeah, well and good," Nance said. "That problem's easily solved, with the one-way mirror. What's wrong with having your wit take a look at Mr. Hargis? Then we can end the speculation."

"He's already had his witness look at my client," Akin said.

Gholer's head snapped around. "And you know that how?"

The lawyer studied his fingernails. "I just, you know, heard."

Gholer's mouth dropped open. He looked at Agent Miller.

Miller was hooking paper clips together to form a chain. "Now don't be acting insulted. No witness is exclusive to any one law-enforcement agency. That's why we've got a task force, to share information. You don't want to share, we have to find out for ourselves." He looked past Gholer, out into the bullpen. "Why don't you introduce your wit to the rest of us, Jerry?"

Everyone inside Miller's office looked out as well. Jinx Madison was bouncing Jason up and down on her lap, while Eddie Frizell had his baseball cap around backward and his eyes crossed and his tongue stuck out at the child. Jason giggled out of control. Gholer thought his staff looked like idiots. Courtney Bedell was in the background, seated by one of the computers. Her windbreaker was zipped all the way up and the hem was snug around her thighs.

Texas Ranger Trent adjusted his Stetson on his head. "Hell, Jerry, you got a *baby* for a witness?"

"Can he talk lucidly?" Dilbergast asked. "How would you interpret his testimony?"

"Not the kid," Agent Miller said. "The woman sitting on the desk, with the jacket."

"I think she's a policeman," Dilbgergast said. "I've seen her before."

Miller seemed to be enjoying himself. "She's a cop *and* a witness. Who Lieutenant Gholer has had transferred to his own command so he can exercise control. Her name is Bedell. Educate us, Jerry, will you?"

Gholer tightened his belt a notch.

Chief Nance got in the middle of it. "Is this true, Lieutenant?"

"Aw," Gholer began, then paused to think and said, "she may've seen some stuff. We're checking it out."

"Some stuff?" Miller was incredulous. "Yeah, some stuff, such as the Fiddleback from a distance of a few feet. That's what stuff." He turned to Chief Nance. "I want that woman assigned to me on a temporary basis, so we can keep track."

Gholer came out of his chair. "Keep track of what? You going to take her to the daily news conference?

Be sure and do that, so the Fiddleback can see her picture in the paper."

"Give us credit for a little sense, Jerry. You think we're going to put a wit in that kind of jackpot?"

Gholer sat back down. "Yeah, I do. Funny I should think that, but yeah."

"Gentlemen, gentlemen." Nance stroked his conservative gray tie. "Let's keep this meeting on track. All this bickering over whose witness is who, that we can work out later. We're here for Mr. Akin's benefit at the moment, which has nothing to do with interagency conflict. Mr. Akin is interested in steering law-enforcement interest away from his client. So, Jerry. Let's have your witness take a look at Mr. Hargis. You see any problem?"

Gholer pinched the bridge of his nose. He said, rather subdued, "No need. She's already looked at the guy."

Nance expectantly raised his eyebrows. "And?"

Gholer rested his ankle on his knee and scooted further down in his chair. "Hargis isn't the guy."

Akin snapped to. "See there, Chief? Harassment, pure and simple."

"But just because he's not the guy," Gholer chipped in, "doesn't mean he doesn't know the guy."

Nance rested his chin on his cupped hand. He had a fresh manicure. "You've established a connection in some way?"

Gholer watched the front of Miller's desk. "Not yet," Gholer said. "But we're working on it."

"I've heard enough," Nance said. "Mr. Akin, our apologies. Won't happen again. Lieutenant Gholer W, you're to discontinue any investigation into Mr. Hargis until you can show concrete reason for doing so. Is that clear?"

Gholer clenched his jaws.

"Is that clear?" Nance said again.

"I'll leave it up to you, Chief, to make it clear," Akin said. The lawyer stood and hefted a litigation satchel. "Good day to you all," Akin said.

As the meeting adjourned and the brass filed out of Miller's office, Jinx Madison was saying up in the bull-pen, "My little sisters used to get colic. Now that was no fun." Jason sat across her knees, facing her. She had one small hand in each of her own as she bounced him up and down.

Courtney sat on one corner of the desk. "You mind if I pay you a compliment?"

"How could I mind?"

Courtney said, "It's just that, you didn't seem the type to be very crazy about kids. Fooled me." She smiled at Jason, who was laughing again at Frizell as he made another face at the child. Something about children, Courtney thought, which makes us all behave like three-year-olds. Even Topper Moore was getting in on the act, the severe redheaded woman making goo-goo eyes at Jason from two desks away.

"You grow up with seven kids in the family and you're the oldest," Madison said, "you learn a lot about babies. I still don't want any of my own, but playing with them? Where you don't have to change their diapers? Dream world."

Jason reached for Madison's weapon. She frowned and pushed his hands away. "Now that, buster, is a definite no-no."

Courtney had instinctively made a grab for Jason as well. The thought of kids coming in contact with guns terrified her. Every night she spent extra time hiding the Glock, so that Jason couldn't possibly get his hands on the pistol. She said, "Jason, why don't you go with Courtney outside. We can play—"

"Officer Bedell?" A man standing behind her interrupted. The voice was tenor, the accent Northern, the words spoken with authority.

Courtney turned. Facing her was one of the people fresh out of the meeting, a man wearing a dove-gray suit. He had wide shoulders and his coat was parted to show skinny hips. His hair was brown, receding into a widow's peak, and his mouth was taut in a look of self-importance. Instinctively, Courtney didn't like the guy. She took Jason's hand and pulled him close. "Yes?" she said.

"I'm Agent Donald Miller, FBI. You and I need to visit, pronto."

Courtney recognized the name. Gholer had warned her about this man, that he'd appear and try to throw his weight around. Jason tried to climb back into Madison's lap, but Courtney stopped him. Both Madison and Frizell were shooting wary looks at Miller. Frizell turned his cap back around, bill to the front. "Visit about what, sir?" Courtney said.

"I think you know what. This is serious business, Officer, and you'd be well-advised to pay close attention to me."

Madison cut in, rocking forward, her gaze steadily on the federal man. "If you want to tell her about the Duluth Dangler," Madison said, "I can save you the trouble and fill her in."

Miller testily turned his back on Madison. She shot him the bird. Miller moved in closer and said to Courtney, "Siding with these jerkoffs will get you in trouble in the long run, Bedell. I know who you are. I want you to give my people descriptions and talk to one of our sketch artists. Today, if not sooner."

Courtney was suddenly furious. "I'd appreciate it, sir, if you'd watch your language in front of this little boy."

Miller's gaze flicked down at Jason. "Yeah, I was

out of line. But that doesn't change you giving us your time. You can ride with me now, downtown to the federal building."

"I'd have to get Lieutenant Gholer's clearance for that."

"Gholer isn't running this investigation."

Courtney tightened her grip on Jason's hand. She'd had it up to here with this guy, and was about to say as much when Gholer walked up behind the agent.

Gholer said, "What's going on here?"

Miller lifted his coattails, put hands on hips, and looked down at the floor.

Madison chimed in. "Donald the Dangler just fired you, Loo. Says you're not in charge of the Fiddle-back case."

Gholer eyed Miller, then gave a hands-up shrug. "Man's right," Gholer said. "I'm not in charge. Neither is the FBI. You want to know who's in charge? The Fiddleback. He thinks we're all clowns. Maybe he's right."

The other participants from the meeting had filed to the front, near the exit. Courtney recognized Chief Nance and Captain Dilbergast. Nance's forehead wrinkled in interest as he watched the exchange between Gholer and Miller.

"I'm taking this witness with me, to have a session with a computer sketch artist," Miller said.

"Hmm," Gholer said. "Let's see, two days with the artist, couple more for the prints to make it out for circulation. How many people can Fiddleback kill in the meantime?"

Miller made a snickering sound. He turned to Courtney. "The child, Officer. Have you got someplace to leave him?"

Gholer stepped partway in between Courtney and the FBI man. "I don't think so, Donald. I need for Officer Bedell to go with me this afternoon."

Miller shot a see-what-we're-telling-you glance toward Chief Nance, then looked back at Gholer. "For what purpose, Jerry?"

"So she can look at some live possible suspects. Also 'cause I don't like having one of my detectives wasting time talking to sketch artists."

"Oh Jesus Christ, Jerry. Your own chief of police just got through telling you—"

"To lay off Hargis," Gholer said. "You see me chasing after Hargis? We're going to look at a brand-new crime scene."

"I'm not wasting any more time with you," Miller said. He stepped toward the exit. "Chief," he said loudly.

Nance was following Captain Dilbergast outside. Neither stopped at the sound of Miller's voice. The door closed behind them.

"We'll see about this," Miller snapped at Gholer, then took off after the police chief.

"Yeah, see about it," Gholer said. "And when you do, make sure Chief Nance tells me in person. Any 'he says' messages from the FBI, I ain't going to listen to."

Agent Miller had barely disappeared through the door when Gholer took Jason by the hand and led him over to Topper Moore's desk. The redhead leaned back from her work at the computer, lifted a hand and waggled her fingers at the kid. "Jason," Gholer said, "this is Mrs. Moore. She's going to let you work the computer."

Jason immediately reached for the keyboard. Moore stopped him, but pulled up a chair. Jason hopped up into the seat, all ears. Gholer gave a come-hither wave and led Courtney, Madison, and Frizell back into his office.

Courtney sank down into one of the visitor's chairs. "Loo, am I going to have to talk to the FBI?"

Gholer gave a limp-wristed, dismissive waggle with

his hand. "Not today, not a chance. You got to understand, we've put Chief Nance in the middle, which he
don't like but which can't be helped. He's pulled us
up from investigating Hargis for political reasons. We
can forget Mr. Hargis unless we can come up with
probablc cause, other than me saying I think the guy
might have done it. But by the same token, Nance
isn't about to turn you over to the FBI, because it'd
make the department as a whole look bad. Not to say
that won't change tomorrow. As soon as Nance turns
Agent Miller down on his request to take charge of
you, Miller's gonna take that slight to the Special
Agent-in-Charge, who's gonna raise hell with the
mayor. The mayor might back down, in which case
Miller may havc you with a sketch artist twenty-four
hours from now. Until then, Hargis is out but you're
still mine."

"And Hargis being out," Frizell said, leaning his
back against the wall, "leaves me and Jinxie standing
around with our thumbs up our asses."

"Your thumb," Madison said. "My thumb is on the
pulse of justice."

"You two," Gholer said, "have got plenty to keep
you occupied. We're not through with Hargis—we just
got to find a different avenue. Maybe through what's-
her-name, Sis Hargis' lawyer."

"Megan Harris," Frizell said.

"Right, Megan Harris. You already got a discrep-
ancy in that she told you she left the auto building
with Mrs. Hargis while the security guard told you
different. Follow up on that. If Harris gets in a bind,
she might give us something we can pursue against
the ex-husband. But without something to go on, don't
come within a mile of Billy Hargis *or* his lawyer unless
you want to wind up busting drunks behind the
courthouse."

While Gholer talked, Topper Moore came over and

stood nearby. Jason remained at Moore's desk, banging away on the computer keyboard though the machine was turned off. When Gholer was finished speaking, Moore said, "The MEs sent this up from the back." She tossed an envelope in front of Gholer and left.

Gholer leaned back, tore the envelope open with his thumb, unfolded a piece of paper from inside, and read. "Well, I'll be damned," he said.

Madison and Frizell looked at each other, then back at Gholer.

"Could be something, could be nothing," Gholer said. "It's enough to follow up on. Says here, in connection with . . . who's the vic from the park the other night? The homeless woman."

Frizell shrugged. Courtney offered, "You mean Trash Rosita?"

"Yeah," Gholer said. "That solid citizen. Anyhow, she's the one with the teeth fixed postmortem. I had Topper do some checking, but turned up no burglaries on dentists' offices or dental supply places. But Harris Sands has come up with something. Seems the caps are made of a porcelain, brand name GraniteBond, manufactured by a company outta Bentonville, Arkansas. The Arkies supply the stuff exclusively to a molder located in Arlington close to the ballpark, and if the molder can have a look at one of the caps they might be able to tell you where the shipment was headed. Dentists take impressions and send 'em in to the molders. The molders make the caps and turn 'em around back to the dentist.

"So, Jinx and Eddie," Gholer said, "go back to Harris Sands' office and pick up a couple of these caps from Trash Rosita's teeth. Take 'em out to Arlington and have this molder take a look. The shot may be longer'n Trash Rosita's odds of winning that trifecta, but if we get lucky we're talking concrete physical

evidence. Which in Fiddleback's case we've got damn
near zero at present." He tossed the paper across his
desk to land, face-up, in front of Madison. "Bedell's
going with me to the scene where they found the fresh
corpse last night. Jesus, we got to move—before Fiddleback decides to kill somebody else."

As Madison and Frizell headed toward the door
leading to the medical examiner's quarters, Gholer left
his office with Courtney a step behind. The thick-
necked cop headed for the exit. Courtney halted in
her tracks. "What about Jason, Loo?"

Gholer spun on his heel and came back, snapping
his fingers. "I forgot. Too much going on." He went
to Topper Moore's desk and held out his hand.
"Gimme that address, Topper, huh?" She wrote something on a scratch pad, tore off the sheet, and handed
it over, Gholer bent and, one-handed, scooped Jason
up and held the child in the crook of his arm. He said
to Courtney, "Let's go," and started to walk away.

Courtney was dubious. "Go where?" She stood
her ground.

Gholer retraced his steps, jiggling Jason up and
down as he did. Gholer handed Courtney the slip from
Topper Moore's scratch pad. "This place," Gholer
said. "It's approved by Duncan Hines, the Sultan of
Swat, George Bush, you name it. It's the day-care center where Topper leaves her two kids. Several of the
people working at the city leave their kids at this
place. Never had a complaint. Jason will love it."

Courtney read from the piece of paper. Rest 'n'
Play. "I know the place, Loo. Every working mother
in town knows about it. But it's high. High as a kite.
No way can I afford—"

"Which is why the department's footing the bill for
now," Gholer said. "Until this case is over one way
or the other, you got child-care courtesy of the city."

He winked. "When things look down, it means they're headed back up, Courtney. Don't ever say we didn't take care of you."

Rest 'n' Play was a single parent's dream, on a half acre of land just south of Brook Hollow Country Club. The day-care center's main building was a story-and-a-half high, red brick with fresh-painted white trim, and sat behind a well-kept lawn and weed-free beds teeming with caladiums. A high wood fence surrounded the property, the back portion of which was divided into separate playgrounds—crawl-through mazes and net-surrounded heaps of colored plastic balls for the toddlers; slides, swings, and jungle gyms for the older kids. Courtney didn't have the slightest idea what the daily charge at Rest 'n' Play might be. She didn't ask, and didn't want to know. As she and Gholer arrived in the motor-pool car with Jason sitting in her lap, a woman parked beside them driving a Jaguar.

As Courtney completed the sign-in form at the desk, Gholer led Jason to a table where three little boys played with Legos. Courtney filled in her name and address. In the blank where she was to name other parties who might pick Jason up, she wrote SELF ONLY. She listened with half an ear as the day-care manager—a pleasant woman in a gray skirt and high-necked white blouse—explained that for children left after seven o'clock, the extra charge would include an extra meal.

"That's okay," Gholer said, walking up. "You're billing the city, right?"

The woman checked a log and nodded that she was.

Courtney said to Gholer, "Give me a minute, huh?"

Gholer said, "Sure, take your time," and turned his attention to Courtney's sign-in form.

Courtney went over to the table where Jason played. The other little boys looked at her and giggled. She got down on her haunches beside Jason and hugged his neck. "I love you, Jason. Have a good time."

Jason was absorbed in building a platform out of Legos. He barely looked at her. His look of intense concentration was a preview of the man, Courtney believed, that Jason would someday become. " 'Bye, Coatney," he said.

A minute later, Courtney felt a lump in her throat as she stood at the exit watching Jason. Gholer finished his business at the desk, then walked over and held the door for her. With a last longing look at her nephew, Courtney went outside with Gholer close on her heels; and the two went off to chase the Fiddleback. Halfway to the car she had a premonition, a horrible sinking spell, and for just a moment it was all she could do to keep from running back inside, grabbing Jason, and heading for home. By the time she'd settled into the front seat beside Gholer the feeling had passed, but she couldn't get that awful moment out of her mind. For just a second she'd been certain that she'd never see Jason again, that before she returned for him she was going to die.

15

Sis Hargis was barely alive. Harold Bays had to bend to within inches of her lips to feel her breath on his face. The thought of having to get rid of her this soon pissed Harold off—not at the woman, because she didn't matter, but at himself. She wasn't even Harold's choice to begin with. The man who gave Harold orders had selected her—and didn't know what the fuck he was doing. She was too thin, and her model's body wouldn't absorb enough poison. Those Harold had chosen on his own had lasted for days, some as long as a week.

Harold clenched his jaws in rage.

The limousine driver had been a shitty choice as well, and, like the woman currently on the brink of death, hadn't been Harold's selection. In the case of the driver, Harold had spotted a more suitable subject—the Mexican woman—as he'd piloted the limo away from the racetrack with the driver secured in the trunk. The Mexican woman had lived until Thursday, absorbing more and more poison, producing the finest sores since the Change had begun. The limo driver, on the other hand, hadn't been worth the effort.

Harold Bays was never wrong when it came to choosing human subjects.

The man who gave the order to take the limo driver

and the model was always wrong. The man who gave
the order was a fuckup.

And now, holding the lantern aloft to better view
the woman who barely breathed, Harold came to a
decision. The man who'd given him orders would have
to die.

It was as simple as that.

The plastic box in Harold's grip vibrated as the spider inside grew more and more restless. Its legs scrabbled and scratched on the plastic surface. The orders
it screamed echoed inside Harold's head like yodeling
in a canyon.

*What are you waiting for, you prick? You insignifi-
cant asshole, let me out of here!*

Harold wasn't fazed. He even smiled as the insults
grew nastier and nastier. Harold Bays, insignificant?
The spider inside the box was merely a worker, without authority regarding the Change, and therefore had
no more status than Harold himself. Less control over
Harold, in fact, than that jackass of a dock boss Melvin Pure. When Harold had called in sick that morning, Melvin Pure had given him shit, and Harold had
slammed the phone down in Melvin Pure's face. If
Harold Bays wouldn't take shit off Melvin Pure, he
certainly wasn't going to let this worker spider get
to him.

Harold Bays believed that he lived in the real
world—*his* real world, where spiders talked to him
and humans were his subjects as he waited for the
Change. The *human* world—where insects didn't
speak, where people held jobs, raised families,
watched television, and went on vacation—was nothing but a fantasy kingdom.

Harold held the box up to the lantern. The spider
grew still. Harold said in a childishly petulant voice,
"I'm not the prick. *You're* the prick, for *calling* me a
prick. I don't have to do what you tell me."

The woman chained to the bench stirred and moaned at the sound of Harold's voice, then resumed her faint breathing.

The spider waved two of its forelegs. *I'm telling on you, you motherfucker. You deformed two-legged cocksucker, you are finished.*

"And *I* will tell on *you*," Harold said, "for yelling at me. She doesn't like for you to yell at me. If I tell Her, buddy, you are fucked. So there." The last part he said without much conviction, for Harold Bays really had no idea what She might do in any given situation. But he'd decided some time ago to stand up for himself when the workers taunted him. Fuck the workers. They were nothing but envious assholes, jealous of Harold because he was the one who got to carry out Her orders. The workers weren't as jealous of Harold as he was of *them*—every time he looked at the spider's magnificent legs, or the beautiful brown of its violin marking, Harold shivered with envy—but if Harold allowed his own jealousy to show, the workers would have the upper hand. And a bunch of stupid workers weren't about to get the best of Harold Bays. Fuck them. Once the Change was complete, every one of them would learn never to mess with Harold Bays.

He decided to let the spider have its way with the woman. The woman was as good as dead, and had little fluid left in her to mix in the bottle for the injections, so the spider for all purposes would feast on a pile of bones. Fuck this worker spider. Harold hoped that the bastard starved.

He dropped the spider onto the woman's body, giving the box a harder shake than necessary, feeling satisfaction that the spider landed on its back and had to struggle to right itself. As the spider began to crawl over the woman's body, Harold made a face and stuck out his tongue.

The spider took its time, circling the sore beneath

the woman's breast, skirting the lesions on the woman's stomach and hip, finally stopping on the woman's thigh. The woman remained in a coma, her chest barely rising and falling as she breathed. The spider came to a standstill.

Harold felt a tightening in his crotch as his erection began. All animosity for the worker spider left him in a rush. Very soon he would please Her. Very soon he would give Her more evidence that he was ready for the Change. As Harold kept his gaze riveted on the spider, he reached down and squeezed himself. He was practically delirious with excitement.

He used a corner of the box to poke at the spider, to irritate it, and sucked in breath as the recluse thrust its probe deep into the woman's flesh. Penetration was the moment Harold lived for—*had* lived for, in fact, since the Change had begun. Once he was changed, Harold would have his own beautiful probe. His now-full erection pulsed between his legs.

Harold quickly scooped the worker spider back into the box and leaned over to inspect the bite. The area around the puncture already swelled and reddened, and soon it would grow and fester. Eventually the red spot would become a beautiful slick-wet wound. Harold would then collect the fluid, dispose of the woman, and She would once again be pleased with him. He firmly grasped his member and flogged himself.

Moving with speed and agility in spite of his limp, his tattoo writhing as his muscles tightened, Harold carried the box out of the room. He didn't bother to lock the door as he had when the woman had first become his captive; she was far too weak to try to get away. Harold closed his eyes and continued to massage his erection as he hurried down the corridor and into the kitchen.

He opened the lower cupboard, knelt before the bottom shelf, and released the worker spider from the box. The recluse scuttled to the back of the shelf and disappeared through a crack in the wall, but Harold barely noticed. His attention was riveted on something closer by.

Strung in between the wall and the shelf was the wispy beige-colored web where, earlier, She had laid Her eggs. He could see them there, hundreds, maybe thousands of tiny dots like pepper grains. He pointed his erection toward the web, his chest heaving, a series of moans coming from his lips, his pelvis thrusting forward as his fist tightened and moved faster and faster.

Thick, grayish semen spurted on the wall, cascaded onto the web, and soaked down to cover the eggs. Harold collapsed on the floor, spent, his lips pulled back from crooked teeth in an expression of pleasure. He remained limp as his breathing subsided.

He was conscious of movement on the shelf. A second spider, larger than the worker, came through the crack and approached in majestic unhurried strides. The big recluse came abreast of the semen-drenched web and stopped.

She.

Harold was speechless. She was more beautiful than anything he'd ever imagined, Her body smooth and parabolic, Her violin marking perfectly shaped, Her life-giving abdomen swollen with eggs. He was practically giddy with pleasure at himself. He had performed once again. Soon She would order the Change.

She spoke to him, her voice inside his head ten times louder than all the others combined.

YOU FUCKING MORON! YOU HAVE THE NERVE TO BRING ME YOUR WORTHLESS COME!

Harold shrank back in terror. He sputtered and stuttered. "I only wanted to please you. What have I done?"

*WHAT HAVE YOU DONE? WHAT HAVE YOU
FUCKING DONE? YOU BRING AN UNCLEAN
WOMAN HERE, AND THEN YOU SPRAY YOUR
WORTHLESS COME ON MY EGGS? GO AWAY,
YOU ASSHOLE!*

The spider turned and started to march away.

Harold leaped quickly forward. "Don't go. Listen to me."

The female recluse stopped and turned.

"I'll make it up, I swear," Harold whined. "It isn't my fault. He made me bring that woman, I didn't want to."

The spider's tone inside Harold's head was a mimicking falsetto. *NOT YOUR FAULT? NOT YOUR FUCKING FAULT? YOU WANT ME TO BELIEVE YOU ARE WORTHY, AND YET YOU BRING ME A WOMAN BECAUSE SOMEONE TOLD YOU TO? YOU'RE NOT WORTHY. YOU ARE A STUPID, DEFORMED FUCKHEAD. NOW GO AWAY.*

Harold sobbed out of control. "You can't send me away. You have promised the Change."

SHOVE THE CHANGE UP YOUR ASS, YOU DUMB BASTARD. She methodically paraded toward the crack in the wall.

"*Wait,*" Harold screamed. "Give me another chance. Jesus Christ, another chance."

The recluse halted again. *YOU CALL ME JESUS CHRIST? I AM STRONGER THAN JESUS CHRIST, YOU FUCK.*

"I know." Harold folded his hands in supplication. "I will bring you one that's suitable. You will see. Oh please, you will see."

The recluse rubbed Her forelegs together as if in thought. *WHEN, ASSHOLE?*

"Now. I will go . . . right . . . fucking . . . now. I will do anything. I have to have the Change."

*THEN GO. WHAT THE FUCK ARE YOU WAIT-
ING FOR?*

"Oh thank you." Harold got up and started for his room. Halfway there he stopped and turned back, and screamed at the top of his lungs, "You will see, Mother! I swear! I can be a good boy! You will see!"

Half blind with tears of rage and shame, Harold tromped into his room and gave himself an injection. None of this was his fault. All the man's fault, not Harold's. He hated the fucking man who'd given him the orders, even more than he hated the stupid worker spiders.

The syrupy mixture coursed through his body. He was strong once again. He lived for the time when he'd be powerful without the aid of the needle.

He opened a dresser drawer. Two pistols lay side by side, the .22 for executing his subjects, the .45 for killing anyone who stood in the way of the Change. The .22 made a smaller entry wound, and left the bodies more suitable for display.

The man who gave him orders wasn't fit to go on display.

Neither was the woman who was about to die.

He grabbed the .45, retreated down the hallway into the closet, and shot Sis Hargis through the head. Her body jerked in recoil. Blood and brain matter spattered the wall.

Harold unlocked the shackles, grabbed the woman's foot and dragged her down the corridor toward the back of the house. A trail of blood marked his path, wetting the planks and shimmering in the dim light filtering in from the living room. He paused beside the kitchen, shouted, "You will see, Mother," and hauled the corpse away.

Harold strained and grunted as he dug Sis Hargis' grave behind the shed, the shovel blade flashing as he slung dirt in all directions. He must hide this woman who wasn't suitable, just as he would soon hide the man who gave him orders. Only the suitable ones went on display; the others Harold buried behind the barn.

Finally the hole was deep and wide enough. He cast the shovel aside, panting from exertion as he looked at the fourteen mounds where he'd buried other bodies through the years.

When the spiders first began to talk to him, Harold Bays had already murdered eleven times. His first victims were convicts from the federal penitentiary down the way, three men he'd befriended through an outreach program. One spring night he'd put on dark clothing, crept through the woods to the perimeter of the prison, and cut a hole in the fence with a pair of loppers. Then he'd retreated halfway to the house and waited. The escapees—a counterfeiter, a bank robber, and a convicted real-estate swindler—had stuffed pillows under their covers to fool the guards during midnight count, had sneaked through the prison laundry and infirmary, and laid in wait beside the baseball field. Fifteen minutes after he'd cut the fence, Harold had blown two short blasts on a whistle and the prisoners had scuttled out through the hole. He'd met them in an open field, led to the house, and fed them each a plate of rice and beans. Then he'd shot all three men in the head and buried the bodies. A couple of days later prison officials had dropped by the house and given Harold photos of the men, telling him that he should consider the escapees armed and dangerous. As far as Harold knew, the U.S. Marshal's Service still had the trio listed as fugitives.

He remembered most of the victims buried behind the shed, but there were a few whom, try as he might, he just couldn't picture. Most had been homeless. A

couple had been hookers Harold had picked up near
the fairgrounds. One had been a girl he'd abducted as
she walked home from school. At first the killings
were totally at random. Maligned and ridiculed all of
his life because of his strange appearance and step-
and-drag manner of walking, Harold had taken his
hate out on the world. He'd killed, buried the bodies,
and disposed of the victims' belongings in Dumpsters
as far as two counties away.

Originally, the spiders hadn't been part of the plan.

Carla Ruth Rabinowitz, the woman he'd taken at
gunpoint from Texas Stadium during a Cowboy football game eleven months ago, had originally been an
experiment. Harold knew her name today only because, along with the rest of Dallas, he'd read about
her in the newspapers even as he'd held her captive.
He'd had difficulty connecting the screaming headlines
and photos blanketing the media with the woman he'd
stripped and chained to the bench in the hallway
closet. She had been the only one he'd really tortured.
Because she was pretty, he'd beaten her senseless
every night for a week. He'd given her just enough
food to keep her alive. He'd tried to have sex with
her, but found he couldn't get an erection.

On the seventh morning after he'd captured Carla
Ruth Rabinowitz, he'd entered her miniprison to find
her sleeping heavily as if drugged. He'd tried to shake
her into wakefulness, but she was limp and nonrespon-
sive. The sounder she slept the angrier he became. He
punched her with his fists and banged her head against
the wall. He undid her shackles, grabbed her under
the armpits, and started to haul her out in the corridor
for a sound whipping. He suddenly froze. On her left
inner thigh was a large glistening sore.

Fascinated, Harold stretched Carla Ruth Rabinowitz out on the bench and knelt down for a closer

look. He'd dragged his hand through the slick-wet wound and licked his fingers. The fluid had a taste like salted bitter lemon.

He retreated naked into the corner, and sat on the floor with the lantern between his legs to watch. He remained there motionless for most of the day. Occasionally she moaned and quivered in her sleep, but otherwise she was still.

It was several hours before a spider appeared out of the darkness and crawled across her chest. Harold tensed with excitement He'd seen these harmless-looking creatures around the house for years, had even killed a few with a flyswatter, but had never paid much attention to them. He'd thought their violin markings odd, but otherwise had considered them just another pest along with the roaches and rats living in the attic and inside the walls. Harold grabbed a splinter of wood from the floor and poked at the insect.

The spider bit Carla Ruth Rabinowitz on the right breast, just above the nipple. As Harold edged closer, the bite reddened and swelled. The spider's legs scuttled on flesh as it tried to get away. Harold looked desperately around, located a wadded piece of cloth in the corner, and captured the spider before it could crawl through a crack in the floor. He carried the insect into the kitchen and imprisoned it inside a jar with at twist-on lid. For the rest of that day and into the next, Harold left both Carla and the spider alone.

Around noon the day after he'd captured the insect, Harold had checked on Carla to find that the second bite had festered into a sore identical in appearance to the one on her thigh, but even larger. He touched the fresh wound and licked his fingers. The bitter taste was the same as with the moisture from the other sore.

He retreated into the kitchen, found the jar, and held the imprisoned spider up to the light. The spider sat motionless, tense as a runner in the starting blocks.

Harold held the jar an inch from his nose. The spider's markings were beautiful, its body round and sturdy. Harold flattened his eye against the glass.

And then the spider screamed, *FUCK YOU!*

Harold recoiled in shock, dropping the jar, clutching at the glass receptacle as it tumbled in midair, catching the jar a foot above the floor. He was terrified, but spellbound as well. He staggered into a kitchen chair and set the jar up on the table.

The spider's words were only thoughts in Harold's mind, but the voice echoing inside his head was just as real to him as if the spider were actually talking. And the voice was familiar, one he hadn't heard in years. The spider sounded just like one of the mean kids back in the reformatory who used to laugh at Harold and call him names.

Harold said, haltingly, "Are you talking to me?"

What other asshole is here? Of course I'm talking to you.

For the next two hours, Harold sat in his kitchen and carried on a conversation with a spider in a jar. The spider thought Harold was a worthless piece of shit, and continued to curse and call him names, while Harold tried to convince the spider otherwise. In a gesture of friendship, Harold carried the insect back into the miniprison and allowed it to feast on Carla two more times. Each time he did, the spider became more and more abusive. Harold finally became fed up with the spider's attitude and decided to mash the insect under his shoe. He'd unscrewed the lid from the jar, raised his foot in the air, and was ready to dump the spider onto the floor when, in the corner of his eye, he spied the Queen.

She.

She'd crawled unnoticed onto the kitchen counter, larger than the spider inside the jar and, in Harold's eyes, a thousand times more beautiful. When she spoke to him her voice was much louder in his head than the imprisoned spider's, and was the mature voice of a woman. *DON'T HURT HIM, STUPID.*

Harold refastened the lid and set the jar back up on the table. He stared speechless at the Queen.

She continued to sit motionless. *WHAT DO YOU EXPECT US TO THINK OF YOU, YOU CREEP? LOOK AT YOU, YOU DEFORMED TWO-LEGGED COCKSUCKER. IF YOU COULD BE LIKE THE REST OF US, WE MIGHT EVEN LIKE YOU. BUT YOU'LL NEVER BE LIKE US. YOU'RE TOO FUCKING UGLY.*

Harold whimpered. He recognized Her voice as well. She sounded exactly like his mother, who'd died when he was ten, and who used to ridicule him in public. Who used to tell others in the supermarket checkout line, total strangers, that her little boy was funny-looking and she couldn't understand why. Who used to leave him at home alone and tell him she didn't want to be seen with him. Who, when she'd catch him outside the house without permission, used to tie him to the hitching post and put him on display.

As a little boy he'd done everything he could to please his mother, but had never received so much as a kiss on the cheek in return. He'd cried himself to sleep a thousand nights in a row because he knew she didn't love him.

The Queen recluse spider was to become a second chance for Harold Bays.

Everything he'd done from that point on had been to please Her, so that someday he could shed his ugliness and become one of Her subjects. He'd be a worker, anything, if only She would love him in return. In fact at this point Harold considered himself one of the workers, and was certain in his mind that the other spiders' insults came through jealousy because Harold could please Her more than they could. All the humans he killed thereafter he dressed up like one of the roaches that the worker spiders presented to Her. He put the humans on display only to please Her. And the injections he gave himself were working. The knot developing on his side was one of his additional legs beginning to grow, he was sure now.

Harold Bays would become the largest, most beautiful fucking spider in the world. And once he did, life would finally be happy for him.

But then the man who gave him orders had come along.

The man who gave Harold orders had discovered the Change taking place, and had forced Harold to do things in order to keep the Change a secret. And because of the man's orders, and of Harold's carrying out of the orders to keep the Change a secret, he was in danger of having Her reject him just as his mother had.

Harold Bays hated the man who gave him orders more than he'd ever hated anyone, even the girl he'd killed for teasing him when he was twelve.

Just the thought of the man caused Harold's teeth to clench in rage. He screamed, raised the shovel over his head, and hit the ground so hard that the shovel broke in two.

Harold wiped his tears on the forearm of his shirt as his pickup rattled its way through the woods. He pulled out through the gate, burning rubber, and headed down the blacktop road toward I-45. He'd changed into jeans, running shoes, a black long-sleeve turtleneck, and a Texas Rangers batting helmet. A ski mask was rolled up on the seat beside him. He was sobbing so hard he could barely see the pavement ahead.

The Queen's final words echoed inside his head. *BRING ANOTHER SUBJECT, YOU IGNORANT*

FUCK! AND THIS ONE HAD BETTER BE SUITABLE.

Harold was terrified. If he didn't please Her, She might very well end the Change forever.

He stopped for the red light at the freeway access road. Idling beside him was a Jeep Cherokee with a woman driving and a girl of about twelve in the passenger seat. Both were blond and fair-skinned, unsuitable for the Change, so Harold paid little attention to them.

He heard a faint scuttling noise. A worker spider crawled out of the glove compartment and sat motionless on the dashboard. It rubbed its forelegs together. *You're in trouble, you prick. The shit is going to hit the fan. After today your ass will be history.*

Harold couldn't take it. "Leave me alone," he screamed.

Leave you alone? Sure, why wouldn't I? Who'd want to have anything to do with such a fuckup?

"Goddammit, I'll kill you!" Harold yelled, and slapped at the spider with the palm of his hand.

The spider scuttled quickly sideways. Harold's palm hit the dash with a sound like a gunshot.

The spider bounced up and down. *Jesus Christ, you are such a fuckup.*

"Am not, you son of a bitch." Harold slid from under the wheel. He kept his foot on the brake as he tried to mash the spider under his thumb.

The spider retreated into the shelter where the windshield connected to the dash. *Fuckup! Fuckup, fuckup, fuckup.*

"You're dead, you asshole!" Harold shrieked. "You are fucking dead!"

Inside the Jeep that idled beside the pickup, the preteen girl said to her mother, "What's wrong with that man?"

The mother looked over her shoulder. The pickup

was maroon and white with an Aggie Twelfth Man bumper sticker. The guy inside the cab had the look of a madman, his shoulders hunched, his sparse hair wild, his teeth clenched in hatred as he flailed at something on the dashboard.

The mother felt a bolt of fear. She gunned her engine, praying for the light to change in a hurry. Her daughter's gaze was riveted on the pickup.

The mother hissed, "Stop looking at him."

The daughter looked scared to death. "But what's wrong with him, Mom?"

"I don't have the slightest idea, sweetheart, and don't want to find out. Best to steer clear of people like that. Some of these Aggies are crazy as bedbugs. Stop looking at him. And if he looks at you, pretend he isn't even there."

16

Courtney Bedell thought that the guy should come up with a better line. She snapped, "Let's just say I'm conducting a study," then moved quickly away toward the barrier of crime-scene tape.

The guy followed after her. "No, I mean, what do you do for a living?" He wore a tool belt and a hardhat.

Courtney paused. He wasn't that bad-looking, but God, hitting on a woman while hanging around a murder scene? If she gave in, he might end up by asking her to hang him, lay the whip to his ass or something. She said, "I'm in training."

He continued to grin under his thick mustache. "Yeah? Training for what?"

"Martial arts," Courtney said. "Breaking men's arms when they try anything."

"Yeah?" He looked her up and down. "Bet you could put up a tussle, huh?"

She'd had it up to here with the verbal sparring. She opened her wallet and held her shield an inch from the guy's nose. "And I'll bet you could put up a tussle with a jail guard. Leave me alone, I'm working here." She walked away again.

This time the guy didn't follow.

For a couple of hours Courtney had circulated

among the onlookers at the scene where the preacher
had dragged the limo driver's body out in the open,
while Gholer stayed with the CSU techs and looked
over their shoulders. Neither the lieutenant nor his
star witness was having any luck—other than Courtney's getting hit on by the hardhat guy, of course.
She'd yet to spy anyone who remotely resembled the
Fiddleback, and the crime-scene technicians hadn't
found a shred of usable evidence. Last night's after-
midnight deluge had turned hard dirt into mud and
washed away already-sparse vegetation. The CSU
workers had located a broken tree limb where they
believed the body had been anchored, and had gone
over the area with rakes, brooms, and handheld vacu-
ums. Thousands of tire tracks crisscrossed among the
trees, and some of the techs dutifully created molds,
but so many Cowboy fans parked here on Sundays it
was impossible to guess which of the tracks, if any,
might belong to the Fiddleback. There'd been bits of
flesh scattered about as if the victim had been muti-
lated, and that, plus the fact that the medical examiners had reported the limo driver's right eye and parts
of his face were torn away, had created a few moments' excitement. But then one of the techs had
looked up, had done a double take, and then had
pointed solemnly at a buzzard perched on a nearby
mesquite tree. The big bird lurked nearby as if waiting
for the workers to leave so he could finish his meal.

Courtney was getting awfully bored—not bored
enough to react to the hardhat guy, but very nearly
so. Gawkers came and went: delivery men, workers
from the road gang resurfacing portions of I-35 a mile
down the road, a guy driving a catering truck, even a
couple of off-duty Irving cops who'd heard through
the grapevine about last night's find. Since she'd been
on the scene, Courtney had sized up at least a hundred
people. She was frustrated and angry, and felt as if

she and Gholer were wasting their time. Her gaze kept drifting north to Texas Stadium, its semidomed roof towering over traffic headed to and from the airport. She thought about Jason, wondered if he was enjoying the day-care center. Thoughts of the little boy drummed up images of Jan. Courtney recalled her older sister's usual shitty attitude as she'd gone off into the night beside her boyfriend. Just picturing Jan and her worthless asshole of a lover made Courtney even madder.

The passing cool front had brought the first hint of fall into the area; the temperature was in the upper sixties and a stiff wind rattled the branches of the mesquite trees. Courtney's windbreaker was zipped halfway up and she kept her hands stuffed inside her pockets.

She left the knot of onlookers, went over to where Gholer leaned dismally against a squad car, and asked, "How long before we check it in?"

Gholer's expression was defeated and hopeless, like a gambler's on a losing streak "I feel like we already have. How can this guy get so lucky? Might have left evidence out the ass, the storm comes along and covers his tracks. I feel like I'll still be looking for this guy when they haul me away to the rest home. To top things off, Fiddleback's ruining my sex life."

Courtney laid a sympathetic hand on Gholer's arm. "Yeah, it's tough to even think about making love with this fruitcake running around."

Gholer snorted. "Tough, hell, it's all I *do* think about. It's just that I'm gone so much my wife thinks I'm the guy that just drops by when he wants a little cooze. I'm lucky I can even cop a feel." He looked toward the knot of spectators. "I guess it's pointless to ask if you're doing any good."

"I got a chance to get laid, Loo. Otherwise, *nada.* One woman sort of reminded me of an aunt I haven't see in a while. Maybe I should drop her a line." She pointed at the hip pocket where Gholer kept his cell. "You hear from Jinx and Eddie?"

"Not yet." Gholer pointed toward the road, where a pickup had driven up loaded with what looked like field hands. Men in overalls and women in straw hats climbed down from the bed and approached the barrier. "Another load, Courtney," Gholer said. "Look 'em over, okay?"

Courtney took a stride toward the barrier, then stopped and turned back. "Jesus, Lieutenant, they look like *Roots* meets *Tobacco Road*. Do I have to?"

Gholer had a crooked grin. "Yeah, you have to. Times like this you never know. Come on, Court, stay on your toes. It's a choice between this and spending your time with the FBI. I don't know about you, but it'd be a no-brainer for me."

Jinx Madison had expected the director of Haver Laboratories to run tests on the porcelain dental caps, maybe do comparisons on a computer screen in hopes of finding a match. Instead, the guy left the caps lying on his desk while he leaned back in his chair and cleaned his glasses. "I don't know if I should talk to you without checking it out with our attorney," he said.

Madison exchanged a look with Eddie Frizell, who was sprawled out on a divan with his knee up in the air. Madison was seated in a cushioned easy chair. The director's office was a homey place, with an old-fashioned roll-top desk and pictures of animals on the walls—a walking horse, two groomed golden retrievers, and a Maltese. The director was named Roland Gibbs and was a paunchy black man with gray kinky hair. Visible through the window behind him was a tree-shaded lawn, and beyond the lawn were the buildings on the northeast corner of the University of Texas at Arlington campus. Gibbs was dressed in a

starched white lab coat, though Madison had already
figured out that Haver Laboratories was more into
sales than any kind of research. She'd yet to see a test
tube, but the director's desk was piled high with in-
come projections and profit-and-loss statements. Gibbs
looked like a family man, wife, kids, mortgage, the
works, things foreign to Jinx Madison's lifestyle. She
concentrated on the work at hand.

Madison said, "This is a homicide investigation, Mr.
Gibbs. You're not a suspect or anything, but if you
think you need a lawyer—"

"Oh, not for that." Gibbs waved dismissively. "It's
just that . . . well, these porcelain caps could become
the subject of a lawsuit."

Frizell came to life, showing a pained expression as
he touched one of the molars at the back of his mouth.
"You mean they fall off people's teeth?"

Gibbs laughed heartily. "All porcelain caps come
loose occasionally, Detective. That's what keeps the
dentist in country-club dues. No, it's this particular
shipment that's in dispute."

"Dispute with who, sir?" Madison said.

"With a dental clinic," Gibbs said. "That's why I'm
wondering if I should be calling our lawyer in on this.
He's told us not to discuss it."

"Discussing it with us," Madison said, "isn't exactly
like gossiping around the neighborhood."

Gibbs picked up one of the caps and rolled it between a thumb and forefinger. He wore a diamond
pinky ring. "An attorney's advice is often confusing
to me," Gibbs said. "I'm just not sure."

Frizell put both feet on the floor. "Well, let me be
*un*confusing. I'll bet we can get a search warrant for
your entire premises before your lawyer can say, 'Let's
go to lunch and talk about it.' "

Gibbs didn't seem flustered. "What would you be
looking for?" He held the dental cap up to the light.

"I'll save you the trouble if you'd expect to find more of these around here. There aren't any."

Madison crossed her legs and smoothed the fabric of her slacks over her thigh. "Maybe we got bad information. Our medical examiners tell us that particular porcelain, trade name GraniteBond, is exclusive to your company, at least in Texas."

"Oh, it is," Gibbs said. "We just don't order much of it."

"It's that exclusive, huh?"

"No, ma'am, it's that *un*exclusive. No one uses that crap except doc-in-the-box dental clinics, may their breed discontinue. It's cheap stuff, for patients looking for a deal. I wouldn't want it in my mouth."

"Dr. Gibbs," Madison said.

"*Mr.* Gibbs." Gibbs touched the lapel of his lab coat. "This outfit is strictly for appearances."

"*Mr.* Gibbs, then," Madison said. "If your company's involved in some kind of lawsuit over the quality of this stuff, that can't have anything to do with what we're trying to talk to you about."

Gibbs held up two fingers. "Actually, there are two bones of contention. One is, one of our customers is being sued over the overall results of their dental work, and has threatened to enjoin us as a counter-defendant. They say it's the materials. We say it's the dental clinic's faulty workmanship."

"None of which," Frizell said, "leads us any closer to catching a nutso killer. What's the other bone of contention?"

Gibbs seemed a little confused. "The other dispute is, quite simply, an unpaid bill. Same customer. We shipped them a sizeable load of dental caps and they haven't paid us. Not only is their workmanship apparently crappy, they're deadbeats as well."

"Maybe," Madison said, "the two disputes are connected. They might be saying, hey, you sold us faulty materials, we're withholding payment until we see the outcome of the people suing us."

Gibbs smiled and shook his head. "No connection whatsoever, Detective. They're not claiming any kind of offset. They claim the shipment never arrived. We think that it did, and that they are lying through their teeth."

Madison and Frizell looked at each other. Frizell said, "Why do you think that? Are there warehouse receipts to back you up?"

"Afraid it's not quite that simple. We use a freighthauler that's always sixty, ninety days in forwarding paperwork. We've asked for copies of the delivery tickets, but so far they haven't turned up."

"So," Frizell said, "you don't really know whether the materials arrived or not."

"No, not a hundred percent certain. But come on, Detective, consider the source. Our freighthauler's reputable. One of their bobtails picked the shipment up from our loading dock and signed for it. From there it went to their distribution center. If the goods had been lost, stolen, or damaged en route, we would've already heard. This doc-in-the-box operation has decided to stiff us."

Madison felt her excitement level rise. "But if the materials *have* disappeared, that's more than a little interesting to us. We're checking out porcelain caps that are unaccounted for. You ever read in the paper about the Fiddleback, Mr. Gibbs?"

Gibbs' nose wrinkled in disgust. "That awful business? What could this possibly have to do with that lunatic?"

"You'll just have to trust us, sir," Madison said. "It could be very connected. What's this dental clinic's name?"

"Westex Associates. But all these murders you're

talking about happened around here. This clinic's way
to hell out west in Midland."

Madison's enthusiasm dropped like a stone. "Oh
hell. That's three hundred miles from here."

"Right. I don't see how it could . . ." Gibbs
scratched his chin in thought. "Our freighthauler's
local, though."

Frizell sat straight up. "And who would they be?"

"Texas Motor Freight. Their dock's on Irving Boulevard, right down the street from your office. But
TMF's been doing business damn near three-quarters
of a century. They've been our shipper twenty or
thirty years, since before I ever came to work for the
company. If you ask me, detectives—not that you are
asking me, but if you did—any thought that TMF has
misplaced these dental caps is strictly out in left field."

Madison and Frizell parked in Texas Motor
Freight's employee lot and crossed a wide expanse of
asphalt headed for the loading dock. Bobtails and
forty-footers were backed up to the dock, side by side,
and, visible on the dock itself, forklifts and mules
whined back and forth. Some of the men had long
hair tied back into ponytails. As the detectives drew
near the steps, Madison said, "I think I'm in heaven."
She was watching a black guy's muscles writhe as he
loaded a box onto a cart.

They crossed the dock to the office, where Madison
passed her ID through a window to a woman in overalls. The woman's eyes widened as she read over the
credentials. She said through a speaker, "Are you
looking for anyone in particular?"

Madison shrugged. "We want to see whoever can
tell us about a Haver Laboratories shipment that
seems to be missing."

"That would be Mr. Spivey. Office in back." The

woman pointed off to one side. "Go to that door down there. As soon as you're ready I'll buzz you on through."

Mr. Spivey seemed to Madison like a no-bullshit operator. He was a rangy white man with graying sideburns, dressed in slacks, white shirt, and tie. When Frizell stated the detectives' business, Spivey marched over to a file cabinet and returned with a folder two inches thick, secured with a rubber band. "Last four months' record on Haver Labs. Every delivery ticket, including the times. One thing we got here is pieces of paper." He dropped the file with a resounding thump.

"The one we're interested in," Frizell said, "is a shipment of porcelain dental caps bound for West Texas. Mr. Gibbs at Haver tells us there's a dispute."

Spivey propped his shin against the edge of his desk, and drank coffee from a cone-shaped cup inside a plastic holder. His cigarettes showed through his breast pocket. Camels. He took out the pack and tapped one out. "That deal's been in dispute for a while. So far we've got no lawyer involved, but it could come to that."

"Okay," Frizell said. "To shorten this meeting, we just need the answer to one question. Did the porcelain reach its destination, or didn't it?"

Spivey lit his cigarette. His hands shook and it took a couple of tries for him to get the Bic disposable to work. He inhaled and blew smoke at the ceiling. One of the women working outside came over and shut Spivey's door, fanning the air as she did. Spivey said, "This is crap. We've told Haver Labs we're investigating. Them getting the police involved is jumping the gun."

Frizell started to say something, but Madison stopped him with a hand on his arm. She moved up nearer Spivey's desk. "Well, sir," she said, "maybe Haver Labs thinks you're not moving fast enough."

Spivey faced his window and waved toward the massive loading area. "We handle millions of items here. Some of 'em get misplaced occasionally. When they do, we track 'em down. But accusing anybody of any kind of theft—"

"What makes you think," Madison interrupted, "that anyone thinks there's theft involved?"

"You cops being here," Spivey said. "Things get stolen, sure. In my fifteen years here we've even had a couple of trucks hijacked en route. But who's going to steal a bunch of dental caps?"

"So maybe motive isn't apparent," Madison said. "What is apparent is that somebody's missing a lot of porcelain. You can make this pretty simple for everybody concerned, Mr. Spivey, if you'll just tell us whether the materials reached their destination. Which according to Haver Labs was Midland, Texas."

Spivey flicked ashes into a black glass tray with a golfer mounted on the edge. "Maybe I should call our lawyer."

"That's the second time today somebody's talked about calling lawyers." Frizell spread his hands, palms up. "So maybe we should call ours. The district attorney. Call your lawyer, and raise you a lawyer."

Spivey nervously squeezed his earlobe. "I've damn sure stolen nothing. Nobody around here we know of would steal anything like that. Jesus, I never had the police out here before."

Madison stood, rested a hip on Spivey's desk, and leaned on her straightened arm. The smoke inside the cubicle was getting thick. She took the cigarette from Spivey's fingers and ground the butt out in the ashtray. "Well, maybe we can help you make this a one-time visit," Madison said. "If you start getting lawyers involved, police investigations have a habit of getting nasty. We're not investigating any theft here, sir. If you took the porcelain home and sold it out your back door, we couldn't care less. But some of that porcelain turned up inside a murder victim's mouth. Now that, we're interested in."

Spivey folded his arms and hugged himself. "Jesus Christ."

"And all the angels," Madison said. "What happened to the shipment, Mr. Spivey?"

"Right . . ." Spivey pointed a quivering finger. "Right over there."

Madison and Frizell looked in the direction Spivey pointed. Stacked in the corner of Spivey's office were four packing boxes. The top box was torn open.

Frizell got up and walked over to the boxes. He jammed his hands into his back pockets and leaned over. He looked at the freight man over his shoulder. "This is the shipment in question?"

Spivey massaged his forehead. "I'm not lying. No way am I hindering any murder investigation. No, sir."

Madison was still seated on the front of Spivey's desk. She said, "Well, just supposing, Mr. Spivey, what kind of investigation *would* you hinder?"

"I cooperate with the authorities, a hundred percent."

Frizell snorted through his nose. "Yeah, I can see that." He went back over and sat down. "I think you better start filling us in, Mr. Spivey. We got no suspects at the moment, and need one PDQ. You don't want to be our first volunteer, you better start talking to us."

Spivey dispatched one of the workers to bring in reinforcements. As Madison and Frizell watched through Spivey's window, the worker approached a paunchy man who stood near one of the trucks. The

man wore glasses along with a pair of white coveralls.
The worker talked a mile a minute while gesturing
toward the office. The bespectacled man looked angry.
He approached the office in long strides and knocked
on a window. The woman buzzed him through. He
came into Spivey's cubicle and said, "Harry, I already
told you I'm not—"

"Melvin Pure," Spivey interrupted, "meet Detectives Madison and Frizell, DPD."

Pure visibly sagged. He sat on a hard-backed sofa
against the wall.

"They're not here," Spivey continued, "in connection with any theft charges. They're here about a
murder."

"Jesus. Whose murder? I already said I had nothing
to do with those missing caps, and I'm sticking to it."

Madison was afraid that this conversation could go
on until daybreak. She said, "Let's try starting on
square one. Instead of you guys pointing the finger at
each other, just tell us what happened. We'll decide
what's important to us."

Pure and Spivey looked at each other.

Spivey said, "Okay. We picked up the shipment
from Haver Labs bound for Midland. Procedure here
is, we deliver the goods and get a receipt. The receipt
goes into a file. Unless somebody questions the deal,
that's the end of it. On this shipment, nobody said a
word about the materials being missing until last Fri-
day. When I got the call from Haver Labs I went
straight to the delivery ticket file. For this shipment
there was none. That's when I got Melvin Pure here
to start running the shipment down."

"Which isn't really my job," Pure said. "Account-
ing's supposed to keep up with this kind of shit."

"Yeah," Spivey said, "but with the instructions we
had . . ."

"Not my instructions," Pure said. "The only orders I got were to find the fucking porcelain. Which I did. You're not putting it off on me, Spivey."

Eddie Frizell looked first at Spivey, then at Pure, and back again. "Tell you what," the detective said, "how about we just ride both of you downtown to talk about it?"

Pure intertwined his fingers in his lap and watched the floor. Spivey nervously carried his cup to the Mr. Coffee and filled the cup with hot liquid.

"We got no more time to waste, guys," Frizell said. "While you two are accusing each other, we might have more people getting dead. So once and for all. What happened with those?" He pointed at the stack of boxes.

Spivey paused halfway between the coffeepot and his desk. "As soon as we found out there'd been a screwup, I got a hold of our Midland-Odessa driver. According to him the stuff never went on his truck. I checked on our warehouse receipt, and the guy was telling the truth. All I could assume was that the porcelain disappeared somewhere on our dock, before it went into the truck. Melvin Pure here supervises the stackers, so that's when I called him in."

Pure looked up from his floor survey. "And that's when I did what I'm supposed to do. I started a search. There was a hangup because my worker who was supposed to load that freight ain't here. He's called in sick today. So I had to do it on my own. The boxes were in bay 14, which is where we put freight we can't identify—you know, the bill of lading has fallen off or something. They weren't hard to locate. As soon as I found 'em I brought 'em in here. They're in exactly the shape I found 'em in."

Madison got up and went over to the boxes. "With this one box partway open?"

"Yeah, right," Pure said. "I was told to find the

freight. I did it. All that's missing is two cartons out of that top box. Thirty fucking dental caps. Why somebody wanted them I got no idea. The rest of it I've got nothing to do with."

Frizell looked back and forth between the freight men like a spectator at a tennis match. Frizell said, "The rest of what?"

"Hold it." Madison sat bolt upright. "You say the worker who was supposed to load that freight isn't here?"

"Yeah," Pure said. "Name is Harold Bays. Now that's one guy you ought to be looking at."

"Oh? Why is that?"

" ' Cause he's a crazy-acting son of a bitch. If it was up to me, he'd, ah, been gone a long time ago."

Madison leaned forward and rested her forearms on her thighs. "Crazy-acting how?"

"Just you know, crazy-acting. Lives up inside a trailer like he's a caveman. Won't talk to nobody. Guy gives everybody around here the quivers."

"None of which is illegal." Madison looked at Spivey. "You folks keep a photo directory of employees?"

"Everybody's got a picture ID. HR keeps one on file."

"Great," Madison said. She produced a pad and pen, wrote down, HAROLD BAYS, then looked up. "We'll need Mr. Bays' photo chop-chop."

"I'll call for it," Spivey said. He picked up the phone. "Bays is a nutty-acting character, all right." He punched in an extension and waited.

While Spivey requested the missing worker's ID from his human resources department, Frizell asked Melvin Pure, "You keep your employees' time card records?"

Pure nodded. His expression was vacant. The man was obviously scared to death.

"Good," Frizell said. "We'll need this guy's in-and-out times over the past twelve months. How long would that take?"

"I've got the last thirty days' time cards here on the dock. The rest would be in payroll."

"I don't guess I'd have to put on much pressure to prioritize that procedure, would I?" Frizell said.

"As soon as Spivey's off the phone, the records are all yours."

"Good. We'll wait for 'em." Frizell turned to Spivey, who had just hung up from HR. "What's our time frame?" Frizell said.

"They're shooting a copy of Bays' picture ID and messengering it up here. Five, ten minutes."

"A-okay," Frizell said. "Your turn, Mr. Pure."

Pure stepped around Spivey and picked up the phone. "Sometimes payroll's a little slow," Pure said.

Frizell showed a buddy-buddy grin. "Well, Melvin, I'll tell you. We're depending on you to see that this time they're a little fast. As in, if they don't get Mr. Bays' records up here in the next ten minutes they're going to have a couple of cops helping them, if you get my drift."

"Reading you loud and clear." Pure didn't require much convincing. He held the receiver against his ear and quickly punched a number into the keypad.

Frizell turned to Madison. "Jinxie, I guess you and me can wait outside. Keep out of these guys' hair so they can perform for us." He got up and stepped toward the exit.

Madison held her position, seated on the edge of Spivey's desk. "We're forgetting something, Eddie," Madison said.

Frizell frowned in thought. "Yeah? What's that?"

"Well, before we got all this cooperation," Madison said, "Mr. Pure and Mr. Spivey were arguing about

who told who to do what. I think I'd like to find out
what that was all about."

Frizell sat back down. Both cops looked at Pure
and Spivey.

Apparently the payroll department had put Pure on
hold. He held the receiver away and said, "I already
told you, I got nothing to do with that."

Madison smiled at Spivey. "I guess that leaves
you, sir."

Spivey took a deep breath. "Jesus Christ."

Neither detective said anything. Pure now had
someone on the line, and spoke softly into the
mouthpiece.

Spivey said, "I can lose my job."

Frizell settled back in his chair. "Last time I checked,
the county jail isn't letting anybody loose on work
release. So where you could be going, you wouldn't
need any job."

Spivey looked at the ceiling.

Madison tried some diplomacy. "How about if we
promise that it goes no further than here."

"No good," Spivey said. "No one knows this but
me. If it gets out to anyone, the guy's going to know
where the information came from."

Madison arched an eyebrow. "What information is
that, Mr. Spivey?"

"Who the orders came from, to keep the lid on
this business."

"Well, since you put it that way," Madison said,
"let me alter what I just said. Even if we might broadcast what you tell us over the radio, you'd best begin
talking, say, within the next five seconds or so."

Pure hung up the phone. "Bays' payroll records are
on the way. Am I finished here?"

"Sure," Frizell said. "As soon as Mr. Spivey tells us
what we want to know."

Pure returned to sit on the sofa.

Spivey said, "Sweet Jesus."

Madison glanced at Frizell. Frizell said, "Well if *Sweet Jesus* gave the orders, I guess we're screwed. Come on, Mr. Spivey, we got no more time to fart around."

Spivey seemed resigned. "You've got to understand. If Mr. Hargis gives the word, well . . ." He feigned cutting his own throat with his flattened hand. "No more me, at least not at this job."

The two cops gaped at each other. Madison said, "Mister *who*?"

"Hargis," Spivey said.

"That wouldn't be William Hargis Jr., would it?"

Spivey's surprise was obviously real. "How could you possibly know that? Billy Hargis' name appears nowhere on our organizational chart."

Madison shrugged with her hands. "So how does he manage to give orders?"

Spivey sighed in resignation. "This company's been in the Hargis family from day one of its existence. They've never been active in management, but they still control over fifty percent. Enough that, when Hargis speaks, we listen."

"And he knew about the missing porcelain how?"

"He called and asked about it. Out of the blue last Thursday. Said he knew there might be a problem with a shipment, and he wanted me to keep him up to date. When the problem came up I notified him, and he instructed me to keep those boxes in my office and tell no one unless he gave the okay. But Jesus, a murder investigation . . ." Spivey trailed helplessly off.

"Right," Madison said. "A *big* murder investigation. So if there's anything else you should be telling us, it'd be better to tell us now."

Spivey wrung his hands and looked to Melvin Pure.

Pure raised up, scratched his thigh, then sank back down on the couch. "Harold Bays is his yard man," Pure finally said.

Madison's gaze snapped back to Spivey. "Puts you right in the middle," she said.

Spivey's tone went up an octave. "Jesus, not *my* yard man. Listen, most of this stuff isn't IRS kosher, but for years the Hargis family's been using crews from here to do private work at their houses. Yards, general repair, you name it. The company's paying the people, but they're really over at one of the Hargises' clearing brush, cutting hedges, you know. It's a rich man's perk, what can I tell you?

"About seven or eight months ago," Spivey went on, "Harold Bays went out to do some work for Mr. Billy Hargis on a Saturday, cost us overtime. Now you'd never understand why those two would hit it off, Bays is such an unpredictable asshole, but they did. Around here you ask Bays to do something, he's liable to tell you to shove it, but Billy Hargis fell in love with the guy. From then on, every week, Hargis demanded yard service. And Harold Bays was the only employee he was interested in. Some days we had nobody to cover the Midland-Odessa hole, but you think Billy Hargis gave a shit? Hell, no, it was Harold Bays or nobody." He leaned back and mopped his forehead. "Listen, can we keep this on the QT? No fooling, anybody finds out I told, Jesus, I'll be pounding the pavement, and at my age . . ."

Madison had noticed something going on out on the loading dock. She got up, skirted Spivey's desk, and stood with hands on hips looking out the window. "Mr. Spivey, we're on the QT if you can give us one more thing."

Spivey shrugged. "I've already put my life in your hands. What else can I do?"

Madison pointed outside. "What's that guy doing?"

Spivey stood and looked out along with her. Over near the edge of the dock, a muscular shirtless man was pouring a powdery substance from a keg into a fifty-gallon barrel. As he lifted the keg, his lats rippled with the effort.

Madison said, "The *Sixteen Tons*-looking guy. What's he doing?"

Spivey massaged the back of his neck. "He's filling the resin barrel. So the people can dip in for some, to get a better grip. Some of those cartons are slippery as hell."

Frizell rose and moved up next to his partner. He was excited. "Like, the same stuff that used to be in a bag by the pitcher's mound?"

"I think the major leagues ruled it illegal, like tricking up the ball some way," Spivey said. "But, yeah, that's what it is."

Madison gave Frizell a great big grin. Then she turned, threw her arms around Spivey's neck, and gave the man a great big hug. Spivey looked as if he couldn't decide whether to relax and enjoy it or defend himself.

"You don't know it, Mr. Spivey," Madison said. "But before this is over we could be seeing each other sort of regular. And don't be so glum about it. The blacker the berry, the sweeter the juice, you know?"

Fifteen minutes later Jinx Madison hotfooted it across the Texas Motor Freight parking lot with Eddie Frizell in close pursuit. Frizell had Harold Bays' picture ID which showed a scowling, slope-shouldered man with thinning hair and a scar on his cheek. Madison carried Bays' time-card records. With her free hand she fiddled with her cell phone, and punched in Gholer's number.

After five rings, Madison got Gholer's voice mail.

She waited for the beep, then, as she came abreast of the city-owned Mercury Sable, stopped and lowered her head. "Loo? Loo? Come on, pick up, will you? Jesus, Loo, we've got the fucking guy."

17

Lately, Harold Bays had ranged a long way from his farm in Seagoville in search of suitable humans. His early kills had been close to home; escapees from the penitentiary right down the road, a schoolgirl from Wilmer practically next door. One day he'd read a quote in the *Dallas Morning News,* from an important detective named Lieutenant Gholer, that serial killers generally stuck to a certain area. Harold thought that Gholer must know what he was talking about, so after that he'd changed his pattern and started taking his victims from fifteen or twenty miles away. Harold Bays knew every section of North Texas and even had most of the back roads committed to memory. As the time for the Change grew closer and closer, Harold grew smarter and smarter. The worker spiders were dumbbells; once Harold had undergone the transformation he would be second in command only to Her. He was sure of it.

Today he took I-45 all the way north to the LBJ Freeway. His forehead creased in thought as he approached the cloverleaf access leading onto LBJ.

LBJ. Lyndon Baines Johnson.

Harold smiled, proud that he could remember.

History class, sixth grade, just before he'd murdered

the girl for laughing at him, and then had gone to live in the reformatory.

Lyndon Baines Johnson had become president after Lee H. Oswald had killed John Fitzgerald Kennedy.

John Fitzgerald Kennedy was from Massachusetts.

Lyndon Baines Johnson was from Texas, and had lakes, highways, and all kinds of other shit named for him. Since childhood Harold had heard men say that LBJ was a crooked politician, had stuffed ballot boxes, pulled all kinds of crap to get elected.

Harold didn't believe the stories. He thought that if LBJ had been dishonest, the people never would have voted for him for president. For America was founded on the principle of equality. Of the people, by the people, for the people.

Whatever else he might be, Harold Bays wasn't dumb. He'd been pretty smart in school, in fact, and might even have made a B in history if he hadn't murdered the girl.

Murdering the girl had really fucked up his education. After that, they'd sent him away.

Once the Change was complete, no one would send Harold away ever again.

He went west on the LBJ Freeway and exited at Preston, and stayed on the access in front of Valley View Mall. The mall was a monstrous two-level affair covering four full city blocks, and housed a Sears where Harold had once bought a pair of coveralls that he'd disposed of after he'd hung Carla Ruth Rabinowitz from a bridge.

It was important for Harold to remember that kind of shit.

Behind the mall on the other side of Alpha Road sat row after row of apartment houses, once upscale singles' places with pools and patios where lawyers, bankers, and stockbrokers had lived. The swimming

pools were still there but the high-stylers had long fled
the neighborhood; within the past decade the feds had
changed the renting rules, and there were no more
specified areas for government-subsidized housing.
Today, any apartment owner who'd gotten financing
from federally insured lenders (and what owners
hadn't, if they dealt with a bank or savings and loan?)
had to rent to anyone who qualified for government
assistance through a system of vouchers.

But Harold Bays didn't know anything about vouchers, federal assistance, or the history of apartment
houses. Harold knew only that he'd driven through
the complexes behind Valley View Mall several times,
and that he'd seen dark-skinned women on the sidewalks he thought were whores. One had even tried to
flag him down, but there had been a man chained up
in the pickup's bed at the time, and Harold had been
in a hurry.

Harold entered the mall parking lot and cruised up
and down between the cars.

On the rear portion of the lot, hidden from the
freeway in between Foley's and JC Penny's, a black
ten-year-old Bronco was parked ten or eleven spaces
from the nearest vehicle. Harold looked around, saw
no one coming, and then pulled his maroon-and-white
pickup alongside the Bronco. He got out, a strong
wind whipping and molding his pants against his legs,
and peered inside at the Bronco's front seat.

On the console was a window envelope with the
return address of McDonald's, Valley View Mall. It
was the same kind of envelope in which Melvin Pure
delivered the paychecks at the TMF loading dock.

The owner of the Bronco must work for McDonald's. Harold pictured the golden arches and smiled.

He went back to his pickup, rolled his ski mask on
over his head until it stopped just above his ears,
jammed his Rangers batting helmet over the stocking

cap, and returned to the Bronco carrying a flat metal
bar, two feet long with a hook on one end, along with
his .45. He checked this way and that, shoved the bar
down between the Bronco's window and door, and
used the hook to jimmy the lock. He got behind the
wheel and hid his gun under the driver's seat. The
metal bar was pointed on one end. He used the point
to pop the key assembly out of the steering column
and hot-wired the ignition.

Five minutes later Harold piloted the Bronco out
the rear parking-lot exit. He'd had trouble getting
used to the vehicle. The transmission was a five-speed
with a clutch, which Harold wasn't used to driving,
and his initial efforts were pretty much pop-the-clutch,
lurch, curse while the motor rattled and died, start the
engine, and go again. By the time he'd gone a hundred
yards he thought he had the hang of it.

He found a side street skirting one of the complexes, and parked the Bronco behind a storage building out of sight from the apartment windows. Then,
taking his time and being casual about it, he made the
ten-minute walk back to the mall parking lot and fired
up his pickup. He drove back to the side street and
left the pickup a few feet behind the Bronco. He got
out, looked, and frowned. The pickup's rear bumper
stuck out a few feet beyond the end of the storage
building.

Harold read his Aggie Twelfth Man bumper sticker
and his frown turned into a cunning grin. People who
noticed the pickup sticking out would just think, typical Aggie, didn't know how the fuck he was supposed
to park.

Since he'd bought the truck, Harold had heard a
lot of Aggie jokes. He thought some of them were
pretty funny.

He went back to the Bronco, got in, and drove off
down the road.

Harold Bays was smart. If any vice cops were hanging around where the whores went on parade, taking down license numbers, they'd next be looking for the Bronco's owner working at McDonald's.

Harold was more than ready for the Change. His spirits were on the upswing since he'd angrily buried Sis Hargis behind the shed and taken a tongue-lashing from the Spider Queen. The injection of venom mixed with body fluids coursing through his veins had restored his confidence. With a fearsome buzzing noise emitting from his mouth, Harold Bays drove around and among the pawn shops, convenience stores, and apartment buildings, trolling for a whore with dark-colored skin.

Roshonda Morgan wasn't no street ho, no way, just a *sometime* ho, depending on whether her boyfriend decided to get his ass out and find a job. Which didn't happen very often, and when it did, he couldn't get hired because every place where he applied tested for drugs. Roshonda was tired of the bullshit and had told him just that morning, "I ain't gonna be yo' ho no mo'."

Which didn't help her much at the moment because she didn't have any money, there was no food in the apartment, and she and her boyfriend were down to their last three rocks of crack cocaine. Hard, hard times. So hard that she'd gotten up before noon, bathed, put on her best mesh stockings and a tight leather skirt she'd shoplifted from the Sears in Valley View Mall, and gotten out hustling to put some bread together. She used her best bring-it-on strut and finger-popping gait, her ankles wobbling slightly in platform heels as she sashayed along, black sequined purse dangling from her forearm, her bottom plump, ready for the dudes to *ride,* sugar. No two ways about it, Roshonda be lookin' *good.*

Problem was, there hadn't been any customers. One old dude all day long was all, and white-assed Priscilla up the block had gotten to the guy before he could drive down to the corner where Roshonda strolled. Damn wind was blowing and messing with her hair. Her legs were getting tired. She'd give it another hour, and then she'd have to settle for going on down to the Quickway. The convenience store's manager was named Rasheed, some kind of sand nigger, and was always good for some French bread, a couple of slabs of cheddar cheese, and a liter of Coke in exchange for a blow job. Rasheed never had any money but knew a way to fix the register tape, balance out the inventory to fool his employers. Roshonda was really desperate. It had been a month or more since she'd stooped to blowing Rasheed.

Her body sagged in dejection. She didn't think she could make it another hour. Strutting her stuff on this deserted patch of street was messing with her head. She'd have to settle for Rasheed after all, then hurry back to the apartment, hide the rocks of crack from her boyfriend, maybe smoke them all herself. Serve his sorry ass right to do without, make him have to get a job. She turned on her heel and fast-stepped up the street in the direction of the convenience store.

And just as she did, a Ford Bronco came around the corner with a white man driving. A really weird-looking dude, peering out from under the brim of a Texas Rangers batting helmet, looking her up and down. Driving slow. Downshifting into a lower gear, the Bronco lurching some as it passed Roshonda and turned the corner in front of her. She waved. The dude caught her signal, and nodded his head as he disappeared from view behind an apartment building.

The man would circle the block, and would pass this way again in a couple of minutes.

Fuck Rasheed, his loaves of bread, and his moldyassed cheese. Roshonda was about to make herself a *score*.

She went over to the curb and made herself present-able, wiggling as she straightened her skirt around her hips and thighs. This funny-looking white dude was just the type to be a money machine; thick-necked, slope shouldered, and with a scar on his face. Ros-honda had been a sometime streetwalker for long enough to spot them; she'd long ago given up ex-pecting any Denzel Washingtons to be trolling for a ho. She thought about fixing her makeup, and even reached inside her purse and touched her compact.

No time. The dude in the Bronco was coming around the corner again.

Roshonda let her purse dangle from her forearm. As the Bronco pulled to a stop and the window came sliding down, she pulled her windblown hair off to the side, out of her face. "Whatcha lookin' for, baby?"

The man had big expressionless eyes. The scar on his cheek was slightly red. He said, "Get in."

Roshonda leaned her hip against the door. "Well, now, I gotta ax ya. You ain't no *po*-leece now."

"No."

"Well, what you got in mind?"

"I want to fuck you." The dude's lips twisted sort of funny, as if he didn't like saying the words.

A warning bell went off in Roshonda's head. Rasheed and his bread and cheese all of a sudden didn't seem so bad. She said, cautiously, "Cost you a hundred."

The dude never batted an eye. "I'll pay what you want."

That pretty well did it where Roshonda was con-cerned; she normally started at twenty dollars and worked up, depending on what she had to do to earn the money. So the dude was a little strange. Shee-it, they were all a little strange. "I got a place," she said.

"Is anybody there?"

"Jes' my boyfriend, but he asleep. He don't be bother-in' us none."

"Well, get in, then." The dude adjusted his batting helmet and sat up straighter behind the wheel.

Looking both ways in search of cops, Roshonda jiggled around streetside and opened the passenger door. She leaned in. "You sure you ain't no *po*-leece now?"

The man never looked at her. "No."

Roshonda climbed in and slammed the door behind her. "Well, what are we waitin' for, baby? My place is right on up there."

Roshonda concentrated so hard on directing the man into the correct driveway that she forgot to pay attention to what he was doing. Her face pressed close to the passenger window, she looked for the yellow Dumpster that marked the entry into her complex. She said, "You gotta make a right here, baby," then leaned back and waited for the guy to make the turn.

The Bronco kept going and picked up speed.

Roshonda looked at the driver and thumbed over her shoulder. "You missed it, baby, it's right back—"

The words stuck in her throat. While Roshonda had been giving directions, the man had removed his Rangers batting helmet and pulled a mask down over his face. The mask had eye and mouth holes. He'd slipped on latex surgeon's gloves. He reached down between his feet and came up holding a pistol.

Roshonda's eyes flew wide open. She cringed against the door. "Oh lawdy-lawd."

The man pointed the gun at her and floored the accelerator, whipping the wheel to the left as he steered the Bronco, tires squealing, onto the road that ran behind Valley View Mall. Roshonda watched curb and parking lot entries flash past in a blur. The mall lot looked to be about a third full, all the cars parked up close to the building, at least two hundred yards away from the street. The road ahead was clear of traffic, and there was no one standing in front of the apartment buildings on her left. Roshonda was all alone with a crazy-assed maniac.

But though her windpipe felt clogged and her fingers trembled, Roshonda wasn't as frightened as she might have been. She'd been in these situations before—all street hos and most *sometime* hos had run into dudes with more than just sex on their minds. It was part of the life. And part of the life was in being ready. And along with the rest of her streetwalking sisters, Roshonda kept up on current events; *especially* those events that dealt with serial killers who picked up people and then set spiders loose to bite the shit out of them. And even as the Bronco sped along behind the mall, Roshonda thought, *This be the mothafuckah right here.*

There would be no begging off with this man, no giving up of the goodies at no charge. If Roshonda didn't do something, she was fucking dead.

Inside her purse, nestled down among her compact, her Jasmine perfume bottle, her condoms and her nail clippers, was a straight razor with tape around the handle. And though she'd never actually cut anyone, she'd had to threaten a few dudes, and kept the razor stropped so that it would shave hair off her arm.

Roshonda continued to make horrific gurgling noises, but she wasn't near as frightened as she sounded. She kept her gaze riveted on the hand that held the gun. Her own clenched fist found its way inside her handbag, relaxed, and then wrapped its fingers around the razor's handle.

The Bronco steamed up Montfort Drive, the driver braking, swinging the wheel to the right, making an arc in preparation for turning left up into Valley View

Mall. The transmission was a five-speed. In order to negotiate the turn, he'd have to downshift. When he did, he'd have to use his gun hand.

Roshonda sat stock-still, waiting for her chance.

The Fiddleback braked again. His left foot pushed the clutch to the floor. His right hand reached for the gearshift, his palm pressing the lever down and to the left as his fingers loosely gripped the pistol. For just an instant the barrel pointed at the floorboard.

Roshonda moved like a whippet. As fast as thought, her hand came out of her purse with the razor. She slashed upward, aiming for the arteries in his wrist. She missed her mark by an inch or so. The blade sliced through his rubber glove and into the fleshy part of his hand.

The Fiddleback yelled bloody murder. As he spread his fingers and blood poured from his palm, the pistol rattled to the floor. He grabbed his wrist and let go of the steering wheel.

The Bronco jumped the curb and rammed into a light pole fronting the mall parking lot. The Fiddleback's forehead banged into the steering wheel and Roshonda slammed against the dashboard. The Bronco rocked on its springs, recoiled from the collision, and came to a halt. The impact had mashed in the grille. Steam jetted from the radiator.

For a heartbeat, Roshonda and the Fiddleback stared at each other.

And then they both dove for the gun. Roshonda got lucky. The gearshift lever was between the Fiddleback and the pistol. His hand bumped the lever and he yelled in pain. Roshonda came off the floor with the .45 leveled at his face.

The Fiddleback's eyes widened behind the ski mask holes, and spittle ran out of his mouth to wet the dark blue wool.

Roshonda's shoulder ached where she'd hit the dashboard, but otherwise she was okay. All in all, she felt pretty strong. And pretty proud of herself.

And pretty pissed off at this dude who'd just been going to kill her, and her just going about her business, trying to scrape some bread together. Which reminded her that she was still just as broke as when she'd left her apartment. Which pissed her off even more.

"Now look," the Fiddleback said hoarsely.

Roshonda looked down at the gun, then back at the Fiddleback. She grinned. "Gimme yo' money," she said.

The Fiddleback gaped in shock. "Huh?"

Roshonda, now in control, pressed the pistol barrel against the ski mask. "I said, gimme yo' money, you white-assed mothafuckah. Right fuckin' now."

The Fiddleback looked as if he couldn't figure out what was going on. Just seconds ago he'd had her, had been going to set the spiders on her ass, shoot her, then string her up from a bridge or telephone pole. Now here she was, robbing him.

The more she thought about it, the more Roshonda liked the idea of holding up this asshole. She eased back the hammer with a soft *click-click.*

Suddenly, a block behind them, a siren pealed. Roshonda looked back over her shoulder. Around the corner came a DPD squad car with flashers flashing.

Roshonda was furious. She wasn't going to score any money. She wasn't going to score any dope. She wasn't going to score a fucking thing. She wasn't even going to get to shoot the Fiddleback. In the wink of an eye, her big moment had turned to shit.

As the police vehicle approached, the Fiddleback looked out the back window as well. His body sagged. He seemed to forget all about Roshonda, all about the fact that she was holding the gun. He made a

weird hissing sound. Slowly, deliberately, he unfast-
ened his seat belt. He pulled on the handle and shouldered open the door.

The fuck is he doing? Roshhonda thought. The dude
was ignoring a gun stuck in his face. She said, "You
ain't goin' nowhere."

He didn't act as if he heard her. He got out of the
Bronco and, as Roshonda sat with the gun trained on
him, skirted the hood, hopped over the curb, and
loped across the parking lot toward Valley View Mall.
Though he limped as he ran, he picked up speed. He
yanked off his ski mask and cast it aside.

Roshonda was too stunned to move. She looked in
disbelief at the gun. Was the motherfucking pistol
carved out of soap or something? She looked once
more over her shoulder as the cop car pulled to the
curb.

And realized that she herself might be in a world
of hurt. Sitting here in this strange car holding a gun.
Wearing her hooker's clothes. A bloody straight razor
on the floor.

Roshonda all at once agreed with the guy who was
running across the parking lot. The Fiddleback had a
point. Hauling ass was a pretty good idea. She wished
that she'd thought of it herself.

Roshonda leaped out of the Bronco and took off in
pursuit of the Fiddleback. She tore her mesh stockings
on the Bronco's door. She kicked out of her platform
shoes and ran in her stockinged feet, waving the gun
in front of her. The Fiddleback's fast-retreating backside neared the entrance to the mall. As Roshonda
watched, he ducked around two women who'd just
come out carrying shopping bags.

"You stop yo' ass, you mothafuckah!" Roshonda
screamed. "You ain't leavin' me for no *po*-leece. You
stop yo' runnin', right fuckin' there." And to make

her point she pulled the trigger and fired a shot at the sky. The noise in the still warm air was like a cannon's boom.

The two DPD patrolmen who'd just driven up in the squad car were named Rayford Bond and Melissa Raker, and they'd been lovers and partners for the better part of a year. Bond was a big-shouldered man going to flab around the middle, and Raker was a thin woman nearly six feet tall with braces on her teeth. Both were married, though not to each other. They thought that their extramarital carrying on affected neither their marriage nor their jobs, though their spouses and employers might have disagreed if they'd known about it.

The two had been traveling north on Montfort Drive when they got the call from the 911 dispatcher. A man standing inside Valley View Mall had witnessed an accident and reported, via his cell phone, some kind of black SUV in a collision with a light pole in the parking lot. The witness couldn't tell if there were injuries, but the vehicle appeared disabled and there was steam coming out of the radiator. An instant later the 911 operator had contacted Raker and Bond.

The duo called for a fire truck, a tow truck, and an ambulance, switched on their flashers and siren, and whipped from Montfort Drive onto the street that ran across the back of the mall. The wrecked Bronco was in plain view, a couple of hundred yards ahead with its grille caved in. The officers discussed procedure. First they'd inquire about injuries. If the passengers weren't seriously hurt, Bond would surround the vehicle with traffic cones while Raker directed approaching autos to detour while the tow truck did its work. Routine deal. Piece of cake. An hour, more or less, and the ambulance and fire truck would be gone along with the wrecker and Bronco. Fill out reports, possibly have time to drop by a motel for a quickie on the way to turn the squad car in to the motor pool As the cops drew near to the scene of the accident, Bond squeezed Raker's leg in anticipation.

And now, this shit.

A black female in a skin-tight leather skirt fleeing the scene of the accident, kicking off her shoes, running toward the shopping mall firing a weapon into the air. Waving her arms, screaming. Mall customers in the parking lot shrinking back, running for cover.

Possible psycho.

Raker called for backup. The dispatcher asked what kind; ambulance, tow, or fire truck? Raker said none of the above, she wanted another squad car. The dispatcher asked her why, and said there was no report of any disturbance, only a traffic accident. Raker told the dispatcher to get more fucking cops, double quick, and disconnected.

Bond was already out of the squad car, running crouched in a zigzag pattern after the woman in the leather skirt. Raker hopped to and ran after her partner, yelling for him to stop. The officers conferred, then split apart and approached the crazy-acting woman from opposite sides. They caught up with her twenty yards short of the mall entry. The police took cover, Bond behind an Acura Legend and Raker behind a Chevrolet Monte Carlo. In the distance, a second siren wailed.

The female suspect seemed out of breath. She was walking now, the gun hanging at her side. She didn't seem to notice the officers.

At a signal from Raker, Bond called out, "Police! Stop right there!" He had his weapon trained over the Acura's hood.

The woman halted in her tracks. She took a step toward Officer Bond, then staggered off in the opposite direction.

Now Raker raised up from behind the Monte Carlo. "Stop there, ma'am. Put the pistol on the ground."

The woman's features twisted in surprise. Caught in between the patrolmen, she lurched away back in the direction from which she'd come. Bond came out from behind the Acura, aiming his service revolver. The woman tossed her own pistol away and thrust her hands skyward. "Y'all done surrounded me. I give up."

Down in the street, a black-and-white parked alongside Raker and Bond's vehicle. Two more cops got out and dashed across the lot toward the mall.

Raker ran her finger over her braces as she approached the woman. Raker reached for handcuffs. "What's your name, ma'am?" the policewoman asked.

"Roshonda. You 'restin' me?"

"Yes, ma'am. You discharged a weapon, for starters." Raker slipped a bracelet on one of Roshonda's wrists and drew Roshonda's other arm around behind her.

"I was chasin' the Fiddleback." Roshonda seemed resigned.

Now Bond walked up, and stood by while Raker gave the suspect her rights. The two reinforcements thundered up, both men. They stopped nearby and folded their arms.

"You never heard of no Fiddleback?" Roshonda said.

One of the newcomers smirked. "I heard of Batman. And Superman. But I 'spect you've been chasing the Dope Man, am I right?" He stuck a pencil in the barrel of Roshonda's discarded pistol, and raised the weapon off the ground. "We've handled Roshonda here a time or two, guys. First time I ever seen her armed this way. It's always been a razor before."

Roshonda stood stiff, her hands cuffed behind her. "I ain't tellin' no lie. The dude just run off into that mall, an' y'all are arrestin' *me*. He the dude been doin' all that killin an' shit."

The new-cop-on-the-scene introduced himself to Raker and Bond as Officer Dunham. He held the pistol, butt in the air, suspended on the pencil. "Where'd you get this gun, Roshonda?"

"Got it offa that Fiddleback."

"And how'd you happen to know him?"

She seemed stumped. Finally she said, "Dude gimme a ride. Tried to take me off someplace."

Dunham checked out Roshonda's skirt. "And you were on your way where?"

"Just doin' my thing, you know."

Bond and Raker stood on either side of the prisoner. Bond said, snickering, "And your thing is what?"

"Just, you know. You standin' here, he's gettin' away while y'all dissin' me."

Raker tugged on the flashlight suspended from her belt. "Now, why would we diss you, Roshonda? You're running around high, shooting off a gun . . ."

"Ain't had no dope! You don't believe me, just look down there." She jerked her head toward the street where the wrecked Bronco sat along with the police vehicles.

Raker followed Roshonda's direction. The lady cop said, "Down where?"

"Dude was wearin' a ski mask. He done dropped it."

Raker looked to Dunham. "Might ought to check it out," she said.

Dunham strolled toward the front of the lot, looking along the ground. Halfway to the street he paused, leaned over, and picked something up. He returned with a hunk of blue wool cloth in one hand and Roshonda's pistol, still suspended on the pencil, in the other.

Dunham looked around at the group. He held up his left hand, said, "One ski mask," then held up the other and said, "One S&W .45 semi-automatic." He looked thoughtful. "We've got fliers on this Fiddleback creep, saying to be on the lookout for a .22 or a .45. What do you think, folks? You think our girl Roshonda might have something here?"

The cops stood around Roshonda in a semicircle. Tension spread through the group. Finally, Bond said, "I don't think we've got a choice. I think if the odds are one in a million, we'd still better get these mall exits covered. Case as big as this one, I don't want to be the one caught standing around making whore jokes while the guy's right under our noses. 'Pears to me, that wouldn't set too well."

Harold Bays entered the wide corridor inside the mall. In here it was much quieter, with no one shooting, with no one yelling for him to stop.

The whore had been screaming something just before he'd heard the gunshot. The explosion had scared the shit out of him.

Jesus Christ, the nigger had cut him almost to the bone. He *hated* the goddamned whore.

His surroundings barely registered on him: Isaac's ahead on his left, U.S. Postal Service on his right, Kay Bee Toy & Hobby straight ahead. He stepped-and-dragged along, gasping for breath. He jammed his injured hand under the opposite armpit and kept pressure on his wound by flexing his bicep against his side. His skin was damp where blood had seeped through the cloth.

His injury didn't matter. The only thing that mattered was escape.

And how She would react to his failure. His failure mattered more than his escape, and because of his failure he had endangered the Change. He didn't have a suitable human to take to her.

Harold was in deep despair. Maybe the worker spiders were right. Maybe Harold Bays was a deformed asshole who'd never amount to shit. Maybe he wasn't worthy of the Change after all.

And if he wasn't, the Queen would deny him. And if the Change was never to come to pass, Harold would as soon be dead.

Spittle ran from the corner of his mouth and his vision blurred. He glanced fearfully over his shoulder at the entrance through which he'd just passed, in search of the whore who now had his gun. She'd already shot at him. He thought that at any second she might come running through the door and begin firing again. Harold would watch for her; anyone, even a whore, who carried a gun was dangerous.

He needed to keep up with that kind of shit. Who was and wasn't dangerous.

Who did he have to fear besides the whore?

The police. Yeah, sure, uniformed cops had stood in the path of the Change ever since day one. They would come bursting into the mall behind the black woman. The fucking whore. The black whore and the police, in search of Harold Bays.

Jesus, he hated being here in this shopping mall. He wished he was back at the farm, where he could find his way through the semidarkness blindfolded. On his own turf he could put the cops and the whore inside the special room, chain them up, let the workers loose, massage his erection while the spiders bit and bit, and then loose his semen in order to please the Queen.

But first things first. If he ever wanted to see the Queen again, he had to escape from this shopping mall. He rounded a corner and staggered on.

He followed the corridor around to the left, toward

the food court where men and women clustered around McDonald's, Sonic, Mrs. Boston's Chocolate Chip Cookies, Johnny Wok's Chinese.

He had some money in his pocket now. Seventeen . . . no, eighteen dollars; he'd slipped four extra quarters in his pocket in case he needed to use the tollway. He might go to Mrs. Boston's in the food court, buy a dozen fresh warm cookies and sit at a table. Eat them all, watch the shoppers stroll by. Glance at the women's legs . . .

No. Can't stop. Can't rest.

What was he thinking of? He had to get the fuck away from here and go about preparing for the Change.

Harold shut his eyes to rid his mind of the cookies. He concentrated on Valley View Mall. Even though the close-by neighborhood where he'd picked up the whore was going to shit, the mall itself remained an upscale place to shop, and somehow the condition of the area made things better for him. Better because Valley View Mall was jam-packed with customers, and the police weren't likely to be shooting off guns in here. And because it was easy for Harold Bays, wounded hand and all, to blend in with the rest of the shoppers. The corridor in which he stood teemed with business; four women chatting gaily and one man with a newspaper walked by, and they didn't so much as glance at him. Seen through a window inside some unoccupied space, two women talked with a man who was likely a leasing agent. None of the trio looked Harold's way. How could they not fucking notice him?

He wondered if he might be invisible.

He thought sometimes that becoming invisible would be part of the Change. In Harold's mind the Change was sort of a fucked-up version of heaven; until you'd been there, you didn't really know what it would be like. There had been a teacher in the reformatory who talked about heaven all the time. Harold would like to set the spiders on her.

He forced the Bible-spouting teacher out of his mind. He had to move on. He shuffled his way east inside the mall.

There were signs ahead, suspended from the ceiling, pointing the way to employees-only restrooms. He followed the signs.

In the restroom there would be running water, paper towels and crap. He could make a bandage to soak up the blood. Use wadded paper towels as a compress and stop the bleeding altogether, so that telltale blood would not attract attention. He could then get away, find his pickup truck, and return to the safety of the farm.

And the anger of the Queen.

No. *Bullshit.* Harold would find a way to please the Queen. But first he must find his way to Her.

Harold cheered up a little bit. He was now using his mind to better advantage.

He ducked down a long narrow corridor with broom closets on either side, and entered the men's room. He went into a stall, locked the door, undid his coveralls, sat on the toilet, stripped off his sliced-through latex glove, and examined his wound.

The cut was a half-inch deep, but hadn't hit a vein, and the bleeding had slowed considerably. Harold opened and closed his hand. His grip was firm and strong. He wadded toilet paper and covered the laceration, buttoned up his clothes, left the stall, went to the sink and turned on the water. He took the toilet paper away from his wound and held his hand under the faucet, washing the blood down the drain.

He felt a sudden bolt of alarm. Jesus, he'd concentrated so on cleaning his wound that he'd let his guard down for an instant. He couldn't do that and survive. Above all else, he must keep alert.

He looked fearfully around. Was there anybody in this restroom with him?

No, he didn't think so. This was the employees' john; the public toilets were on the other side of the food court.

He got on his haunches and peered under the stall doors but spied no feet. The urinals stood white and bare, with dull green pucks resting in the drains. Harold flushed one of the urinals, watched the water cascade over the disinfectant tablet. He liked the odor.

Quit standing here sniffing disinfectant, you dumb shit. Look for people hiding behind the toilets, under the urinals. Anybody's capable of fucking with you.

But there was no one. Harold was alone.

Good.

He felt better. He would hide here until the whore and the police were gone. Wait till after dark. Things were easier then.

The door hissed open and a man came in.

Just as swiftly, Harold hustled back to the sink, shoved his injured hand under the faucet, and watched the newcomer from the corner of his eye.

Jesus, a cop. Harold was dead. The Change was dead.

Not a cop. A security guard. A rent-a-cop. Wearing pale khakis instead of a navy-blue DPD uniform. Dropping a billed cap on the counter and walking toward the urinals. This was an older man, fifty at least, with steel-gray hair and marks on the sides of his nose where he'd just removed his glasses. Pale, freckled skin. Short and stout.

And armed with a pistol.

Harold wanted the man's pistol. He needed something to even the odds against the whore.

He continued to wash his wound while the rent-a-cop went to the urinal, unzipped his fly, and stretched

out his dong while holding the head between a thumb
and forefinger. The newcomer massaged his nose with
his free hand and stood with his back arched, his pelvis
thrust forward. Nodded at Harold and smiled, then
hunched over and ducked his head to watch himself
pee.

Harold knew what came next. The rent-a-cop was
about to babble some senseless shit, typical of what
men said to each other in the john. Something about
pussy. Or something about the Dallas Cowboys. Or
something about how badly they'd needed to take a
leak. Conversation that always occurred while men
were pissing or taking a dump. Harold hated bathroom talk. On the loading dock he wouldn't even go
in the toilet unless he was the only one in there.

The rent-a-cop winked and looked at the ceiling.
"Ah, the pause that refreshes."

The pause that refreshes? Harold would enjoy killing
this fucker.

The guard pressed the button to flush the urinal and
stood there shaking his dong. He glanced toward the
sink. "That's a nasty-looking cut, bud. You oughta get
it looked at."

Looked at by who? Harold washed his hand and
didn't answer. Water poured into the laceration. Stung
like hell.

Now the rent-a-cop approached the sink beside
Harold, turned on the hot and cold, and adjusted the
temperature. "People don't watch where they're
going," the older man said. "Right out back they got
a Bronco run into the guardrail. You see it?"

Harold's jaws tensed. "No."

"I ain't had an accident in fifteen years." The rent-
a-cop pumped soap into his palm and rubbed his
hands together under the faucet. "My old lady has
enough wrecks for the both of us, though."

The guard's weapon was holstered at his waist, not three feet away. The gun was a revolver. Harold wondered where the man kept his extra bullets.

The rent-a-cop shut the water off and reached for the paper towels. "One more hour and I'll have it made." He mopped his hands, wadded the towels, tossed them into the trash. "You take care of that hand, now." He started to walk away.

Harold stepped back from the sink. "Wait."

The guard turned. Brows lifted in mild expectation. Expression friendly, mouth turned up at the corners.

Harold hugged the older man and pinned his arms. "I want your gun," said Harold Bays.

Harold had never strangled anyone before, having only killed people by shooting or beating them to death. He didn't like the injury to his hands that beatings caused, and he didn't like the way the rent-a-cop's swollen tongue protruded while Harold choked the life from him. He didn't like the crunching sound when his thumbs pulverized the man's windpipe. It would have been better to have shot the guy, but firing the gun would have made too much noise. He snugged his cut latex gloves down over the guard's lifeless wrists, left the corpse wearing his discarded coveralls, exited the bathroom, and closed the door.

The rent-a-cop's khaki pants were too big in the waist and too short in the legs. Harold had cinched the belt up tight through the loops, and wore the pistol holster high to cover the sagging folds in the trousers. The rent-a-cop had the feet of a woman; Harold couldn't fit his own heel into the heel of the uniform shoes. Finally he'd given up and put his Adidas sneakers back on.

He pictured someone asking him in the mall why he was wearing running shoes. If they did, he'd answer that the tile in the corridor was hard on his feet.

Or maybe that wouldn't be a satisfactory reason for

him to be wearing sneakers. He'd have to think on
the answer.

But he had to be ready for the question. He had to
be ready for anything.

The revolver was a .38 Police Special, and extra
rounds were in the uniform pants pocket. The rent-a-
cop's name was Fred Porter, and he had a gun permit.

Good. Harold Bays could be Fred Porter for a
while. No one looks closely at ID photos. Besides, if
anyone asked Harold for ID, he'd probably shoot
them.

Harold Bays was flexible. Prepared for anything.
Definitely worthy of making the Change.

She would be pleased with him. Pleased enough that
She wouldn't listen to the workers when they trashed
him. Fuck the workers. Harold was as good as
Changed.

The real Fred Porter was dead and wore the lunatic's clothing who'd had the problem with the whore.
Also he wore the cut latex gloves. When someone
found the corpse, they'd assume that Fred Porter was
the lunatic.

Or at least they'd think he might be, for long
enough that Harold Bays, dressed as Fred Porter,
could get away from the mall.

Harold tried on the billed uniform cap. The band
flopped down over his eyes. He stuffed toilet paper
into the crown. The cap wasn't a perfect fit, but it
would have to do.

Harold left the men's room and walked through the
mall. He stumped his way to the food court and
bought a Big Mac with cheese, looking around at the
McDonald's employees and wondering which one
owned the disabled Bronco. Harold wasn't sorry he'd
wrecked the car. It was really the whore's fault. He
thought that someday he might apologize to the
owner. The owner might understand about the whore.

The Big Mac tasted good.

No one paid any attention to him or even glanced at his shoes. They passed him by carrying their shopping bags. Likely they felt safe. Everyone trusted a security guard.

Harold decided that he liked being a security guard.

He pictured himself helping children aboard a school bus. He'd ridden the bus to school when he was little, and he'd always respected the crossing guard. A crossing guard was different from a security guard. But it was the same idea—people looked up to him.

No. He *wasn't* a fucking security guard *or* a crossing guard. He was supposed to be making his getaway.

His mind had wandered again. He needed to concentrate even harder.

Why was he standing around McDonald's eating a cheeseburger? What the fuck was he doing?

He wadded his Big Mac, half eaten, into its wrapper, and stuffed the whole mess into a trash can. He retraced his steps and proceeded toward the parking lot.

Fred Porter the security guard was simply going to walk out of here. Harold pushed open the glass-paneled entryway.

And halted.

Ahead on the sidewalk, looking closely at everyone who entered or left the mall, stood three uniformed policemen. And in their midst . . .

The whore.

Jesus, the fucking whore again. Harold *hated* her. He touched his thumb to the cut on his hand.

The whore was looking at passersby as well. Shaking her head at the cops to indicate, No, that's not him. Watching to see if Harold was one of the departing mall customers.

Angry and frustrated, Harold retreated into the mall and tried another exit. Just like at the other door, cops were checking people over. Only these cops were holding pictures up and comparing them with each person who entered or left the mall.

Harold went back to the food court and walked around, nodding and smiling, the safety-conscious security guard. He'd wait for nightfall, if he had to.

In the meantime he'd be a smiling, friendly security guard. With people looking up to and respecting him.

He'd wait patiently for darkness.

By the time the mall closed, the police would have all gone home.

18

Courtney Bedell, fumbling in her excitement, checked the clip in her Glock while Gholer drove like a madman toward Valley View Mall. This was it. This was the guy.

The call had come a half hour ago as Courtney wandered around among the onlookers near Texas Stadium. She hadn't seen anything out of line the entire afternoon, except for two girls in high school band jackets who surreptitiously passed a joint back and forth, giggling because they were smoking dope right under the cops' noses. Courtney was bored enough to bust the girls, write them up, and give them a warning, and had just made up her mind to do so when Gholer came barreling down the incline from the road.

"Got 'im, Court." Gholer's tone was up a couple of octaves.

She looked toward the CSU truck. "Got who?"

"The guy." He yanked hard on her arm. "Come on. I'll fill you in on the way."

Which he did as the four-door motor-pool Chevy burned asphalt on the way down Grauwyler Road toward I-35, with the lieutenant driving and Courtney clinging to the door handle as the car rocked on its springs.

"Guy picked up a whore in one of those complexes

behind Valley View Mall," Gholer said. "Pulled a pistol on her, and apparently she didn't like the idea. Cut the holy shit out of him, took his gun, and chased him into the mall. He's still in there and we got the exits all covered. Jesus, I'm going to kiss that whore."

Courtney looked at him.

"Well, I might," Gholer said. "Or at least I'll give her a candy bar or something." He floored the accelerator and barreled on.

As the lieutenant ran the light at the interstate and turned onto the northbound ramp with two wheels off the pavement, Courtney yelped, "God, look out!" Then, as she settled back down in the seat after very nearly banging her head on the ceiling, she said, "You might be getting your hopes up too high."

"Naw. Not this time. There's more." Gholer watched her like a man with a hard-to-keep secret.

"Okay, Loo," she finally said. "Cut the suspense."

Gholer passed a bobtail truck in the inside lane. "Jinx and Eddie. They have a picture of the guy."

"Taken where?"

"His photo ID. Taking on his job, fuck the FBI profilers very much, where he works five days a week. On a loading dock three blocks up the street from our office, can you believe it? At a company owned by guess who."

"Okay, I give up. The mayor the police chief . . . ?"

"William Hargis Jr. His family, anyway."

Courtney turned toward Gholer and stared.

"Who everybody thought I was full of shit," Gholer said, "for wanting twenty-four/seven surveillance on. Maybe in the future my troops will pay attention to me. Anyhow, they got the guy's ID and've been calling me all afternoon, only I got my head too far up my ass with those CSU techs to check my messages. Finally talked to Eddie about thirty seconds after the disturbance call came over the radio, and sent him

and Jinx hauling ass out to Valley View Mall to show
the whore the picture. It's the guy. According to Jinxie, the whore's got no doubt it's him."

"And he's still in the mall?" Courtney drew the
Glock and popped the clip out of the handle.

"Well . . . he *probably* is." Gholer looked a bit
unsure. "Look, Jinx and Eddie and the patrol shift
lieutenant got a plat from the mall office. There's eight
main exits. Plus your individual department stores,
Sears and Dillard's, Foley's, and JC Penney's, got their
own outside doors, not to mention basement, service,
and covered parking accesses. I guess the guy's capable of flapping his arms and flying off the roof, the
way he's been running us around. But we got every
mall access covered as of now. Jinx and Eddie took
copies of the guy's photo to our people at every exit,
thank God for patrol car fax and copy machines. Took
us maybe twenty minutes to surround the place, so if
he wasn't already gone by then . . ."

Courtney hit the clip home with the heel of her
hand. "Might take a room-to-room search of the
building, Loo. He could be in the restroom."

Gholer shook his head. "Too much danger right
now, civilians running around buying shit. The whore
took one weapon off of the guy, but for all we know
he's got four more strapped to his ass. After closing
time, maybe. If he didn't get away during the window
it took us to cover the joint, he's got to be still wandering around. So like I say, he's probably in there."

Courtney holstered her weapon, leaned back and
folded her arms. "You mean, *maybe* he is, don't you?"

Courtney didn't think she'd seen this many black-
and-whites since she was in the academy, when they'd
spent a day at the police lot learning vehicle mainte-
nance procedure. God, half of the force seemed to be
at Valley View Mall. She counted five squad cars out-

side Sears alone, three more parked in front of the
Foley's entry at the northwest corner. Three uniforms
were at every door, attentive, with photos in hand.
She spotted Rainey and Trevino by one of the exits,
the two muscle-men likely still arguing over Michael
Irvin. The day she'd spent working the fair seemed as
if it was a hundred years ago. When all of this was
over and the Fiddleback was in jail, she'd look up
Rainey and Trevino and inquire how they were doing.
As Gholer drove like a wild man toward the rear
parking lot, Courtney promptly forgot the two guys.
She had more on her mind.

Gholer drove to the lot between Foley's and JC
Penney, where most of the firepower seemed to be
gathered. Or make that *brass* power, Courtney
thought. Captain Helen Dilbergast was there along
with Miller, the FBI agent who'd been up in Gholer's
face earlier at the office. There were also mobile news
units, parked a distance away, and men hoisting minicams. On-the-spot reporters carried mikes, fooling
with their hair as they made a beeline for Miller and
Dilbergast. Jinx Madison and Eddie Frizell were hanging around as well, keeping their distance from the
federal man and the captain. Three cops lurked near
the mall entry, and with them stood a saucily dressed
black woman in a tight leather skirt.

Madison and Frizell approached before Gholer
could get his door open. He stood halfway out of the
vehicle as Frizell told him, "You're not going to believe this," while thumbing over his shoulder toward
the FBI agent and Captain Dilbergast. Agent Miller
was talking to one of the TV reporters. He struck a
we-the-people pose.

Gholer's mouth wrinkled in distaste. "I'm not going
to believe what, Eddie? I'll believe the TV stations
have showed up because Miller called 'em. Am I
right?"

Frizell gave a so-what shrug. "That goes without saying. But you won't believe what they're telling us about this Hargis asshole."

Gholer left the car with Frizell while Courtney fell in step beside Madison as they headed toward the mall.

Walking fast, Gholer said, "I bet I'll believe that, too, Eddie. I'll bet they're telling you to leave Hargis alone."

Frizell jammed his hands into his back pockets. "The way they put it is, we lay off of him until we get stronger evidence. What stronger evidence is there?"

"A photo of the guy and the Fiddleback cutting a birthday cake might do it," Gholer said. "And even that might not satisfy all these politicians getting donations from Hargis' folks. So exactly who is it that's telling you Hargis is off limits?"

Frizell kept his head down. "I heard Dilbergast and Miller talking."

"Yeah, right." Gholer stopped in his tracks and turned to Courtney and Madison. "All you guys gather 'round."

They formed a semicircle around Gholer. Visible in the periphery of Courtney's vision, Agent Miller glared in the detectives' direction. Courtney was sure that if the agent hadn't been giving an interview, he would have hustled on over and butted in.

Gholer lowered his voice, all business. "Okay, listen up. Jinx and Edie, as of now, has the captain told you personally to keep away from Hargis Jr?"

The athletic black woman and the wiry male cop looked at each other. Madison said, "Dilbergast never said jack to me, Loo. All I heard was second hand, her talking to Donald the Dangler."

"And did Donald the . . ." Gholer paused, then grinned. "There you go with that name again, Jinxie. Eddie, did *Agent Miller* say anything directly to you?"

Frizell seemed to think it over. "Not straight up.
Me and Jinx told Dilbergast about what happened at
the loading dock and how we got the suspect's ID
photo, and that Hargis' family owns the trucking company. That's about as far as we got with her, because
then Dilbergast and Donald the Dangler put their
heads together and sort of excluded us from the
conversation."

Gholer's eyebrows moved closer together. "And
you never heard them say not to go after Hargis?"

"Yeah, we did," Frizell said. "We were standing
there and heard 'em—"

Madison yanked on Frizell's arm, stopping him. She
was watching Gholer.

Gholer moved up closer to Frizell. "You never
heard 'em say anything directly to you, did you,
Eddie?"

Courtney inwardly grinned, getting it.

Now Frizell got it as well. "Never heard a thing,
Loo."

"And since you didn't," Gholer said, "you never
could have told me anything about Miller and Dilbergast's conversation. And since I got no orders to the
contrary, if I tell you two to go sit on Mr. Hargis
you'd haul ass, wouldn't you?"

Madison and Frizell stepped closer together.

"Which is what I'm telling you now," Gholer said.
"Go and sit on that guy. Go to his house. If he's not
home, wait. You do not move until you see this guy,
or until I tell you different."

Frizell glanced toward the street. "You mean, now?"

Madison leaned an elbow on Frizell's shoulder.
"You are one dim son of a bitch, Eddie," she said.

"That is one potent observation, Jinx," Gholer said.
"So while Miss Bedell and I go about catching this
asshole in the mall, you two do an about-face and
head for the Hargis estate. And what I mean is, right

fuckin' now. With no interference from captains and Donald the Danglers and shit, okay?"

Courtney stayed to the rear as Gholer walked in between Agent Miller and the television journalist. The journalist was a pretty blond woman about thirty, with coiffed hair and chic clothes. Captain Dilbergast waited off to the side. Courtney watched the reporter's eyebrows lift in surprise. Lieutenant Jerry Gholer chinning with the press was something seldom seen.

Gholer showed the journalist a big pancake grin and lifted a hand to her. "How you doing?" He squeezed the back of Agent Miller's neck. "Ol' Don here keeping you filled in?"

The reporter was too surprised to answer. She stared down at her mike.

Gholer said, "You know, if it wasn't for Don and his group of agents, we would have really been in trouble on this one."

Miller looked as if he wanted to push Gholer's hand away, but was afraid to do so with the press standing by. The FBI man gazed past Courtney toward the parking lot. Miller said, "Hey, what happened to—?"

"Yessir," Gholer continued to the reporter, "if it hadna been for Don and his profilers, we never would have figured out that our suspect was likely to be shopping here at Valley View Mall on this very day. These profilers are something else, and I—"

"Excuse me," the reporter broke in. "But, Lieutenant Gholer, our information is that he tried to abduct a woman near here and she somehow disabled him." She gestured with her mike toward the hooker in the leather skirt. "That woman, right over there, unless I'm mistaken."

Now Agent Miller's look turned frantic. "Where did those two—?"

"Well, what I was about to say," Gholer cut in, "is that, without the profilers' information we wouldn't have known the suspect would be *abducting* in this area. Any credit here should go to Agent Donald Miller. I got to spell that?"

Miller's cheeks were turning red. "Dammit, Jerry, did you send those—?"

"And now," Gholer said, striding toward the mall and beckoning for Courtney to follow, "while we take care of apprehending the suspect, which I'm sure the FBI has set up so it's a piece of cake for us, Agent Miller can answer any questions you might have. And believe me: Any quote from Agent Miller goes absolutely double for me."

Courtney stood outside the mall entry and listened to Gholer tell the stragetic weapons shift commander, "No SWAT. If the guy sees a uniform I want it to be the janitor's. A pizza guy's or something."

Captain Helen Dilbergast stood blandly by. "Plain-clothes detectives would be better. But we seem to be missing a couple of those." She favored Gholer with a look that might melt cobalt.

"Yeah, they seem to be out of pocket, captain. Too bad they're not around." Gholer turned to the SWAT commander, also a lieutenant, a tall rangy man in a squared-off hat and jack boots. "No fooling," Gholer said. "We're dealing with a suspect here that we got no history on, as far as hostage or pursuit situations. If he's our guy, we know what he's like in private. In a public place he could be a pussycat. He also could be Jackie Chan with a pound of dynamite strapped to his leg. We just don't know."

The SWAT boss looked to the dark blue van in which he'd arrived just moments ago. Inside sat a half-dozen men and women wearing squared-off hats like their commander's, their arms cradling ropes, AR-15s, and grenade launchers. The commander gave a mild palm-up gesture.

"Okay, Jerry," Captain Dilbergast said. "You've told us what you don't want. So what *do* you want?"

Gholer placed a hand firmly on Courtney's shoulder. "Me and this young lady here," Gholer said, "take the mall proper. She can identify the suspect, Captain. She's got his picture, she's conferred with this other woman"—he pointed at the hooker, who stood nearby looking confused—"and they've agreed that this is the guy."

Courtney idly took out the Fiddleback's work ID, and looked over the photo for the fourth or fifth time since one of the uniforms had handed it to her. Harold Bays. She pictured him near the fairgrounds, just before he'd shot her, standing alongside a pickup truck with a screaming woman inside. She slipped the photo back in her pocket and folded her arms, her expression deadpan, staring at the pavement. She'd recognized the Fiddleback the instant she'd laid eyes on the picture.

"As for the perimeters," Gholer went on, "I'd ask you to go with mall security. They know the utility, broom closets, employees' restrooms, places we didn't even know existed. A rent-a-cop in a tan suit isn't going to attract any attention, but one of our guys could set the suspect off. But please tell those people, if they spot anyone suspicious, leave him the hell alone and get back to us. That's all we need, a private cop in the morgue." He winked at Courtney. "Ready, Officer Bedell?"

Courtney fastened her windbreaker, pulling the garment down over her hips to cover the Glock. Just as she nodded that she was ready to go, her cell phone buzzed in her pocket. She looked to Gholer in alarm.

"Take it," Gholer said. "The phone's registered to

me, so it could be my old lady. If it is, tell her I've
gone for coffee. If it happens to be for you, you're on
your own."

Courtney drug out the phone, flipped it open, turned
her back and lowered her head. "Hello?"

A female voice on the line said, "Officer Courtney
Bedell?"

Courtney frowned in surprise. "Yes?"

"This is Topper Moore. You know, back at the
office?"

Courtney was stumped for an instant. Oh yes. The
admin, came in for half-days, had set Jason up with
the day-care center. Courtney said, "Yes, how are
you?"

"Well, I'm fine, but . . . listen, Rest 'n' Play's calling
for you. I'm going to patch them through, okay?"

Courtney listened to a series of clicks on the line,
at the same time experiencing dread. Jason? God if
there was something wrong . . .

A pleasant woman came on, saying, "Hello, Miss
Bedell?"

Courtney took a deep breath. "This is Courtney."

"This is Mrs. Atcheson, Rest 'n' Play." The woman
paused.

Get it out, lady, Courtney thought. Her nails dug
into the fleshy part of her hand. "It's nothing major,"
the woman said. "But sometimes these little ones get
upset. It's our policy to contact the adults when they
do . . . I hope you don't mind."

Courtney's sigh of relief sounded awfully loud to
her. She said, "No, of course not."

"We think it would calm Jason to talk to you."

Courtney glanced at Gholer. His expression was
tight. Courtney showed Gholer a casual thumbs-up
sign as she said into the phone, "Sure. Put him on."

There was a second more of silence, after which
Jason said, "Coatney?"

"*Court*ney, you . . . What is it, baby?"

"You know what, Coatney?"

"No, I don't. What, sweetheart?"

Jason giggled. "I do not like green eggs and ham."

Courtney's teeth were on edge, but at the same time she had a pang of sympathy. Jason had pulled this stunt several times on Mrs. Bailey. Any time Courtney was out of his sight he tended to panic, and pulled every trick imaginable so that someone would get her on the phone. Considering his mother's history, her disappearance from Jason's life, Courtney more than understood. She thought that sorrow—and, in her own case, possibly guilt—over Jan's behavior was the bond that held her and Jason together. Courtney said reproachfully, "Oh, Jason . . ."

"I do not like them, Sam I Am."

Courtney looked toward the mall. Of all the freaking times. She said, "You're being silly. Courtney's working now." She recalled the feeling she'd had when she'd left him at the center, the stab of fear that she'd never see him again. "Jason?" she said.

"I am Sam I Am." More inane giggles.

"Okay, Sam I Am, or whatever your name is. Courtney loves you very much. Now you go with the lady and quit being a toot. You behave yourself, Jason, you hear me?" She disconnected. There was an odd emptiness in the pit of her stomach. It was all she could do to keep from calling the day-care center back, getting Jason on the line, telling him over and over how much she loved him.

You're being a little overdramatic, aren't you? she asked herself.

She closed the phone, put it away, and stepped forward. "Ready, Loo."

Gholer watched her closely. "You sure?"

"Yeah, let's get it over with."

Gholer stepped toward the mall entry. He raised his voice. "Ma'am? Excuse me, ma'am?"

A woman and a little girl had just come out and passed the cops who were checking out the comers and goers. The woman was laden down with three shopping bags.

Gholer went over, flashing his shield. "Sorry, but I'll need those."

The woman said, "What?"

Gholer gently took two of the bags from her. "These," he said. "Your receipts are in here, right?" He offered one of the bags to Courtney, who slipped the strap over her arm.

The woman said, "Listen, cop or no cop . . ."

"The department," Gholer said, "will reimburse you for damages. Cheer up. You can say you were instrumental in bringing a major case to a close." He grinned at her and let one of the bags hang by his side. "I'm not near as pretty a shopper as you are, ma'am," Gholer said. "But under the circumstances, I'll have to do."

The clerk inside the upper-level bookstore asked Courtney, "Something I can get for you?"

She moved self-consciously off to one side, still holding a paperback copy of *The Coffin Dancer* by Jeffery Deaver. The clerk had her view blocked, so that she couldn't see out into the mall. She raised up slightly and peered past the clerk. "Just looking," she said.

The clerk didn't seem to buy it. He was a soft, college-graduate-looking type, about Courtney's own age, with thick brown hair flopping down. "Well, if you see something you're interested in . . ." He continued to look dubious as he slipped in behind the register.

He thinks I'm a shoplifter casing the joint, Courtney thought. Under the circumstances she didn't blame the guy; for twenty minutes she'd been wandering around the store, handling the merchandise, buying nothing, gazing out into the mall like a woman in silent communication with an accomplice. She flashed an apologetic grin and slid the paperback in beside the other books. She strolled casually over to the self-help section, feeling the clerk's gaze on her every step of the way. Jesus, one end of this mammoth shopping mall to the other, twice, and the most suspicious-looking person she'd run across thus far was herself.

Except for Gholer, of course. She could see him across the wide second-level expanse, a thick-necked man in a rumpled suit carrying a—*God,* Courtney thought, *why didn't I notice it before?*—shopping bag from Nancy Madison Maternity Wear. *I think you're just a hair out of your element, Loo,* she thought. But there he was, looking like an ex-pug or maybe a mafia hit man, carrying a bag from a store for pregnant women while looking in the window at Harris for Teens. If Courtney were in uniform and on patrol duty, and didn't know the lieutenant, she'd stop Gholer and ask him a few questions.

More than an hour after entering the mall, Courtney's apprehension had given way to complacency, and now approached plain old don't-give-a-shit boredom. At the other end of the four-block-long building, where the mall was built on a single level, she'd seen security guards in khaki uniforms hustling unobtrusively around the perimeters. Here in the two-story shopping cavern, however, there was no one but civilians. Mothers, daughters, fathers, sons, hurrying briskly along, stopping, looking, conversing with clerks, ruefully shaking their heads while reading price tags. Nothing unusual, nothing out of line.

As Courtney watched from within the bookstore,

Gholer left the teen shop and moved down to a pricey-looking gift store where two women stood side by side. Gholer took up station beside the ladies. They glanced his way, then moved rapidly on.

Item One, Courtney thought. *Characters such as Courtney Bedell and Lieutenant Jerry Gholer hanging around the premises is bad for business in general.*

Item Two: The Fiddleback is gone with the wind.

They now had the guy identified and each of them carried his picture, yet she didn't feel as if they were any nearer to an arrest than on the night he'd shot her. For all they knew he was fifty miles away, headed for his lair with some helpless victim in his grasp. Driving hell-bent-for-leather toward wherever it was that he kept all those fucking spiders.

Jesus Christ, those hideous, hairy, little eight-legged creatures.

Courtney pictured the craterlike sores on Trash Rosita's legs. She shut her eyes tightly to chase the image from her mind.

The clerk continued to keep an eye on her. She decided that she'd worn out her welcome. She hefted her own dummy shopping bag from one hand to the other as she left the bookstore and crossed the second-level platform over to the rail. She subconsciously reached to the small of her back and touched her Glock through her jacket as she peered down.

The main arena of Valley View Mall was the size of Texas Stadium, with a twelve-foot walkway around the perimeter halfway up, and rows of shops above and below. At one end of the vast room, a flat ramp extended between levels at a thirty-degree angle. Courtney and Gholer had agreed to keep on opposite sides of the second level, so that between them they'd have a 360-degree view of the bottom floor. For all the good it was doing; Courtney suspected that the lieutenant was every bit as fed up as she was. Gholer turned and caught her eye across the chasm between them. Courtney shrugged, shook her head, and stifled a yawn.

A flash of color far below caught her eye. Downstairs and across the way, a pudgy man held thirty or forty multicolored, helium-filled balloons by a host of strings bunched in his hand. As Courtney watched, two little boys bought balloons from the man. They carried the balloons, a green one and a red one, over to show their mother. She wagged a disapproving finger. Courtney supposed that the kids had just blown a couple of bucks that they weren't supposed to. She raised her head to search for Gholer across the chasm.

Gholer had vanished.

Courtney's gaze swept to the right, to the end of the landing. No lieutenant. She looked down the other way.

And there he was, running top-speed toward the ramp leading down, his coat flapping behind him. He'd dropped the shopping bag he'd confiscated, and he had his cell jammed against his ear. As he thundered around the rail and started down, he saw her. He swept his free hand over his head like a traffic cop and pointed for her to haul ass after him.

But Courtney was already on the move. She'd left her own shopping bag against the railing. As she ran she dug at the small of her back, mall shoppers in front of her cringing in fear as the Glock came out, Courtney's breath whistling between her teeth, her jaw set in determination. Her weapon held pointed up, her sneakers slapping the tile, Courtney Bedell followed Lieutenant Jerry Gholer to the lower reaches of Valley View Mall. As she dashed down the ramp, she had the distinct impression that she was headed for an up-close view of hell.

19

In Gholer's view it didn't begin as hell, but more as a Chinese fire drill. He told Captain Helen Dilbergast over the phone that he was on his way as, in his mind, he cursed Agent Donald Miller and all of his ancestors. Gholer ran full speed even as he talked to the captain, his words interspersed with grunts and thudding noises as his feet collided with the floor. He spied Courtney Bedell across the way in front of the bookstore as he charged onto the ramp leading down to the mall's ground level. He gave Bedell a come-on wave, and caught movement in the corner of his eye as she sprinted down the opposite walkway toward the down-ramp. Gholer wasn't sure but thought she'd drawn her weapon.

If Miller had fucked up the Fiddleback's apprehension, Gholer was going to take a swing at the guy. Bust Miller in the mouth, and not give much of a shit if Lieutenant Jerry Gholer wound up in a federal jail for assault. What the hell, he'd heard that the food was pretty good.

His tie flapping in the breeze of his own momentum, Gholer dashed through the lower level and into the corridor leading back to Foley's and Penney's. On the way he very nearly leveled a woman pushing a stroller, and did in fact overturn a handbag display, scattering beaded purses from here to hell-and-gone. As he charged through the food court his elbow knocked a slice of pizza out of a teenager's hand and his flying hip turned a chair over. People eating at tables stood and protected their meals.

Finally Gholer slowed to a rapid walk, huffing and puffing. Up ahead, a narrow walkway branched off from the main corridor. At the head of the walkway hovered four or five security guards and a half-dozen blue-uniformed patrolmen, along with three heavily armed DPD SWATs in squared-off hats. In front of the SWATs stood Agent Donald Miller like Teddy Roosevelt leading the charge. Captain Helen Dilbergast was backed up to a wall, fooling with a shoulderboard, and wouldn't meet Gholer's gaze. Gholer came abreast of the group and squinted down the narrow corridor past brooms, mops, and a couple of trash barrels on wheels. Four more SWATs were down there, two on either side of a closed door. The SWAT lieutenant led this group, and was just about to tell his troops to kick the door wide open and go in blazing.

Gholer stopped at the head of the corridor and cupped his hands in front of his mouth. "You people hold it, right there!" He'd attracted quite a crowd. A dozen or more shoppers had followed him in from the food court, and another dozen halted in their tracks coming out of a Kay Bee Toy Store, all wondering what this lunatic was up to next.

Down at the end of the narrow walkway, the SWATs backed away from the door. Their lieutenant came halfway down to where Gholer stood. "I got orders to go in there, Loo," the SWAT lieutenant said.

Gholer swaggered forward. "Not from me, you don't, *Loo*. Who gave 'em?"

The SWAT lieutenant pointed in Agent Miller's direction.

Gholer glanced at Miller, then looked back at the SWAT leader. "Yeah? You on the federal payroll now?" He then walked over and stood nose to nose with the FBI man. "The fuck you doing, Miller?" Visible at the periphery of Gholer's vision, Courtney Bedell trotted up. She took in the situation and solemnly holstered her weapon.

Gholer glared at Miller and waited for an answer.

Miller blurted out, "I've got equal authority with you in this task force, Jerry."

"Yeah, okay, equal. So fill me in equally. What the fuck are you doing?"

Miller pointed toward a security guard who stood off isolated from the others. "That man," Miller said, "reported to us that there's a suspicious character hiding in the employee's restroom. We're just taking care of business."

"By going into the toilet shooting? If the Fiddleback's in there, where do you think he's going to go? There's no other way out but through here."

"Yeah, but we have to corral the guy."

"Jesus Christ, Miller, if he's in there he's already corralled." Gholer gestured with his head toward the six uniformed cops standing by. "Did you jerk these guys away from the mall exits and bring 'em down here?"

Miller's look was suddenly unsure.

"I'll take that as a 'yes,'" Gholer said. "So if the guy in the bathroom happens to be somebody just taking a dump, you've cleared the exits so the Fiddleback can just walk the fuck out of here." He glanced at the SWAT lieutenant, then stared at Miller once more. "So as the man in charge of this operation, Mr. FBI, fill me in. What's with the SWAT team?"

"Firepower," Miller said defensively. "I cleared this with your captain, Jerry."

Gholer looked around. Captain Dilbergast had now

walked over by Courtney Bedell. The two seemed to be discussing something by a Nintendo display across the walkway in the hobby store.

Gholer said, "In this operation you don't clear anything with the captain, Miller. You clear it with me. So now, suppose whoever's in the john is really the Fiddleback, and suppose those Green Berets go charging in and blast him off the throne, killing the fucking guy. Then what are you going to do?"

Miller had lost his backup, Captain Dilbergast, and went at it alone. "The case will be cleared. We can make an announcement."

"Yeah, great. And what about the Hargis woman, who he's had a couple of days, plus anybody else he might have chained up waiting for his spiders to bite 'em? What you going to say to those people? '*Adios*, motherfuckers, been nice knowing you'?"

Miller stepped back. He opened, then closed, his mouth.

"We need this asshole alive, Donald," Gholer said. "He's got one hostage we know of plus God knows how many others. So recall your troops, bud. SWATs and all."

Miller backed down, but remained petulant. "And what? Wait for him to come out whenever he feels like it?"

Gholer reached inside his coat and drew his revolver. He held the barrel pointed down while he checked the cylinder. "No, Donald, I'm going in there. Me, myself, and I. And if it's him, me and Fiddleback are going to have a little talk among ourselves about where he's keeping these people. If I gotta shoot him, I gotta. But first we got to give him a chance to surrender. So get those SWATs out of my way. I'd as soon not have 'em busting in and shooting me while me and Fiddleback are having a go, if it's all the same to you."

*   *   *

Gholer stripped out of his coat and put on an armored jacket brought up from one of the squad cars, at the same time getting what briefing he could from the security guard who'd seen the suspect hiding in the john. According to the rent-a-cop, a twenty-something youngster with a gap between his two front teeth, he hadn't really seen the guy. He'd been checking out the restroom and noticed feet from under one of the stall doors. The hiding man's pants were navy-blue, so he couldn't be part of mall security, and no one other than an employee was authorized to use this particular restroom. No, the security cop had not tried to talk to the man; he was under orders to report any strangers and that was what he'd done. Gholer secured the final strap on the armored vest as he nodded and thanked the young man.

Gholer handed his suit coat to Courtney Bedell. She carefully folded the jacket and draped the garment over her forearm. Gholer went to the employees' washroom door, flattened his back against the wall, grinned while nodding right and left at the SWAT team, shouldered open the entry, and stepped inside. The door swished shut behind him.

He was in an alcove, behind a tiled head-high barrier. The bathroom opened out on his left. The ceiling was pale green. The floor was done in inch-square light beige tiles. Somewhere up ahead, water dripped.

Gholer stayed in place and raised his voice. "Can we talk some? Hey, I know you're in here." The ceiling wasn't acoustical, and there was a faint echo.

Silence.

Gholer held his .38 Special pointed up beside his ear. Tension bristled in his neck. Sure he was frightened, but he felt a little silly as well. "So you'll know," Gholer called out, "there's about two dozen armed cops outside. Hey, we all want to live through this. But if the shit hits the fan, well . . ."

More silence. Maybe a faint scratching sound, nothing more.

Gholer stuck his head around the barrier and looked down the length of the bathroom. Sinks and urinals on the left, stalls on the right. The security guard had said the last stall on the end.

Gholer said, "Don't make me do this the hard way."

The faucet continued to drip.

Gholer pictured the guy crouching down behind a toilet with a pet spider riding on his shoulder. Maybe a bazooka, too, or a flamethrower or something.

Gholer came out in the open, gun extended, held in both hands. He got down low and looked underneath the partitions. The rent-a-cop hadn't been kidding, there was a pair of feet down there. Above the feet were dark blue cuffs.

Gholer straightened and walked down until he was in front of the water closet. The feet hadn't moved.

Gholer said, "Okay, no more bullshit, now. I'm coming in there." He hopped to his right and pushed inside the stall next to the hidden man, hopped up on the toilet seat, and looked down over the partition. He relaxed and let his pistol hang at his side. "Shit," he murmured to himself. He was looking down at a man wearing navy-blue coveralls, staring up at him. The man wasn't moving, his eyes open and unblinking, his tongue protruding between his lips. The guy sitting there on the toilet was stone-cold dead.

Gholer couldn't resist a parting shot as he and Courtney walked away down the corridor toward the exit. He backed up a step and pointed a finger in Agent Miller's direction. "On you, Miller. Everything he does from now on, directly on you."

Miller and Captain Dilbergast were at the head of the corridor leading to the employees' washroom, where uniformed cops stood in a semicircle, securing yet another crime scene. CSUs and EMUs were on the way. Again. *They'll find more resin,* Gholer thought, *maybe a couple of carpet fibers, body hairs clinging to the perp's clothing which he'd put on the dead man.* The usual shit. Another stiff, the Fiddleback long gone. Another innocent somebody sent to hell.

Courtney Bedell put a hand on Gholer's arm. He looked down at her, her soft brown eyes pleading for him to shut up, not make things worse. She was right. Gholer lowered his head.

Captain Dilbergast stepped in front of the FBI agent. "We should all meet, Jerry. Discuss what's next."

Gholer inhaled, let it out slowly. "Yeah, right, Captain. In the morning, if it's all the same. My place?"

She nodded. "Nine A.M." Dilbergast looked at her watch. "The mall doesn't close for another hour. We've still got the exits covered in case."

"Yeah, right," Gholer said. "In case." He shuffled off down the corridor as a knot of onlookers parted in front of him. He stopped and pointed a finger back. "On you, Miller," he said, and resumed his tired walk toward the exit.

Courtney Bedell stood frozen for a moment, then hustled to draw abreast. "There's still the Hargis guy, Loo."

"And as soon as his lawyer finds out Jinx and Eddie are shadowing the guy, he'll come whining to the city council and that'll be the end of that. Jesus, we don't really even have probable cause to question Hargis. Up until Miller shot his mouth off to the press, we had a chance to catch the nutso just by waiting at his job. But now this mall thing's going to be all over the papers, plus a picture of the guy. You think he's just going to report for duty tomorrow? You think we'll find him at home? Hell no, the next thing we'll hear is, bodies found in Seattle, Washington or someplace. It's over, Court. The guy is fucking gone." He trudged ahead, turning down the corridor that led to the parking lot where they'd first entered the mall.

"Likely," Gholer went on, head down, "the fruitcake was already twenty miles from here before we got to the scene. He had plenty of time to get away before we had the mall exits covered, plus I'm not all that sure our people would have recognized the guy even if they'd seen him. You ever try to ID a suspect in person on a mug shot? Half the time the guy and his photo don't even resemble each other, and Fiddleback's work ID is an even shittier picture than a mug shot." He slowly raised his head as he neared the row of glass doors opening outside. "Harold Bays. Who'd have thought the guy would have such a crappy name, huh?" He pushed open a door and held it for Courtney to go on through.

She stepped with agility into the alcove and turned to face him. "We could revisit evidence. Maybe get some idea where he keeps the vics before he . . . We do have his home address, Loo."

"We've already sent people. They're out there now, in case the guys show up." He came on into the alcove and favored her with a grin. Visible behind her and beyond the next row of doors, three cops stood by on the sidewalk with a photo, checking out people as they left the mall. The hooker had apparently decided to go home. It was dark now, and hard to believe that when they'd entered the mall the sun had been halfway above the horizon. Gholer said to Courtney, "And what's this 'we' shit?"

She frowned at him.

"This morning," Gholer said, "I had to kidnap you just so's I could get you to help look for the guy. You come over to our side now?"

She seemed to consider the answer. Her hands in her windbreaker pockets, she said, "I guess it sort of grows on you."

Ten yards outside the mall, they stopped and faced each other like parting lovers. Or, Gholer thought, like suspects ready to split the loot. Gholer said, "Does that mean you're not going to turn me in for having you transferred?"

"It means . . ." Her expression turned solemn. "It means that it grows on you. And until further notice, that's all it means."

"Yeah, it grew on Jinx Madison, too. The first two weeks after I took her out of Patrol, I slept with one eye open for fear she'd sneak up and blow me away. Now, you couldn't get her to transfer with a gun to her head. Listen, Court."

She arched an eyebrow.

"There's things going on I ain't told you," Gholer said. "About continuing the unit on Irving Boulevard even after the Fiddleback case is over. As sort of a special-crimes detail. You ought to think about it."

She checked her watch. "Right now I have to think about getting Jason. Come on, Loo, drive me back to the day-care, all right?" She walked toward the parking lot.

Gholer caught up with her quickly. "No, wait. I'm not kidding, I want you to . . ."

He trailed off in puzzlement as Courtney Bedell went into a crouch, reaching to the small of her back and bringing out the Glock. Her gaze was steady, ahead and twenty degrees off to the right. Gholer followed her gaze and drew his own weapon as she yelled, "You! Stop right there!" Gholer went into a shooter's pose of his own as she hissed, "The security guard. The one with the limp, right up there, looking this way. Jesus, Loo, that's the guy."

HER. *I WANT* HER, *YOU IGNORANT, DE-FORMED FUCK. YOU GET HER FOR ME, GOD-DAMN YOU.*

The Queen, screaming inside Harold Bays' head.

Louder than he'd ever heard her, reaching out to him from many miles away. From the farm, from her realm inside the cupboard, controlling his every movement as though she was right here with him. The all-powerful She.

YOU ARE DEAD IF YOU FUCK THIS UP, YOU ASSHOLE. YOU BRING HER. YOU BRING HER NOW.

The Queen.

Or was it Harold's mother?

One and the same.

She wanted the human female. The small, lithe, pretty, dark human female. A perfect instrument for the change.

The perfect instrument.

But a cop. *She's a cop, Mother . . .*

I DON'T GIVE A FUCK IF SHE'S THE PRESIDENT. BRING HER TO ME.

Harold uttered a helpless sigh.

The human female was a cop, all right, and she was armed. And she'd just called out to him as he made his escape from the mall, after he'd stood by disguised as a security guard and watched the big ugly detective go into the washroom and find the real rent-a-cop, the one Harold had killed. After the body's discovery, Harold had used the ensuing furor as cover to stroll casually out of the mall, past the three uniforms at the exit who were comparing his picture with passersby. The uniformed cops had barely glanced his way.

Because cops, like everyone else, looked up to and trusted security guards.

Harold was going to miss being a security guard.

And now he stopped halfway between the exit and the parking lot, looking back toward the perfect human female. Miss Perfect had drawn her pistol. The big ugly cop stood there along with her, reaching for his weapon as well. It was the same man who'd gone in the washroom and found the dead security guard.

Detective Gholer. Harold had seen Gholer's picture in the newspapers and on television. Gholer was a really smart detective. There wasn't another human alive more dangerous to the Change.

There's another cop here with her, Mother. A dangerous cop.

THEN KILL THE FUCKER. BRING HER.

Harold's features softened in rapture. The female human cop was beautiful, with such perfect skin. The ripest sores of all would fester on her.

She had her gun pointed at the center of Harold's chest.

Detective Gholer suddenly lowered his weapon and yelled out, "No, ma'am! No, don't . . ."

Harold frowned. What ma'am? Where? Ma'am don't what?

The detective was speaking to an older gray-haired woman as she walked past Harold, headed toward the mall. Head down, oblivious, carrying a shopping bag. She stopped as the detective shouted his warning, and gaped at Harold from three feet away. Her gaze fell on the gun holstered at Harold's side.

Harold grabbed the woman as a shield. Her shopping bag fell and overturned, spilling out boxes. Harold cupped his hand under her chin. She screamed.

Harold drew the .38 Special from the security guard's holster. He said, "I have a permit."

But he was lying. Harold didn't have a permit. The guard he'd killed had a permit.

Harold wondered if he was about to get a ticket for not having a valid gun permit. He'd never gotten a ticket before.

Fuck. He had to concentrate. He had to stop his mind from wandering.

The woman screamed louder, squirming in his grasp.

The noise was confusing. Harold wanted to shoot the woman in the head, just to stop the screaming.

NOT YET, YOU STUPID ASSHOLE. YOU NEED HER ALIVE FOR A LITTLE BIT LONGER.

Harold smiled. The Queen was there inside his head to protect him, give him direction.

The big detective came forward, Miss Perfect at his side. "Don't be dumb, Harold," Gholer said. "You can't get away. Let the woman go."

Detective Gholer knew Harold's name. *How?*

Gholer spoke again. "You are surrounded, Harold. Now drop the gun. You're just making it worse."

Harold frowned. Surrounded? Oh yes, three more cops. The ones in uniform who'd been outside the mall, comparing Harold's picture with the shoppers exiting through the doors. The same ones who'd returned Harold's nod as he'd walked by them dressed as a security guard. The three had spread out across the walk and now moved toward Harold with their weapons out.

But Harold knew he wasn't surrounded. There were no cops behind him, only between him and the shopping mall. Detective Gholer was bullshitting. The Queen would be proud of Harold for not falling for Gholer's bullshit.

But he wasn't sure what to do about the three uniformed policemen.

Do we need those other three cops alive, Mother?

FUCK NO. KILL THEM.

Harold changed his grip on the woman, now pulling her tight against him with his forearm across her chest. He then shot one of the uniformed cops. A gaping hole appeared in the policeman's chest, and he went down kicking his feet. From all around came screams as passersby scrambled for cover.

Detective Gholer jogged toward the fallen officer.

Leaving Miss Perfect standing alone.

Harold dragged his captive backward, toward the parking lot. Spittle ran from her mouth and wet his shirtsleeve.

Miss Perfect slowly followed, crouched, her gun extended. "Let her go, Harold," she said. "Killing more people won't help you."

She'd spoken his name just as Gholer had. *How did she know my name?* He had the queasy feeling that he'd seen Miss Perfect before. Somewhere . . .

Her knowing his name was good. He would talk to her about it as the spiders sacrificed her body to the Change.

And to the Queen. Harold would be almost as powerful as the Queen Herself. He was suddenly giddy with excitement. He made an angry buzzing sound.

Miss Perfect watched him. Her lips parted in shock. Harold's battle cry must be frightening to her. She would soon belong to the Change.

But first things first.

Shall I kill another policeman, Mother?

NO. SHOOT THE WOMAN YOU'RE HOLDING. THEN RUN. THE PERFECT FEMALE WILL FOLLOW YOU. BRING HER, YOU FUCK. BRING HER TO ME.

Harold shoved the older woman away from him. She tried to run in high heels on weak scrawny legs. Harold shot her in the back. The impact knocked her forward on her face. Harold turned and sprinted through the parking lot, running low between the cars.

Behind him, a pistol cracked. Something whined overhead. He ducked even lower and ran even faster.

Miss Perfect yelled, "Goddamn you, Harold, you stop right there!"

At the curb beside the light pole where he'd earlier wrecked the Bronco, Harold did stop. He turned and

looked toward the mall, where Detective Gholer was
bent over the fallen uniformed policeman, and where
Miss Perfect stood near the wounded older woman.

Two kills for the good of the Change. The Queen
would think Harold a really fierce warrior.

He waited on the curb in plain view. He wanted
Miss Perfect to see him.

Harold suddenly grinned from ear to ear, and began
to get an erection as Miss Perfect sprinted toward him.
She could run very fast, Harold noted as he jogged
off toward the apartments where he'd left his pickup
truck. He was careful not to move too quickly, for
fear that Miss Perfect would lose sight of him. If he
failed to bring her, and right fucking now, he'd answer
to the Queen.

Mother of God, Courtney thought.

All around her was pandemonium. Panic. People
running for cover in all directions. Shouts of terror.
Gholer on his haunches beside the downed cop,
Gholer on his radio, talking fast. The poor innocent
woman shot in the back, pitched face-forward on the
ground at Courtney's feet. The Fiddleback hauling ass
across the parking lot.

*Your call, Officer Dumbshitz. Aid the woman or
chase the suspect. Which is it?*

The woman tried to crawl. Her knees came up and
then her legs stretched out. She clutched at empty air.
Courtney's heart went out to the woman. But . . .

*Take the suspect. Take the fucking suspect, Officer,
you can't help the woman.*

Courtney dodged around the prone, struggling figure, struck a two-handed practice range pose and fired
off a shot at the fleeing figure. Her aim was far too
high, not even close. The Fiddleback continued to run.
He paused at the curb the other side of the parking
lot.

Courtney ran after him, down two steps and across the asphalt.

Behind her, Gholer yelled, "No, Court, hold it."

"No time, Loo! Take the victims!" Her own words sounded faint and far away.

The Fiddleback seemed to be waiting. Taunting her. She made it past two rows of cars, cutting his lead in half before he moved again. He jogged through a crosswalk, dodging traffic. Horns honked and cars swerved from their paths. The Fiddleback reached the other side of the road, and headed east along the sidewalk. His pace was leisurely, practically a walk.

Courtney ran into the middle of the street. *Oh, Jesus Christ, I'm dead,* she thought as a minivan bore down on her left, its headlights blinding her, its brakes squealing. At the last instant the vehicle jumped the curb and bumped to a standstill, missing her by a hairsbreadth. She ran on across the street and up on the curb.

The Fiddleback was now crossing traffic-clogged Alpha Road fifty yards ahead. Courtney stopped and aimed her weapon. Autos crossed her line of sight in a parade. She couldn't chance a shot, no way. She ran on, her heart threatening to pound its way through her ribs. Jesus, her injured ribs. Pain rocked her side. She reached the curb at Alpha Road.

The Fiddleback had already crossed to the other side and stood near a driveway leading into an apartment complex, beside an open gate.

Courtney yelled, "Police, Harold! You are under arrest. Do not move."

She marveled at how fucking silly she sounded, even to herself. And was glad she hadn't said anything really stupid such as, "Things will go easier for you if you give it up." Nothing would ever go easy for this asshole if Courtney Bedell had anything to say about it. She dashed across Alpha Road as the Fiddleback loped off among the apartment buildings. He ran step-and-drag, moving rapidly nonetheless, and disappeared in the shadows.

Courtney took out after him, leaving the noise and the lights on Alpha Road, running past the open gate into the complex. She stopped, her breathing ragged, and waited for her vision to adjust to the darkness. Two- and three-story apartment buildings lay ahead on both sides of her. The honking of horns and the chugging of engines, loud enough seconds earlier to shatter eardrums, were faint and distant background noise.

She stood there, straining to hear something. Anything. Somewhere up ahead, a cricket *whirred*.

She felt dreadfully alone. And there was no sign of Fiddleback.

She thought of Berlin, the alley behind the Tattered Angel. She recalled the terror that clutched at her as she crept up on the men who were about to rape the woman. One guy stood in front of the woman, bare-assed, his pants down to his ankles, while another man entwined his fingers in her hair and forced her to her knees.

Courtney recalled sharply the feeling of total fear. After she'd turned the trio over to the Berlin police, her hands had trembled for hours. She hadn't slept peacefully for a month or more.

And now, once again, she felt total fear.

Her throat constricted as she moved in a crouch through the courtyard in between the apartment buildings, stopping every fifteen feet or so to do a complete turn with the Glock extended. A pool lay on her right, with underwater halogens casting a blue-green glow on sidewalks and walls. A volleyball net flapped in the breeze. Tall green ferns, elephant ears, and caladiums grew all around the perimeter.

Cover. Hiding places out the ass.

Was he in front of her? Behind her? Jesus, he was nowhere.

It was as if he'd vaporized.

She stayed close to the westernmost row of buildings, her hands tight around the Glock, her own breathing loud in her ears. She passed the pool, giving a wide berth to the diving board, and neared the end of the courtyard.

There was sudden movement overhead on her left. Courtney whirled in that direction. A girl came out of an upstairs apartment and stood on her balcony, getting some air. Courtney yelled out, "Police officer, miss. In pursuit of an armed suspect." The young woman ran inside as if she suddenly realized she was naked.

Courtney went down an open breezeway with apartment entries on both sides and came out in the open. She was in the resident parking area. Corrugated tin strung over pillars sheltered numbered spaces. Standing there in the moonlight were a Dumpster overflowing with garbage, a freestanding laundry room, and a small storage building six or seven feet high.

She first tried the laundry room, pointing the Glock around at washers and dryers. One of the dryers was on, damp clothes tumbling.

Not here.

She exited the laundry room and approached the storage building, frowning.

What's that? That vehicle, what's it doing there?

The tailgate and rear wheels of a pickup stuck out beyond the storage building's eastern wall. She moved past the building and stood behind the tailgate. The truck was two-toned, with a covered bed. An Aggie Twelfth Man sticker adorned the rear bumper.

In her mind she was back at the park near the fairgrounds. Standing inside a phone booth as the Fiddleback dragged a woman toward a waiting pickup.

This truck.

Jesus. It's his.

She extended the Glock and flattened against the storage building. Spun to the left. Spun to the right. No one.

Keeping her weapon ready, she squeezed in between the truck and the storage building and peered in through the window at the rear compartment. It was dark in there. She pressed her nose to the glass. Moonlight glinted from shackles that were bolted to the floor. She wiggled her way up beside the driver's door. There was a bench seat inside the cab, and a box on the floorboard on the passenger side.

Suspect's vehicle sighted, Officer. What now?

Report.

Slowly, Courtney took her cell phone from her pocket. Using both hands, the Glock pointing off to one side, she flipped open the mouthpiece and punched in the first two digits of Gholer's number.

Hold it, dummy. You forgot to check on top of the building.

She tilted her chin, looking up.

The Fiddleback dropped on her from the storage building's roof. He pinned her down between the pickup and the wall. The Glock flew in one direction, the phone in another.

First there was the pain, his full weight pressing down on her as her legs resisted, the agony in her ribs so fierce that she blacked out for an instant. When she came to she was facedown on the pavement with the Fiddleback straddling her back.

Oh, Jason . . . baby . . . Courtney is so, so sorry. Whatever will happen to you now?

The Fiddleback grabbed her under the arms and hauled her halfway to her feet. His chin pressed into the side of her neck. His breath was putrid, the stink of death.

The pressure jarred her ribs again. She screamed at the top of her lungs.

He dragged her backward toward the rear of the truck. Her heels scraped concrete. She made her body go limp. The dead weight didn't faze him; he bore her along as if she was made of balsa wood.

He wrapped one arm around her and pinned her against his chest while he opened the tailgate. Then he backed up, sat on the ledge, and hoisted her up inside.

She closed her eyes. A shackle clinked in the pickup's bed.

Without warning a noise like a firecracker split the night. The Fiddleback froze.

A husky male voice said nearby, "Don't move a muscle, Harold."

Gholer.

Courtney opened her eyes. Gholer stood twenty steps behind the pickup, lowering his weapon after firing a shot into the sky. He leveled his pistol toward Courtney and the Fiddleback.

She said faintly, "Loo?"

Gholer spread his feet farther apart. "Now listen, Harold. You let her go and stand clear."

The Fiddleback kept his seated position in the pickup's bed with his feet dangling and Courtney on his lap like a daughter at story time. He drew a gun from his holster, clicked the hammer back, and put the barrel against her head.

Gholer moved his feet closer together and stood up straighter. His pistol hung loosely at his hip. He extended his free hand, palm out. "This is dumb, Harold."

Holding Courtney in front of him, the Fiddleback slid down to a standing position and backed up between the pickup and the storage building. He took her, one slow step at a time, toward the front of the truck until they stood beside the driver's door.

Gholer walked a couple of steps toward them.

Courtney hissed, "Shoot the fucker, Loo. Don't worry about me, just kill the bastard."

The Fiddleback opened the door and started to climb in along with his captive.

Courtney raised her foot and stamped down on the Fiddleback's instep. He grunted in surprise. His grip around her shoulders loosened.

She dove forward on her face. "Kill him, Loo!" she yelled.

Gholer's gun went off. Glass shattered. A split second later tiny shards rained on the back of Courtney's neck and into her hair.

A door slammed. A starter chugged and the pickup's engine caught. The truck lurched forward, the rear wheel spinning and burning rubber less than a foot from Courtney's head. Then the truck was clear of the storage building, speeding away toward the exit from the parking lot.

As Courtney rolled onto her side, Gholer came up beside her. He fired off a final shot at the retreating vehicle. The pickup listed as it turned to the right and disappeared behind an apartment building.

Courtney struggled to her feet and stood beside Gholer. He touched her shoulder. "You okay?"

She threw her arms around him, the two of them alone in the parking lot, tears running down her face to wet his jacket and drip on the pavement.

She was, unbelievably, alive.

But the Fiddleback was once again long gone.

20

Megan Harris, naked in her office. Tiny sagging tits, big ugly nipples. Flabby protruding belly. Big fat thighs spread out as she sat on her desk. Ass like cottage cheese. Head tilted back, lips parted in ecstasy.

Billy Hargis thought, *Christ, I can't take it anymore.*

The grunting and the groaning. Her yelps of passion, more like oinks.

Fucking her in the standing position so he wouldn't have to get on top of her and feel that blubber against his own smooth-muscled body. Her on top? No goddamned way. *Let's get this over with . . .*

Over by the bookcase filled with Federal Seconds and Vernon's *Annotated Civil Statutes,* the fax machine dinged and whirred. A page rolled slowly out of the platen.

Hargis glanced at the incoming fax as he continued to pump her. She threw pudgy arms around his neck. She wailed. "Oh yes, darling. Oh yes, darling, yes, yes. *God . . .*"

Hargis finished with his eyes closed, faking his own cry of lust. Christ, he deserved a medal. Navy Cross or something.

She kept her legs wrapped around his middle and her arms around his neck, squeezing. Christ, she might strangle him.

He had to see the fax. Had to disentangled himself from this love-starved elephant and get down to business.

Not that humping Megan Harris wasn't business. *Only* business. One of the low points of putting the deal together.

The other low point: hassling with the lunatic who went around buzzing like an insect. The guy who heard voices. The guy who believed that he was turning into a spider. Thought that someday he'd be spinning webs, with silk stringing out of his ass. Thought he'd be stinging people. Christ, what a maniac.

Which chore was the most disgusting? Fucking Megan Harris or putting up with Harold Bays?

It was a toss-up.

Both were equally necessary.

Christ, the things that Billy Hargis had to endure.

He firmly grasped her upper arms and took them from around his neck. "Good, baby?"

She settled back and leaned on her hands. "Oh wonderful. Great." She uttered a long and soulful sigh.

He slipped out of her and walked naked over to the fax machine. "I think this is it."

She drew her legs up and sat on her ankles like a walrus-sized teen queen. "That worries me, Billy. There'll be a record."

Hargis lifted the fax out of the tray. "A record of what? My lawyer faxing Sis' lawyer?"

"I mean, of the fax itself. I think they have a way of retrieving those."

He shrugged and gave her a confident smile. "So get another machine. Smash this one to pieces. You give these police too much credit." He examined the fax of Courtney Bedell's picture under a table lamp. "Christ, she was there that night."

Megan Harris scootched around in anxiety. "A black woman?"

He looked at her.

"One of the detectives who came here was a black woman," she said. "I think she might've been suspicious."

"Oh? A big, strong-looking gal?"

"Looked like she might've played basketball."

"Yeah. I met her, too," Hargis said. "She works for the hard-nosed fuck. The black chick and the other one, the rat-faced fuck she calls Eddie. Is he the other one that came here?"

"Eddie? Yeah, I believe. Frielander? No, Frizell."

"That would equate. The woman took Larry over for a look at the body while the rat-faced fuck and the hard-nosed asshole stood around staring at me. Shit, everybody seems to work for this hard-nosed fuck." Hargis turned the fax around so that Megan could see. "This one stayed in the background, behind the yellow tape. I thought she was watching me awfully closely. Christ, the dark eyes, the skin. Old Harold will get a boner just looking at this picture."

Megan's lashes fluttered. "God, you call him by name?"

"Well, what would you call him?"

"What he is. Evil."

Hargis spread his hands. "We're all evil, Megan. Harold just looks the part."

Her chin sunk down to her chest. "I can't forget those eyes. His grotesque body."

I'll bet he can't forget your body, either, Hargis thought. *Christ, the guy is better off fucking a bunch of spiders.* He dropped the fax on Megan's desk, then picked up striped boxer shorts and stepped into them, snapping the elastic against his taut-ridged abs. He turned sideways and examined his reflection in the window. Perfect. "Harold has a purpose," he said. "Never know when you're going to need a Harold, you know?"

Megan slid off her desk and hung her head. She slowly raised her gaze to him. "I want this to be over. So that our lives can finally merge. So that we can be together openly."

Hargis slipped a pale yellow Polo shirt on over his head. Be seen in public with her? Was she kidding? Christ, he was in a hurry to leave, afraid she'd want him to fuck her again. Heather waiting at home with her toned legs and tight twenty-two-year-old ass, while he stood here with this hideous-looking woman in a law office. "It will be over soon. Just one more little thing to take care of."

She picked up the fax. "Bedell. Italian?"

"Something foreign. Spanish?"

"No, Italian. I knew a guy with that name. A lawyer. I'm not familiar with this home address."

"Neither am I. East Dallas someplace, Larry says. Out of the loop. Poor people's neighborhood."

"Like, around the fairgrounds?"

"Christ, not that fucking poor. She's got a job. Don't worry, though, Harold will find it. He'd find her in Israel, that one. Trust me." Hargis picked up flat-front Tommy Hilfiger slacks and shook them out in preparation for putting them on.

She looked unsure. "I don't want to go to his place, Billy."

He paused before stepping into the pants. "We have to. I need you to wait with the engine running. Christ, you think I'm talking to Harold without a gun on him or a getaway driver outside? First thing you know he'll be putting one of those spiders on me."

"It made my skin crawl just to be within yards of him. The day he picked up Sis I thought I'd faint."

"But you didn't, Megan. You did good. Without you standing there, Harold might not've found her. Used you as a landmark, someone he'd recognize."

Megan looked away. "Jesus. That detective."

Hargis buttoned his slacks. "Her?" He indicated the fax.

Megan laid the fax on the desk. "No, the black woman. I may have screwed up."

Hargis had his zipper halfway up. He stopped and cocked his head.

"Something I told her," Megan said.

"Oh? What is that?"

"I told her I left the building with Sis."

"And you didn't?"

Her mouth tightened. "You know I didn't, Billy. I left her modeling on the platform while I went outside and called you. So you could send that awful . . . Jesus."

"And you met her later, so you'd be standing there when Harold drove up. So he could recognize you. I don't see that as any big deal."

"It may not be. It's just that detective—you could tell she didn't believe me. She scares me, Billy. She's pretty intelligent."

"Smart enough she isn't picking cotton." Hargis was dressed now, modeling for his own benefit, turning this way and that, watching his reflection in the window. Christ, the rugged good looks . . . Michael Douglas. No, Christ, not that fucking old. George Clooney, only a better set of abs. "Get dressed, Megan," he said. "Before we sleep we've got miles to go."

Hargis watched Megan Harris struggle into her pantyhose, wiggling her enormous ass in his face as she pulled the mesh up over her thighs. Christ, he couldn't stand the sight. He turned and looked out the window. Highland Park Shopping Village teemed with business, chicly dressed WASPy men and women bustling in and out of the stores, carrying packages. No niggers, no Mexicans. Maybe a few queers—sometimes you couldn't tell, but if there were fags in Highland Park they were all in the closet. Beyond the shopping center lay the country club, and behind the country club lay the mansions on Beverly Drive. Dallas' version of the rich man's world.

Billy Hargis' world.

Or, more explicitly, William Hargis Sr.'s world, up until he died eighteen months ago. Billy Hargis' world now that he'd inherited everything. Or such was public perception.

The truth was that Billy Hargis was broke as a toad. B-R-O-K-E. Couldn't pay attention. If pussy went down to two bits a throw, he couldn't buy a hand job. Of the jokes his father and his buddies used to tell around the country club, half of them were about poor people, the other half about niggers and queers. Jew jokes as well, though in more select company; Christ, there were all kinds of Jews on boards of directors of banks, insurance companies . . . piss one of those guys off, forget about it.

Christ, but he missed his old man.

But even more, he missed the twelve million dollars he'd squandered since the old man had croaked. In Vegas. On the Riviera. Some on Wall Street, the dot-com stocks, maybe a hundred thou, chump-change, blown on women, flying them around the country, paying their apartment rent.

Christ.

A shade *over* twelve million, actually. In a drawer at home he had a bill from Caesars Palace, fifty grand worth, plus a notice that as soon as he settled the account they'd consider reinstating his now-revoked credit line. He wondered if they'd send someone after him, fuck up his face. These chiseled features . . .

All these insignificant assholes were demanding their money. Even Larry Akin the lawyer was bitching about his unpaid fee. Hargis had had to argue with the guy, just to get him to fax the info on the witness.

Christ, the witness. Courtney Catherine Bedell. The

policewoman who'd stumbled on Harold Bays as he hauled Sis away, and who now could identify the guy as the Fiddleback. And the fruitcake Bays, who could in turn identify Billy Hargis as the man who'd set his own wife's abduction in motion.

If the cops believed the insane asshole, that is. A guy that talked to spiders? Fifty-fifty that he'd have the sense to become a snitch, odds even less that the police would listen to the guy. But why take the chance?

Christ, but Billy Hargis needed money. *Had* to have money.

Sis' life insurance policy would take care of everything, and then some. He wondered when Harold Bays was going to hang her from a bridge, tie her ass to a tree or something. Unless her body turned up, the insurance company wouldn't pay for five years, presumption of death and all that jazz.

Billy Hargis couldn't wait five years. He couldn't wait a week. Christ, he'd be lucky to last a couple of days.

It was a good thing he'd decided to fuck Megan Harris, bring her over to his side. Otherwise she never would have filled him in on Texas law.

Written in stone, right there in the family code: In the event of divorce, any provision in a life insurance policy naming the ex-spouse as beneficiary is void, the idea being to keep recently divorced couples from killing each other. Which was the reason Sis had to die before the divorce was final, so that Billy could remain her beneficiary.

Sis had thought the reason for delay in the divorce proceedings was her demand for the house and a few other items, but in truth, her claim to the house had nothing to do with it. With the five-million-dollar proceeds from life insurance, Billy could buy another house. Pave things over with Caesar's. Fly to Monte

Carlo, get hot on the dice table, get his money back. Live as it was his God-given right to live.

Billy Hargis' real reason for having his lawyer file delay after delay was to give him time to have Sis murdered. He'd even met with a couple of button men. But those insignificant assholes had been as bad as the bookmaker, demanding cash in advance. Obviously not knowing who they were dealing with.

Thank God for Megan and her flabby gaping hole.

And, in other ways, thank God for sending Harold Bays.

Christ, the lunatic and his schizophrenia. His buzzing noises. The way he walked, like a lurching Frankenstein. Scarred face, wide sloping forehead. Hair combed over to hide his bald spots. What an ugly shit.

But extremely useful.

The first time Billy Hargis called the dock super at Texas Motor Freight, threw his weight around and demanded a worker to dig some flowerbeds, the dock boss sent over Harold Bays. The crazy asshole had scared the shit out of Hargis on sight. Dragging his foot around. Not speaking to anyone around the property. Did a good job on the beds, but it wasn't worth it to have the guy hanging around. After Bays had finished the job, Billy Hargis had vowed never to lay eyes on the fucker again.

Bays had frightened Sis as well; as long as Harold Bays was on the premises she wouldn't step outside the house. But she'd stepped outside the house right quick when she'd slapped Billy with a divorce petition.

Sis had been gone a month before Billy Hargis, strictly by accident, watched Harold Bays abduct a woman.

Or *was* it strictly by accident? Billy Hargis believed in fate. And part of fate, as his old man used to say, is that the race belongs to the strong. Or was it the swift? Whatever—the guy with his ass in gear always wins.

Humping Sis' divorce lawyer certainly wasn't an accident. And neither, probably, was discovering that Harold Bays was the insane fuck the police were calling the Fiddleback.

The ballpark in Arlington, middle of July, one of those ninety-degrees-at-midnight kind of days. Devil Rays in town. Rangers 6, Tampa Bay 2. Kenny Rogers a four-hitter. John Wetteland the save. Billy Hargis would never forget the game.

After the top of the fifth he'd excused himself from the liquor-leeching assholes partying in his luxury box and had taken a stroll outside the stadium to settle with his bookie. Jerry the Fin, another disgusting fuck questioning Billy Hargis' credit, demanding money before he'd accept more action. At one time Billy Hargis could've bought and sold the fucker.

Nonetheless he'd swallowed his pride, met Jerry the Fin outside a southeast gate, forked over a roll of bills, gotten down on the Dodgers and Mariners in late-starting West Coast games, and then had walked in between mammoth stadium support pillars on his way back to rejoin the liquor-leeches.

Harold Bays had been lurking in the parking lot, seated behind the wheel of a two-toned pickup truck. It was the truck that first caught Hargis' attention, the same vehicle in which Bays had arrived at Hargis' home to dig the flowerbeds.

Billy Hargis' first reaction was, Christ, that Neanderthal was a *baseball fan*?

Hargis ducked behind a pillar. What if the guy saw him, wanted to talk or something? He decided to stay in hiding until the fucker drove away. And that's what he did for the next ten minutes, peering occasionally around the pillar to see if Harold Bays had gone. The pickup never moved.

And from that vantage point, Hargis had a face-on view of the black girl who walked in toward the stadium from the far reaches of the parking lot.

She was a stadium employee of some kind, concession vendor or ticket taker, dressed in pale blue slacks and a Rangers jersey showing number 25, a Raffy Palmeiro fan. Her hair was braided into a ponytail that stuck out over the adjustment band in her baseball cap and waved between her shoulder blades. She was very pretty, with smooth black skin and confidence in her step. Hargis would guess her age as somewhere between twenty-five and thirty (though, as his old man used to say, with niggers it was hard to tell).

As she drew abreast of the pickup, Harold Bays opened the door and stood outside. Now Hargis had to laugh; at least the ape was human and was trying to score a little poontang. Nothing wrong with that. He waited for the girl to tell Bays to leave her alone.

Harold Bays walked up to the girl, put a gun to her head, and made her get inside the pickup truck on the driver's side. She begged him to let her go, her voice drifting to Hargis' ears in his hiding place. Harold Bays climbed in after the girl, put the pickup in gear, and drove away.

Just like that. The entire incident was over in fifteen seconds. Hargis had jerked out his cell phone, punched 911, and then paused with his finger ready to punch the send button that would summon police emergency. His gaze had followed the direction in which the pickup had gone. His eyes had widened as a lightbulb flashed inside his head. He'd closed up the cell phone and put it away.

Harold Bays was a lunatic who went around kidnapping people.

And, as of that moment, Billy Hargis owned the fucker's balls.

Hargis was suddenly sweating, just remembering the night. Perspiration darkened his shirt, both at the waist and under the arms. He turned away from the window as Megan Harris strained to fasten her bra. She looked at him, her moon face relaxed in an expression of fear. "I'm afraid to go, Billy," she said.

He stepped behind her and hooked one of the catches on her bra. "Nothing to worry about," he said. "I control the bastard, remember? What, you think I'd let anything happen to you?"

As Billy Hargis' Cadillac SUV neared the gate that marked the entry to Harold Bays' farm, Hargis glanced sideways at Megan Harris. She had a death grip on the door handle and her mouth was partway open. Her skirt was hiked up, exposing her chubby knees. Every time the car went over a bump in the asphalt, she uttered a tiny yelp of fear.

Hargis grinned to himself. Not that Harold Bays wasn't one scary son of a bitch, because he was. You just had to know how to handle the guy.

Such as four days after the incident at the ballpark, when Hargis had once again demanded free labor from the freight dock line. And this time he'd specified Harold Bays—not by name, because that would be a dead giveaway, but by telling the dock boss to send the squatty-bodied crippled guy. Was Hargis sure that's who he wanted? the dock boss had asked, because Harold Bays acted a bit crazy at times. Of course, Hargis had told the guy, the last time he'd come to the house, Harold Bays had done one helluva job.

And, later, with Harold Bays, shirtless, wielding clippers as he trimmed the hindmost row of hedges on the Hargis estate, Billy had walked up behind the guy and dropped that day's newspaper on the ground. On the front page of the paper was a photo of a pretty African-American girl, under a headline reading, MISSING WOMAN FEARED FIDDLEBACK VICTIM.

The hedge clippers skipped a beat as Harold looked down at the picture and the headline.

Billy Hargis said casually, "Hey, Harold. Ever seen her before?"

Harold whirled, hissing. He opened the clipper blades.

Hargis had a gun pointed at the Fiddleback's face. "I can kill you, Harold. Or we can talk."

Harold continued to hiss and scowl, but he eventually dropped the clippers on the ground. His dark eyes smoldered with silent hatred.

"Much, much better." Hargis clapped the Fiddleback on the shoulder, in mock good cheer. "Better me than the cops, Harold. Christ, how can I teach you? You've got nothing to fear from me."

Hargis' thoughts came back to the present as the entrance to the farm loomed on the left. He braked, pulled off the asphalt, and left the engine running while he opened the gate. He jogged back, got in the car, and doused the lights. "This is the trickiest part, driving in the dark. Piece of cake after that." He grinned at Megan and dropped the lever into gear.

Megan Harris continued to whimper as the Cadillac passed the gate and bumped in among the mesquite trees. The wind had picked up, rattling branches and whipping leaves and pieces of paper against the windows. The moon shone brightly through the foliage; the twin tire ruts leading through the woods were as easy to follow as if it was daylight. Hargis traversed the distance into the clearing at a steady ten miles an hour. Once clear of the trees, he stopped beside the ancient barn. The WWII-vintage harvester hulked on his left.

Hargis could see clearly all the way up the muddy gravel drive. The house stood silent, with sagging roof and shutters hanging from single hinges. A lone bulb glowed over the door. Harold Bays' pickup truck wasn't parked anywhere in sight. So Harold wasn't home. Likely out snatching someone off the street or hanging a body from a bridge. The usual crap for the guy.

Hargis shrugged, and allowed a little smile. Harold not being home was good. Meant that Hargis wouldn't have to confront the deranged asshole. He gave the SUV a little gas, drove on up to the house, and parked in the curved driveway in front of the porch.

He slammed the gearshift into park, reached inside the glove box, and pulled out the fax containing Courtney Bedell's photo and home address. Then he brought his own Smith & Wesson .32 automatic from beneath the seat, along with a flashlight. He grinned at Megan. "Be easier than I thought," Hargis said. "He's not even here." He shouldered open the door.

She reached over and clutched his arm. "He could drive up at any minute. Don't leave me here alone, darling."

Darling? Christ . . .

Hargis moved her hand away. "Wouldn't dream of it. Come with me, Megan. This is going to be so easy you won't believe." He brandished the .32. "And in case he should show up . . . oh hell. Just stick close to me, okay?"

Harold Bays is one filthy fuck, Hargis thought. Dust on the furniture like dirty snow. Wastebaskets overflowing. Rat poop on the floor. The smell inside the house like steaming dog shit.

The flashlight's beam shined on dirty hardwood floors, across ancient sofas and chairs with cotton stuffing poking out, springs exposed. Hargis had been inside this spooky old house three days earlier, when he'd held a gun on Harold Bays and directed the Fiddleback to show him Sis. Which Bays had done, his eyes glaring hatred as he'd led the way down the hall and opened the door. One glance had been enough for Hargis, seeing Sis sleeping naked and chained to a

bench, a spider bite festering on her ribcage. He'd
demanded to know when Bays was going to do her
in. Bays had just hissed at him. Hargis had decided to
let well enough alone.

And exactly where was that fucking hallway leading
to that minidungeon? Hargis shone the light this way
and that. Past the staircase. *There.* Back there, beyond
the open archway was the corridor.

Hargis started to go past the banister. Megan
grabbed his shirt and hung on for dear life. Christ, but
this hippo of a woman was strong. She panted in his
ear and made terrified little squeaking noises.

"This way," Hargis said. "And relax, will you?"

"I can't relax, Billy. God, this place. The things he's
done here."

Hargis did his best to walk on toward the back of
the house, with Megan dogging his steps. She stumbled in the dark and fell against him. She'd damned
near knocked him over. He steadied himself with one
hand against the wall. She stood there whining, clutching his arm.

"Look," he said. "I've got an idea."

"What, darling?"

Christ, there was that word again, enough to make
you puke. He said, "You wait here, where it's safe.
I'll be through in a minute." He pointed the flash at
her, her eyes wide, her mouth slack.

Her grip tightened on his arm. "Safe? Here? Oh,
Jesus, Billy, don't *leave* me."

He aimed the beam toward a dusty chair. "Just sit
there. Nothing can get you."

She wildly shook her head. "I'm afraid to."

"Well, okay. Come along if you want to. But I'm
warning you, it isn't pretty. Back there is where he's
kept them. Blood all over the place. All kinds of those
fucking spiders crawling around."

She took a step back. "Spiders? Oh God, I can't."

"Exactly my point." He grasped her upper arm and ushered her firmly over to the easy chair. "Just sit there, Megan. Here is scary, that I'll grant you. But just sit and wait. You'll see. It'll be over before you know it, Megan. Just trust me, okay?"

It was as if he'd cut the rope and loosened the dangling albatross from around his neck. Moving free as a bird down the corridor toward the back of the house without Megan clutching at him, he halfway hoped that Harold Bays jumped out of a closet and yelled *Boo!* at her. Give her a fucking heart attack.

More rat shit here in the hallway. *Fiddleback my ass,* Hargis thought, *the guy should be Rat Man.* Or Cockroach Man, one of the hideous fuckers that scuttled across the floor and ran through a crack underneath the wall. And in the middle of the corridor were drops of . . .

Christ. Was it blood?

Hargis bent nearer to inspect the round glistening puddle. It was blood, all right, and, up ahead, more drops formed a trail leading away from him. The door on Hargis' right was the room where the lunatic had been holding Sis.

Had he already killed her? *Christ, I hope so,* Hargis thought.

Hargis tried the door. It wasn't locked, so he pushed it open and pointed the flash inside the dungeon. The bench where Sis had lain in a coma was bare. As the light flashed on hard splintery wood, a spider scuttled for safety. It was one of those fucking arachnids the guy was always talking to. Hargis swallowed his revulsion and stepped inside, nearer to the bench. He shined the light around.

Blood and grayish matter had spattered the wall.

The goo was still wet, glistening in the glare from the flashlight. Dripping and puddling on the bench in a series of soft dull plops.

Super, Hargis thought, *he's blown her fucking brains out. And those drops of blood leading down the corridor . . . Christ, he's dragged her away.*

And he is somewhere right now, stringing her up from a bridge or tying her to a tree.

Her head down, bare ass in the air. An ass worth five million dollars in life insurance.

Hargis grinned from ear to ear.

He went down the hall and into the lunatic's bedroom, looking for something, anything, with which to hang the poster. He shined the light around, on a metal bed with a sagging mattress, a dresser whose drawers were partway open. On the dresser was a small jar filled with knickknacks; paper clips, safety pins . . .

And thumbtacks. Two or three stickpins. He reached inside the jar, fumbled around, pulled out a tack with a yellow head. He went back out in the hall and closed the door.

He unrolled the fax from Megan's machine and steadied the flashlight. Courtney Bedell's police academy photo was at the top of the page over her birthdate, rank, and home address.

He laid the flashlight on top of a hallway cabinet and, steadying the fax against the door with one hand, pushed the thumbtack through paper and wood. He stood back and shined the flashlight on Courtney Bedell's picture. It was in plain view, where even an insane fuck such as Harold Bays couldn't miss the damned thing.

Megan Harris thought she might not be so terrified with her eyes closed. She tried it, squinching her lids tightly together. The walls creaked and the wind rattled the shutters. God, she was even more frightened than she had been. She opened her eyes and peered through the darkness. Something moved in the far corner of the room. Or did it? No, it was only a tree branch waving in the breeze outside, outlined in shadow from moonlight slanting in through the window.

The chair in which she sat faced the front of the house. Through the window she could see the porch, Billy Hargis' Cadillac SUV parked in the drive, and the ribbon of gravel road leading past the barn and old harvester into the woods. On the other side of the woods lay the road leading to the interstate. The moon was full. Bright and round as a pumpkin.

A witches' moon.

God.

She thought about running down the hall in search of Billy. But what if she stumbled and fell into a nest of spiders? She could practically feel them, brown recluse spiders crawling over her naked body, stinging her, her skin sloughing away and melting into puddles.

She thought of Sis. Poor Sis . . .

No, no, fuck poor Sis. Megan had wanted Sis' husband, and now she had him.

Or did she? Did he want her, or did he want his mindless teenybop girlfriend?

Did it matter?

God, but she was scared. Her whole body trembled. Her sinuses ached.

She heard a noise, a creaking sound like footsteps in the hallway. Billy. Billy returning to protect her. She turned hopefully toward the archway at the head of the corridor.

But no one came. Had she really heard the noise, or was her mind playing tricks?

Oh, Billy, Billy, come back to me.

She turned and looked out through the window

once more. Maybe she should go and wait in the car. Maybe she should . . .

Far in the distance, headlights glowed. A vehicle was coming through the woods, headed for the barn. The lights bobbed up and down, disappeared behind a thick row of mesquites, and then reappeared entering the clearing.

Coming here, Megan thought. Coming straight for this house.

Harold Bays.

God, he'd kill her. Rape her time after time while turning his spiders loose to scuttle across her belly, her legs . . .

Out of her wits in terror, Megan Harris threw back her head and screamed at the top of her lungs. Across the room, hidden in the darkness, rats scrambled for cover and cockroaches scurried into the walls.

Harold Bays drove through the night with tears of shame blurring his vision. He had had Miss Perfect in his grasp and had let her escape. Had run like a coward from Detective Gholer. Had failed. Had utterly failed.

YOU BLEW IT, YOU WORTHLESS FUCK. I SAID I WANTED HER. WHAT ARE YOU BRINGING ME? NOTHING, YOU PIECE OF SHIT. NOTHING.

The Queen, screaming inside his head. He had to make her understand. *I will bring her, Mother. You'll see.*

YOU'LL DIE, YOU ASSHOLE.

Harold sniffled and continued onto his property, so upset that he didn't even notice that the gate was open. He drove wildly through the woods, missing a tree by the width of an eyelash, the pickup's hood bouncing as he raced over tire ruts at thirty miles an hour. He rolled into the clearing, sped up, and whipped past the barn and ancient harvester. The house was a hundred yards ahead.

Where She waited.

She had to forgive him.

FORGIVE *YOU? I DON'T EVEN KNOW YOU, YOU WORTHLESS FUCK.*

Oh please, Mother . . .

SHUT UP. DON'T EVER SPEAK TO ME AGAIN.

He sobbed uncontrollably as he followed the curve in the drive, slammed on the brakes, and listed sideways as the pickup came to a sliding halt in front of the porch. He snatched the keys from the ignition and threw open the door. Shards of glass flew from his bullet-splintered window and tinkled on the gravel.

Harold froze in mid-stride.

A Cadillac SUV was parked there, facing him. Jesus, *he* was here. The man who gave Harold orders. And whose fault it was that Harold had lost face with the Queen.

Harold's features pinched in hatred. He unholstered the .45 and, bellowing in anger and waving the gun before him, thundered across the driveway, over the porch, and used his shoulder as a battering ram to blast open the door.

Billy Hargis heard Megan Harris scream as he stood at the far end of the corridor, shining the flashlight on Courtney Bedell's picture. Christ, Hargis thought, what was wrong with that fucking buffalo? Scare the shit out of a guy.

She screamed a second time, the noise loud enough to puncture eardrums.

That does it, Hargis thought. *Absolutely fucking . . . does it.*

He stomped back down the hallway toward the living room. His S&W .32 hung loosely at his hip. The flashlight's beam was pointed straight ahead. Yet another insane woman in his life. He was going to slap her silly, stuff rags in her mouth, anything to shut her up. Maybe chain her to the bench where Sis' brains were spattered on the wall, leave Megan Harris for the Fiddleback. Anything to get rid of her.

He passed beneath the archway and stepped into the living room. And there she was, the helpless walrus of a woman seated frozen in a chair. Christ, she might cut loose with another yell at any minute. Hargis swung the flashlight around the room, looking for a board, a baseball bat, something with which to bash her over the head. As he did, the front door burst open, rocked on its hinges, and hit the wall with a noise like a thunderclap. And, as Hargis watched in disbelief, Harold Bays came thundering in. Hargis pointed the flashlight at him, seeing that he was dressed as a cop or security guard or something. And his look was wild, out of control.

Harold blinked in the glare of a flashlight shining in his face. He had a partial view of the dirty floor, the sofa and chairs, and of someone sitting down over by the staircase banister. A woman he'd seen somewhere.

Where, Mother?

No answer. The Queen had deserted him.

Howling in sorrow, Harold pointed the dead security guard's gun and pulled the trigger. Flame spurted from the barrel, the blast deafening inside the room. The top of the woman's head disappeared and the rest of her fell from the chair and crashed to the floor.

Billy Hargis recoiled in shock as Megan Harris dropped like a stone. Christ. The insane fuck had shot her. *Dingdong, the witch is dead.* Or was she? Hargis didn't know and didn't really give a shit. He had a singular thought—get the hell away from here. He even forgot that he had his own pistol in his hand, and that Harold Bays was a sitting duck framed in the open doorway. The flashlight slid from his grasp and rolled across the floor, shooting its beam this way and that. Hargis turned tail and ran.

Down the hall toward the rear of the house he thundered, through the kitchen, and out into the yard. He stopped and looked wildly about, at a shed near the back of the property, at federal prison fences in the distance. His car was in front; did he chance circling the house and diving in behind the wheel, or did he take to the open fields in the direction of the prison?

He had to make up his mind. The lunatic could be on him at any second. Panting in terror, mucus flowing from his nose, Hargis ran to the house's eastern edge and down the side toward the driveway. Christ, the lunatic was going to get him. Christ, Billy Hargis was as good as dead.

He came around the corner at the front of the house. His SUV sat in the drive in front of Harold Bays' pickup. Sobbing with the effort, Hargis charged to the SUV, yanked open the door, and threw himself inside on the seat. He reached for the ignition and his hands froze in terror. He clenched his teeth and forced his fingers to turn the key. The engine caught immediately and the automatic sensor turned on the lights. Hargis jammed the lever in gear and pushed the gas pedal to the floor. His rear wheels spun on gravel as the SUV fishtailed away toward the barn.

He was going to make it. Unfucking believable. His gaze frozen on the landscape ahead, on the woods coming toward him at ever-increasing velocity, Billy Hargis clutched the wheel and plunged on toward the safety of the highway.

Harold Bays never even noticed Billy Hargis fleeing. Harold's gaze was frozen on the dead woman with the

top of her head blown away as he listened to the
Queen.

*YOU INCOMPETENT FUCK. WHY DID YOU
SHOOT HER?*

She was a danger, Mother.

*A DANGER? A FUCKING DANGER? SHE WAS
A WOMAN SITTING ON HER ASS. SO WHAT'S
SO DANGEROUS?*

I was trying to protect you.

*YOU FUCKING NINCOMPOOP. YOU COULDN'T
PROTECT YOURSELF FROM A KICK IN THE
BALLS. JESUS CHRIST, NOW YOU HAVE TO
GET RID OF HER.*

I will, Mother.

*YOU BET YOUR SWEET ASS YOU WILL. NOW
GET MOVING.*

In a trancelike state, Harold stooped and picked up
the flashlight. He shined the beam in his own face, then
turned the light around and directed its beam on the
woman. Her face was turned up toward the ceiling. It
dawned on Harold where he'd seen her before.

She was a friend of the man who told Harold to do
things. She had stood beside the other woman at the
fair, so that Harold would recognize her. And then
Harold had brought the other woman to this house
and chained her. The other woman had displeased the
Queen, so Harold had shot her and buried her behind
the shed.

So the woman who now lay dead at Harold's feet
was an enemy of the Change. It was good that she
was dead. Harold would now bury her behind the shed
as well. Harold stuffed the flashlight into his pocket,
grabbed the dead woman's ankles, and dragged her
away down the corridor.

I'll get rid of her, Mother.

YOU'D BETTER, YOU FUCK.

Head down, grunting with the effort, Harold plodded on. The woman was heavy, heavier than any of the others. A fat worthless slug and an enemy of the Change.

He drew abreast of his room, dropped the woman's feet with a thud, and plodded over to open his door. His shovel was in his closet, kept there so it would be hidden in a place known only to him. He grasped and turned the handle.

And stopped. A letter-sized piece of paper was thumbtacked to his door. He drew out the flashlight, thumbed the switch, and directed the beam. His mouth gaped open.

It is her picture, Mother.

HER?

The one you want. Miss Perfect.

HER?

Yes, Mother.

WELL, THEN, BRING HER TO ME.

Harold looked wearily toward the dead woman in the corridor. *Should I bury the body first?*

FUCK NO, YOU ASSHOLE. YOU BRING HER TO ME, RIGHT NOW. QUIT STANDING THERE GAPING, AND GET YOUR ASS IN GEAR.

21

Courtney kept to herself amid the pandemonium outside Valley View Mall. Her throat ached and her body trembled. Through her fear and depression, anger boiled.

What had been a media watch had turned into a circus; the two mobile news units had multiplied into half a dozen. Two Emergency Medical Unit vans stood near the mall entry, one team of medics hovering over the fallen policeman and the other over the woman the Fiddleback had shot in the back. Both victims were alive. The wounded lady's husband, a portly, bespectacled man in his sixties, was giving hell to medics and cops alike. His wife was laid out on a gurney with a blanket covering her from the neck down. As two techs rolled the gurney toward a waiting ambulance while a third medic walked alongside holding a transfusion bottle, the husband told a reporter nearby that the cops had endangered his wife with their fumbling. The husband followed the gurney inside the ambulance, stepping up and sitting down beside his wife. She reached out to him and he took her hand. Flashes flashed and minicams whirred.

Courtney didn't much blame the husband. She even agreed with the guy; law enforcement had blown this one, big-time. Or more to the point, FBI Agent Miller had blown it. Courtney was sure that she and Gholer would have eventually run the Fiddleback down inside the building and captured him without any bloodshed. Maybe they wouldn't have, but Miller's dumbass decision had cost them any opportunity to try. Agent Miller wouldn't shoulder the blame, of course. Neither would the chief nor Captain Dilbergast. Eventually they'd all point the finger in Gholer's direction. Involuntarily, Courtney's upper lip curled.

Gholer stood on the steps talking to Captain Dilbergast. Or listening to her, actually; the lieutenant stood with hands on hips, head bowed, as the captain talked a mile a minute. Occasionally, Gholer would nod. Sometimes he'd paw the ground with his foot. Each time the reporters approached, Gholer would wave them away.

Courtney was frustrated, and she felt like a fool. The guy had hidden practically in plain sight on top of a six-foot-high storage building, and Courtney had been so busy playing movie cop, flattening against walls and whirling this way and that, that she hadn't bothered looking in the most obvious place. Her own stupidity had almost gotten her killed. Jesus, if Gholer hadn't happened along . . .

None of which would be any consolation to the man whose wife was down. Or to the wounded cop's family. It was a miracle that both shooting victims were going to live. *And next come the lawsuits,* Courtney thought.

A nearby female voice called out, "Courtney Bedell?"

Courtney turned. It was the same coiffed and cool-looking on-the-spot reporter who'd been interviewing Agent Miller when Courtney and Gholer had arrived at the mall. The reporter approached, mike in hand, cameraman in the background. "Courtney Bedell?" she said again. "I'm Candace McCord, Channel 6."

Of course she was. Courtney had seen her a zillion times on the ten P.M. edition, standing in the rain in the wake of a tornado or outside a burning building with sparks falling all around her, interviewing victims and witnesses. Candace McCord was North Texas' version of the Disaster Lady.

Courtney hugged her windbreaker tight around her shoulders and didn't say anything.

The reporter moved in closer as the cameraman positioned his lens above her right shoulder. "Word is," McCord said, "that you've been face to face with the fiend. What could that possibly have been like?" She offered the mike.

Courtney's lips parted. Maybe thirty feet from where she stood, visible behind the newswoman and the cameraman, Agent Miller was holding court with several mikes thrust in his face. More reporters left the FBI man and moved toward Courtney, following Candace McCord's lead. Miller glanced in Courtney's direction, then looked quickly away.

You son of a bitch, Courtney thought. She glanced down at the microphone. "Is that turned on?" she asked.

The reporter came up beside Courtney, and faced the camera with a smile straight from an ad for whitening toothpaste. McCord said, "Doris, we're here with Detective Courtney Bedell, who's twice faced off in person with the suspect known only as the Fiddleback. Detective Bedell, could you comment on your harrowing experiences?" She pointed the microphone.

Courtney wanted to say, Who the hell is Doris? and almost did, but closed her mouth. Sure, Doris the Breast Arness, the sex-goddess-turned-anchorwoman who sat in the studio and turned it over to Candace McCord at the scene. Two babes getting ahead on brains and guts, not to mention a show of leg.

Courtney said, "Look, I can't comment on this."

McCord went on as if she hadn't heard. "Detective Bedell, as the only person who's ever seen the Fiddleback up close and lived to tell about it, please share with our viewers what it's like. Did the monster speak to you? And if so, what did he say?"

Courtney had a surge of stage fright. Four more reporters had now moved over and stood facing her, along with their accompanying cameramen. Agent Miller had finished his interview, and now watched the proceedings with folded arms. Courtney resisted the urge to shoot the FBI man the bird. Visible in the corner of her eye, Gholer had left the captain standing on the steps and was headed this way.

"Detective Bedell," McCord continued, unruffled, "what's it like being a central figure in this manhunt, and trying to balance that with life as a single mom?"

Courtney wasn't certain she'd heard correctly. "As a *what*?"

"I'm sure," McCord said, "that with such a nemesis stalking our streets you have the same concern as all parents."

Courtney faced the reporter. "I'm not a—"

"But unlike the rest of us," McCord said, "you not only have a child to protect, you're charged with the burden of protecting society in general. So what's it like, trying to balance the two?"

Gholer was halfway there, coming fast.

Courtney had had it up to here. She showed the camera her sweetest smile. "Well, I'll tell you, Candace," she said, "it's really cool."

Candace McCord's painted-on smile began to fade.

"I think chasing the Fiddleback's the neatest thing in the world," Courtney said. "And even cooler than that is all this coverage you're giving him. And me. Gee, now that you've got my name out over the air,

why not add my address and phone number? That
way he'll be sure to find me."

Candace McCord looked suddenly very nervous.

Courtney leaned over so that her lips were inches
from the microphone. "I just love chasing this guy,
Candace. And in a lot of ways, I feel really close to
the Fiddleback, you know? So if you'd give me your
business card I'll see that he gets in touch with you.
In private. How will that be?"

McCord just looked into the camera, not knowing
how to respond. She finally opened her mouth. "This
is Candace McCord, Channel 6 News. Back to you,
Doris."

Courtney got up in McCord's face. "Back to Doris?
What are you giving it back to her for? Why, I'm just
getting started here."

McCord tucked the mike under her arm and walked
away, fast. The other reporters trailed after her, apparently wanting no part of this wildwoman Courtney Bedell. Courtney was mad enough to follow, and actually
took a step in pursuit. Gholer stopped her with a hand
on her arm.

She whirled to face the lieutenant. "That asshole
Miller gave them my name, Loo. Please tell him if
he's going to spout off, he should at least get his facts
straight. He told 'em that Jason was my kid."

Gholer stepped in between her and the fast-
retreating reporters. *"Shh."* He put a silencing finger
to his lips.

She tried to step around him. He got in her way.
"In addition to the detective's exam," he said, "I'm
enrolling you in a public-relations class."

Now she turned her anger on Gholer. "Coming
from Mr. No Comment himself, that's pretty good."

"Not making a comment, that's one thing. Blowing
up on the evening news is another. Look, Court, it

happened. Stay in this job long enough, more bad stuff
will happen. A lot more bad stuff than good stuff.
You gotta learn to deal with it."

She inhaled deeply and then let it out through her
nostrils. She took a step back. "Oh Jesus, I had him.
All I had to do was look up on top of that building,
and he was a dead pigeon. Now, every other person
this nutso kills, it's right on my shoulders. My fault.
Oh hell. Just get me out of here, Loo, willya?"

On the ride down Stemmons Freeway toward the
industrial district, Gholer got on the cell and talked
to Jinx Madison. He said, "uh-huh" and "yeah," a
few times, finished by saying, "Well, stick on him,"
and then disconnected. He kept his eyes on the road.
"No sign of William Hargis Jr. The butler insists he's
not there, and Jinxie says his Caddy SUV isn't anyplace on the property."

Courtney was looking out the window, at the lights
of Las Colinas in the distance. She said, "Do me a
favor, will you?"

Gholer changed lanes, moving in between a bobtail
truck and a Ford Explorer. He glanced at her
expectantly.

"I don't ask much from people," Courtney said.

Gholer draped his wrist over the wheel, steering
teenager style. "Maybe if you'd ask more often, you'd
find out you got more friends than you think you
have."

Courtney watched him thoughtfully, then said, "It's
not much of a favor. Just, when you get home, call
my house and check on Jason and me. I'm being
hyper. But with Miller getting my name broadcast all
over hell and gone . . . I'm just a little nervous
about it."

"I'll do better than that. I'll have a couple of patrolmen check you out once an hour, all night long. And, yeah, I'll call you, but I won't be home for a while."

Courtney was able to smile for the first time since the incident with the Fiddleback. "Why, Loo? You got a woman on the side?"

"As if I could afford one. Naw, after I drop you off I'm going to have a look at Fiddleback's place."

"Huh? What place? The Fiddleback's got a place?"

"I already told you, but I guess you forgot. The address on his employee ID at the motor freight company. We've had people on the residence since fifteen minutes after Jinx and Eddie got their hands on the ID. Won't be anything to it, but I'm dropping by for a look around."

Courtney tilted her head. "Not without me, you're not."

"Hey, you don't have to. The guy won't be there, Courtney. I doubt he'll ever come there again. But we might find something to lead us to the guy. You should go home. You've been away from the little boy too long already."

She grasped the door handle and sat up straighter in the seat. "I'm going with you, boss. You already told me the day-care center will keep Jason until I can get there."

"Yeah, they will. But what happened to 'this is all a pain in the ass'? For somebody not one of us, you're damned sure getting involved."

She kept her gaze frozen on the freeway ahead. "Involved? Yeah, Loo, you might say that. You've gotten me involved. Now the Fiddleback's gotten me involved." She looked at him. "As of the moment he tried to kidnap me, then almost ran over me getting away. As of then I am totally involved. This bastard's mine, Loo. And the mayor, the chief of police, the

FBI, anybody else. You can tell them Courtney Bedell said so, if any of 'em wants to know."

The apartment was a block off of Illinois Avenue in Oak Cliff, a mostly black area where hard-working people lived next door to dope dealers and street-walking hookers. The three black-and-whites parked outside Harold Bays' address wouldn't attract much attention in this particular neighborhood. Cops in uniform stood guard at Harold Bays' door.

Gholer stopped in the breezeway and looked the unis over, two guys in their twenties standing straight like palace guards. Gholer peered toward the lighted courtyard and swimming pool, then out at the darkened street. He touched one of the unis on the shoulder and nudged him forward. "About a foot further up," Gholer said.

The uniforms stood at ease and looked nervously at each other.

"What I'm saying is," Gholer went on, "that you guys are only in view from the sidewalk and the back parking lot. If you move a foot further up, then the guy can see you from down at the end of the block. Give him more of a head start when he decides to haul ass away from here."

One of the unis, a fair-skinned youngster with a mole on his chin, eyed Gholer with a pissed-off attitude. The uni said, "This is a police operation, fella. I suggest you move along." He glanced down at Courtney, then looked back at Gholer.

Gholer stepped back and jammed his hands in his pockets. "A *police operation?* Okay, I'll bite. Who told you guys to stand out here? And, oh yeah, by the way. I'm Lieutenant Jerry Gholer, and this is Detective Courtney Bedell. We ain't exactly the curious public, guys."

The uni's attitude changed in a hurry. He said humbly, "The sergeant, sir."

"Who is where?" Gholer said.

The uni looked nervously toward the black-and-whites in the street. "I think he might be . . . well, he could be . . ."

"Gone for doughnuts?" Gholer said. "Or gone home? Which is it?"

Both unis snapped back to attention. The spokesman said, "He just told us to stand here, Lieutenant. I don't know the sergeant's current whereabouts."

Gholer exchanged a look with Courtney. "Yeah, okay," Gholer said, "I'm buying that one. Though I gotta tell you, this 'blue wall' shit can get old. But you don't want to snitch on your sergeant, that's okay. But in case you haven't been told, you are waiting here in an attempt to surprise a dangerous suspect, and not as a police recruitment ad. So move your act into the living room, will you? And also, one of you park those squad cars across the street out of sight someplace. Detective Bedell and I are going to look around inside. And while we do, you two try to keep from scaring any potential suspects away. If you will. You guys understand? If you don't, I can make sure that you do."

The two uniforms sat sheepishly inside the apartment as Courtney left the kitchen and went out into the breezeway. Mailboxes hung on the wall about halfway back toward the pool. She bent from the waist and squinted to look inside the box with Harold Bays' apartment number. The mail receptacle was stuffed full of pamphlets, ads, and a couple of envelopes that looked like bills. About what she'd expected. She went back inside, nodded to the cops, and went into the bedroom to find Gholer. Gholer had a dresser open and was rummaging around inside.

"He hasn't been here in a while," Courtney said. "The mailbox is stuffed. No dirty dishes. A six-pack of beer in the refrigerator, nothing more."

Gholer held up a pair of Jockey underwear. "I don't think he's ever been here, not to live. Out front you got two beanbag chairs, no TV, no couch. In the bedroom is this one ratty-assed sleeper sofa. No food in the joint. In the cabinets there is one plate and one saucer, two glasses, and he's got a fork and a couple of spoons. And that"—he pointed at the sofa—"is something even a spider wouldn't sleep on. So that's what's here. What's *not* here tells you even more. No clothes except for two pair of underwear and some coveralls. This address is strictly a front for this guy. There's one phone, the number of which is listed in the book under our man Bays' name. We can ask for luds, and I'm betting he's never made a call from here."

Courtney started to sit down on the sofa, then noticed a stain which could be urine and thought the better of it. "Something else isn't here, Loo. Notes. People make grocery lists, write down phone numbers, winning lottery numbers, directions to places. There's not a single scrap of paper anywhere in here with anything written down. He's got two wastebaskets, one empty and the other with a wadded Kleenex at the bottom."

"And even worse," Gholer said, "according to those uniforms, the apartment manager doesn't even know what the guy looks like. She's been working here six months, and Bays has had this place rented for a year and a half. Since the manager's been here she hasn't laid eyes on the guy. The rent comes through the mail." He ruefully dropped the underwear back inside the drawer. "So this is wild goose chase number seven thousand with this character. No ceremonial candles, no spooky music playing on the stereo, mainly because

the guy doesn't even *have* a stereo, no newspaper stories about his crimes. So how come the movie cops
always find crap like that in the killer's lair, Court,
and all we got is a pair of Jockeys with droopy elastic?
Jesus, you'd think the guy could afford new underwear."

"He lives somewhere, Loo. Somewhere with a place
to imprison people. Someplace out in the country,
away from everything."

Gholer stood looking around, arms akimbo, palms
facing the rear. "We're wasting time. I'm sending the
uniforms away. We can have somebody check this
place periodically, but I'm laying ten to one Fiddleback's seen the last of it. With Miller popping off to
the TV people the guy's name is going to be out, so
he won't be back at his job, either. The only person
I can think of likely to know Bays' location is William
Hargis Jr., and we're going to have to battle through a
thousand yards of bullshit just to look at him." Gholer
watched Courtney wearily, through half-lidded eyes.
"Let's go home, Court. Chalk it up as one more day
won by the Fiddleback. And beginning in the morning,
Mr. William Hargis Jr. is going to face heat that even
his lawyer won't believe."

Courtney sat with every muscle relaxed as Gholer
steered into the driveway in front of Rest 'n' Play.
She was limp with fatigue, coming down from an
adrenaline high. It was a couple of minutes after midnight. Only two cars sat in front of the day-care center.
The building was dark except for a lone light in a
downstairs window and a floodlight that came on automatically as Gholer pulled in.

Courtney was so freaking tired that she wondered
if she'd have the strength to get Jason home and tuck
him in before she collapsed. At this hour the little boy

would be sound asleep. Courtney debated whether to wake him up and lead him out by the hand, or to carry him to the car like a sack of potatoes. Thanks to the fresh mauling the Fiddleback had given her, her ribs were on fire. No way could she lift Jason, much less tote him to the car. She wondered if Gholer would mind going in after the child, and started to ask as much.

Gholer beat her to the punch. He jammed the lever into park and shouldered open the door. "I'll get the little guy, Court. You just relax here."

Gholer continued to amaze her with his tough-guy/sensitive-guy act. She gave him a weary smile. "Sure you don't mind?"

"Nah. Send you the bill." Gholer exited the car, closed the door with a solid thunk, and half walked, half jogged up to the day-care entrance. He pressed the night buzzer, then stood back with hands on hips.

Courtney scootched her rump forward, propped a knee against the dash, and rested her head in the corner formed by the door and the seatback. Her eyelids drooped and she began to softly snore.

And once again was back in the apartment complex parking lot, and once again felt the Fiddleback's weight pressing on top of her, pinning her down between the pickup and the wall. She balled her fists and gasped for breath.

The mininightmare brought her instantly awake. She sat bolt upright, and for a couple of seconds forgot where she was. She sighed in relief, her gaze drifting back to the day-care center's front door.

She blinked, uneasiness growing within her. Something was wrong.

Gholer stood outside, talking to the attendant through the screen. The lieutenant waved his arms around. The woman pushed the screen partway open and showed Gholer an in-and-out log. Gholer bent his head to read. He said something to the attendant. The attendant vigorously shook her head.

Courtney was out of the car, running up on the porch. She came up behind Gholer and said, "What is it, Loo?"

Gholer turned, his face ashen, and firmly gripped her shoulders. "Get back in the car," he said.

"No." She was trembling now, her hands suddenly cold. "No. What in hell is going on?"

Gholer's look was one of total helplessness. "No need for you to— "

"What in hell is happening?" Courtney was screaming. The day-care attendant, a light-skinned black woman wearing slacks and a blouse, recoiled as if slapped. Courtney got up close to the screen. "Where's Jason?" Courtney said.

The woman read from the log, then looked up. "You are Miss Bedell?"

"Damn right I'm Miss Bedell. Now where's my nephew?" Courtney said. Gholer grabbed her arm. She pulled away from him.

The woman seemed terrified. "He's gone, ma'am."

Courtney didn't quite grasp the meaning. "What do you mean, gone? Gone where?"

"He was signed out two hours ago, Miss Bedell."

Courtney was near hysteria. "This isn't funny. Now you get Jason, right now."

"He isn't here. I told you, signed out."

"Signed out by who?" Courtney screamed.

The woman passed the log out through the screen. "Signed out by you, Miss Bedell. Now, I wasn't on duty when you brought the child in. Mrs. Taglibue was. She signed you in, and she was here when the little boy went home. She approved it."

Courtney's vision blurred. She was afraid she might faint, and leaned on Gholer for support. "Home is with me," Courtney said. "He couldn't have gone home. Who in hell signed him out?"

"That's what I'm trying to tell you, ma'am," the woman said. "According to the log there, you did. And Mrs. Taglibue identified the lady as you. We don't turn these kids over to just anyone, ma'am. The woman signing Jason out was either you yourself, or you have an identical twin."

22

Six hours earlier James Wheeler said to Jan Bedell, "That's all? That's fuckin' *all*? Can't be, no fuckin' way." He was sitting at a worm-eaten table beside the motel room window, with the contents of Jan's purse—a pack of Certs, a tube of lipstick, eight round earrings, two wadded Kleenex, and a rotten apple core—strewn out in front of him. He held the apple core up by the stem. "What's this? Where's the rest of the money?"

Jan was on the bed wearing black bikini panties, sucking on a crack pipe, her knees in the air, needle tracks on her ankles. "I think we spent it, baby."

James was in his droopy-crotched jockeys. He had skinny arms and thighs the size of softball bats. His hair as ratty and hung to his shoulders, and he had a pimple on his chin. A ring of thorns was tattooed around his bicep, nothing original, the same thing he'd seen on basketball players, Olympic swimmers, and guys in the penitentiary. He dropped the apple on the floor. "We ain't spent no *hunnerd dollars*." He turned up the purse and shook it. Nothing more fell out. He looked in disgust out the window toward the motel office, at a sign reading OUTRIGGER INN, with the *U* and one of the *N*'s dangling upside down. Up the street were a few beer bars, a liquor store, and a glassfront shop named Condoms to Go.

Jan sucked in crack smoke, inhaled deeply, blew it out. "The room was fifteen dollars. We gave seventy dollars for four rocks. There was the cheeseburgers." Her voice was slurry, dopey.

"Don't no cheeseburgers cost no fifteen dollars, not at no Sonic. Where's the rest of it?"

"I can't remember every fuckin' penny, James. You bought those cigarettes."

James got up and stumbled over to the dresser. He picked up a crumpled pack of Marlboros, dug inside with his index finger, made a pissed-off face, wadded the spent pack and dropped it on the floor. He tore the cellophane from a second unopened pack. "What kinda sister you got? Shit, we're broke. Call 'er for some more."

Jan laid the crack pipe on the end table and rolled over on her stomach. "She won't give me any more. Said it plain as day."

"Shit. She's livin' in that house, an' it half rightfully yours."

"She owns it legally. Screwed me out of it when Momma and Daddy died."

James dangled a cigarette between his lips, and went to the table for a yellow Bic disposable. "What kind of person would do that to her own sister?"

"Her kind. She's always had it in for me like that, even when we were little. Never came to see me in prison, not one single time. Had all those legal papers fixed up so I got nothin'." Jan reached for the pipe, took another hit. "That is good stuff. That is fuckin' good stuff."

"And we ain't got no more dope, neither. Think, Jan. We gotta get some money together. She's at work, ain't she? There's somethin' in that house we could sell, don't tell me there ain't."

"Nothin' I could find when we were over there. She even hid her mad money. There's nothing you could get anything for. Some old figurines Momma used to paint, but not worth shit as far as money. Bitch sister of mine, gimme a hundred dollars, acted like she was partin' with the world."

James lit his smoke with shaking hands. "She's still got one thing that belongs to you." He took a drag, and then held the cig between his thumb and forefinger, rolling the cigarette around, looking it over. "Your kid. Now that's somethin' belongs to you a hunnerd percent."

Jan came up on her haunches. "Now what are we goin' to do with any kid, James? We can't fend for ourselves, much less any little boy." She examined the needle marks on her inner arms, gingerly touching them one at a time.

James sat back down at the table, and propped one bare foot up on the radiator. His toenails needed trimming. "There's places that'll pay good money for a little kid."

"*Shee*-it. You think I don't know it? But that's my little boy, my own flesh and blood. Besides. What's good money these days?"

James sneered at her. "Enough so's you won't have to ask that bitch for any, not for a long, long time. I heard twenty thousand dollars, some places."

"Bullshit. You must be dreamin'. Who's going to pay any twenty thousand dollars for any little kid?"

"Sell 'em to rich people that don't want to wait on those adoption agencies. Some of those people will pay about anything."

"And we just know thousands of rich people lookin' to buy a little boy, don't we?"

James' look was suddenly crafty. "A friend of mine knows a few of 'em."

"Oh yeah? What friend is that?"

"A guy I knew in Darrington Farm."

"Sure, James. All kinds of rich people hanging with dudes that just came from some prison farm."

"I ain't shittin'. Guy's named Cordell Wilson. He does this through his lawyer."

"Does what?"

"Shit, what're we talkin' about? Finds little kids for rich people to adopt, no questions asked."

"And I guess this Cordell told you all that. You believe him?"

"Never known the man to lie," James said. "Besides, I know somebody that took him a kid. A fuckin' jungle bunny, white people are adoptin' them a lot now. People paid ten thousand for a little nigger, so a white boy's bound to be worth twice as much. Come on, get your bitch of a sister on the phone."

"And tell her what? That, hey, don't think anything about this, but I've decided to sell the kid. She's a cop, James. Have us under arrest before I could get the words out."

"No, you don't tell her nothin'. You take your opportunity and take the kid. Possession's ninety-nine percent of the law."

"I've already been down for dope, James. Have you got any idea the time I'd get, a two-strike felon, for kidnapping?"

James had the cigarette smoked halfway down. He thumped ashes on the floor. "How you think a prosecutor's goin' to justify any kidnappin' beef when you're the kid's mother? No way that's going to happen. Nice-lookin' little Eye-talian boy, can't nobody say he don't look like his mother. Plus you'll be showin' your shitty-actin' sister a thing or two."

Jan thought it over, her smile spreading. "But I don't even know where she drops him off while she's working."

"So you do it at night, when she's not expectin' it.

You begin by calling her up, right now, an' tellin' her how sorry you are for what you done. Tell her you're on the road to fuckin' recovery."

"Get in her confidence," Jan said.

"Yeah. Act right, she might even float you another hundred or so. Tide you over until you can snatch the kid."

Jan adjusted the black elastic at her hip with a snapping noise. "She works in a patrol car. I doubt I can get her on the phone."

"So leave her a message," James said. "Say it's an emergency, leave the number for this motel. She'll call you back 'cause she's curious, if nothin' else. Come on, it's the best money-makin' idea I ever had. You want to be smokin' any of that good shit anymore, for the rest of your life, you get your ass on the phone."

The switchboard person in the Patrol Division, DPD, told Jan that her sister was no longer with the unit, and gave her another number to call. It pissed Jan off that Courtney hadn't told her she'd changed jobs within the department. The bitch didn't want her own sister to know how to get a hold of her. What were sisters supposed to be for, anyway? Seething inside, Jan called the second number.

After several rings and a few clicks, a woman picked up. "Four-three-four-two," the woman said. Which were the last four digits of the number Jan had just punched into the keypad.

Jan wondered why the woman hadn't told what department the caller had reached, maybe given her name or something. This might be a secret operation, but more than likely it was Courtney again, trying to hide her whereabouts from the only sister she had. After another puff on the crack pipe Jan said testily, "Courtney Bedell." Her tone was flat and emotionless. Jan was going to like putting her hot-shit baby sister down, taking her precious nephew away. Jan's own child living with her, Courtney not showing a speck of gratitude . . .

The woman on the line, obviously misinterpreting, said, "Hi, Courtney, this is Topper. Did you talk to him?"

Jan sank down on the bed, eyes wide, with James hovering over her puffing on a cigarette. The woman thought she was talking to Courtney and not someone *calling for* Courtney. Jan coughed, and then said, "Yes." Deciding to play along, pretend to be Courtney and see how it went.

The woman spoke rapidly. "Hey, I'm glad you did. And listen, I'm sorry I had to bug you on the job, but I've got kids that get nervous in day-care myself. I was pretty sure you'd like to talk to the little guy. You get him calmed down?"

Jan couldn't believe this was happening. She tried to recall Courtney's speech patterns, her inflection, but then decided that disguising her own voice wasn't necessary. When the sisters were in high school, callers got them mixed up over the phone all the time. So Jan said to Topper, "That's sort of why I'm calling you. I think I got him straightened out, but I wanted to call and talk to the lady keeping him. But, hey, I've lost the number, could you . . . ?"

To which the woman named Topper replied, "Sure, here it is," and then recited the number for the day-care center.

Jan said, "Thanks," and disconnected. She blinked in disbelief, winked at James, and then got busy on the keypad. She waited patiently through five full rings, and then listened to an older female voice answer with, "Good afternoon, Rest 'n' Play. How may I help you?"

Jan hung up immediately and stretched out fully on the bed, staring at the ceiling. Oh Jesus, Rest 'n' fuckin' Play. She raised up on one elbow and showed James a broad Bedell grin. "The little fucker's resting and playing, James," Jan said. "That's the name of the place, Rest 'n' Play. We'll look up the address. Damn, get me a phone book. I saw one last night, in that drawer over there."

By the time Jan took a final drag from the crack pipe, left James in the parking lot with the motor running, and went into the day-care center lobby acting as if she owned the place, she was just zonked enough to get away with impersonating her sister. Dope had always given her courage, made her feel as if she was floating, in free fall, what-me-worry, let it all happen. Couple of lines up her nose, or a hit or two from the magic dragon, and Jan Bedell was good to go.

She walked straight to the desk, signed Courtney's name with a flourish in the in-and-out log, then sat in a row of waiting chairs along with three or four moms. The moms had hundred-dollar hairdos, wore designer slacks and soft leather Easy Spirit shoes, and one had even come in her tennis dress and held her racket between her thighs. Women without a fucking thing to do, dropping their kids off while they went shopping at Neiman's, played tennis, went to historical society meetings. Jan had dressed in a clean pair of jeans and a man's shirt with the tail out. She'd brushed her hair down over her ears, to hide the multiple piercings. She showed one of the moms her best zonked-out grin. The mom looked quickly away, got busy reading a *New Yorker.*

Jan thought she should try to blend in. She looked over the array of magazines on a nearby coffee table. There were several issues of *Time,* some *Newsweek*s, more *New Yorker*s, a couple issues of *Entertainment Weekly,* nothing that Jan gave a shit about. She was wide awake, alert, and on her toes. Ready to spring from her chair, pretend that she was just one of the moms, take the kid Jason by the hand, lead him out to the car . . .

Except that he wasn't only *the* kid. He was *her* kid. Her own personal property. Hers to sell, if that's what she wanted to do.

She considered herself a better-than-average actress, and had already planned the performance she was about to put on in this waiting room. As loving aunt, Devoted Relative of the Year, all weepy-eyed over picking the kid up from this day-care. As if her sun rose and set with this kid.

The dope she'd been smoking was awesome shit. Awesome.

The kid himself could be a problem, and might even resist leaving with her. Jan had thought about that one, and still wasn't sure how she'd deal with such a situation. The best plan she could come up with was to pretend that the kid was merely having a tantrum, that he behaved this way all the time when he was tired.

As for the kid, he wouldn't recognize her. His own mother, whom he hadn't spent time alone with since the day he was born, now a total stranger.

But Jan had planned out how to cope with the problem. The key was in who the day-care people believed that she was. As long as she was Courtney Bedell, picking up her ward, fuck how the kid happened to feel about it. And Jan was prepared to play the role of Courtney to the hilt.

Beginning right now.

Because, as Jan sat there with the phony-looking moms who were reading all these phony-looking magazines, a handsome older woman entered the lobby from inside the daycare. She had two children with her, holding their hands. One of the kids was Jason Bedell.

Jan recognized her son instantly because of his coppery skin and facial features. He could have been hers and he could have been Courtney's; the family resemblance was that strong. Looks inherited from the grandfather's dominant genes. The little boy looked expectantly around, his gaze moving from one mom to the other. When he came to Jan he stared at her.

And she stared back at him. I look a lot like Courtney, Jan thought. Don't I? But I'm not quite her. Not quite her at all. Messes with your head, doesn't it, kid?

Jason's keeper came forward and smiled. "Miss Bedell. So nice to see you." And then dropped Jason's hand and moved on to one of the plastic moms.

Just like that. Jan couldn't believe it was going to be this fucking easy. Now to handle the kid.

Jason watched his birth mother with a look of confusion, as if he knew her but he didn't. As if he couldn't understand why she looked so much like Courtney, yet wasn't Courtney. A four-year-old little boy, mixed up and frowning. But not yet afraid. That would come later.

Jan moved in a hurry. She squatted in front of Jason and hugged his neck. "Darling," she said, loudly enough for the daycare woman to hear, then bent close and whispered in Jason's ear, "I'm your mommy. Don't you know me?"

Jason pulled back and gave her a searching look. Touched her chin in wonderment. "My mommy?" His smile was uncertain. "Coatney come, too?" He looked past her, scanning the room.

Jan said quickly, "Outside, sweetie." She firmly gripped Jason's hand and led him toward the exit. "She's waiting outside," Jan said.

Jason needed no further prompting. He lunged for the exit, tugging on Jan's arm, his eyes bubbling with excitement. "My mommy, my mommy," he said over and over, giggling in delight, literally quivering as he led the way through the door into the parking lot.

Every step of the way Jan expected someone to stop her, expected the day-care woman to step in her path, give her a questioning look. Ask her for some form of identification. Call the police, have her arrested. But nothing of the sort happened. As she followed the kid through the door, Jan glanced back over her shoulder. The day-care lady had forgotten her and was busy with one of the well-dressed moms.

Jan wondered dreamily if James had left her any of that awesome shit to smoke. Not much, just enough to get her by until the sale was final. For twenty thousand dollars, they could buy all the awesome shit in the world.

A couple of hours later, inside a run-down frame house near Love Field, James Wheeler almost went ballistic. He pounded his fist on the table. "A deal's supposed to be a fuckin' deal! You didn't tell me any of this shit."

Cordell Wilson was a fat man around forty with tattoos on his arms, bare-chested under a leather vest. He wore diamond pinky rings on both hands, his thinning hair cut short and combed straight forward. He said, "You didn't *ask* me any of this shit. You just showed up over here with this kid."

James flopped down in a slatted armchair. "How long's it take to get this money?"

"Depends on whether my man's got a spot available. If he's dealing with someone right now, hey, no sweat. Sometimes, though, he's got to find somebody. Takes longer then. But longer, shorter, you still got to have a birth certificate." Wilson was drinking strong hot tea. He lifted the string and dipped the bag around inside the cup. It was dark inside the house except for a single lamp, both men hunkering low in order to see each other clearly.

"Sounds like bull hockey to me," James said. "People wanting to buy a kid on the black market, the fuck they need a birth certificate for?"

"You want black market? Bring me a girl, I'll show you black market. Get you cash right away."

"That's some perverted shit," James said.

"I don't know if it's perverted or not. But a girl I can move without a birth certificate. This boy, you're talking legal adoption."

"If it's legal, how come we got to go through you? Why aren't we down at some adoption agency?" James moved in closer, intense. "Come on, you know me. We got the merchandise right outside in the car."

Cordell lifted out the teabag, set it down on his saucer, and sipped from the cup. "Read my lips. The adoption is legal. What isn't legal is you getting paid. That's under the table. We ship the kid the fuck away from here, Portland, Tacoma, or someplace, for the final home he's going to be in. These adoptive parents got to have a birth certificate to be sure the kid isn't one we've kidnapped, that the person doing the transaction has legal authority. Now if this girlfriend of yours . . . what's her name?"

"Jan."

"Yeah, Jan. Now if this Jan is the birth mother and the certificate says so, then she's got the authority to sign the kid over. No problem with that. The money comes and nobody knows about it but you and the parents. And the lawyer and me, but we don't figure into the equation except for, you know, our commission. But the adoptive parents got to have that birth certificate to make it all legal, enroll the kid in school, get him a Social Security number."

James gripped the edge of the table. "And suppose I can't get no birth certificate."

Cordell had his cup halfway to his mouth. He paused. "Then you are fucked, my friend." He sipped. "So go get me the certificate, or let's quit wasting each other's time."

While James and Cordell talked things over inside the house, Jason Bedell sat in the backseat of James' old Plymouth amid the smell of motor oil and Taco Bell burritos. Jan was in the front, smoking one cigarette after another. The little boy's legs were straight out in front of him and his arms were stiff as boards.

He was afraid that the lady in the front seat had told him a fib, and that she really wasn't his mommy. He knew she'd fibbed when she'd told him that Courtney was waiting outside the day-care center. Little boys and girls told fibs, especially near bedtime when they were watching TV and didn't want to go to sleep. Jason sometimes didn't believe other children when they told him things, but he'd never before doubted a grown-up's word. Adults always told the truth.

But in the future he was going to doubt this. The woman had told him a fib, and that was all there was to it. Jason would tell Courtney on the woman. He would, and then Courtney would probably punish her.

The lady in the front seat was puffing on a cigarette, blowing smoke out of her nose, holding the butt out the window occasionally to thump her ashes onto the sidewalk. They were parked in a neighborhood of small frame and brick houses with pickups in the driveways and weeds growing in the yards. As Jason watched, an RV cruised slowly by, reached the end of the block, turned left, and disappeared behind a house.

Jason hated the smell of cigarette smoke. Smoking was bad for people and gave them cancer. Jason was never going to smoke when he got grown. Courtney had told him that smoking was dumb.

Jason decided that the woman couldn't be his mommy, because his mommy would never do anything so dumb as smoking a cigarette.

But if she wasn't his mommy, who was she? And why had she and her man-friend brought Jason to this neighborhood? He was really tired of this game. He wanted to go home.

"Mommy?" he said timidly, calling her that because he didn't know what else to call her.

The woman ignored him and fooled with the radio, looking for a station that played music. Jason liked Courtney's music, the golden oldies, but didn't like what the woman had played thus far. Jason hated heavy metal. He'd heard that people who played heavy metal did a lot of dope, and he knew that dope was bad for you. People who did dope were every bit as dumb as people who smoked cigarettes. Maybe even dumber.

He wondered if the woman in the front seat took dope, and decided that she probably did. Because she was smoking a cigarette, which was bad for her, and because she listened to heavy metal. People who did one or two bad things probably did other bad things as well.

He wanted to ask the woman when he could go home to Courtney. "Mommy?" he said again, a little louder this time.

Now the woman turned around and leaned toward him over the seat, exhaling smoke in Jason's face. She had poked some earrings through her lobes, which made metallic clanking noises. "Let's get one thing straight, little man," the woman said. "I am not your mommy, not any longer. I don't have time to be your fucking mommy, you understand what I'm telling you?"

Jason was right after all. The woman wasn't his

mommy, and she did bad things. Jason was going to tell Courtney on this woman.

If he ever saw Courtney again.

Jason sniffled, wiped his nose, and began to cry.

The front door to the house opened and slammed, and the woman's man-friend came walking down the sidewalk. He looked mad. Jason could tell by the way he walked, really fast with his hands swinging. The man climbed inside the car and banged his fist on the steering wheel. "God*damn*," he said. Jason didn't mind cussing all that much. Sometimes Courtney cussed, but only when she didn't think Jason was listening. Courtney's cussing didn't sound bad. The man's cussing sounded vicious and mean.

The woman in the front seat said to the man, "What'd he say, baby?"

"We gotta have a fuckin' birth certificate. You ever had a birth certificate on this kid?" The man thumbed toward the backseat, toward Jason.

The woman took a deep drag from her cigarette. "No," she said, picking tobacco from her front tooth. "But, you know what, baby? I'll bet I know where one is."

As the old Plymouth left southbound I-45 and entered the East Dallas neighborhood where the Bedell sisters grew up, Jan worried some about James' driving. He was hunched over the wheel, squinting to see over the hood, and the car was weaving in the road. He ran a stop sign and bounced through an intersection, scraping both bumpers on the pavement because he was going too fast. Jan thought she knew what was wrong with her boyfriend. He was getting shaky because the crack was wearing off.

Jan knew, because she felt it herself. Her fingers were beginning to tremble and her forehead was numb enough that when she inched the skin together really hard, she barely felt it. They needed more money in a hurry, to buy more rocks to smoke. If both of them were laid out in detox, twenty thousand dollars wouldn't do them much good.

To make matters worse, the kid was really bawling. Tears streaming down his face, crying so hard he had the hiccups. *Boo-hoo, boo-hoo, hic-hic-hic.* Jesus Christ, getting pregnant with this kid had been a mistake. But one that twenty thousand dollars would more than make up for. Jan thought about reaching over the seat and slapping the shit out of the kid.

She turned up the volume on the radio, heavy metal drumbeats now filling the car's interior and vibrating dashboard. She yelled at James, "Take the next left, then it's the third house on the right."

James applied the brakes and whipped into the turn. "I know, I been there. Last night, remember? You sure she's got a birth certificate for this mutt?"

"She's gotta. Gotta be able to enroll the kid, get him shots and shit. Got to have a birth certificate to do any of that. She keeps a lockbox in her closet."

James pulled up to the house, catawaumpus, the front wheels scraping the curb and the rear of the car sticking out in the street. "She got any money in the box? I'm starting to hurt real bad."

"Yeah, me, too." Jan shouldered the door open and put one foot out on the sidewalk. Courtney had left the porch light on. Jan scanned the street. Courtney's Lumina was nowhere in sight. Which didn't mean that Courtney wasn't home; she usually parked out back in the freestanding garage. The only vehicle on the block was a two-toned pickup truck with a bumper sticker, parked two doors down. Jan peered in that direction. There was no one behind the pickup's wheel, no one in the passenger seat. She took a deep breath. "This shouldn't take long, baby," she said.

"And for God's sake, see if you can shut up that fuckin' kid."

Harold Bays crouched down in Courtney Bedell's dining room and peered out the front window toward the street. He'd been waiting half an hour for Miss Perfect to come home, so he could take her for the Queen. His excitement grew as the car pulled to the curb and the woman got out and hurried up the walk toward the house.

Harold believed that the woman approaching was indeed Miss Perfect, though she wasn't close enough for him to see her clearly. She was the right size, the right body shape. The walk was the same, light and graceful, though this woman seemed to stagger occasionally. Maybe Miss Perfect was injured. Harold doubted if she was drunk. He'd be surprised, in fact, if she drank at all. He hoped he hadn't hurt her in the parking lot near Valley View Mall. If she was injured in any way, the Queen would be furious.

Harold could make out a man's shape, seated in the car at the curb. He wondered if it was the same man who'd shot at him. The man who'd stopped him from taking Miss Perfect in the apartment house parking lot.

Detective Gholer. If the man in the car was Detective Gholer, Harold was going to kill him. Not because he hated Detective Gholer. Only because Detective Gholer stood in the way of the Change. And the Change was all that mattered.

The woman was halfway to the house now, quickening her pace.

Harold stood away from the window and peered in the darkness through the den and living room. Bright moonlight shone through the window he'd broken in order to climb inside. To find the address he'd needed a city map. He'd left his pickup two houses down, crept between the houses into the alley, and approached the home from the rear.

Harold had followed instructions to the letter. No way could the Queen be anything but proud of him. For the past half hour he'd toured the house, gone into her bedroom, touched her things, her underwear, smelled her scent on her bed. He'd seen some clothing that belonged to a little boy. He hoped that the little boy wouldn't be with her when she came home. He'd never killed any children before. But he would if he had to.

He left the dining room, walked quietly down the hall, and waited for the woman just inside the entry. He would take her very quickly. He pulled his pistol and held the weapon in the ready position.

As he waited, he cocked his head and listened. The Queen hadn't spoken to him since he'd left the farm.

Harold smiled. The Queen had stopped yelling inside his head. It was Her way of showing Her confidence in him.

There was a rasping noise as the woman reached the front porch and pulled the screen open. The door handle rattled, then there was the sound of a key sliding in a lock. The deadbolt turned.

Harold crouched in the alcove, ready to spring. He was excited but steady on his feet. The Change was very near.

The door swung inward and she stepped inside, so close that Harold could feel the draft from the swinging door. Light spilled in from the porch. She stood blinking, trying to adjust her vision to the darkness inside.

Harold stepped toward her, then stopped. The Queen all at once screamed inside his head.

NOT HER, YOU IGNORANT FUCK. NOT HER, NOT HER, NOT HER!

Harold sobbed in disappointment. This woman re-

sembled Miss Perfect, yet wasn't her. This woman had
earrings dangling from both ears. Her features were
similar to Miss Perfect's, but harsher. More coarse.
An older version. Crow's feet around the eyes.

*YOU HAVE FAILED AGAIN, YOU FUCKER.
YOU ARE NOT WORTH A SHIT TO ME.*

Belching in rage, tears welling up in his eyes, Harold
pistol-whipped the woman across her nose. There was
a crunching sound. She fell on the floor, gasping.
Screaming in frustration, Harold jumped on top of
her. He grabbed her by the ears and pounded her
head against the hardwood floor over and over, as the
Queen's insults continued to pierce his brain.

23

On the beat, Courtney Bedell had always felt sorry
for the victims' families who'd come to the scene of
an accident, and who could do nothing but stand helplessly by. And now she knew the feeling. Grief, frustration, total despair.

On learning that Jason was missing, Gholer had set
up a command post inside the day-care center. He'd
recalled Madison and Frizell from their watch outside
William Hargis' house, and had gotten on the phone
and ordered the day-care employees back in to work.
At the moment he and Madison had Mrs. Taglibue, the
manager, inside the office and were asking her questions.
Frizell was working the custodians and part-time child-
care providers back in the playroom, holding court on
tables stacked high with alphabet blocks and Legos. All
three detectives' faces were drawn in concern. Gholer
had told Courtney over and over how sorry he was, that
he felt at fault for getting her mixed up in all of this.

None of which was helping. Questioning the day-
care employees was procedure, nothing more. These
people wouldn't have any useful information, and
Courtney knew it. Jan had walked right in, imperson-
ated her sister, and had snatched Jason away. The only
question was where.

It was pangs of guilt that stabbed at her sore ribs

now. If she hadn't been so rough on Jan at the house last night, this might not have happened. Maybe she should have invited Jan to stay with her. If she'd only shown more concern for her sister's predicament . . .

But a predicament that Jan had brought on herself. To hell with Jan and her problems, Jan was the enemy. Always had been. Had been her parents' enemy, her sister's enemy, and now was directing her venom on her only son. Jason . . .

Courtney, seated in a waiting room chair inside the day-care center, tried to control her emotions. Flying off the handle wouldn't help. Only logic would.

Okay, drugged-out, sociopathic sister of mine. Where have you taken him?

Jan was, as always desperate for money, and the hundred bucks Courtney had given her wouldn't have taken her and her jerk of a boyfriend very far. Only as far as the nearest street corner where the crack dealers congregated. And once both of them had gotten high, there was nothing they wouldn't do to score more dope in order to keep their buzz from fading.

Courtney harbored no illusion that Jan gave a damn about her son. In fact Jan had tried to sell Jason before he was born, something Courtney had learned while her pregnant sister was in jail and Courtney was making arrangements to take the baby home with her. So Jan's motive for taking Jason now probably had to do with money.

Courtney shuddered and covered her face with her hands. Not even Jan could do this to her own child.

Oh yes she could, Courtney Codependent. She could, and you know it.

She tried to remember the names of Jan's old prison mates, ones that Jan had mentioned in passing. Someone Jan, or more likely her boyfriend—and where had Jan come up with *that* lovely son of a bitch?—had known in jail, someone with connections in . . .

Kiddie porn?

Courtney didn't even want to think about it. But she had to. Had to control her emotions and think rationally. Make connections.

Courtney's head shot up as the door burst open and Captain Dilbergast walked in with Agent Miller on her heels. Trailing the captain and the FBI agent were five men and two women, all in dark suits. Fibbies. Courtney looked at the clock on the wall. It was almost eleven. What were the captain and all these federal people doing running around at this time of night?

Agent Miller approached, nodding seriously. "Word is Gholer's here."

Courtney nodded toward the open day-care center office. Visible through the entryway, Gholer talked to Mrs. Taglibue while Jinx Madison took notes on a spiral steno pad.

Miller pointed a finger at Courtney. "Don't get away," the agent said. "I'm going to be needing you." Then he walked back to the office entry and said loudly, "Hey, Jerry. Got a minute?"

Gholer was seated with his back to the doorway, across the desk from Mrs. Taglibue. The lieutenant glanced over his shoulder, did a double take, and then nodded for Madison to take over with the day-care center manager. The athletic black woman leaned over the desk and began to ask more questions. Gholer came out into the lobby, softly closing the door behind him. "Yeah, what is it?" Gholer said.

Miller opened his mouth as if to speak, then paused and called out, "Captain?" Captain Dilbergast came over and stood beside the FBI man. Miller then said to Gholer, "I want you to hear this from her."

Gholer folded his hands in front and raised his eyebrows.

Courtney got up from her chair and moved over

close to the trio. She was boiling inside. She had no idea what these people wanted, but was certain it had nothing to do with Jason. The feds and the captain were here to interfere.

Captain Dilbergast had a solemn look about her. "This is straight from the chief, Jerry. You're off the case. As of now, it's all theirs." She nodded toward Agent Miller.

Gholer scrubbed his stubbly cheeks with his knuckles. "Yeah? What case is that?"

Miller took charge of the conversation. "You know exactly what case, Jerry. Now the only thing left to say is this." He pointed at Courtney. "I need her. Do I get her voluntarily, or do I have to go through channels?"

"Jesus." Gholer looked at the ceiling. "How did you guys find me, anyway?"

"Radio channels," Miller said. "Your dispatcher knew, you called in."

"And you got no idea," Gholer said, "why me and my detectives are here."

"And don't really give a rat's," Miller said. "Look, you've had every chance to do something about this guy, and haven't. He's got to be stopped. And your witness, she goes with us. So answer my question. Voluntarily, or otherwise?"

Courtney stepped forward. She was so mad her ears were ringing. "Otherwise," she said.

All three looked at her, the captain, the FBI agent, and Gholer.

"If I've got to resign from the force," Courtney said, "then I resign. I'm not interested in the Fiddleback. Listen, my nephew's missing here. And until he's found, the DPD, the FBI, each and every one of you can go straight to hell."

Miller looked confused. "There's someone missing? Did the Fiddleback take another one?"

Courtney favored Miller with a murderous look. In an isolated corner of her mind, she was glad for the interruption. She was just angry enough so that her emotions would no longer interfere with her thinking. She opened her mouth and started to tell Miller to get the hell away from her.

Gholer stepped up and gently grasped her upper arm. "Let me handle this." He turned to Miller. "You are one dumb son of a bitch, you know that?"

Miller looked to the captain for help. In the background, the seven FBI agents traded self-conscious grins. Miller glared at them. The agents straightened up their acts in a hurry, showing deadpan Mount Rushmore expressions.

The day-care center office door opened and Jinx Madison came out. She was waving her cell phone. "Loo, you'd better take this. They said they tried you first, but your phone's turned off." She came up and handed Gholer the phone, then looked around at the host of federal agents and showed Courtney a puzzled look. "What the hell is this all about?" Madison said.

Gholer jammed the receiver against his ear. "Yeah?" He dug his own cell from his pocket and looked at it. "Yeah, mine's turned off. Sorry. What . . . ?" He listened, glanced at Courtney, and then said, "Yeah, that's her address. Why?"

Courtney forgot all about the FBI, Captain Dilbergast, and the Fiddleback. Icicles paraded up and down her spine.

Gholer lowered his head and turned his back. He said, "Yeah?" Then he listened some more and said softly, "Jesus." He disconnected and said to Madison, "Go in there and get Eddie, Jinx. Jesus Christ, we got to move on this."

Miller and Dilbergast exchanged confused glances.

Courtney jerked on Gholer's coatsleeve. "What is it, Loo?"

Gholer took her by the shoulders. "You'd better sit down over there."

Courtney stood her ground. "What is it?"

"There's . . ." Gholer licked his lips. "There's been a disturbance at your house, Court. Shots fired. A patrol car's on its way over there. We don't know what it is as yet, but . . . Courtney, dammit, don't be flying off the handle. We don't know anything right now, okay?"

The street in front of Courtney's house was lit up with the flashing lights of an ambulance and several squad cars as Gholer rounded the corner and parked, bumping his front tire up on the curb. Yellow tape was strung across the sidewalk. There was an ancient Plymouth parked at the curb with CSU people hovering around. Courtney already had the door open and one foot out on the grass before Gholer could turn off the engine.

He grabbed her arm. "You listen to me. Whether you realize it or not, you're too involved in this. Let us take care of it." Visible in the rearview, Jinx Madison had parked her vehicle behind Gholer's. Madison and Frizell were halfway across the yard to the house. Medics had rolled a gurney out on the front porch.

Courtney tried to yank away. Gholer tightened his grip. She lowered her head and began to sob.

Gholer looked back over his shoulder. Jesus, half the police force and most of the FBI had arrived, Miller and his agents in two cars, Captain Dilbergast and her driver in a third. The captain's dress uniform stood out among all of the suits now crossing the lawn toward Courtney Bedell's house.

"Okay, here's the drill," he said to Courtney. "You stick close to me. I know the pain inside is ripping you apart right now, but you've got to be in control." He let go of her arm. "You ready?"

She silently nodded.

"Let's go, then," Gholer said. He got out and escorted her across the yard.

They reached the sidewalk as the medics pushed the gurney past. There was a woman on the gurney with olive-complexioned skin and deepset dark eyes, covered with a blanket from the neck down. Gholer stared at the woman, then at Courtney, and then back at the woman again. The woman had lacerations on her face and chin, and purple bruises on her cheeks and forehead. Her left eye was practically swollen shut. Even considering the distorted features, the resemblance was unbelievable. If Gholer hadn't known better, he'd have sworn they were twins. The woman was awake, groggily looking around.

Courtney pulled away from Gholer and went up beside the gurney. Gholer wanted to grab her, to pull her back, but something stopped him. Courtney's expression was oddly calm. Gholer walked up beside her and looked down at the injured woman.

Courtney spoke to the medic in charge. "How is she?"

The medic in charge held up a hand and the other two medics halted with the gurney. The medic in charge said, "Beat to hell. We'll have to X-ray, but bet me that both her left arm and right leg aren't broken. So's her nose. Nothing life-threatening, but she'll be out of commission for a while."

Courtney's mouth tightened in thought. She looked to Gholer. "Place her under arrest, Loo. I'll fill out the burglary complaint, for starters. The kidnapping we'll have to talk to the DA about. She's Jason's birth mother. She signed him over into my custody, but I'm not sure she doesn't retain some legal rights. But the burglary goes without saying. She had no permission to go in my house."

Gholer hesitated. The sister was a new wrinkle in

the Courtney Bedell equation, one he knew nothing about. In his original interview with Courtney, she'd told him not to ask about her sibling. He wondered about their relationship, about what in hell could have gone wrong. "You sure that's what you want?"

Courtney's expression was firm. "You betcha."

Gholer looked to the medic in charge. "She goes to the jail ward at Parkland. Under arrest."

Courtney was now beside the gurney, leaning over. "Jannie? Get straight for a minute and talk to me."

Jan Bedell rolled her head toward her sister. She tried to focus. "Courtney?"

Courtney inhaled, let it out slow. "I'm here."

"He hurt me, Courtney. This guy . . ."

"I can see that. Where's Jason?"

"I was just taking him for a drive. Was going to buy him ice cream."

"Jesus Christ, Jan. No more lies, okay? Nobody around here's going to believe you. Where is he?"

Jan began to beg. "I didn't hurt him, Courtney. I'd never do that."

Courtney bent even closer. "Look at me. You're in a world of shit, and this time I'm going to see that you stay there. You can help yourself one way, and that's by telling me where my nephew is, and right fucking now."

"He's just fine. James is watching him out in the car."

"Oh Jesus. Loverboy James?"

"He likes little kids." Jan's tone shifted to a begging whine. "Don't be mad at me, Courtney."

Courtney stepped back, head down. "Mad? I'm not mad, any more than I'm mad at cancer. Or scorpions or cockroaches. Things whose existence we can do nothing about." She looked to the medic. "Jail ward, right? And if you jostle her on the way, I don't think anybody would care."

*   *   *

Gholer tried to talk Courtney into going inside the house and sitting down somewhere, but he was wasting his breath. She stuck close by as he went down to where the Crime Scene Unit had the old Plymouth surrounded. The car's driver-side window was shattered. The CSU people had the door open, and were poking around. A skinny, long-haired man was behind the wheel, head thrown back, unmoving. There was blood on the seat and more splatters on the broken window.

Gholer walked over to the patrol sergeant who was supervising the securing of the scene, and pulled the guy aside. The cop was tall and broad with a graying mustache, a veteran with dandruff on his uniform shoulders. Gholer was conscious of Courtney on his left as she raised up on tiptoes to peer anxiously inside the vehicle.

Gholer said to the sergeant, "Gimme a thumbnail."

The sergeant looked away from the car. "The guy in there is dead. One gunshot through the window, hit him in the left temple. The 911 call came from one of the neighbors, that lady there." He jerked his head toward the house next door, where a lady in a bathrobe stood talking to two uniformed cops. The cops had pads and pencils out, taking notes.

Courtney moved in between the patrol sergeant and the lieutenant. "There was a little boy," Courtney said.

The sergeant turned toward her. "And how do you know that, miss?"

Courtney's tone grew demanding. "*Detective* Miss, Sergeant. And it's my house. Now, was there a little boy?"

The sergeant backed down and touched the brim of his hat in a two-fingered salute. "Yes, ma'am. The witness says she watched from the bedroom window.

That woman there"—he nodded toward the gurney as the medics loaded Jan into the ambulance—"got out of the car and went inside the house. A minute or so later, this guy comes running out, acting crazy, and shoots the driver through the window. According to the witness, the guy left in a two-toned pickup truck. Now, she's not sure of the make. Says there was a bumper sticker of some kind, and—"

"Dammit, Sergeant, the little boy!"

The sergeant nodded his head. "There was a child, ma'am. Crying to beat all. According to the witness, the perp shot the driver, reached over the seat, and took the little boy along. We got no identity on the child, ma'am. If you could help us with that, we'd all be much obliged."

Courtney's words were strained as she choked back tears. "I can't see that anything's missing. Just . . . oh God, he's been walking around in here, touching everything." She looked helplessly around her bedroom. The dresser drawers were pulled open and clothing was strewn across the floor—some bikini panties, a few bras, her police academy T-shirts, some of Jason's romper pants.

Jinx Madison stood in the center of the room in a hip-cocked posture. "Be sure. What's important isn't what's missing, but what he might've left around here. Anything to give us some idea of where he might be headed."

Courtney exhaled and touched Madison on the shoulder. "Listen, you don't know how much I appreciate all you're doing. You've been up twenty-four hours straight, I know you're dead tired. Maybe you and Eddie should take some time."

Madison shook her head. "Naw, we're fine." She bent and picked up something from the floor, saw that it was just a safety pin, and laid the pin on the dresser.

Courtney said, "You sure?"

Madison's features softened in sympathy. "Hey, I can't believe you're worrying about me at a time like this."

"It's just that what you're doing is so far above and beyond," Courtney said.

Madison moved up closer. "The deal is this. You're one of us. Something happens to one of us, it happens to us all. That's the way it is."

Gholer came into the bedroom with Frizell on his heels. Gholer said, "They found some of the backyard fence wire mashed down where he climbed over. He broke out a window to get in the house. They're dusting for prints, but we already know who he is, don't we?"

Courtney stared blankly off into space. "How he knew who I was and where I live, that we don't know." She picked up a pair of Jason's pants and folded them over, smoothing the creases repeatedly as if in a trance.

Frizell moved up beside the lieutenant. "It's a starting point," Frizell said. "Find out who told the guy where to find Courtney, and that person likely also knows where to find Harold Bays. So who did we tell?"

"We didn't tell anybody," Gholer said, then looked at the ceiling and breathed in through his nose. "Wait—Hargis' lawyer. That pow-wow inside the office earlier, he was sitting there when Agent Miller . . . Jesus, I'm going to murder that son of a bitch."

"Donald the Dangler?" Madison said.

"Who else?" Gholer said. "Eddie, you two sat on Hargis' house today for how long?"

"Two or three hours, anyway," Frizell said.

Madison pulled her notepad from her pocket and thumbed through the pages. "We arrived at seven

minutes after five, Loo, right after we left Valley View
Mall. Stayed right there until you called us to come
to the day-care center, which was at . . ." She squinted
at her notes. "Nine minutes after eleven. That's more
like six hours, Eddie. We saw nobody but the guard
at the gate, who swore up and down Hargis wasn't
there. And you know what? I believe the guy. That
Caddy SUV Hargis drives wasn't around anyplace we
could see."

Gholer pinched his chin. "So during the time the
Bays asshole was running around the mall, and for
sometime thereafter, Hargis was out of pocket. He
could've been in touch with the lawyer and found out
Courtney's name. And since she's a cop, her personal
data would be public record. He shoots the Fiddleback
Courtney's address . . . Jesus, I wonder."

Courtney continued to pick up things from the floor,
dropping one of her bras back in the drawer, stooping
to pick up a pair of black lace panties.

Madison flipped her notebook closed. "Where are
you coming from, Loo? We already know Hargis is
mixed up some way."

"I'm wondering about probable cause. Which I
don't think we got. The fact that the guy wasn't home
all afternoon doesn't equate to any kind of warrant.
We got no one on him at the moment, right?"

"You called us off, Loo," Frizell said.

Gholer took out his cell. "You got his address? I'll
call downtown and send somebody else. Eventually
he's got to show up."

Madison thumbed through her pad, then laid it open
on the nightstand. "That's the address there, Loo."

Gholer squinted to read Madison's writing as he
punched a number into the cell. A uniformed cop
came in from out in the hall. Gholer stopped dialing
and looked up. "Lieutenant?" the cop said. "This FBI

guy out here's looking for you. You, too, Detective
Madison, and Detective Frizell. He wants you all front
and center."

Gholer snapped his phone shut. "Yeah, well, I want
to see that son of a bitch, too. Jinx and Eddie, you
guys come with me." He stepped toward the door,
then stopped and turned. Courtney stood in the middle of the room, staring blankly at a pair of Jason's
underwear. Gholer went over and put his arm around
her. "We'll just be a minute, Court. You get your
things in order." He squeezed her shoulder. "And,
hey, look at me. We're going to find Jason, you got
my word. No way is anything going to happen to that
little guy, you understand?"

Agent Miller was in the living room giving directions
to CSU techs and his own agents as they rifled through
the kitchen cabinets. Gholer walked up to Miller. Madison and Frizell flanked the lieutenant, Frizell smirking
and Madison lifting her coattails to put her hands on
her waist. Captain Dilbergast came out of the bathroom and moved in between the detectives and the
federal man like a football official ready for the coin
flip.

Gholer said to Miller, "You're looking for me?"

Miller rested his elbow on the mantel and rested
his chin on his cupped hand. "Yeah. I'm going to need
whatever notes your people have strung together, plus
any physical evidence in your possession. Come tomorrow morning I'll have a truck out at the Irving
Boulevard location to move things to our office downtown. I've never been a big believer in the separate-
office task force bullshit to begin with."

Gholer folded his arms and looked at the floor.
"Meaning, if any of us want to know what's going on
in with this case we can read about it in the paper."

Miller gave a condescending wave. "Quit looking so glum, Jerry. Hell, you got hundreds of homicides going. You should be glad to have this one off your hands." He looked at Madison. "I saw you a while ago with a steno pad, detective. That's part of your notes, right?"

Madison adjusted the badge pinned to her belt. "That, or a grocery list. It's up to the lieutenant what I do with it."

"Not anymore it isn't," Miller said. "Everything about the case is now up to me."

Madison half turned to Gholer. "Donald the Dangler has spoken, Loo. Give me the word. I comply or I don't, it's up to you."

Gholer rolled his eyes and didn't say anything.

Captain Dilbergast cut in, speaking to Madison. "I'll furnish the answer, Detective Madison. Straight from the top. Whatever Agent Miller says."

Madison stood her ground. "Loo?"

Gholer exhaled, long and slow. "Give him the notes, Jinxie. And whatever else he asks for. In the morning I'll go to main headquarters and see if there's anything I can do about it. I doubt if I can."

Madison held the lieutenant's gaze for an instant, then dropped her own. "Yeah, right," she breathed. She dug in her pocket, came up empty-handed. "I left the notebook in the bedroom. I'll get it." She looked defiantly at Agent Miller. "You want to send a couple of your fibbies along as an escort?"

"Enough," Gholer put his hand on Madison's arm. "Just get 'em, Jinxie, okay?"

Madison stalked off toward the bedroom. Frizell watched her go, then looked at the floor.

Miller extended a hand toward Frizell, while speaking to Gholer. "I'll want this detective and Madison at my office in the morning for debriefing. After that, my people will be taking charge. Occasionally we might need some input from you. Any problem with that, Captain Dilbergast?"

Dilbergast flicked a glance at Gholer, then looked back at Miller. "None at all, Agent. None at all."

"Good. Then we'll—" Miller stepped forward, extending a hand as Madison returned from the bedroom. He said to her, "You bring 'em?"

Madison had a puzzled look. "Funny thing, but no. I didn't."

Miller frowned. "Now this time I'm not asking for cooperation. I'm demanding it."

"I'm cooperating," Madison said. "My notes aren't cooperating. They're gone."

The FBI agent, the captain, Gholer, and Frizell all looked at her.

"Vanished," Madison said, spreading her hands. "Along with Detective Bedell. The bedroom window's wide open, Loo. I think Detective Bedell has fled the scene."

24

Harold Bays hated being confused, hated trying to get his thoughts in order. The asphalt road flashed past underneath the pickup and the speedometer needle pressed toward seventy miles an hour. With the voices inside his head now talking to each other, and not to him. Talking about him, but leaving him out of the conversation.

Whatcha think She'll do?

To this stupid prick for taking the kid? I think he is fucking dead.

Yeah, right. She'll eat him alive.

Harold mopped his tears with a handkerchief. "Shut up!" he screamed. "You don't know. You're just stupid workers." He flipped on the interior light and opened the glove box. "I'll find you and mash you stupid bastards."

The answer inside his head was a high mimicking falsetto. *You stupid bastards. He hates us. Ain't that too fuckin' bad?*

He won't hate us for long. He'll be dead.

"Will not. I will explain to Her." Harold jerked the wheel to the right, barely missing a dead skunk in the middle of the road.

The mimicking falsetto again. *I will explain to Her, he says. The prick can't even explain to himself, how*

*will he explain it to Her? He'll mash us, he says. He
ought to mash his own fuckin' self. Save Her the
trouble.*

He is so fucking dead.

Harold pounded the side of his head, behind his
ear. He wanted the workers' voices to go away. He
wanted to hear the Queen's instructions. But the
Queen hadn't spoken to him since he'd left Miss Perfect's house. Since he'd thrashed the woman who'd
looked like her, shot the man inside the car, and taken
the little boy.

He didn't know why he'd done any of it, only that
he'd been confused. He'd waited inside the house, ex-
pecting Miss Perfect, and this other woman had entered instead. Looking so much like Miss Perfect that
it was as if she was mocking him. Harold had been
infuriated.

After he'd attacked the woman he'd run screaming
out of the house and down the sidewalk, waving his
pistol, and then this other man had been sitting there,
inside a car that was parked at the curb. The man had
looked at Harold through the window. A skinny man
with tattoos on his arms, too pale to be suitable for
the Change. Harold hadn't even realized it when he'd
pulled the trigger. The scene had unfolded before him
as if in a slow-motion video, the bullet shattering the
window and drilling a hole through the man's head,
blood spurting out, the man watching as if dumb-
founded, staring, then going limp. And then there was
the child, crying out of control.

Harold hadn't expected a little boy to be involved,
and hadn't known what to do. Kill the child or take
the child.

Harold liked children and didn't want to think of
killing one. He wished that he could be a child again.

He'd scooped the little boy out of the backseat and,
lugging the kicking and struggling child under one

arm, had run to his pickup and opened the tailgate. He'd tossed the child into the pickup's bed, locked the boy inside, and then climbed in the truck and drove away.

Now he hurried in frustration toward his farm to beg the Queen for forgiveness. To ask Her for more direction. To ask Her what to do with the child.

But the Queen was no longer speaking to him, only the workers. The fucking hated workers. The workers who were jealous of Harold and his closeness to the Queen.

The gate fronting Harold's property loomed on his left; he braked and spun the wheel in that direction. The pickup fishtailed into the drive. Harold floored the accelerator and smashed through the gate, wood and wire splintering and twisting, winding around the pickup's grille and hood. Harold barely noticed. He steered on through the woods, the truck bouncing and careening from side to side, Harold holding the steering wheel in a death grip, rehearsing what he would say to the Queen. If he could form the words correctly, She would certainly forgive him. If he could get back on Her good side, She would still permit the Change.

Jason bounced from side to side in the pickup's bed, skinning his knees and elbows, bumping his head on one of the shackles bolted to the floor. He'd cried until he had no more tears left; he was sobbing and hiccupping, but his eyes were dry. That afternoon at the day-care center, the teacher had led the children in prayer. Jason now prayed that this would soon all be over, that the strange-looking man would take him home.

His shirt and little romper pants had dots of blood on them, and there were more drops of blood in his hair. He was exhausted. His time at the day-care cen-

ter had been fun. What was happening to him now
wasn't fun at all. He wanted Courtney.

Sometimes at night he had bad dreams, and he
chased the bad dreams away by imagining himself in
a fantasy world. In the fantasy world he rode on Pegasus, the winged white stallion, high above the clouds
drifting to faraway lands. And now in the back of the
strange man's pickup truck, Jason tightly shut his eyes.
And soon he was aboard Pegasus, riding away to a
world where there were no adults, no horrible man
shooting people through the head; no one, in fact,
except Jason and his wonderful friends. He liked the
kingdom where Pegasus soared. He would stay there
until Courtney came for him. He had no doubt that
she would.

Billy Hargis wanted his girlfriend Heather to go to
sleep. Christ, he had things to do she couldn't know
about. He had to bathe and wash his clothes. Get rid
of all traces that might connect him to Megan Harris
or Harold Bays.

Hargis had arrived home three hours ago—five minutes, the guard at the gate had told him, after two
detectives had left. The tall black woman and the
skinny guy, Frizell. They'd been watching the house
all afternoon, parked in their unmarked car across the
street. Smiling and waving at the guard. Questioning
the guard about Hargis' whereabouts.

Hargis knew that the two detectives were following
orders from that hard-nosed fuck, Gholer, stalking
Billy Hargis, trying to make him nervous. Which he
was. More than nervous, terrified. The depth of his
fear would be known only to his laundry man, when
he found the stains in Hargis' underwear.

The lawyer Akin had told Hargis that the police
didn't have shit for evidence, that all they could do
was bug him, and that Hargis should sit tight until

they went away. But Billy Hargis' old man had taught
him early on not to pay any attention to lawyers. If a
lawyer predicted doom, more than likely the client
had nothing to worry about. But if the lawyer told
him, no sweat, then the client should prepare to take
it up the ass.

Billy Hargis wasn't going to take it up the ass alone.
If Billy Hargis took it up the ass, the lawyer should
bend over and spread his cheeks as well.

When he'd walked into the upstairs bedroom
Heather was on the canopied four-poster king-size,
drinking vodka and smoking grass. Laying around in
bikini panties, posing, giving him little shots of her
twat while she poured herself more liquor. Trying to
use her youth and her body to keep him under control. Which worked most of the time, but not today.
For one of the only times in his life, Billy Hargis had
more on his mind than pussy and gambling.

And now, finally, the booze and the dope had taken
their toll and Heather had begun to snore. Not quite
sound asleep, but almost, rolling onto her side and
pulling her legs up against her chest, a burning joint
dangling from her fingers. Hargis took the roach from
her hand and ground it out in an ashtray. He went
into the bathroom and flushed the ashes down the
toilet, then returned to the bedroom. Now Heather
was hugging her pillow. Hargis decided it was safe for
him to move.

He went in the master bath, stood beside the sunken
tub and removed his clothes. The bath had his-and-
her showers and lavatories, and opened out into separate areas. In one corner, across from the toilet, there
was a bidet.

His shirt and pants showed tiny spatters of blood.
Megan Harris' blood; evidently Hargis was standing
closer then he'd thought when the crazy had blown
off her head. Hargis recalled the ear-drum shattering

blast, Megan's head vanishing, bone and brain matter spraying the walls as she dropped like a stone. Now that Sis was out of the way, Hargis was going to sneak up on Harold Bays and blow the fucker away. Then make an anonymous 911 call, tell them Bays was the Fiddleback, give them directions to the farm.

He dropped his clothes into a plastic bag and secured the neck with a twist-tie. Later on he'd take the shirt and pants out back and burn them. Hargis' estate bordered White Rock Creek, and across the creek was the Preston Trails Golf Club. Late at night there'd be no one around to see the flames. When he was finished, Hargis would bury the ashes.

He turned on the shower and held his hand under the faucet, waiting for the water to warm. Had he forgotten anything? Kill Harold Bays. Let the cops find Megan Harris' body at the farm, add her to the list of the Fiddleback's victims. As soon as someone found Sis' body, make a claim on her life insurance. Take part of the money, settle up with Caesars, fly to Vegas for a week or two.

Sis would be dead. So would Megan Harris and Harold Bays. The hard-nosed fuck, Gholer, would be so tickled at ending the Fiddleback's reign that he'd forget all about Billy Hargis. Larry Akin couldn't talk because his conversations with Hargis were covered under attorney-client privilege. Not to mention that Akin was likely an accessory. Hargis' old man had taught him to always make lawyers an accessory and guarantee the fuckers' silence.

Christ, almost there. Almost fucking there.

Hargis bathed, scrubbing his fingernails and underneath his pecker very carefully. He'd read up some on DNA; often a woman's juices remained on a man's balls for days, weeks even, unless the guy really scrubbed, and most incriminating trace evidence came from under the suspect's nails. Christ, there could be nothing to tie him to Megan Harris. In the months prior to Sis' death, no one had seen him and Megan together.

He dried off, came out of the bathroom and stepped into boxer shorts. He felt pretty good. Heather's ass was sticking up as she lay on her stomach. Hargis wondered if he was up to humping her, decided that he was. He walked to the bed, reached out, and halted with his hand an inch from her behind as the intercom buzzed.

Hargis stared at the wall speaker, which was a direct hookup to the guard at the gate out front. Christ, who could be coming by at this time of night? Maybe the detectives again. Damn Gholer the homicide cop all to hell. The hard-nosed fuck just wouldn't give up, would he? He'd sent the black woman and the skinny fuck, and they were outside hassling the guard to let them in. Fat chance of that happening.

Hargis walked toward the speaker, watching Heather's firm ass over his shoulder. He depressed the speaker button and said, "I hope this is important. It's after midnight, you know."

The guard was a retired Plano cop named Terrance. He had a smoker's voice, cracked and hoarse. "Mr. Akin out here to see you. What would you like me to do?"

Christ, what could Akin want now? Middle of the night, the fucker would double his fee. "Anyone with him?" Hargis asked.

"No, sir, he's alone. Hey, Mr. Hargis, you know I wouldn't bother you at this time of night for just anybody."

"Yeah, sure. Let me think a minute."

Hargis let the receiver hang by his hip. Akin must have something important. You normally couldn't wake the fucker at this time of night with TNT.

Hargis put the phone against his ear. "Okay, send him on back."

"He says you should come up here to the gate, Mr. Hargis."

"Shit. Why?"

There was a moment's hesitation, Terrance the guard's voice faint in the background as he talked to Akin through the guard-station window as the lawyer sat in his car. Terrance came back on the line. "Says it's about the insect, Mr. Hargis. Said you'd know what he meant."

Christ, the insect? Didn't Akin have any more imagination? Meeting outside the grounds did make sense; both Hargis and the lawyer had talked about the possibility of the house being bugged, tiny microphones hidden in the flower pots, chandeliers . . .

"Tell him to give me ten minutes," Hargis said. He disconnected and walked over to the closet. He stood for a moment looking at Heather's gorgeous ass as she murmured something in her sleep. Dug in his closet for a red-and-white striped parachute silk jogging suit and running shoes. Christ, the things Billy Hargis had to put up with.

But he was almost there. Almost fucking there.

Billy Hargis exited through the front door into a strong, cool fall breeze, crossed the brick porch, descended the wide stone steps and skirted the fountain. The fountain was circular, with stone cherubs all around spraying water through seashell horns. When Billy Hargis was a kid, he and his buddies from St. Mark's Private School used to stand behind the cherubs and make jokes about how, from a certain angle, the cherubs looked as if they were pissing into the fountain. Some of Hargis' old school chums were doctors, others lawyers, while others did nothing but live off trust funds. Most of them lived close by, and as long as they had money they were still in the loop. Being broke was the same as being in exile.

The thought of being broke made Hargis shudder inside. Christ, having to get a job. Even worse, having to resign from Preston Trails Golf Club.

He left the Cadillac SUV and took the Porsche, driving the sleek black sports car down a winding blacktop, over a bridge spanning the creek, and down a lane lined with cedar trees. The guardhouse loomed on his right, the gate standing open onto Westgrove Road. Hargis looked around for Larry Akin's white Mercedes, but the lawyer's car was nowhere in sight. Hargis pulled up to the guardhouse and pressed the button to lower his window, the Porsche's engine throbbing under an October moon, headlight beams illuminating asphalt pavement, a strip of gravel between the end of the drive and the road.

There was a light on inside the shack, Terrance's head and shoulders visible, the brim of his hat shading his cheeks and nose. Hargis thought the guy looked tense, bent out of shape. Hargis said, peering around, "Where's Larry Akin? He drive off or something?"

The guard didn't reply, his gaze shifting down and to the right, the guardhouse door opening, a slim, lithe form emerging and—*Christ!*—the facial features becoming clear as she leaned in through the window. Courtney Bedell, the hard-nosed fuck's eyewitness, extended a hand holding a gun, pressing the barrel hard inside Hargis' ear as she said, "Larry's not here, Mr. Hargis. Just me. And you and I are going for a ride."

25

Courtney's grip was firm and her gaze was clear. There was a tightness around her eyes from squinting to read Jinx Madison's notes under her Lumina's dome light, thumbing through the steno pad to find Hargis' address as she drove down the alley in back of her house.

She'd taken the notes from her nightstand and climbed out her bedroom window, and then had crept into her freestanding garage. She'd backed her Lumina out and driven down the alley with her headlights off. All the way to the expressway she'd expected Gholer to come up behind her, yelling and honking his horn.

She'd made the half-hour drive to Hargis' estate with aid from a road map. Once there she'd parked half a block down, walked casually up to the guardhouse and poked her Glock in through the window. Her knees were slightly stiff from crouching behind the counter, holding her gun trained on the guard while waiting for Hargis to appear at the gate. The cover story about Akin coming to call was something she'd dreamed up on the spur of the moment, assuming that the one person Hargis would be willing to see at that time of night was his lawyer. She had guilt pangs over pulling a gun on the guard; the guy seemed likeable and was only doing his job. But Hargis was different. She could shoot this bastard without a qualm.

The guard's .38 Police Special was in her pants pocket. She pulled out the revolver and, working with one hand while keeping her Glock trained on Hargis with the other, opened the cylinder and dropped the bullets on the ground. Then she tossed the .38 off into the bushes. She reached in her hip pocket, produced a printed business card, and handed it through the window to the guard.

His chin dropped slightly as he read the card over. He lowered the card and looked at her.

"You're going to do what you're going to do," Courtney said. "And probably you'll ignore what I'm about to say and call 911 anyway. But the number written on the card is for a cell phone, which DPD Lieutenant Jerry Gholer has in his pocket. Calling that number will get you a quicker response than calling police emergency. Tell Lieutenant Gholer that Detective Courtney Bedell has been here, and that I've abducted Mr. Hargis at gunpoint. Also, if you would, tell Gholer that my own cell's turned off, so he's wasting his time calling me. Tell him I'll get to him when I can." She put one foot in on the Porsche's floorboard, then turned to the guard again. "Oh," Courtney said. "And I'm sorry. I've never pulled a weapon on anyone except criminal suspects before. You won't believe this, but under the circumstances I had no choice. If I live through this I'll buy you a drink." She ducked inside the Porsche and sat, smelling new leather, and slammed the door. She steadied her Glock on the console, pointed at Hargis' midsection. "You drive," she said.

He was hunched over the wheel, his handsome features blank. "Drive where?"

"For now, halfway down the block. You'll see a little clearing on the right, with a dark blue Lumina sitting there. Pull in behind the Lumina."

Hargis pulled jerkily onto Westgrove Road. Visible in the periphery of Courtney's vision, the guard inside the shack picked up the phone. She hoped he called Gholer first. But whether he did or not wouldn't affect what Courtney was about to do. The Porsche toured a hundred yards, then left the road and pulled into the clearing where Courtney had parked fifteen minutes ago.

"Now kill the engine," Courtney said.

Hargis turned the key. The Porsche's motor rumbled and died. The wind stirred bushes, rattled branches, and rustled leaves. The Porsche's headlights reflected dully from her Lumina.

"I estimate," Courtney said, "that we've got about five minutes to sit here before some squad cars come rolling up, responding to that guard's call. What happens in that five minutes is up to you. You can cooperate, or you can get shot."

Hargis continued to grip the wheel with both hands, his gaze straight ahead. "You won't shoot. You're a policewoman, for Christ's sake."

"Not exactly. What I am is someone raising a little boy your friend Harold Bays has kidnapped. That makes me something besides a cop. He's just a little kid, for God's sake. What you're going to do now is drive us over to Harold's house. Not his setup house, the Oak Cliff apartment, but his real house. Where he takes people and murders them. You know which one I'm talking about, don't you?"

There was a tremor in Hargis' voice. "Who the fuck is Harold Bays?"

Courtney watched him through unblinking eyes. She moved her Glock slightly to the right, and shot him in the hand.

The explosion within the confines of the sports car

was eardrum-shattering, the odor of burned gunpowder strong enough to singe Courtney's nostrils.
The bullet pierced the fleshy part of Hargis' hand,
ricocheted from the dashboard and exited through the
driver's side window, leaving a neat round hole.
Hargis yelled and doubled over, pressing his hand
against his belly. Blood darkened his jogging suit and
dripped on the floorboard.

Courtney bent close to Hargis' ear. "Listen to me,"
she said. "Did that hurt?"

Hargis was in tears, his chest heaving. "Christ!
Christ, Christ, Christ . . ."

"Now," Courtney said, "do you feel like finding us
Harold Bays' place? For your sake I hope you know
where it is, because I'm going to think you're lying if
you tell me otherwise. And next I'll shoot you in the
kneecap. This isn't police brutality, sir. This is *aunt*
brutality, which in this case is as brutal as it gets. Are
you going to take us, or aren't you?"

Hargis sobbed and nodded his head.

"Good," Courtney said. "I aimed for the fat of your
hand between the thumb and forefinger so as not to
break any bones, so you shouldn't have any trouble
driving. Keep pressing your hand against your chest
whenever you can. That will act as a half-assed tourni-
quet to stop the bleeding. And please get us there as
fast as possible, before that bastard hurts that poor
little boy. Your life depends on it, Mr. Hargis. Believe
me it does."

Courtney thought she'd visited every nook and
cranny in Dallas County at one time or another, but
the road that Hargis took from I-45 near Seagoville
was a new one to her. A quarter-mile past the federal
prison, he made a left onto bumpy asphalt. The road
was a two-lane, not a house visible in any direction,
low-slung mesquite forests on either side.

She sat bolt upright and alert, watching Hargis' every move. Other than to moan in pain and mutter "Christ" occasionally, he hadn't said a word since they'd left the clearing where her Lumina was parked. She glanced at the odometer. Since they'd left Hargis' place they'd traveled twenty-six miles. The Porsche's dashboard clock read eight mintues after one in the morning. She thought of Jason, and prayed that she was in time.

Hargis braked and turned into a marshy gravel drive on the left. Fifteen feet off the asphalt was what had been a wire gate. The wooden supports were broken as if someone had smashed on through. There were fresh tire marks in the mud.

Hargis stopped and let the engine run. "This is it."

Courtney squinted up ahead. The headlights illuminated twin ruts leading off into a grove of trees. She said, "What's back there?"

"It's an old farm," Hargis said, holding his wounded hand. "There's a barn, a house . . . Christ, I need a doctor."

Courtney said, "I don't know the way, Mr. Hargis, and you're my guide. Drive us on in, please."

"You don't understand. This guy is a cold-blooded killer."

Courtney didn't flinch. "At the moment, so am I. Let's go."

"I'm not going in there." He leaned back from the wheel. "Shoot me if you want to, I don't give a damn."

She pointed her Glock at his knee. "I'll break bones this time, sir."

Hargis sat unmoving. His lips trembled.

Courtney eared back the hammer with a soft double click.

"Wait. Christ, okay, I'm going." Hargis pressed on the gas and the Porsche moved ahead.

They bumped slowly through the woods with the headlights reflecting from small animals' eyes like points of fire, and with crickets whirring and owls hooting away. They reached a large clearing with a rotting barn and an ancient harvester standing like a skeleton. Hargis stopped beside the barn and pointed ahead. "The house. Right there."

Courtney looked through moonlight bright as early dawn. The house was a hundred yards away, a two-story with cantered shutters and a louvered roof. A single bulb glowed on the porch. A two-toned pickup sat in a circular drive in front. Courtney held her breath, then firmly nodded her head. There was a sticker on the pickup's bumper.

His truck.

She told Hargis, "Okay, kill the engine and douse the lights."

Hargis clicked off the headlamps. He turned the ignition switch and the engine died. Courtney took the keys and dropped them in her pocket. She took handcuffs from her belt and cuffed Hargis' good hand to the steering wheel. From her right hand pocket she produced a penlight. She flicked the light on and off, making sure it worked. She moved her lips up beside Hargis' ear. "Pray that the little boy in there isn't harmed, Mr. Hargis. It's the only way you're going to live through this."

He gasped.

Courtney opened the door a crack to turn on the dome light, then took out her cell. She checked the monitor for messages. Gholer had called seven times. She punched in his number and put the receiver to her ear. He answered after the first ring.

"Loo?" she said.

"Jesus, where are you?"

"Someplace out by Seagoville."

"Is Hargis with you?"

She breathed. "The guard called you, huh? Where are you, Hargis' place?"

"Yeah. Courtney, you got any idea what kind of shit you're in?"

"Some. Got a pencil?"

Gholer said that he did.

"Okay. I'm at a farm, and I can see Harold Bays' pickup from where I'm sitting. Take I-45 to Seagoville and exit at the federal joint. Take a right. There's an asphalt road on your left about three-quarters of a mile off the interstate. Take it until you see a gate on your left that's broken down and a path leading through some mesquite trees. Follow the path through the woods to a clearing. You'll see a barn and an old harvester. Hargis' Porsche will be parked beside the barn, and you'll find Hargis, in person, cuffed to the steering wheel. Unless I've killed him before you get here."

"You listen to me. Wait right there until I can get some backup. Do not move, Detective Bedell, I'm ordering you."

"No good, Loo. I'm going in. Just get here as quick as you can, okay?" Courtney disconnected, shot Hargis a final glance, exited the Porsche and jogged toward the house. There was a fluttering rush of wings as an owl flew from its perch. Somewhere to her left, a mile or so in the distance, something bayed at the moon.

Coming across the open field, Courtney was in plain view to anyone inside the house. She knew it and had taken that fact into consideration. Better a single person running silently than a Porsche with its engine throbbing and its headlamp beams stabbing the darkness. As she reached the circular drive, the house towering like a witch's castle, she took cover behind the pickup and waited for her breathing to subside.

She raised up off her haunches and shined the penlight into the pickup's bed. No one in there, nothing,
just the shackles bolted to the floor. She clicked off
the light, duckwalked to the truck's nose and peered
around the bumper toward the porch. The distance to
the front door was less than thirty feet. She debated
shooting out the bulb over the porch and plunging the
area into darkness but decided not to. If the Fiddleback was watching her approach, he already knew her
position; on the other hand, if he hadn't seen her, a
gunshot would alert him that he had company.

I'm coming, Jason. Hold on, baby, Courtney's here.

She gulped in air and sprinted across the porch, and
flattened herself against the door frame. She turned
the handle. The door was unlocked. She ducked inside
and crouched, Glock ready. Total blackness enveloped
her. Somewhere nearby, tiny clawed feet scrambled
for purchase as something ran away.

She stayed put and waited for her pupils to dilate.
Shapes appeared; hulks of furniture, stumpy ottomans,
a staircase leading up. A corridor beyond the stairs,
branching off toward the back of the house.

Upstairs or downstairs? *Which?*

Carefully placing one sneaker-clad foot at a time,
she skirted the banister and reached the corridor. She
stepped in something wet and sticky, and froze.

Did she dare use the penlight? She had to.

She pressed the button and directed the beam to
the floor. She was standing in a pool of blood, with
more big smears leading away in a trail, as if someone
had been dragging something toward the back of the
house.

Jason? Oh Lord, please, no.

She went down the hallway, keeping to the right to
avoid the blood. She passed a hallway cabinet, then a
few doors. The bloody trail seemed to pause here,
the drops coagulating in larger puddles, then the trail

leading away again. She tried one of the doors, pushing it open and shining the penlight inside. The beam illuminated an old refrigerator and a gas stove.

Slowly, carefully, shooting glances back over her shoulder, she entered the kitchen and flashed the light around. There was a rickety breakfast table, and on the table was a jar with a screwed-on lid. She pointed the beam at the jar. Inside the jar a spider wiggled and tried to scurry away from the light. Courtney bent over for a closer look. On the spider's back was an upside-down violin, clearly outlined in brown.

She shuddered as she reached out to lift the jar. As her hand brushed the table, something with tiny legs hurried across her flesh. She gasped and straightened, and shined the light around the room.

Spiders were everywhere, running up the walls, on the floor, scuttling over the counters.

She whimpered and drew back. Her hip struck the table. The jar teetered and fell to the floor, shattering to bits with a loud crashing sound.

Harold Bays heard the jar break from his position behind the shed. He was stark naked in the moonlight, bent from the waist with a grave half dug, and Megan Harris' corpulent body laid out on the ground beside him. He stood up and cocked his head, his tattoo prominent on both sides of his hideously curved spine. The sound was faint but distinct. Someone was inside the house.

DON'T JUST STAND THERE, YOU ASSHOLE. DO SOMETHING.

It was the first time the Queen had spoken directly to him since he'd left Miss Perfect's house with the boy imprisoned in the back of his pickup. So the Queen hadn't forgotten him. His spirits soared.

What, Mother? What do you want me to do?

THEY'RE HERE TO DESTROY US, YOU PRICK. KILL THEM. KILL THEM ALL.

He dropped the shovel and ran toward the house, his bad leg dragging, his lips pulled back in a snarl, his testicles bouncing between his legs. As he traversed the back stoop and flung open the door, he opened his mouth and made an angry buzzing sound.

Courtney heard the back screen door open and slam as she stood in the kitchen, spiders running away from her in all directions. Footsteps sounded from the back of the house, coming toward her. She took a two-handed grip on her Glock and whirled toward the kitchen entry. As she did, a hand reached around the jamb and flipped a switch, and the overhead light came on.

And there he was. Harold Bays, the Fiddleback, framed in the doorway, stark naked, horribly stooped, hissing at her. His tongue protruding slightly as a buzzing sound came from his mouth. He stepped inside the kitchen. He held no weapon that she could see.

You are one ugly son of a bitch, Fiddleback, Courtney thought. She leveled her weapon. "On the floor. Now. You are under arrest." Heard on all sides, tiny legs whispered as the spiders scrambled for safety, hiding under the walls and inside the cabinets. God, there seemed to be thousands of them.

Harold Bays stood there unmoving, his gaze riveted on the floor beneath Courtney's feet.

She followed his gaze. Beside a table leg sat a brown recluse spider, larger than the one she'd seen inside the jar, its markings distinct, sitting there waving its feelers.

Harold Bays said softly, "Mother?"

Courtney mashed the spider under her shoe. She slid her foot sideways, tiny legs and feelers scattering, the spider's body fluids smearing the dirty linoleum.

"No!" Harold Bays screamed. "No, no, noooo . . ." He got down on one knee and covered his eyes.

Courtney pointed her Glock at him. "Facedown on the floor. Now, sir."

Bays didn't seem to hear her. "No," he said again, this time more softly, then turned, ran from the room, and sprinted away down the hall.

For a second Courtney was too stunned to move. She went out in the corridor as the Fiddleback ran into the living room and skirted the stairs. "Halt!" Courtney yelled. She pulled the trigger and, as Harold Bays disappeared in the darkness, a bullet lodged in the staircase and splintered the wood.

You stupid prick. You've gotten Her killed.

You're not worth a shit. You've ruined everything, you asshole.

"Did not," Harold whined as he ran through the living room and out the front door. "Did not, did not. You're just jealous of me. Always have been."

He stopped at the edge of the porch, panting. Miss Perfect had killed the Queen. Now the Change could never come. He must avenge Her. His pickup truck sat near the porch. He charged from the porch, pulled open the driver's door, and lifted his .45 from off the seat. As he turned to face the house, Miss Perfect came outside, struck a two-handed pose, and fired at him.

There was sudden numbness in Harold's shoulder. He looked down in shock as bone splintered and blood ran down his arm. He turned toward the woman, hissing. She pointed her weapon again. Harold Bays ran around the side of the pickup and limped off toward the barn. The Queen was dead and Miss Perfect had injured him. Harold was cold, alone, and, for the first time in his life, totally afraid.

*   *   *

Christ, here the fucker comes, Billy Hargis thought. Naked as a fucking jaybird, limping up the incline toward the Porsche. And with that bitch in pursuit, running after the guy, waving her gun.

Christ, what was wrong with her? She was a cop, wasn't she? Supposed to protect poor people like Billy Hargis, not fucking shoot them and haul them around wounded.

Hargis opened the door and got out of the car, yanking hard on his handcuffed wrist, his eyes wild, his gaze riveted in fear on the Fiddleback.

The Fiddleback halted twenty feet away, blood running from a wound in his shoulder. He glared at Hargis, and then lifted his hand. In his hand was a gun. Hargis held his arms up as a shield.

Harold Bays fired twice, then ran on past the Porsche headed for the woods, the gunshots and pounding feet the last sounds that Billy Hargis would ever hear. Hargis slumped to the ground, murmured, "Christ," one final time, then slowly emptied his lungs.

The caravan rolled into the clearing with Gholer in the lead, Madison and Frizell riding his bumper, and three black-and-whites bringing up the rear. The cop cars fanned out and came to a halt. Madison, Frizell, and the uniforms all came out with their weapons ready. Gholer shouldered his door open and hit the ground running.

Up ahead sat a dark-colored Porsche with its door open and its interior light burning. A man was slumped on the ground beside the driver's seat with his hand thrust inside the car. Gholer heard running feet on his left. He turned.

Harold Bays, buck naked, was running through the clearing clutching his shoulder. Blood poured from a wound in the vicinity of his collar bone. He was dragging one leg but moving fast. Jesus, the guy had a violin tattooed on his back. Really playing the fucking part.

Gholer yelled, "Police, Harold. Stop right there."

Bays halted and turned around, pointing his weapon. Madison and Frizell came over, the three detectives now forming a semicircle with Harold Bays in the center. The uniformed cops trotted over as well, six of them. Bays was trapped. The unis all knew that this guy had shot a cop earlier in the day, and Gholer wondered if someone would get trigger-happy all of a sudden. "Throw down your weapon, son," Gholer said. "It's over. Come on, Harold, put it down."

Bays just stood there, chest heaving, looking wildly about as if searching for an escape route. Jinx Madison blocked the path to the woods. Gholer and Frizell stood between the Fiddleback and the house. The unis stood on the path leading to the barn.

Bays said, "You killed my mother." And raised his weapon toward the sky.

A shot sounded on Gholer's left. A hole appeared as if by magic in Harold Bays' temple, another in the back of his head above the ear as the bullet exited. The Fiddleback seemed to hang suspended for a full second, then crumpled slowly to the ground. His right leg twitched, then was still.

Gholer walked slowly up and looked down at the guy. Jinx Madison came over, putting her weapon away. Frizell joined them. The uniformed cops stood by.

Gholer, Madison, and Frizell looked at each other.

"He was gonna shoot you, Loo," Madison finally said. "I had no choice." She looked around the clearing. "That okay with the rest of you guys?" she said.

Gholer led the way, circling the pickup, approaching the house, stepping up on the porch. Madison and

Frizell stopped beside the truck and shined a light inside. Gholer started to enter the house.

The front door opened and Courtney Bedell came out, carrying a sleeping little boy. His head was cradled on her shoulder. She stepped very carefully, as if she was afraid she'd drop him.

Gholer sighed in relief, and draped his arm over Courtney's shoulders. He said, "Is he—"

"*Shhh.*" Courtney spoke in a harsh whisper. "Not a mark on him that I can find. He was in a room in there, sound asleep. A room with blood and brains on the wall. Little guy's in a trance, Loo. Let's let him sleep, okay?"

26

Gholer pulled a few strings and spread a little grease around to make Courtney's problems over kidnapping William Hargis disappear, and he was glad to do so. The FBI and the chief of police were fairly easy to deal with, considering that Gholer could've leaked it to the press that the guy Agent Miller and the chief were shielding for political reasons was in fact the Fiddleback's closest buddy. The chief's blessing was conditional; he wanted to be certain that the young policewoman wouldn't commit any further crimes while on the job. Gholer assured the department head that wouldn't be a problem; Officer Bedell was now under Gholer's command, and he'd certainly keep an eye on her.

Attorney Larry Akin was a different story. Hargis' lawyer, backed by the gate guard's testimony concerning what had happened that night, stated openly that he'd sue the shit out of everyone concerned on behalf of William Hargis Jr.'s estate, and stuck to his guns until one afternoon when Gholer paid him a visit. Sitting calmly in front of Akin's desk with his thick legs crossed, Gholer made the following speech:

"You know, Mr. Akin, you're probably right about departmental liability. You are also right in that a case against your client Hargis would have been a tough go for us, probable cause and all. You have definitely got us by the balls, and if you do file suit the city attorney's probably going to offer one helluva settlement. So the only glitch is, and my detectives are really hot on this point, is how Harold Bays got Miss Bedell's name and address. It's a good question. We do know a fax containing that information came over Megan Harris' fax machine, and I don't gotta tell you where the fax came from. Your own little fax, that little machine I passed on the way in here, which we can subpoena in a heartbeat. Now that, coupled with the fact that Megan Harris is dead out at Harold Bays' place, and that we know Hargis took Megan Harris out there to die, there's a possibility you could face some conspiracy charges. They're likely charges you can beat, you being this really smart lawyer and all, but look. You want to read all about what you did in the newspapers? So the way it goes is, you fuck us and we'll fuck you. That's the way you lawyers do it every day, isn't it, bud?" Shortly thereafter, Akin's firm announced that it had elected not to pursue the matter.

And two weeks after the Fiddleback case was history, Gholer talked his wife Toni into letting him throw a barbecue. The lieutenant lived in a nice house in Arlington off the turnpike, with a swimming pool paid for with Toni's inheritance from her grandmother, though Gholer joked that he'd funded the pool with his bribe money. It was the second Saturday in October, one of the last warm days they'd have in the year, hot enough that everybody could still go swimming. Gholer cooked burgers on the grill while his teenagers, Rusty and Ed, tossed a football back and forth and pretended not to watch Jinx Madison flouncing around in a yellow bikini. Gholer pretended not to watch as well, though, Jesus, it was hard not to.

Around four in the afternoon as the sun began to

sink, Gholer said to Courtney Bedell, "No question, the guy was hearing voices. They all hear voices. Schizophrenics. Son of Sam listened to a dog. Our guy listened to a spider. You know he was injecting himself with some weird concoction of body fluid and spider venom?"

Courtney shuddered and hugged herself. She wore a blue one-piece French-cut swimsuit and a thigh-length terry-cloth robe. Her hair was damp. Gholer thought she looked pretty good in a bathing suit. Not quite flashy like Jinx, but pretty damn good. Toni Gholer was on a metal chaisse longue, twenty yards away, reading *The Cat in the Hat* to Jason Bedell. Jason wore a blue bathing suit, flippers, and water wings. Toni kept glancing over occasionally, her sharp looks telling Gholer to keep his fucking eyes to himself. He responded by leering at his wife who, at forty, looked pretty damned good as well. Hell, *life* was pretty damned good. Gholer reached for the spatula and flipped a couple of burgers, and wiped his fingers on his apron. The apron said CHIEF COOK AND BOTTLE WASHER across the front.

"The autopsy tells us," Gholer went on, "that this guy was about finished, anyway. All those toxins, he was ate up with cancer. Had spread to his liver and lungs. According to Harris Sands he had only a few months, six at the most. Already had a good-sized tumor on his hip." He gestured with the spatula toward the lounge where Toni read. "How's the little guy holding up?" Gholer said.

Courtney poked at the charcoal with a metal rod, spreading the glowing coals more evenly. "The psychologist swears he doesn't remember a thing after Jan took him out of the day-care center, but I don't know. He wakes up a lot at night, Loo. He could have damage we're not seeing, and may not see for quite some time."

"That's the part about the case I hate the most, Court. And your sister?"

Courtney didn't answer. Her strokes with the metal rod grew longer and firmer.

"I got to know," Gholer said, "because a guy from the DA's office called me. You're their case. If you're not going to stand up, press the charges, the prosecutor wants to know."

"I'll stand up, Loo," Courtney said.

"You know what they say about blood and water."

Courtney watched him with a steady gaze. "I'm not sure there is any more blood between me and Jan."

"She's got a parole violation," Gholer said, "in addition to the burglary with you as the complainant. She's likely to be gone forever and a day."

"So she'll have to be gone, then."

"And you're not going to suddenly break down and start hiring her another lawyer or something?"

"Not this time. As far as I'm concerned, I no longer have a sister. It'll be a lot of years before that changes, if it ever does."

"Your life, kid." Gholer reached for a platter and ladled a couple of patties off the fire. He set the platter aside. The odor was mouthwatering. "You know a couple of patrolmen named Rainey and Trevino?"

Courtney laid the metal rod on top of the grill. "Sure, guys I rode with."

"How about a Jimmy Bethancourt? White Rock Precinct."

Courtney tilted her head. "Where's this going, Loo?"

"Where do you want it to go?"

"You tell me."

Gholer shrugged. "Rainey called the other day, looking for you. Said Bethancourt is throwing another party tonight and wants you to come."

"Jimmy Bethancourt's cute. But I've got Jason. No time for guys hitting on me."

Gholer looked over toward Jason, who now sat on Toni's lap. "Little guy looks fine to me," Gholer said. "Look, we got a bunk in there. The boys got video games out the wazoo. He could spend the night, you know."

One corner of Courtney's mouth turned up. "You in cahoots with Bethancourt or something?"

"No way. I'm in cahoots with you, Court, you know that."

Courtney picked up the platter and stepped toward the picnic table set up at one end of the pool. She stopped and turned. "Well, Jason would sure appreciate the invite. And I suppose I could use some partying in my life." She winked. "I appreciate ya, Loo. And let me think on it. You know what, I just might go." She continued on toward the table.

Gholer raised his voice. "Oh. And, Courtney."

She turned around once more.

"Listen," Gholer said. "I know I put a lot of pressure on you. Had to be done. I don't want you to think I'm forcing you to stay in my unit, not if you don't want to. If you want to transfer back to Patrol, just let me know."

She seemed deep in thought. Finally she showed a wide grin. "You mean, '*our* unit,' don't you?" Courtney said.